$8.00
signed

"Maybe the girls knew each other, maybe their babies had a common father. Maybe they all got together and jilted him. On the other hand, and this is the frightening part of it, there may be no logical answer at all. We may have a maniac loose in the city. And in that case, my dear, you'd better speed up your education and learn about serial killers. As a psychiatrist, you just might get involved in this some day."

"That's police business in there," and Lt. Lenhart pointed toward the patient's room. "You cain't keep me out."

"Don't bet on it. All I have to do is get her chart and write 'No Visitors Allowed' and I'm going to do that right now."

He was upset after last night's scene at home and more concerned than he wanted to admit. He hurried through the remaining office appointments and left abruptly at eleven-thirty. Skipping lunch, he drove directly home and was three blocks away when he saw the moving van parked in front of the house. "Son of a bitch. I can't believe that," he said. "What in the hell is she doing?"

Unseen or unnoticed, the right arm of the large rain coat was raised for just a second. Mary Ann's baby died before the light turned green. Number four and counting.

Jon took the scalpel from the nurse and made a deep cut across the lower abdomen about an inch and a half above the protruding weapon. The small bleeders in the skin and subcutaneous fat were quickly cauterized and the incision continued down through the fascia.

A minute later the warm glow of candlelight eased the darkness. Reassured, she decided against checking the fuse box, assuming the same wind which had caused the noise in he bedroom had knocked out the power and telephone lines. Lights from the neighbor's house were burning brightly, but she failed to notice this and started back toward the bedroom.

DEATH BEFORE LIFE

a mystery novel

Robert C. Jackson, M.D.

Strawberry Hill Press

Strawberry Hill Press
3848 S.E. Division Street
Portland, Oregon 97202

Cover by Ku, Fu-sheng
Cover concept by Carol Schieno
Book edited by Kristi Burke
Typeset and design by Wordwrights, Portland, Oregon

Manufactured in the United States of America

Library of Congress Cataloging-in-Publication Data

Jackson, Robert C., 1923-
Death before life : a mystery novel / Robert C. Jackson.
p. cm.
ISBN 0-89407-120-3 (tradepaper : alk. paper)
I. Title.
PS3560.A2434D43 1997
813 .54--dc21

96-29797
CIP

ACKNOWLEDGMENTS

An author must be motivated to first write, then rewrite, then revise a manuscript. This motivation has come from many friends and acquaintances, five of whom have made major contributions. First is the book doctor, Jerry Gross of Croton-on-Hudson, New York. "Doctor Gross" was responsible for a significant change in the formulation of this novel. Next is David H. Morgan of Richmond, Virginia. David is a teacher and helped me understand how a mystery evolves properly from the first chapter through the last. My friend, David Alexander, read one of my early drafts and suggested the title *Death Before Life*. I am grateful for the advice and confidence of Jean-Louis Brindamour, the president of Strawberry Hill Press. The book is in print because of his efforts. I am indebted to my editor, Kristi Burke, of Lake Oswego, Oregon. Her suggestions have done much to smooth and strengthen the novel.

I also wish to acknowledge the contribution of the Pacific Northwest Writers Conference. Their meetings attract experts in all aspects of the writing profession and have been most informative and helpful.

Sept 15, 01
Thanks for
coming by.
Bob Jackson

CHAPTER I

She was only fifteen years old, eyes accentuated with heavy eye shadow, lips scarlet—and pregnant. Few of the shoppers in this metropolitan area had even noticed her. Those who did had quickly looked away and silently expressed disgust at a child, her abdomen swollen with a near term fetus, wandering the streets of the city during a rainstorm. The maternity clothes she wore were obvious hand-me-downs and she appeared completely oblivious to the rejection of those around her. Life had not done her any favors as yet and she had no reason to believe her fortunes would change in the future. Aimlessly window shopping, envying those who could buy, she felt something hit her distended, pregnant belly. Surprised and hurt, she stumbled then fell.

Sprawled on the wet sidewalk she instinctively knew that something had just happened to her baby. Suddenly she screamed with horror as her hand, covered with blood, came away from the sharp pain in her side. Now she could no longer be ignored. A large number of people quickly gathered around and someone pulled her beneath a store canopy, away from the torrential downpour.

At that very moment, had anyone chosen to carefully observe the crowd, they would have seen varied reactions among the people surrounding the girl with the bloody hand. Some were curious, some were helpful, some even rather ghoulish in a nosy sort of way. But one was different. The difference wasn't marked; the raincoat was a little too large and a wide brimmed hat pulled down too far in front and in back. Underneath that hat there was a slight, satisfied smile. From the left sleeve of the oversized raincoat a brown envelope was dropped unnoticed to the sidewalk.

Police and ambulance arrived, each with their different sirens blasting through the traffic. The little victim received emergency treatment and was whisked away to the University Hospital. The police didn't stay much longer. A pregnant teenager down and bloody was no longer a shock to them. There would be a calling card, an envelope, they were sure of that. It would be found and carefully placed in a plastic bag to be opened and studied at headquarters. Many of the people in the crowd were questioned but no one had really paid any attention to the girl until she fell to the sidewalk and started to scream. No, they didn't know exactly what had happened to her, just that something must have struck her suddenly. No, they hadn't noticed anyone pointing at her before she went down. Names were taken and the people were informed they might be asked to come down to police headquarters in the future to see if more information might be obtained. But the police were not very optimistic and soon the traffic, both auto and pedestrian, had returned to normal. The splotch of blood on the sidewalk was all that remained and even this was gradually disappearing under the continuing onslaught of the rain. The shoppers that walked by now, unaware and unconcerned about the origin of the red stain, merely stepped over it and went on their way.

In the operating room, surgeons were removing a dead baby from the womb of the teenager. A four-inch stainless steel knife had penetrated the abdomen of the mother and lodged in the chest of the unborn baby. While they were thus occupied, and not far away, a large raincoat was hung in the back of a closet. A weapon—mounted on a slim piece of aluminum and a spring-loaded mechanism—had been removed from the coat and placed in a nondescript shoe box on the closet floor.

THIS IS NUMBER THREE
FOR ALL TO SEE
A BASTARD BABE
ITS DEBTS UNPAID
BEST TO DIE UNBORN
THAN TO LEAD A LIFE FORLORN

This gruesome poem was the headline in the next day's morning paper, a paper which served a metropolitan area of over a million anxious souls. An account of the macabre crime, listed as Feticide Number Three, was described in great detail on page one and was limited to this particular occurrence. The editorial page felt no such restriction and gave the readers a general description of the victims, past and present, and exercised the self-imposed right of the editors to be highly critical of the authorities in charge of the investigation.

> FETICIDE, the purposeful killing of a fetus. This city has now seen three of these horrible crimes. The first didn't rate even so much as a line on the editorial page of this newspaper. There was a second some four months later and we began to suspect a serious problem. Now, a third baby has been destroyed. They all fit a set pattern:
>
> 1. All three babies were male and near term.
> 2. The mothers were in their teens.
> 3. The mothers were on welfare.
> 4. All mothers were in a special clinic at the University Medical School.

5. None of mothers were married.
6. The attacks invariably occur during a heavy rain storm.
7. An envelope containing a poem has been found at the site of each attack.

Young, unmarried, poor and pregnant—a group which as a rule does not arouse a great deal of sympathy or compassion among the leading citizens of the community. Unfortunately, a lack of concern for this particular segment of society has also been demonstrated by the police department and specifically by Lt. Billy Ray Lenhart. Lt. Lenhart is in charge of the homicide division at police headquarters and accordingly, heads the team investigating these murders. The Lieutenant is a recent import from a law enforcement agency in rural Georgia and likes to carry his authority in the form of a pearl-handled .38 caliber pistol beneath his civilian jacket. This police officer also carries with him the type of bigoted religious fanaticism so peculiar to that area of the nation in which he was born and raised. He is an avowed, dedicated born-again Christian and when interviewed yesterday following this latest fetal death he did not mask his contempt for those of lesser religious convictions which, of course, included the three feticide victims. In fact, this scorn, this derision for the pregnant teenagers overshadowed the entire interview. Not once did the Lieutenant appear to analyze the crime itself and attach any significance to the glaring fact that all the babies were male and all the mothers attended the same clinic at University Hospital.

We are also concerned with the dedication and zeal of the entire police force, including Chief Michael O'Neal and Police Commissioner Richard Braun. Either the Chief or the Commissioner has the authority to relieve Lieutenant Lenhart of all responsibility in this case and it seems they are slow in doing so.

In sharp contrast to the work of the police, the staff at University Hospital demonstrated excellent teamwork in the manner in which they handled this emergency. We hope they are not called on to exercise similar skills in the future.

Jon Spencer Erickson, M.D. was the surgeon who performed the emergency surgery on the latest feticide victim. The morning the editorial appeared, he casually parked his car in the "Doctors Only" zone of the University Medical School and walked into the hospital to see how his little charge had fared through the night. Dr. Erickson had read the newspaper before leaving home that morning and felt reasonably proud of his role in the drama. He was only six years out of his residency training in Obstetrics and Gynecology and was now in the private practice of that specialty. He rather curtly shouldered his way through the visitors and ancillary staff in the hospital lobby on his way to the stairs and the fourth floor of the hospital. Jon was a good-looking young man, lean, but not thin. He was slightly above average in height with strikingly light colored hair which, on his explicit instructions, the barber cut unfashionably short. He wore a dark blue blazer, white shirt with striped tie and neatly pressed gray slacks, a sartorial showing of his conservative personality. "He's definitely not the type to wear a showy neck scarf or a gold necklace," was the appraisal given by one of his friends.

The patient was in surprisingly good spirits considering what she had suffered the night before. She had been transferred from Intensive Care to room 401 on the Obstetrical floor with stable blood pressure, and normal pulse and temperature.

"Tough little nut, isn't she?" Jon remarked to one of the nurses as he was writing orders and jotting down a progress note in the chart.

"I'd say she's doing pretty well," the nurse replied. "Particularly when you figure someone tried to kill her last night."

"No, I don't think that's true. I don't think anybody tried to do away with her. It's the baby they're after but don't ask me why. She's the third one, you know. All of them hit in the side of that big old term-sized belly. Pretty good target if you're out to muck up a pregnancy."

"Same weapon?"

"Same one. The cops call it a ballistic knife. Fires a little stainless steel dagger and just lethal as hell from a short distance."

"And the police don't have a clue."

"Not as far as I know." Jon slid the chart over to the nurse. "Here are some more orders for her. I'm headed over to St. Elizabeths to check on a couple of post partums who had their babies in a more acceptable fashion. Let the resident know I've been around and have him call me if he has any questions."

On the way out of the hospital Jon stopped in to say good-bye to the patient in 401 and was surprised to find a man sitting beside the bed. He was a stranger to Jon and obviously not hospital personnel.

"You the doc on this case?" the man asked as Jon appeared in the doorway.

"Yes, I'm Doctor Erickson."

"That's fine, Doc. Ah'm Lootenant Billie Ray Lenhart, homicide."

The police lieutenant was middle-aged and when he stood up a somewhat fleshy paunch bulged over low riding pants. His eyes, heavy lidded, gave him a sleepy, disinterested appearance. And the drawl was straight from rural Georgia. "Ah guess this here makes the third one, don't it," he said. "Makes me think somebody out there don't much like them girls."

It was not a good beginning. Jon was immediately put on guard by the bad English and southern accent and he was offended with the indifferent manner in which the policeman approached what to Jon had been a tragedy.

"Let's step out of the room for a minute, Lieutenant. I want to ask you something."

When they found a quiet spot in the hall Jon turned and faced the Lieutenant. "Let me tell you something, Lieutenant Lenhart. That young lady in there was one hell of a case last night. I've never seen anything quite like it before and I hope I never do again. I think she is one gutsy little kid. But she's apparently just one of 'them girls' to you. Tell me, sir, tell me what you think of 'them girls.'"

"Well now, Doc, it's mah nature to be somewhat aggravated, shall we say, toward these little chippies."

"That's about what I thought, but I'm not concerned about your nature, Lieutenant, I'm concerned with you doing your job. And as I understand it, your job is to investigate murders. Looks like we have three of them now—all unsolved."

"Now, Doc, don't get all riled up." The drawl, if anything, was intensified. "Not good for your blood pressure, you know. You sew 'em up and I'll look around for the responsible party. Could be a mutual boyfriend, and we're checkin' on that. Lot of people to run down. We just don't have the time or the machinery to follow up on all them kids in a day or two. You right, Doc, these killins' is messy things. But Ah sort of like to look at the whole picture. Let's be honest, Doc, we ain't lost much yet. Them three little boys for certain goin' to be on welfare soon's they is born."

The two men stood about two feet apart, one growing increasingly agitated, the other placid and calm. They were a study in contrasts, most noticeably in their physical appearance and dress, Jon in his tailored and conservative clothing—Billy Ray wearing a flashy jacket with the obvious bulge of a shoulder-holstered revolver. None of this lessened Jon's contempt.

"You are starting to make me a little sick, Lieutenant. Despite your opinions to the contrary, these are human beings and now three of them are dead."

"There you go agin, gettin' your bile a boilin'. We'll get movin' on this. Maybe not so fast as you'd like but we'll eventually find the crazy who done it. And somethin' else, Doc," the heavy eye lids opened slightly. "You may not think so but I was one crackin' good cop down in Georgia. Busted a lot of tough cases. Guess that's why they hired me up here in your little city."

"Then I suggest you do what you were hired for. Seems to me if I were a cop I'd have one ambition—get the Poet."

"But you ain't a cop. Y'all tend to the doctorin'. I'm the guy with the gun."

"Don't worry, I'll take care of the patient, but I've got sort of a one-track mind—right now I can't think of anything I want more than to see that crazy bastard in jail. What I don't want is another rhyme left on the street and another bloody little teenager brought in for me to sew up."

"That's your job, Doc."

"Yes it is and while I'm in charge of that patient you are not to see her again while she's in the hospital. You'll be able to get a copy of the hospital record after she's discharged providing all the proper release forms are signed."

"That's police business in there," and Lt. Lenhart pointed toward the patient's room. "You cain't keep me out."

"Don't bet on it. All I have to do is get her chart and write 'No Visitors Allowed' and I'm going to do that right now."

Before Lt. Lenhart could reply, Jon turned and walked back to the nurses station where orders were given to bar the police or any other visitor from visiting Bobbie Morris without express permission from the medical staff. With that done, he took the stairs down and started again to his previous goal.

St. Elizabeths was a private hospital where Jon and two hundred other physicians from the metropolitan area took their patients. Here he was well-known and over the past six years had gained the confidence of the other doctors in his specialty. They knew him as a very competent and superbly-trained obstetrician and gynecologist.

Among the nurses, however, he was recognized for his chauvinistic tendencies as well. Usually his banter with the nurses was good-natured and somewhat superficial but it left no doubt as to who was in charge. On rare occasions, especially when he was tired or moody, he could cut deep. There were those who said the real Jon Erickson was revealed during these moments when his guard was down. This morning he was tired. The surgery on the feticide victim was followed by two deliveries at St. Elizabeths Hospital after midnight. He was also a little moody and thanks to Lt. Lenhart, the mood was bad.

When he made post partum rounds he found nurse Atwood in charge of the floor. Despite her physical attributes—and they were considerable—she was not one of his favorites. Her beauty and her magnificent body were not adequate compensation for an intellect that was, according to Jon, definitely on the low end of the scale. As head nurse she allowed herself the privilege of occasionally finding fault with the doctors who visited her floor.

She was not always correct in this evaluation and today was a particularly bad day to question Dr. Erickson's patient care—and be wrong. Her criticism was based on a faulty knowledge of anatomy. Jon directed her to the classroom on the floor and using the models and large illustrations in that room he stabbed at the pictures of female anatomy showing her precisely and pointedly just where and how she had blundered. As to the "why," he had no idea but as a parting shot, he quoted Alexander Dumas when he said, "Maybe Mr. Dumas was right. He calculated that God must have made woman on Saturday night as the end product reveals his fatigue."

Leaving a seething, but silent, Nurse Atwood, Jon found his way to the doctors' surgical lounge for a cup of coffee. He hadn't been there long and wasn't really involved in the talk of politics and politicians when Ted Ashley, his office partner, walked in.

"Jesus," was Ted's comment when he saw Jon. "What the hell did you do to Atwood? I was just down on post partum and she's damn near frothing at the mouth. That woman would gladly kill you if she had half a chance."

"Atwood and I don't get along. I think she has PMS about three hundred and sixty days of the year."

Another obstetrician in the room ventured his opinion. "Jon, Atwood's from South Carolina. That's the only reason you don't get along with her. What's with you and the rebs, anyway?"

"Yeah, Jon," someone else broke in. "I've always wondered about that. Never have heard you say anything good about the South or any of its citizens. Some sweet little southern belle turn you down when you were a lusty and vulnerable youth?"

"Well, to begin with, that's a contradiction in terms, an oxymoron, if you will. I've never seen a sweet little southern belle. I've seen a number who pretend to be but somehow they all seem to get the clap and herpes just like anybody else. And when you tell 'em their disease is sexually transmitted, they look up at you with those big innocent eyes and in their sweet little voice they tell you, 'why Doctor, Ah just don't understand where I could of got this.'"

Jon was a good mimic. He was wringing his hands in fake despair and everybody in that room could identify with his falsetto impression of the cute little southern sweetheart.

"Okay, so you don't like southerners. How come?"

"Blame my father," Jon said. "He was in the military police during his service career and spent most of the time in the South. In fact, we were all there for quite awhile. I remember how he hated that so-called justice system they have down there. White man could screw any good looking black chick he could find, very macho you know, but let a black man even look sideways at a white girl and bingo, bring out the rope."

"That's all changed now, Jon."

"Not completely. It isn't just the black/white issue, it's their way of life. Look at their politics, for God's sake. We're bad enough out here in Oregon but those southern politicians are a breed apart."

Ted Ashley had heard most of this before. "Come on, Jon," he said, "get off the soap box and go to the office."

"Jon, before you go," one of the other doctors said, "what's the deal with the latest feticide? I hear you operated on that girl at the University yesterday. How'd you get involved?"

"I know Doctor Johnson, the Chief of Ob-Gyn up there. I've been in surgery a couple of times with him. And I teach a class of junior medical students on a fairly regular basis. Just happened to be in Doctor Johnson's office when that patient came in. He was busy and so were the rest of his senior men so he asked if I'd take it. Quite a case. The report in the paper was pretty accurate and I was glad to see they took out after that police lieutenant, Lenhart. Now there is a real red-necked son of a bitch."

"How'd you meet him?"

"Had a little chat with him in the hospital this morning."

"From the sound of things in the paper, he sounds like a real Georgia cracker. Did you have a nice, pleasant conversation with him, Jon?"

"Not exactly."

"How about the girl. Is she going to be okay?"

"I think so unless she gets a hell of an infection."

"That's the third one of those, isn't it?" Ted Ashley asked. "There's a real kook out there with a nasty weapon. If they don't catch him he's apt to kill somebody. What do you think, Jon? Could that knife kill an adult if it hit them in the right spot?"

"Oh, hell yes. Believe me, that is one sharp instrument. I don't know who makes them but whoever it is, he knows his business. If I had the time I'd sure spend some of it trying to catch the bastard. Shouldn't be too hard. Must be somebody who knows the patients in that Clinic."

"Or, knows somebody who does work up there and shares the information."

"I know," Jon admitted, "all sorts of possibilities. It obviously isn't so simple as I'd like to imagine. But I've seen the disaster that knife can cause. Irritates the shit out of me that they haven't caught him yet. But," and Jon threw his paper coffee cup in the waste, "I can't do anything about it today so I'd better go to the office. See you lads and ladies later."

"What's with that guy, Ted?" one of the women surgeons asked when Jon had left the room. "You see him every day. Should know him pretty well. He really has a burr up his butt when it comes to southerners."

"Well, as he said, his whole family was down there when his dad was in the service. His dad was a detective from Cleveland before he got called into the army military police. A real straight arrow from what Jon tells me. And Jon, I think had plans to go into police work, too. Even went to a police academy for awhile when they were down in South Carolina. Learned a lot about police work, so he told me. Still one of his hobbies, I think. I don't know why he gave it up and went into medicine. Maybe had something to do with the attitude of the instructors and other cadets at the school. He definitely has this thing about the South."

"Hasn't he heard about the civil rights movement? Been a few changes since he lived below that Mason-Dixon line."

"Oh, sure. He just doesn't believe that down deep they really have changed. He told me once, and he was about half serious, that Lincoln made a mistake. Should have let the whole damn lot of them secede."

"Well, I hope his office is full of Yankees today."

"So do I. And I'd better get down there, too. Have to make a living somehow."

Jon's secretary buzzed him as soon as he came in the back door of his office.

"Good morning, Doctor. I understand you had quite an evening in the University's operating room. Any other excitement to report?"

"Nothing quite like the feticide, but I did deliver Mrs. Larkin and Mrs. Boothe early this morning at St. Elizabeths."

"Good. I'll get the details later. You'd better pick up line one.

Some man wants to talk to you about the little girl you operated on—the one whose baby was killed."

"Who is it?"

"Didn't say. Sounded sort of official so I thought you'd better talk to him."

"O.K." Jon released the intercom button and pushed number one. "This is Doctor Erickson," he said.

"Good morning, Doctor. Sorry to bother you but I wanted to ask about the latest feticide victim. I understand you were the surgeon last night on that case."

"Who is this speaking, please?"

"I'm Lawrence Miller. I have a doctorate in counseling and spend some of my time at the medical school in the Special Procedures Clinic. I am particularly interested in their current project. Are you familiar with it?"

"Yes, somewhat."

"Well, the young lady you operated on was registered in that Clinic."

"I know that," Jon said. "But of course it didn't matter much at the time."

"Right, I understand that," Lawrence Miller said. "But I think it will today. The girls in that Clinic know each other pretty well and when I meet with them this afternoon I suspect they'll be quite upset."

Jon was on guard. He had little or no contact with the Special Procedures Clinic and was not acquainted with a Lawrence Miller. Instinctively he was reluctant to discuss any case with a total stranger. "And?" he said.

"Well, I was wondering, you know. They're such happy, innocent souls. I was wondering if you could give me some information to help calm them down. Hopefully something encouraging about last night's case. I'm really quite worried about how they're going to react."

"Doctor Miller, I'm no psychiatrist, but I suspect those kids will react just like anyone else their age. They'll be a little shocked but teenagers are pretty well protected by that age-old philosophy of theirs, you know, it's the 'can't happen to me' syndrome."

"Oh, I suppose. I was hoping your patient might have told you something I could use to reassure her friends in the Clinic."

"No, I'm sorry. She was under anesthesia when I saw her last night and didn't volunteer any information when I made rounds this morning."

"Well, sorry to bother you, Doctor."

"No bother. You might talk to the police. This is the first one of these things I've been involved in. They've seen a couple more."

"Yes, I know. I might do that. And thank you, Doctor."

"Good-bye, Doctor Miller."

Jon put down the phone and turned to Nell Bullard, his nurse, who had come into the office. "That's an oddball if I ever heard one. Name of Lawrence Miller. Sound familiar?"

"There's a Lawrence Miller who's a state representative from around here someplace."

"Can't be the same one. The state rep is an arch conservative—part of the far right crowd. Just doesn't fit, a Jerry Falwell type befriending a bunch of pregnant teenagers."

"No, I think it's the same one, Doctor," the nurse said. "I remember his opponent in last fall's election made some comment about the dual personality of the incumbent. Seems he supports all the ultra-conservative causes in the legislature then turns around and acts like a flaming liberal at the medical school. I hear he makes a little money on the side as a right wing preacher."

"Takes all kinds, I guess, but I wouldn't turn my back on a guy like that. I think I'll wander over to that Special Procedures Clinic some day and see what goes on. I think that's where all the information on those girls is stored. So, if my thinking is right, there's got to be somebody around there who knows more about this feticide business than I do. But in the meantime, back to basics—who's my first patient?"

"Mrs. Van Osborn. She's new to the office, Doctor. Twenty-three years old and she requested an infertility evaluation when the appointment was made."

Stephanie Van Osborn was an attractive, very blonde young woman and it was obvious from the way she walked into Jon's office that she knew the value of her beauty and how to display it in a provocative manner. It was also obvious that she expected to command attention. Slightly pouty lips, Jon would reflect later, was her only physical detraction. A routine history revealed she had never been pregnant and had been off birth control pills for over a year. Further questioning led to a suspicion of gonorrhea or chlamydia sometime during her teens but with some indignation, she denied this possibility. She also denied any previous infertility evaluation and when asked by Jon if her husband was willing to be tested, she replied, "No, he's too busy. He runs a small arts and craft shop. Makes little metal toys and games. He's already starting to get ready for Christmas so I know he won't have time to come in. I guess you'll just have to deal with me," and she gave a coy little flip to her hair.

Dealing with Stephanie was not going to be easy. Infertility patients rarely were and somehow Jon sensed this one would be particularly difficult. The initial physical exam was negative after which he instructed his nurse to schedule the usual tests. These preliminary investigations were designed to find damaged tubes or ovaries; other more exotic and expensive studies would come later if indicated.

"That's a spoiled little beauty if I ever saw one," was the nurse's comment after Stephanie had left the office. "And I can't say that was an appropriate looking blouse, either."

"Appropriate or proper?" Jon asked.

"Neither one. I would say if she's not pregnant it's not for lack of exposure."

"Nell, you're too straight-laced."

"Not me, Doctor. You know better'n that. You forget I was raised on the black side of Detroit. Wasn't much we didn't see—and do. But we knew right and wrong. My mama, bless her soul, taught us that. That little honky wouldn't dress like a high-priced call girl if my mama had raised her."

"Her white skin and yellow hair might look sort of out of place in your family," John teased.

An easy smile settled over the nurse's face. "I suppose it would, Doctor, but I suspect between me and my four brothers and sisters we could have taught her more acceptable manners."

"I'll bet you could. Don't think I ever asked you before—you the only one of that bunch of kids to wander out west?"

"Oh, no. Nobody left in Detroit, Mama saw to that, too. She was a pretty pushy woman—we all got out. I'm the only one in this area. The rest are up and down the coast. And since we're asking personal questions, I've always wondered why you hired me, a black nurse. Your practice isn't exactly lily white but there's not too many soul sisters coming in here."

"That's easy, Nell. You know your job. You're a damn good nurse. Who got you started in this business?"

"My mother."

"I could have guessed that."

"And you, Doctor, you told me once that before you went to medical school you wanted to be a cop. What changed your mind?"

"Well, if your mother played an active, pushy role, I guess you could say mine played a passive role. Her influence came from the grave. She had a tubal pregnancy and bled to death on an operating table."

"I'm sorry. I didn't know that."

"Pretty rare now. And even though tubal pregnancies are more common in this day and age, I've never seen anyone die from one—other than my mother. Even then, and I was about twenty, I had a hunch somebody in the hospital botched the diagnosis and treatment."

"Influenced you in many ways, didn't it?"
"Indeed it did."

"Well, I'm glad I asked. Thank you for telling me. Now I'd better get those rooms filled so you can get to work."

It was still raining when Jon headed out of the city after finishing the office and making rounds at the hospitals. He was anxious to get home as he remembered his wife had invited the Judge for dinner tonight. But there was a measure of caution in his driving. He was not a native of this part of the country, but six years had taught him the streets were slippery and dangerous during the first heavy rains of the season. He had nearly spun out only two blocks from his home last year after a November storm had knocked down most of the leaves from the maple and oak trees which lined the street.

The Judge, State Supreme Court Justice William L. Donovan, was the father of Joseph Donovan, M.D. Joe Donovan had been Chief of Ob-Gyn in the Boston hospital where Jon trained. When Jon and Kathy were married after he had completed his residency, Dr. Donovan learned they planned to move to the Pacific Northwest where Jon would start his practice. "You must meet my father," he told the young couple. "I'll write to him and tell him you'll call when you get settled." The elder Donovan, a widower of forty years, had spent most of his professional life in the state's judiciary system. Now at seventy-five he remained on the bench simply because he liked the law, had a remarkably keen mind—and kept getting re-elected.

His was a vigorous and dominating personality, but he was lonesome and had become somewhat irritable before Jon and Kathy moved into his jurisdiction. He started to soften only a month after their first dinner together. Very soon a bond of mutual trust and admiration developed between this elderly jurist and the young physician. With Kathy, the feelings went deeper. Dr. Donovan had told Jon that Kathy looked much like the pictures of his mother at a similar age—the same black hair, flawless skin and strikingly pale blue eyes. An exquisitely detailed portrait of Kathy hung above a large fireplace in the living room; it had been painted by Joe Donovan's wife.

Judge Donovan always paused for a moment in front of the picture whenever he was in their home. His emotions may have been influenced by the resemblance to the wife he knew so many years ago or it just may have been because Kathy was Kathy. She was a vibrant young woman who loved this irascible old man just as he loved her. Roses were his hobby and tonight he brought a dozen from his greenhouse. They were long stemmed, deep yellow and Kathy had put them on the dining room table.

Jon noticed the bouquet as soon as he walked in. "Good evening, Judge," he said. "Those nice looking little posies from your private stock?"

"Jon, please," the Judge said, "those posies, as you called them, are hybrid tea roses and that particular one is called 'Oregold.' It's a rather recent addition to the rose family—1975, I believe."

"Thank you, Judge. Seems I get a lesson in horticulture every time you come around. Good to see you again."

Kathy had heard Jon's car drive into the garage so when she came out of the kitchen she carried a martini for her husband and a refill of bourbon for the Judge. "Can you drink this, hon?" she asked, "or are you on—" Jon's greeting kiss stopped the question in mid-sentence.

Few wives are capable of displaying a flash of passion while standing with a drink in each hand. Kathy, even after six years of marriage, was equal to the task. Jon just winked at her as they separated and he reached for his glass.

"I'm not on call 'till midnight, if that's what you were going to ask."

This brief display of intimacy was not missed by the man in the big leather chair who was waiting for his drink. He got up slowly and walked over to where Jon and Kathy were standing. He accepted the drink and promptly set it down on a nearby table then put his arms around his two young friends.

"You two," he said. "I love to come here and see you together. I've told you before and I'll tell you again, I'm so very glad you came to my part of the country. You've really made a difference in my life."

Kathy put her hands on his cheeks and kissed him lightly on the forehead. "You old darling," she said, "I don't know what we would've done without you. Now you and Jon enjoy your drinks. I'll join you in a minute."

"We dining gourmet tonight, Kate?"

"No, nothing elaborate tonight and it's about ready. I'll just fix the salad and be back with my scotch."

"How's she do it, Jon?" the Judge asked after he had settled back into his chair.

"Do what, Judge?"

"Go to school, keep house, entertain—"

"Oh, you mean just the simple little day to day things that all women are supposed to do."

"Yes, something like that. I might have expressed it a little differently, though."

"Judge, you know me. I try to maintain my reputation as a chauvinistic S.O.B. even around Kate. I suppose, down deep, I'm sort of proud of her."

"Well, I hope so. And there shouldn't be any doubt about it. I'd say she's done pretty well since you came to Oregon. Graduated from medical school and now in her second year of a psychiatry residency. I think that's making very good use of her time."

"Yeah, you're right. She tells me she wants to stay in academic life. Work her way up the teaching ranks. She'll make a good professor if she stays at it."

"She will. She'll stay at it and she'll be good at it. Maybe with all that training she'll be able to figure you out some day, Jon."

"What's to figure out, Judge? My life's an open book."

"Not quite, Jon, not quite. You're a fairly complicated young man and I wonder if you know it. Here you are a very successful obstetrician and gynecologist but a self-proclaimed chauvinistic S.O.B. Doesn't fit, does it? And Kathy seems to tolerate your attitude. Tell me about her, Jon. Seems to me when the three of us sit around we're always talking about you and your practice and we never get around to Kathy. I wonder if she sort of resents it."

"Oh, I doubt it, Judge. Kathy was a nurse, you know, before she went to medical school. And nurses are used to doctors being the center of attention. And I think nurses in general, young ones particularly, want to be in a male-dominated world. They may resent it later on when they get older and male doctors are still giving orders, but at the beginning I really believe that is one reason girls go for an R.N. degree when they leave high school."

"And Kathy fits into that category?"

"Yes, probably for very similar reasons. She comes from a Boston Irish Catholic family and little Irish Catholic girls live in a male-dominated world—their father and above all, their priest. They are not apt to cross either one."

"Well, having a name like Donovan, I understand what you're talking about, though my family was all from Northern Ireland so I've never had any allegiance to Rome. But what made Kathy different? What gave her the drive to go beyond the subservient calling of the nursing profession?"

"Probably her mother. I think her mother resented her own role as the submissive member of the family. She wouldn't tangle with her husband or the Church—afraid to do that—but she sure pushed her kids to get ahead. I really wasn't too all fired hot for Kathy to go to medical school but, by God, her mother was."

"What do you think about it now?"

"Well, it's a different life, home life, from what I thought I'd have with Kathy. But she wants that specialty certificate in psychiatry and I guess she'll get it."

"You say she comes from a strong Catholic home, what happened to her religion since you were married?"

"What do you mean, what happened to her religion?"

"I don't hear about Catholicism from Kathy and I don't see Catholicism in your home. Have you destroyed her religion, Jon?"

"No, I don't think so. We have some minor clashes over it now and then. Nothing major yet. As long as she doesn't start hanging icons all over the house I think we'll be okay. And she understands that."

"Say, Jon," came a voice from the kitchen, "tell the Judge about that case you had at University Hospital last night. I'm sure he's read about it in the papers, but you can make it more dramatic."

Through another drink and all of dinner, the conversation revolved around the killer Poet and the feticides. At one point the Judge asked, "Kathy, give us a little psychiatric background on a case like this. What do you think causes somebody to act in such an abnormal way and how should we treat him after he's caught?"

"How do you know the killer is a 'he'?" Kathy said.

"It must be, Kate," Jon said. "Women just don't attack other women, especially in this fashion."

"Oh, Jon, yes they do. Women can be terribly vicious toward other women. All the more so if they're a little mentally unbalanced to begin with. And I think, male or female, the individual involved in this feticide business is not operating from a full deck. What's your opinion, Judge?"

"You didn't answer my question, Kathy."

"Your Honor," Kathy pleaded, "you forget, I'm only in my second year of training. How many years have you been on the bench? Thirty some odd? I'll bet you've had more experience with crazy killers than any ten psychiatrists. I only know that our killer Poet doesn't like pregnant teenagers, but I don't know why."

"I suspect the 'why' will turn up in a few days," Judge Donovan said. "Maybe the girls knew each other, maybe their babies had a common father. Maybe they all got together and jilted him. On the other hand, and this is the frightening part of it, there may be no logical answer at all. We may have a maniac loose in the city. And in that case, my dear, you'd better speed up your education and learn about serial killers. As a psychiatrist, you just might get involved in this some day."

"I hope not, Judge. Besides, Jon's already involved. He can sew up those girls after they're slashed by that psychotic. But I think he'd like nothing better than to be part of the hunt. In his heart, Jon's about three-quarters doctor and one-quarter cop and that one-quarter is just aching to be heard."

CHAPTER II

```
THIS IS NUMBER FOUR
    JUST A WHORE
TAX DOLLARS SUPPORT HER
    AND ALL OF HER FUN
NOW THE BURDEN IS LESS
    BY THE COUNT OF ONE
```

The poem was still in the typewriter and had been laboriously pecked out with the index finger of the right hand. There were five pages of computer print-out on the desk beside the old portable machine, each page headed:

University Hospital
Department of Obstetrics and Gynecology
Special Procedures Clinic

The door to the office was double locked, the office itself barren of any distinguishing features showing only an obvious fetish toward neatness on the part of its occupant. The standard metal desk was uncluttered except for the old typewriter and the packets of reports which were stacked in an orderly manner off to the side.

The Poet had completed the verse and remained seated, studying individual case histories of patients registered in the Special Procedures Clinic. The Clinic was a unique gathering of pregnancy patients which had been established at the University Hospital to study the effects of alcohol and drugs on the developing fetus. The Poet was looking for a patient who would mirror the rhymes which were dropped at the scene. The chart of Mary Ann Harper was selected. Mary Ann's use of drugs and alcohol early in her pregnancy made her an ideal candidate for the Special Procedures Clinic—and for the Poet's knife. Her pregnancy wasn't due until late January, over two months away. And January was usually a month of rain.

Jon's sleep had not been disturbed by calls during the night and he was in good spirits as he drove to University Hospital to make rounds on Bobbie Morris, now listed officially on the police blotter as Feticide #3. This was her second post operative day and there were no complications reported in the chart or by Mrs. David, the charge nurse. But that was the last good news for the day as she also reported that Lt. Lenhart had been in to see the patient early that morning. "It was before we came on duty, Doctor Erickson. There was a new nurse on nights. She told me he really came on strong—pulled rank, flashed his badge and all that. Said a police investigation takes precedence over anything but emergencies. Anyway, he got in. Stayed there about a half an hour."

"I'll be damned. Don't written orders mean anything in this hospital?" Jon asked.

"Of course they do, Doctor. But frankly, I wouldn't have wanted to be in that nurse's place. Fresh out of nurse's training, first job and some big cop comes along, shoves his badge in her face and demands to see a patient."

"She should have called the night supervisor."

"That would be Bertha Hill and she called in sick at midnight. Next one up the line would be the day supervisor at home. Nobody likes to wake up the day super, especially just to get permission to let a detective in to see a patient."

The nurse had been trying to type out a laboratory request on the computer but now she turned to face Jon directly. "Did it really matter all that much, Doctor Erickson?" she asked. "The patient seems to be doing very well this morning."

"It mattered to me, Mrs. David," was Jon's reply and he left to go visit Feticide #3. The nurse's report, he found, was only partly true. Physically Bobbie Morris was better than could be expected for the trauma she had sustained, but the Lieutenant's visit had affected her emotionally.

"He wasn't very nice to me, Doctor Erickson," Bobbie said and started to cry. "I think he was mad that I didn't see anything that day, anything that might help him find the guy who did this to me. And he made me feel like sort of a slut. He's not supposed to do that is he?"

"No, but that's Lieutenant Lenhart. There were orders to keep him out of your room but he managed to slip by. It won't happen again, Bobbie, at least not while you're in the hospital. Now, let's get rid of those tears and tell me how you are really doing."

"Pretty good, I guess. I got up twice already this morning."

"Good for you. We'll have you out of here in a couple of days. By the way, besides upsetting you with his comments, what all did the Lieutenant have to say? Did he ask anything about the other two girls who have been hit?"

"Oh, yeah. He wanted to know if we were close friends. When I told him I knew both of them he came right out and asked if we had the same boyfriend. Something else I didn't think was any of his business, he wanted to know if any of the girls were screwing around with some of the staff people in the Clinic."

"You're right, it isn't any of his personal business, Bobbie, but you never know what little bit of information might help keep some of your friends from winding up in the hospital."

"Well, I told him I don't know anything and that's when he got mad. Even threatened to put me in jail if I knew something and didn't tell him."

"I wouldn't worry too much about it, Bobbie. You've got better things to do than fret about Lieutenant Lenhart. I'll see you this evening."

Jon went to St. Elizabeths from University Hospital and found more bad news. The abdominal hysterectomy he was scheduled to do had been delayed by emergency surgery and it was two o'clock before he arrived at his office. The waiting room was full and his first patient, an unmarried teenager, became absolutely hysterical while the nurse was checking the fetal heart with the ultrasound. "It feels like a knife," she screamed. "You're trying to kill my baby. It's a boy, I just know it's a boy and you're poking holes in it with that machine. Oh, my God, I'm going to deliver a dead baby boy just like the ones in the paper."

It took Jon nearly an hour to calm the panicky young woman and by this time he had lost all hope of an orderly office schedule. By six o'clock when the last patient had been seen, Jon turned to Nell and just shook his head. "Tough day," he said, "and I'm afraid we're going to have more of the same if the Poet pays the city another visit."

"You're probably right, but we'll deal with it somehow. Take one day at a time, my mamma used to say. See you tomorrow, Doctor."

It was after seven by the time Jon finished rounds at both hospitals and drove home. It had been an unpleasant and tiring day. To make matters worse, Kathy's day had not been easy and she was anxious to talk with her husband about some of her problem patients. One had been particularly nasty and resistant to any of her suggestions or counseling. When she attempted to describe the session with the patient, Jon cut her short.

"God damn it, Kate," he said, "you're a long way from being a full-fledged shrink. Learn your limitations. Let the attending staff handle some of those goofballs. The world would be a hell of a lot better off if most of your patients had wound up as abortions instead of crazy adults."

"Be careful, Jon. That's a touchy subject and you know it."

"You going pro-life on me, Kate?"

"Don't be an ass. Of course not, but sticking a vacuum cleaner in the uterus is a lousy method of birth control."

"Good thing I rescued you from the Catholic Church when I did. God knows what you might have developed into."

"Jon! Enough! I'm going to bed."

Their tempers had cooled by morning. Kathy thought about apologizing but decided not to. Jon didn't even consider it. A few days later the episode had been mostly forgotten. Their professional lives were too busy to carry on a feud at home, but Kathy was aware of a growing indifference on the part of her husband. Despite the occasional evidence of a deep affection, he had never been very sensitive to her needs and she had accepted this right from the start. Now it seemed the disagreements and arguments were more frequent and it was always she who gave in first and apologized. And she admitted, at least to herself, her subservient role was growing tiresome.

There never was an appropriate time to raise the subject for discussion; Jon was frequently at the hospital until late at night and mornings were a blur of activity as each hurried to get to their respective appointments. The holidays were coming. Surely things would improve then.

They didn't. It was not a very merry Christmas and in rather depressing contrast to her years in Boston, there was not one flake of snow to be seen in the valley. By January, Kathy saw matters getting worse because of Jon's increasing interest in the feticide cases. What little extra time he had in the evenings was spent reviewing all the available details of the three cases plus studying text books dealing with unusual and bizarre crimes. One night, completely exasperated, she accused him of accepting too many challenges. "You want to be the best obstetrician in this city," she said. "You also want to be the best golfer, have the best kept lawn in the neighborhood, drive the fastest car. Now you want to solve the mystery of the feticides. Enough, Jon. Relax a little."

Jon rarely showed any emotion in his response to Kathy's complaints. He did now.

"Damn it, Kate, you bet I want to be a good obstetrician. And I don't like to be embarrassed on the golf course. You mention the lawn. I suspect you'd be the first to bitch if I let it go to seed. And my car is not the fastest in town. You can hassle me all you want about those things, but don't get on my back about the Poet. I want that son of a bitch put down and if the police can't do it, by God I'll find a way."

Somehow, despite these very unpleasant interludes, they did manage to continue as husband and wife and to even occasionally divide the newspaper and report to one another on any item of significance in the section they had read. On this particular day Kathy gave Jon the good news that, despite this being January, a brief spell of sunshine was predicted. Maybe a chance for a round of golf. Jon, in turn, briefed an item which reviewed the three feticides. The article involving the feticides was definitely low-key and on page six. It was obvious that the purpose of the piece was to calm and reassure the city. The writer theorized the existence of a sex-crazed boyfriend who now had his fill of revenge and would seek no more retribution against his teenager lovers. It implied the author had access to evidence that led him to this conclusion.

As it turned out, the paper was mistaken that day—not once but twice. Somehow the meteorologist had overlooked a very significant "low" in the weather pattern. He hadn't really missed it as it was in plain sight just off the Queen Charlotte Islands. The computer had it moving east across Canada, then dipping down over the plains states. Nature, not completely computerized as yet, swung the "low" suddenly and dramatically down into the valleys of the Northwest. Seventy-mile-an-hour winds hit the city accompanied by the heaviest rainfall of the year. Four-thirty traffic caught the brunt of the storm. Traffic lights malfunctioned and the snarl of cars and wet pedestrians stretched for blocks in all directions.

The Poet had not expected the storm. Sunshine, unusual for that time of year, had prevailed during most of the afternoon. But now, the sky was dark and wind-driven rain pelted the windows. Plans could be changed and the print-out of Mary Ann Harper was reviewed. It was four o'clock, just about the time patients would be finished with Clinic. But they frequently dawdled and talked before taking the bus downtown. It was short notice and a gamble, but the shoe box was taken from the closet. The knife was fit into the spring mechanism, a mechanism designed in such a manner that minimal strength was needed to create lethal tension. Now the coat. The weapon was carefully concealed in the sleeve, the pocket was checked for the envelope. With that, the Poet started on another mission of mercy—to end a life before it began and before it suffered from being born into poverty. As usual, there was a final look into the shoe box at the faded snapshot of a tiny baby. **James Leroy** had been printed, crudely, on a small wooden cross, and James Leroy was pictured going to his final resting place in a homemade casket. There was a date, hand-painted, on the cross. James Leroy would have been twenty-one years old this year. It was just a quick look, then the top was carefully placed back on the shoe box.

Mary Ann Harper's exit from the Clinic, as predicted, was delayed by the usual "girl talk" and the bus ride down into the city was slowed by the storm. She lived on the east side of the river and this required a transfer from the bus to rapid rail system. Usually she was able to alight from one conveyance and board the train about a half block down the street. Today the bus was stalled in traffic and Mary Ann decided to get off and walk the remaining five blocks.

The large rain coat and oversized hat blended inconspicuously with the wet and somewhat testy crowd around the transit station. When the buses failed to arrive on time the Poet, sensing correctly that the prey would leave the bus and walk toward the train, joined those who were braving the storm and started down the street to find her.

Mary Ann was an easily identified target. Her thin coat stretched over her full-term belly and offered scant protection from the cold rain and wind. She was first spotted about three blocks from where the bus had come to a stop. Even her youth could not hide the splay-footed duck walk of the very pregnant. She was lost for a few minutes when the Poet crossed over the street in the middle of traffic. It was not a conspicuous move as there were many others crossing between the slow-moving cars. The unmistakable profile came back into view when she, and most of the pedestrians, stopped at the curb awaiting the erratically functioning lights to signal a safe crossing. Unseen or unnoticed, the right arm of the large rain coat was raised for just a second. Mary Ann's baby died before the light turned green. Number four and counting.

Jon was only vaguely aware of an ambulance siren as he sat in a small classroom close to the outpatient clinic of the medical school. His official title there was Assistant Clinical Professor of Obstetrics and it was his day to spend an hour with the students. He had hardly started the session when the clinic intercom buzzed:

"Doctor Erickson, this is Mrs. Connors, operating room supervisor. Do you have the third year obstetrical students with you?"

"Yes, they're all here."

"Good. Send them down to the operating room right away. There's been another one of our Ob patients brought in by ambulance. Doctor Johnson says it's very similar to that case you operated on before. He said since you're here, maybe you'd like to take this one, too. And of course he wants the students to see it."

"Sure, I'll take it. Who's available to help?"

"Second year resident and an intern."

"Be right over."

Dr. Johnson, Chief of the Department of Obstetrics and Gynecology at the University, met Jon in the surgeons' dressing room. "Glad you were available, Jon," he said. "My senior residents are all busy or on vacation. Besides, you've had some experience with these cases."

"Oh, sure, one case. But I appreciate your asking me and I expect I can patch this one up, too. Patching them up is a small part of it, Doctor Johnson. The big question is why the hell are we getting these ripped up young women? Do you think someone in this University complex is using the information available up here or maybe inadvertently giving it to somebody else?"

"God only knows, but I hope we find out soon. Well," and he gave Jon a friendly pat on the shoulder, "I'm supposed to be in a meeting with the Dean. Mrs. Connors will know where I am if you need me."

"Thank you, Doctor Johnson. I'll take care of the post-op on this one."

"Yes, I knew you would. See you later."

Jon quickly changed into a scrub suit and went to the sinks where he was joined by Dr. Hansen, the second year resident, and one of the interns assigned to obstetrics.

"Bill Hansen, isn't it?" Jon asked.

"Yes."

"Weren't you with me when we operated on Bobbie Morris? I think that was her name—the number three feticide."

"I was second assist, Doctor Erickson."

"I thought I recognized you. Did you scrub on the first two?"

"I worked with the Chief Resident on number one."

"Good. We should be able to move right along on this. How 'bout you?" and Jon turned to the intern.

"No, sir. This is my first."

"Have you ever scrubbed on a cesarean section?"

"Yes, sir. Two last week."

"Fine. If the wound of entry is high on the uterus like the last one, we'll treat this very much like a section, then repair the extra hole left by the killer's weapon."

But number four was different. The previous cases had a neat little wound on the side of the abdomen where the projectile had entered. Very little tissue damage resulted from this and minimal blood loss. This victim was not so lucky. She was in obvious shock when Jon first saw her. The operating room table was turned to a steep, head down position to allow more blood and oxygen to the patient's brain. Two transfusions, one in each arm, were being pumped in simultaneously. Later it was determined the projectile had grazed her wrist watch on its deadly path toward the fetus. This resulted in a slight deviation in course and a tumbling action as it hit the bulging abdominal wall. At first glance it appeared as though half the front of the abdomen had been torn off. The muscles were ripped apart and bleeding profusely. A small, pale hand was plainly visible through this mass of blood and torn muscle. The lethal weapon had cut a jagged swath through the uterus and placenta. The fetus, desperate for oxygen and in a frenzy of activity, had managed to get one upper extremity free from this now totally inhospitable environment. Then it died.

As Jon was being gowned and gloved he studied the patient and determined a surgical approach which he hoped would at least salvage one life. Then he glanced at the scrub nurse who was holding his surgical gloves. Tears were streaming from her eyes and disappearing under her mask.

"What's your name?" Jon asked the nurse.

"B—Burton, Joan Burton," she replied, stifling a sob.

"You want to be relieved, Miss Burton?"

"No, sir."

Jon looked straight at the nurse for a few seconds then turned toward the operating table. "Knife," he said.

Exactly three minutes later Jon delivered the dead baby through a new incision made separately from that of the Poet's weapon. It was a little boy, pale and flaccid but otherwise unmarked. He handed the lifeless body over to the circulating nurse. "Poor little devil," Jon said, "died before he had a chance to live."

The projectile lay free in the lower part of the uterus. It had expended all of its energy in destroying the baby's sterile home.

"Okay, let's get this uterus contracted down as best we can. Its pretty torn up but maybe we can save it. Put about four ampules of pitocin in that I.V. solution. That's the best we can do right now to clamp down the muscle. How much blood have we used so far?"

"Eight units with two more going in," the anesthesiologist answered.

"How's she doing?"

"Hell of a lot better than when she first came in. At least I can get pulse and blood pressure now."

"Good. How 'bout you, Miss Burton?"

"I'm okay, Doctor, thank you. This is the first one of these I've scrubbed on and that little hand sort of got to me."

"I think it got to all of us. Now let's see if we can get this mess back together again."

And that took about an hour, after which Jon gave instructions to Dr. Hansen about post-op care and walked out of the O.R.

"He was almost human today," the scrub nurse said as soon as the O.R. door was closed.

"Isn't he supposed to be?" Bill Hansen asked.

"Not according to my friend down at St. Elizabeths. She called him an arrogant, chauvinistic son of a bitch."

"Pretty strong words," the intern said.

"She ought to know," Joan persisted. "She's worked for him in both Ob and surgery. He's good, my friend admits that, but he can be tough on the nurses."

"Maybe the nurses down there just aren't as pretty and talented as you are, Burton."

"And you cried," the intern added. "Awful hard to berate somebody who has tears in her eyes."

"Go to hell, both of you. I had reason to cry. Now give me a hand putting a dressing on this belly."

Uncharacteristically, Jon's head was down as he walked slowly down the hall away from the operating room. The O.R. supervisor stopped him as he walked by her desk. "There is a Lieutenant Lenhart in the visitors' waiting room. He asked to see you as soon as you were through in surgery."

Jon's head jerked up and he slapped his hand down hard on Mrs. Connor's desk. "Damn him," he said. "I'll see him but he won't like it. Would you call in there and tell him I'll be along as soon as I check the post-op orders? And Mrs. Connor, if there are any patient's relatives in that visitors room tell him to go to the surgical lounge. I'm pretty sure that's empty."

"Sure."

The police lieutenant was alone in the visitors' room when Jon walked in a few minutes later. He looked up from the magazine he was reading and saw the blood which had soaked through the surgical gown and stained Jon's scrub suit.

"Hi, Doc. I hope that ain't your blood there."

"No. I expect it's a mixture of the mother's and the dead baby's."

"Dead, huh?"

"Yes."

"The mama?"

"I think she'll be alright."

The information did not seem to visibly affect Lt. Lenhart one way or another. He merely shrugged his shoulders and asked, "Same kind of weapon?"

"Looked like it to me."

"Well, Ah reckon we guessed wrong on this one, didn't we?"

"Meaning?"

"Us boys in homicide. We didn't figure to get another case like this."

"You ever do anything about the previous deaths? There were three, as I recall."

The Lieutenant shrugged his shoulders again. Naw," he said. "Oh, we made the routine rounds but didn't turn up nothin'."

"How hard did you try?"

"Now, Doc. You and me, we jawed about this once before. Y'all just tend to your sewin' and Ah'll do the police work."

"I hate to mention it, Lieutenant, but it seems to me that my sewing is a hell of a lot better than your police work."

The heavy eyelids of the southern policeman opened wider as he met Jon's level stare. A little smile played at the corners of his mouth. "Screw you, Doc," he said. "Ah don't have to take that kind of shit. You just make damned sure your little old photographic department in this here University Hospital takes lots of pictures of that dead bastard baby. Some of our folk will sign for 'em and for copies of the chart and your dictation. Do Ah make mahsef perfectly clear?"

"Oh yes, Lieutenant, you do have a way about making yourself perfectly clear. I also think it's clear that somebody is dragging their ass when it comes to solving these murders. I wonder what the reaction would be if I sent a full report of all four cases—plus our conversations—to the Police Commissioner?"

"You just go right ahead and do that, boy. That's the man that hired me and Ah don't figure he's gonna fire me over these cases. You got me pegged wrong, Doc. Ah ain't no fool. Ah gotta a drawer full of reports on them chippies and there'll be more on this one you operated on today. Showed the others to the Commissioner. He didn't raise no fuss at all."

Lt. Lenhart shifted his weight a little and folded his arms over his ample belly. He smirked as he asked: "If you are so all fired worked up about this Poet and the girls, why don't you just go and ketch him yusef?"

"By God, I think I can do a better job than you're doing."

The smirk was gone. "Careful, Doc," he said. "I really wouldn't interfere in police matters if I was you. That Poet fellow might just use one of his little stickies to slit your throat."

Jon was no fool either. He sensed real malice in the Lieutenant's remarks and chose not to challenge him further.

Lt. Lenhart also knew when a conversation was over. He turned and walked toward the elevator.

Jon stood for a moment staring at the back of his adversary. He felt more than contempt for this disappearing figure. He had come out a poor second in a verbal jousting—and in a hospital setting. Challenged and bested on his own grounds. Pride was a factor and his had been damaged. He went in to the dressing room to change clothes and noticed that his hands were actually trembling. "Damn, I let that guy get to me again," Jon said to himself. "He may not want any competition finding that rhyming killer, but by God, he's got some."

Mrs. Collins paged him just as he was buttoning his shirt. "Doctor Erickson, you still there?"

"Yes. Just about ready to leave, why?"

"There's a call for you from the emergency room at St. Elizabeths."

"Okay, I'll take it in here."

Jon picked up the phone as soon as it rang. "This is Doctor Erickson," he said.

"Doctor, this is Mrs. Jasper, E.R. at St. Elizabeths. Are you backup physician for obstetrics and gynecology tonight?"

"I'm the lucky one, yes."

"Good. There's a young lady here with vaginal bleeding. She thinks she may be pregnant. Doesn't want to see any of our emergency room physicians. Insists on seeing you."

"She one of my regular patients?"

"I don't know. She's not very communicative. Just said she wanted to see Doctor Erickson."

"What's her name?"

"Sarah Tompkins."

"I don't recognize it but that doesn't mean anything. I'd better come on over. What's the weather like? I've been over here at the University for the past two or three hours. Haven't even looked outside."

"It's still raining, of course, but the wind has died down. There are some lines down on the streets so be careful."

"Thanks. Get a little history on this Sarah Tompkins while I get dressed and drive over. Run a quick pregnancy test, too."

When he arrived at St. Elizabeths' Emergency Room, Jon was directed to one of the many exam rooms. The chart outside the door gave the usual and routine information required of all new patients. This patient was not destined to be routine and Jon sensed such a future when he read through the face page of the chart.

Name:	Sarah Tompkins
Age:	26
Occupation:	Unemployed
Insurance:	None
Religion:	None
Marital Status:	Single
Height:	5'4"

Weight:	115 pounds
Blood Pressure:	108/65
Pulse:	80
Respiration:	20
Temperature:	99.2 F
Chief Complaint:	Vaginal bleeding
Last Menstrual Period:	Approximately six weeks ago
Method of Contraception:	None
Blood Count:	No abnormal findings, see attached report.
Urinalysis:	No abnormal finding, see attached report.
Pregnancy Test:	Positive.

There was also a brief note by the E.R. nurse to indicate the vaginal bleeding was not excessive and was not accompanied by cramps.

Jon quickly scanned the chart. Nothing of significance. Sarah Tompkins—the name definitely was not familiar. He opened the door and called her by name.

"Miss Tompkins?" he asked.

"Yes. Doctor Erickson?"

"I am."

Sarah Tompkins was seated on the exam table dressed only in a hospital gown. Quite probably by design, she had put the gown on backwards, the ties in front. The loops of cloth were very loosely tied, the top two entirely open revealing a major portion of remarkably beautiful breasts.

Jon did not recognize her. While he noticed her breasts and was properly impressed, he was more startled by her eyes. Gray, colorless, set close together in a thin, almost homely face, they were the dominant factor in an expression of vaguely masked defiance and challenge. Jon, for all his arrogance, was aware of the pitfalls of his profession. He walked behind the patient and pressed a button to summon a nurse. Sarah didn't seem to be bothered by the addition of a third party in the exam room.

Other than the brief introduction, Jon had not spoken to Sarah. Now he did.

"Miss Tompkins, the nurse tells me you are having some vaginal bleeding and think you may be pregnant. Is this so?"

"Yes. I assume my last menstrual period has been recorded in your chart. I've had no vaginal bleeding since then until today. It's not very severe and not associated with any cramps. But I know any bleeding is abnormal. That's why I'm here."

"Did anything precede the onset of flow?" Jon asked. "Any trauma? Sex relations? Did you fall or did the bleeding just come on by itself?"

"I've not had any sexual intercourse for over a week. No falls, no trauma to the abdomen, but I did move a large branch off my driveway during the storm. I might have strained myself at that time as the bleeding episode occurred shortly thereafter."

"Where did you go to school, Miss Tompkins?" Jon's question was unexpected and completely out of context with the previous inquiries.

Sarah frowned. "Why do you ask?"

"Oh, I'm always a little curious about someone who has no job, no insurance, no visible means of support but who speaks English as well as you obviously do."

"Do you think, Doctor, that you could confine your curiosity to the fact that I am pregnant and bleeding? My mastery of the English language is of no concern to you."

"It's not idle curiosity, Miss Tompkins. Let's just say I'm always interested in what makes my patients tick. And," here Jon paused to look at his patient, "I like to determine why one source of information is at odds with the other."

Abruptly then, he turned to the nurse. "You may get Miss Tompkins ready for an exam now," he said. "I'll be taking the usual cultures."

"Wait a minute. Cultures for what?" Sarah asked.

"We routinely take cultures for sexually transmitted diseases," Jon said.

"Am I to infer," Sarah Tompkins said, "that just because I am a patient in the emergency room that I must submit to the indignity of such laboratory tests? Am I to be treated as a second-class citizen merely because I have no medical insurance?"

Jon finished putting on his rubber gloves and turned again to face the patient. He spoke very slowly so she wouldn't miss a word. "Miss Tompkins, you are a patient in the emergency room of a large metropolitan hospital. We have no precise knowledge of your background or your recent activities. It is a fact, statistically proven, that young women who arrive unannounced at such a facility with complaints referable to their pelvic organs have a much higher incidence of venereal disease than normal. Also the presence of a small rose tattooed over your left breast merely increases the odds of such infections. At least it used to. Tattoos on young women are so common these days that it might not make any difference. But I don't like to take any chances."

Sarah was not easily intimidated. "Then I was right," she said. "I am considered a second-class citizen. Tell me, Doctor—your wife, if she were alone in a strange city with symptoms such as mine, would she be subjected to the same degrading tests?"

"If the doctor who treats her is worth a damn, yes she would. And like you, she would probably be incensed. Does that answer your question?"

Sarah did not reply but instead, still looking directly at Jon, she casually fastened the remaining ties on her hospital gown.

The exam Jon conducted was gentle but extremely thorough. When he had finished he told Miss Tompkins to get dressed and wait. He would return shortly. As he walked from the exam room to the small dictating booth to record his findings, the nurse who had assisted at the exam stopped him in the hall.

"Where'd you get that one, Doctor?" she asked.

"Don't know. Never saw her before."

"She's different."

"You bet she is. She's shrewd and smart as hell and I suspect a little mean. Certainly not the type I'd like to meet in a dark alley."

"Oh, I don't know. Might be exciting."

"Nurse, my life is exciting enough as it is. Besides, I really don't think I need the kind of thrills she might provide."

He went on to dictate and afterwards returned to the exam room. Here he found a Sarah Tompkins almost exactly as expected. She was off the exam table and sitting somewhat belligerently on the exam room counter top. She was wearing a man's shirt—too large, jeans—too tight, and tennis shoes without socks. A raincoat and hat made a formless pile beside her.

"You O.K.?" he asked.

"About the same as when I came in. No better, no worse. I just feel like I've been violated by a very condescending physician who has yet to tell me anything about my condition."

Jon sat down in a corner chair and looked over at this contentious young female. "And that is why I am here now," he said. "To begin with, you are pregnant but you already know that. There is some slight vaginal bleeding which means you may be threatening to abort. You could have a tubal pregnancy and there are some tests we should run to rule that out."

"Do you think the pregnancy is in my tube?"

"No, I don't. But I can't overlook the possibility."

"Do you think I will lose this pregnancy?"

"Do you want to?"

"No. I may want to keep this baby."

"*May* want to? Why?"

"That is none of your business, Doctor."

"Miss Tompkins, when you entered this emergency room tonight you asked for me specifically. I think that grants me the privilege of asking why an intelligent young woman with no husband and no job wants to keep her baby. Your chart shows no religious preference so that sort of rules out a moralistic approach to the problem."

"Maybe I just want to see if I can have a baby. I've done about everything else."

"That's a lousy reason."

"Okay, Doctor Righteous, do you want to do an abortion on me? Remember, I don't have any money."

"Well, as I said, you are threatening to miscarry. Maybe you won't need my help."

"Let's assume I quit bleeding. Same question. Will you abort this pregnancy?"

"If that's what you want, yes."

"So you do abortions then?"

"Occasionally. Let's just say I'm pro-choice. It's not a major part of my practice."

"Actually I was just testing you. I don't want an abortion—unless I'm carrying a boy. If that's the case I want the little shit out of there right away."

There was no smile on Sarah's face when she said this. It was a statement of fact and not offered for its shock value.

"As I recall, Sarah, the odds favor a male—fifty-one to forty-nine I think. You plan to find out ahead of time?"

"Yes I do. There's a Special Procedures Clinic at the University. They do amniocentesis and chorionic biopsies. They'll check it out for me."

"Wait a minute. Do you have any idea what you're talking about? Do you know what those tests are? Amniocentesis? Chorionic biopsy?"

"Of course I know. Amniocentesis is where they jab a needle into the uterus and take some of the fluid the kid is swimming around in. When they ream out a chunk of the placenta, that's a chorionic biopsy. Did you think you doctors were the only ones who could read a medical dictionary?"

"I might have known, but what makes you think the University will take you as a patient?"

"Simple. I don't have any money and I know an orderly who works in that Clinic. Besides, I'm their type. They'll love me. Blow a little dope, snort coke and have an uncle who's a Mongolian idiot—that's Down Syndrome to you, Doctor. Can't you just see those super scientists up there? They'll have an orgasm when they hear my history."

"How much of it's true?"

"Who cares? I'll get those tests run and if it's a male, that little sucker'll get vacuumed out of there—pronto.

"Your business, I guess. A little callous though, don't you think?"

"I have reason to be."

"You hold men in such high regard, I'm amazed you ever got pregnant."

"Oh, men have a purpose. Besides, the lesbian bit doesn't turn me on."

"Well, to each his own," Jon said. "And what role do you propose I play in this charade? You are obviously going to get up to the medical school. Do you want me to refer you and make it easier?"

"Maybe. I'm not sure of the best time for those tests. You'd know more about that. But actually, I want you to take care of me if I stay pregnant. Just refer me to that Clinic for the tests."

"Why me? I'd think with your attitude you'd prefer a woman obstetrician."

"I've heard about you—good things. And that's all I want, somebody competent, male or female. Doesn't make a bit of difference to me."

"Well, thanks for the vote of confidence. And yes, I'll take care of you. I don't think I've ever turned anybody down who's made a point of asking for me. But I admit, Miss Tompkins, with your attitude it's tempting to ask you to find another physician."

Sarah completely ignored Jon's last comment. "O.K., that's settled," she said and slid off the counter to stand in front of him. "So now, what kind of magic therapy do you have for this bleeding?"

"Frankly, not a hell of a lot. If you are destined to miscarry you will do so no matter what treatment I prescribe. Maybe lack of exercise improves your chances of staying pregnant and there are physicians who advise their patients to abstain from all sexual activity when the pregnancy is a little shaky. Nobody knows for sure."

"So it's sort of do your own thing but be careful?"

"That's about it."

"Should I call your office for an appointment?"

"Right, and before you leave tonight I want an ultrasound and a special pregnancy test done."

"Okay."

Jon held the door open for her but she didn't move.

"Just a minute, Doctor. I want you to get something straight. I'm not a complete deadbeat—or as the British would say, a shiftless ne'er-do-well. I want you to know that. And something else—do you have a computer in your office?"

"I share one with another obstetrician, yes."

"I understand those things. I can handle any computer in this town—no sweat. If you have any trouble with yours just let me know.

I'll have the little hummer fixed before you know it." Then with just a slight trace of a smile she added, "No charge."

"Thank you. I might take you up on that offer some day. Now let's get you started off toward ultrasound. I'll see you at the office in a day or two unless you have increased bleeding or pain in the meantime."

Three hours later it was still raining but now, any Northwest native would describe it as "just a little mist." The Poet, a little "high" from seeing Mary Ann go down and then the ambulances and police, was wandering the streets. There was another target in mind, but no hurry. It would take a little planning and the storm had passed. Rain was a curse. It had been hated from early childhood. But now it served a purpose and more would fall before the year was out. And there was always the possibility of snow in the valley. Snow. White snow and red blood. The Poet smiled at the thought. What a dramatic way to show the rewards of sin.

CHAPTER III

The weather was still overcast and somewhat dismal a few days later when Kathy came home late after attending some important evening seminars. Jon was reading in the living room so she made a quick sandwich and went in to join him.

"Jon, do you know a Doctor Miller?" she asked. "He's a Ph.D. psychologist. Spends some of his time counseling unwed pregnancies in the outpatient clinics. I had quite a run in with him today."

"Talked to him over the phone once. That's the only contact I've had with him. He called after I operated on the number three feticide patient. Sounded like sort of a strange duck but I wouldn't know him if I saw him."

"Strange is right. More like paranoid schizophrenic. He came over to the psych department today and accused me of stealing one of his patients. He caught me out in the hall, right in front of some of the other residents, and just ripped into me. Patients were around, too."

Jon had been deeply engrossed in a journal article concerning laser treatment of cervical cancer and hadn't bothered to look up at Kathy when replying to her question on Dr. Miller. His irritation at having his reading interrupted was obvious when, still without raising his head, he asked: "So, did you steal one of his patients?"

"Jon, damn you. I think this is important. Some unbalanced moron on the staff at the medical school acts in a highly unprofessional manner toward your wife and you sort of off-handedly take his side. Of course I didn't steal one of his patients. She called for an appointment in the psych clinic and was assigned to me."

"And I suppose you stood out there in the hall and told him this in no uncertain terms."

"I most certainly did."

Jon just shook his head. "Kate, you've got to learn not to get emotionally involved in these things. Christ Almighty, you're training to be a shrink. Time you started to act like one."

"Oh, don't worry about me, Jon. I'm not nearly as emotionally involved as you think—in the Clinic and maybe not even at home—anymore. Now please go back to your reading. And forgive me, sir. I apologize for disturbing you."

"Don't be nasty, Kate."

"Me, nasty? No, just hurt." Kathy turned and without another word went down the hall to their bedroom. She was more than hurt. She was very much aware that this was the second blow-up in the past week. And Dr. Miller's behavior had truly frightened her. She had hoped to receive some help, some compassion from her husband, but that was out of the question now. He was, she reflected, capable of so much love but it seemed he lavished it on his terms only. She was growing tired of catering to his moods and she was two weeks late with her menstrual period—pregnant. She desperately wanted Jon to be pleased and remembered he had rather liked the idea when they talked about it last year.

Things were still tense at the Erickson home the next morning but neither Kathy nor Jon had time to take much note of it. She had Tuesday morning grand rounds with the Chief of Service starting at seven o'clock and was out of the house just after Jon got up. Jon always said his best thinking came when he was taking a shower—clean thoughts, all the dirt and nastiness being washed down the drain. This morning with the hot water hitting his face and chest he somewhat begrudgingly admitted to a little guilt. Not enough to apologize, but he did resolve to use his connections at the medical school to check on this Dr. Miller. Couldn't be quite as bad as Kathy had made him out to be, she always exaggerated things a bit, but it wouldn't take too much effort to find out. If I volunteer to work in that Special Procedures Clinic, Jon thought to himself, I can find out all I need to know about Miller and that will give me the chance see who else works up there. There had to be a connection between that Clinic and the four dead babies. "If it's there," he said aloud, "I'll find it."

The guilt was gone and his day quite well-planned when Jon got out of the shower. He contacted Dr. Johnson at the medical school who was very pleased to have Jon volunteer to serve in the Special Procedures Clinic. One of the other Clinical Instructors had resigned and it was arranged for Jon to take his place the following Friday. That matter was settled early in the afternoon and there were no additional interruptions in his office routine until a call came at four o'clock. Jon's secretary buzzed: "There is a police lieutenant on the phone for you, Doctor," she said.

"Lenhart?"

"That's who it sounded like."

"What the hell does he want? O.K., I'll take the call," and Jon pushed the button for the incoming call. "This is Doctor Erickson," he said.

"Doc, this is Lieutenant Lenhart. Y'all remember me?"

"Oh, yes. Definitely."

"Little problem down here at headquarters. One of them dumb secretaries misfiled your surgical report on the last kid that got a knife in her belly. Got one there in the office?"

"I'm sure we do, yes."

"That's good, real good. We need a certified copy. Mind sendin' it down? Just stick mah name on the envelope."

"No problem, Lieutenant, except I can't certify it. I don't have anyone in the office who can do that."

"That's a mighty big buildin' you're in there, Doc. Sure to be a notary public around somewheres. Lawyers always have 'em. You just drop down to one of them legal friends of yours. They'll do it. Probably won't cost you nothin'."

"I don't have time to do that today, Lieutenant."

"Well damn it, Doc, send one of your girls down."

"If I'm busy, Lieutenant, they're busy. I'll bet you have a notary around headquarters there someplace. She can pick up that gadget she stamps things with, bring it up here and take care of the whole thing with minimal bother."

"Doc, you don't seem to understand. I need that in the mail today and nobody down here goin' to run up to your office. You tryin' to obstruct justice or somethin', Doc?"

"Nothing of the sort, Lieutenant. Very simple. You want it from this office, you come and get it. You can always call the hospital, you know. They'll send you one after you sign about a dozen forms. Probably get it in a week or two."

There was a pause, then, "You win this one, Doc. Be a patrolman there with a notary in fifteen minutes."

Nell had been standing next to Jon's desk with a chart in her hand during most of the conversation. When he hung up the phone she asked, "That your buddy, Lieutenant Lenhart?"

"The one and only."

"He was here yesterday afternoon while you were gone. Couldn't hide the surprise on his face when he saw me."

"The Lieutenant is not color blind, Nell. That's just one of his many faults."

"I know. I've seen that look before. But it's time to go to work now," and she handed him the chart.

Near the end of office hours, Jon was called to St. Elizabeths to see a patient in labor. He was spared additional confrontation with Kathy by remaining in the hospital until early in the morning when the patient finally delivered.

Both Ericksons avoided controversy of any sort for the next two days, neither one wishing to disturb a fragile peace. Kathy had a pregnancy test to confirm what she already knew. It was positive and now she was beginning to fear Jon's reaction. She was trained to direct mind games in her patients but Jon was not her patient and she could not decide on a proper time or place to tell him of his approaching fatherhood. Her excitement about the pregnancy was tempered by her concern for the future of the family.

Jon started his duties at the Special Procedures Clinic the following Saturday. The Clinic's short term purpose was to detect any abnormalities in the developing fetus. If any gross deformities were found, abortion would be offered. To this end, ultrasound studies, amniocentesis and biopsies of the placenta were routinely performed on nearly all of the patients who had been referred to the Clinic. The directors of the Clinic hoped to study the physical and mental development of the babies for many years to detect any damage if the mother admitted to the use of drugs or alcohol during the pregnancy. Jon had known of the Clinic for over a year and, along with other local physicians, had referred an occasional patient. Most were unwed teenagers with a drug and alcohol history and they remained with the Clinic for the duration of their pregnancy.

The Director of the Clinic was Frances McGraw, B.S., R.N. Ms. McGraw ran an efficient organization and did not tolerate any challenge to her authority. She had been told of Jon's appointment to the Clinic staff and was not especially pleased. She had met him briefly and by chance in the hospital room of the latest feticide victim. She had heard that he was arrogant and patronizing toward nurses. Their brief contact at the hospital did nothing to dispel these rumors. Jon's initial impression of the Director was none too favorable, either.

Their paths crossed and clashed only two hours into the afternoon Clinic. Frances McGraw, uninvited and without knocking, walked into the ultrasonography room where Jon and the radiologist were literally sweating in their efforts to finish an amniocentesis.

"Doctor," the Clinic Director said, "you're next patient has been waiting for over thirty minutes. You are going to have to hurry."

Jon was studying the ultrasound screen when he answered. "Ms. McGraw, this is not a routine case."

"Well, perhaps you'd better have the resident physician relieve you then. He's done several and understands the need to move right along."

Jon did not answer immediately. Instead, he continued to guide the needle into the uterus with the aid of the ultrasound image.

"Did you hear me, Doctor?" It was a tone of voice which had rattled many young residents and even a few attending physicians.

Jon still did not answer. He found the amniotic sac surrounding the tiny fetus and carefully withdrew the prescribed amount of fluid. In a quick movement the needle was removed from the uterus and abdomen. This done, he methodically washed the needle puncture site with antiseptic, waited for it to dry, and covered it with a small Band-Aid. He got up from the stool then, snapped off his surgical gloves and turned toward the Director.

"Ms. McGraw, I don't appreciate being bothered by administrative staff when I am performing my duties to the best of my abilities and—"

"I am here to—" Ms. McGraw tried to break in.

"And don't interrupt me. I was about to say the radiologist and I accomplished this particular amniocentesis as quickly as it was prudent to do so. If you had asked, I would have told you that we are dealing with a twin pregnancy. Therefore, as you might remember, there are usually two amniotic sacs and for your information, a little less room in which to maneuver."

An exam stool was all that separated the two adversaries. Jon pushed this aside and stood face-to-face with the Director. "Now," he said, "let's get one thing straight between physician and Nurse-Director. You are never—repeat, never—to barge into one of my exam rooms again. If I need you, I will call you. We have worked very hard with this case for over half an hour and finally got fluid out of both sacs. To the best of my knowledge the needle didn't damage either cord, either placenta or either fetus. And that, I'm told, is what we're here for."

Ms. McGraw was a big woman and she was not fat. At that point she was obviously furious and looked quite able to physically rid her Clinic of this annoying doctor. Flushed, she opened her mouth to reply, then snapped it shut and abruptly turned and walked out.

Frustrated in her efforts to dominate the newest staff member she vented her wrath on an unsuspecting receptionist who was chatting with a handsome medical student.

"Well, what are you getting paid for?" she said. "It's not just to sit there and look pretty, I can tell you that. Get another patient into the ultrasound room and do it now. And you," she said glaring at the medical student, "quit bothering my help and get where you belong."

The student took his cue from the sheer size of Ms. McGraw and the fact that she was advancing toward him in a most belligerent manner. Without so much as a backward glance at the petite but chastened receptionist, he found and utilized the nearest exit.

With the Clinic Director out of his hair, Jon greeted his next patient. She was only fourteen and very pregnant.

"You are Janie Manson," Jon said.

"Yes, sir."

"You scared?"

"Yes, sir."

"It really isn't that painful a test, Janie. It usually takes just a few minutes. You do understand we are going to use this machine—this ultrasound—to help me guide the needle into the fluid that surrounds your baby?"

"Doctor, I'm not afraid of that," Janie said. "I've had it done before—when I was about three months along. You want another test now, that's O.K."

"But you're trembling, Janie. What's wrong?"

"It's McGraw. She scares everybody, specially when she's mad and she's sure mad today."

"Why should Ms. McGraw frighten you? She's an administrator, hired to manage the Clinic. She really shouldn't have much contact with the patients at all."

"She don't like us, Doctor."

"Come on now, Janie. I suspect McGraw is about ninety-nine percent bluff and just wants to run an efficient Clinic."

"No, sir. I mean she probably knows how to run this place but she really don't like us kids. I seen her hurt a couple of my friends."

"Miss Stanford," Jon called out to the receptionist, "is my next patient here?"

"No, Doctor. She phoned and canceled just a few minutes ago."

Jon turned back to Janie Manson. "O.K., young lady, let's get this test over with and since I have some extra time, you and I are going to have a little chat. Maybe you can tell me what you mean when you say Ms. McGraw hurt two of your friends."

The sample of amniotic fluid was collected quickly and without incident. The radiologist secured the ultrasound machinery and went out for a cup of coffee. When he was gone Jon told Janie she could get up and take the chair which the radiologist had been using.

"No, I'm okay," she said and tucked her slim legs beneath her to sit guru fashion on the exam room table.

"Alright, now tell me, how did Ms. McGraw hurt your friends?"

"She did rough exams on them. She was mean. She meant to hurt."

"Janie, no one likes a pelvic exam. Ms. McGraw was probably being just a bit too thorough. Sometimes it's difficult to find things in the pelvis. Pelvic organs, like the ovaries, sort of hide, you know. Some examiners keep trying to find a particular organ and sometimes they try too hard. And it hurts. That doesn't mean they are rough or hurt you on purpose."

"Doctor, how would you like to have your tits pinched if you was pregnant? And how would you like to have somebody as big and strong as McGraw pushing the baby around in your belly?"

"Wait a minute, now. Let's take these one at a time. Breast stimulation is frequently done for at least a couple of good reasons. One being to make the uterus contract so the baby's heart beat can be checked and the other is to get the breast and nipple ready for nursing."

"Oh, yeah, sure," Janie said with all the cynicism a teenager can muster. "You look here. Lemme show you something." And she gripped the little finger of her left hand between the knuckles of the first and second fingers of the right, pushing with her thumb. "You try that, Doctor. You try that on your skin any place. It hurts and that's exactly what McGraw did. She made black and blue marks around both nipples of my friend Rachel. Her tits were so sore she couldn't even stand to have the shower hit 'em."

Jon was quiet for a moment, studying the angry girl sitting upright and cross-legged on the table. There were none of the telltale facial expressions or body movements which would indicate that the story was a wild exaggeration of the truth. And she hadn't looked away from Jon, not for one second.

"Go on. Tell me about the business of pushing on the baby."

"That's another friend. She was two weeks from her time and McGraw told her the baby was upside down—butt first. Breech, is that what you call it?"

Jon nodded.

"Said it had to be turned so's it would come out head first when she went into labor. Well, she had my friend crying she pushed so hard. Left bruises. I seen where she dug her fingers in. One of the doctors came in—I guess he heard Bobbie Sue crying—and when he found out what was going on he asked McGraw if she knew what kind of a breech it was. I always thought butt first was butt first. Are there really different kinds?"

Again, Jon just nodded.

"The doctor also asked McGraw if she knew where the afterbirth was. McGraw said she was just checking to see if she could gently turn the baby. Gentle, my ass."

"What did the doctor do?"

"Not much. He just felt around a little and told McGraw he would order some studies before anyone tried to turn the kid again."

"Did his exam hurt?"

"Bobbie Sue said he had the softest hands she'd ever seen and he hardly pressed at all."

"Has she delivered yet?"

"She lost her baby."

"Lost it?" Jon said. "What do you mean?"

"Doctor, you operated on her. Her baby was killed. Don't you remember?"

"Oh God, yes. Little blonde girl. Sort of timid. Bobbie Morris."

"Yeah, that's Bobbie Sue."

"What's Rachel's last name? Has she delivered?"

"Rachel Johnson. And she's still pregnant. Bigger'n a house."

Jon opened a drawer of the desk and took out a pad of paper. "You don't mind if I make a few notes, do you Janie?" he asked.

"No, please don't do that, Doctor."

"Janie, I need something to help me remember what we've talked about."

"No, Doctor, please. If McGraw finds out I've been talking to you, she'll fix me for sure."

"No way for her to find out. I won't use your name. O.K.?"

Janie bit her lip and looked down. There were tears in her eyes when she faced Jon again and whispered, "I guess."

"Good girl. Now, just another question or two and I'll let you go. Do you know of any other times when Ms. McGraw was rough on the girls?"

"I hear some stories, Doctor, but I don't really know many of the girls. Bobbie Sue and Rachel were my friends from school."

"Well, why Bobbie Sue and Rachel? Why did she want to hurt them?"

"I don't know about Rachel. She's rougher'n a cob herself. Maybe McGraw was just trying to teach her who was boss around here. But Bobbie Sue, she's like a little flower, sort of delicate. She was a virgin long after the rest of us were screwin' our brains out."

"What does that have to do with Ms. McGraw? Why would she want to mistreat someone like the Bobbie Sue you describe?"

Janie cocked her head over and looked at Jon. Her expression was part quizzical, part annoyance.

"How long you been working on females, Doctor Erickson?" she asked.

"Several years, Janie. Why?"

"I don't think you know much about 'em."

"Oh?"

"Don't you know some women screw around with other women?"

"Janie, are you trying to tell me Ms. McGraw is a lesbian?"

"No—queer."

"I don't think so, Janie. She may be rough on you kids and she may even get a little sadistic pleasure out of it, but that is a good-looking lady. Big and strong, yes, but I don't think she's butch."

"Don't bet on it."

"No, I won't, but for a kid of fourteen you seem to be pretty well-informed on various life styles."

"Doctor, I've been on the streets since I was ten. My mother's a hooker—has been I guess for years. She used to bring her pimp home occasionally and give him a freebie. I'd hear them bumpin' and grindin' away in her bedroom. I'd just turn the TV up louder."

"How about your father?"

"Never met him."

"No idea where he is—or even who he is?"

Again, her eyes filled with tears and she just shook her head.

Jon put his hand on her shoulder. "O.K., my friend," he said, "this conversation is strictly between you and me. And for the record, I believe you. Now, wash your face and put your clothes on. I'll be back in a minute. There's something else I want to talk to you about."

Janie didn't answer. She just clutched Jon's hand briefly then jumped off the table to do as she was told.

Jon had a definite purpose in coming back to talk to Janie, but after twenty minutes he had gained perhaps a little insight but no specific information regarding the mystery which was occupying more and more of his thoughts and time. Four young women had been struck by an unseen killer. Four babies were dead. Yet, with one exception, not one of the patients he had seen in the Clinic this afternoon talked about these tragedies. The exception was Janie when she told him about Bobbie Sue. Even then, there didn't appear to be any emotionalism about it—Bobbie Sue's baby was dead, but it seemed more important that her nipples had been pinched. By now the specter of the Poet and the rhyming evidence of his dislike—hatred—for unwed teenage mothers should be imprinted on the minds of all who attended the Clinic. But it wasn't. There was even a hint of defiance when Janie said, "If I want to go walking in the rain, I'll go walking in the rain. Nobody's going to stop me, not even that crazy guy with the dart gun."

It was frustrating, increasingly so. And Jon couldn't help but feel some of these kids he had seen today were in real danger. No teenage mother had been killed yet by the spring-loaded weapon. It had been a close call with the last case. A slightly more errant course and the knife could slash a big artery and the next day's obituary column would list both mother and baby.

It was now nearly dinner time and since Kathy was attending an out-of-town psychiatry meeting Jon decided to get a quick bite at the hospital cafeteria. Still wearing the long white coat which identified attending and staff physicians he made his way along the serving line. There were no familiar faces in the dining room so he went to a small unoccupied table near the windows. He was nearly finished eating when another diner, obviously heading for a separate table, stopped and looked at the name tag attached over the left pocket of Jon's white coat.

"You are Doctor Erickson?"

"Yes."

"I'm Doctor Miller. I spoke to you a short time ago on the phone. It was right after the third feticide. Do you remember?"

"Yes, of course."

"I saw in the University newspaper where you'd been assigned to the Special Procedures Clinic. I was hoping to meet you. May I sit down?"

"Please do."

Jon's dinner partner was a somewhat overweight man appearing to be in his late forties. His hair, modishly long, nearly covered both ears, and in place of a tie there was a heavy gold chain draped around his neck. His jacket was a rumpled brown corduroy with leather patches over the elbows. Jon was prone to first impressions. He made them and, good or bad, he usually retained them. Months after this initial meeting he would say he tried not to be influenced by what he had heard about Lawrence Miller from Kathy and others. But he did remember coming away from that encounter with a very clear sense of having dined with a charlatan.

Dr. Miller did not neglect his food tray. He was able, between bites, to tell Jon of his capacity at the Clinic as a counselor, a guide and a friend. He especially valued his role as a friend to these young people who, he said, were in such desperate need of a compassionate individual to lead and direct them. Jon listened politely and assumed—incorrectly—the man would eventually discuss just how the Clinic patients were reacting to the murder of four little unborn babies. And he thought Kathy's name might come up in the conversation. It didn't.

Somewhere between a large helping of mashed potatoes and his dessert Dr. Miller revealed that his Ph.D. degree was from a small mid-western school of divinity, but he emphasized that he had majored in psychology. Yes, he knew all the girls quite well. He knew of their abysmal living conditions and their family backgrounds and was so involved in their emotional well-being that whenever possible he arranged to be present when they delivered.

The veneer of the ultra-compassionate social worker slipped only twice during the hour-and-a-half of the one-sided conversation. Once was when he angrily denounced the occasional lack of appreciation by some of the girls for the work he was doing, the second instance, Jon thought, more clearly showed Miller's character. It came when Jon, tiring of the near soliloquy and faintly suspicious of the counselor's motives, purposely set a small trap. Dr. Miller was describing some of the antics of the teenagers when Jon, quite offhandedly, remarked, "They are sexy little devils, aren't they?"

"Oh, indeed they are," was the instant response of the

psychologist. "They are the most sensuous group of young people I've ever worked with. Pretty, pretty things." He was silent then for a minute or two, just leaning back in his chair looking out the window. Abruptly, his mood changed and he banged his fist down on the table. "But of course they use their sexuality in a most depraved and degrading manner," he said. "Personally, and don't repeat this, I think most of them should be put into an institution and supervised until they are at least twenty-one. Be a lot less abortions in this country if we took a strong hand to them."

Any response Jon might have had to this revelation was interrupted by the appearance of a man whom Jon did not recognize, but whose long white clinic coat identified him as a University Hospital staff member. He greeted Lawrence Miller.

"Hi, Larry. Didn't see you in Clinic today."

"Hello, Donald. Oh, I was there but just for a short time. And Don, I'd like you to meet Doctor Erickson. He's an obstetrician here in town and just started working at the Clinic. Doctor, this is Donald Parker. He heads up the lab for all of the outpatient clinics but right now is indispensable for his efforts in the Special Procedures Clinic. He's the one who directs the high-tech analysis on the blood and amniotic fluid of the patients you see."

The lab director was a short man with a round, clean-shaven pleasant face, a face without any distinguishing characteristics. He was also very neat, his starched white coat showing only a few dye stains—a mark of his profession.

"Good to meet you, Mr. Parker." Jon reached out to grasp the hand offered by the lab director. He noted the other arm was in a sling with a cast covering nearly the entire hand. "Looks like you and some orthopedist got together. What happened?"

"Good to meet you, too, Doctor. And yes, I did give an orthopedist a little work to do. Broke two of the metacarpals when a five gallon can of solvent fell off the shelf."

"That'll take a while to heal," Jon said.

"Yes, quite awhile. Got infected and had to have surgery. I can use the left hand a little but not very much. But I do just about everything with my right hand anyway, so it won't interfere a lot. Most of the lab work is done by technicians. I just give them the proper directions. Worst thing is I'll miss most of the ski season. And that's the main reason I moved out to this part of the country."

"I don't ski but from what I see on television, you'd have a tough time coming down those slopes with only one ski pole."

"Very tough. Not worth the risk. I may get in some spring skiing and there's always next year. But welcome to the Clinic, Doctor. We need all the help we can get. It's an interesting project. Eventually we'll get a handle on what drugs do to babies. Hell of a note we even have to spend money on research like this. Dumb kids should know better but they don't and I guess their stupidity keeps us busy."

"I guess so," Jon said. "Maybe it keeps them out in the rain, too. The little devils, they don't seem to worry very much about being a target, do they?"

"Apparently not, but it does make the Poet's job a little easier, doesn't it," Donald Parker said.

"Too easy," Jon said. "Either one of you have any theories about our rhyming knife thrower? Since his target is always a Clinic patient and you've both been around there for quite awhile, I thought you might have heard something."

"Well, he's obviously crazy," Dr. Miller said. "Nobody in his right mind would do what he's doing."

"Oh, I don't know, Larry," the lab director said. "You have training in psychology. Take a little time and read his poems. They were written by somebody with a lot on his mind. Something is really bothering him."

"Do you think he's had his fill of this slaughter," Jon asked, "or are we going to see some more of those Clinic patients come into the hospital with a knife in their side?"

"I don't see any sign of him quitting. I think he'd give us a clue in the poems. Do you agree, Larry?"

"You obviously study those poems more than I do, Donald, but for the sake of the teenagers here, I hope you're wrong. Unfortunately, I don't know why he should quit now. But, of course, we don't even know why he started."

"And that, Doctor Miller, is exactly what I'd like to find out."

"What do you mean?"

"I mean I'd like to find out why this guy started all this. Last winter, wasn't it? I think he hit the first one in February. If I knew why, maybe it would help nail him and I really would like to do that."

"I don't think you'll catch him, Doctor," Donald Parker said. "Sounds to me like he has a mission to fulfill and nobody is going to get in his way. But if you'll excuse me, I still have a little work to do."

"Some of these days, if you have time, Mr. Parker, I'd like to have you show me around over there."

"Be glad to. Do you want to come over now? I just have a couple of things to check on then we can go on a tour."

"Great. I'll make rounds at St. Elizabeths later."

For the next hour the Laboratory Chief took Jon through a neat, well-organized lab explaining the various tests performed on the blood, urine, amniotic fluid and placental tissue of the Clinic patients. When the trip was finished Mr. Parker summed it up by saying, "There's a lot of data here, Doctor Erickson. It's all very preliminary but eventually I hope to publish a worthwhile paper which will examine the results. Then maybe we'll know more about how drugs taken by the mother can affect their babies."

"I'm impressed, Mr. Parker. I suppose all this information funnels into a computer someplace?"

"Oh, yes. But I'm not the computer expert. I just supply the facts to the whiz kids and they go to work with their microchips."

"You enjoy the work, Mr. Parker?"

"Doctor, I've studied laboratory procedures for years. I'm what they call a test-tube lab man. I'm not a clinician. I was fairly happy when they had me in charge of the entire outpatient laboratory. But I'm not happy here in the Special Procedures Clinic."

"Oh, how come? This is great research work you're doing here—original. I don't think anybody else in the country has anything similar going."

"It's not that. I love the research. I love my lab. It's the patients. I've never had to deal with them before. I've always been down in the basement of a hospital with my test tubes and microscope. Never saw a patient. Now I'm here in the Clinic with all these people running around. Been here since the Clinic started—nearly a year now and I don't like it. I'm offended by all the vulgarity and promiscuity. And I'll tell you frankly, Doctor, I'm not dealing with it very well."

"I can understand that. There are some things about these kids that none of us like but we try to take care of them as best we can. Maybe help get their life straightened around a little."

"You're more of an optimist than I am, Doctor. They depress me. There was one here just the other day; came in three months after her baby was born for a checkup and some blood work. The technician who usually draws the blood was gone so I did it myself. After she was gone I looked at her chart. Mostly I wanted to see the comments by the social worker assigned to her case. Very interesting. Sad, really. Made me angry just reading them. The report told of the girl and her baby moving in with her parents—small house over on the east side of town. Too small. Too much stress. Too much of a disruption in the lives of the grandparents. The old man, the grandfather, took off. Hasn't been seen or heard of for three weeks. And that's what I see." Mr. Parker just shook his head and sighed. "You know," he said, "sometimes I think that Poet is smarter than all the rest of us."

"Oh, my God. That's a depressing thought."

"Is it as depressing as more and more babies having more and more babies?"

"You have a point but I'm sure we agree the Poet's method of taking care of all this is a little extreme to say the least. And I'd better go, Mr. Parker," Jon said as he got up from his chair. "I have rounds to make at St. Elizabeths and then I've got to get home. Thank you very much for showing me around."

"Thank you for coming and thank you for your interest. Hope to see you in the Clinic from time to time."

Jon had time to reflect upon his afternoon at the Special Procedures Clinic as he drove across town. The concept, the purpose, was excellent and despite his run-in with the Clinic Director, he had to admit that Ms. Frances McGraw was efficient. He and Frankie might never be friends but they would get along. He was concerned over Janie's story which indicated that McGraw could be physically abusive to maintain discipline over the rebellious teenagers. He thought he should talk to the Director about this in the future.

Lawrence Miller, now there was a strange one. His relationship with the Clinic patients seemed a little weird, the compassion faked. And he didn't even mention his previous confrontation with Kathy. There surely weren't that many Doctor Ericksons around University Hospital. Jon decided it was best to avoid the counselor whenever possible. Plainly stated, there was just something about him that could not be trusted and to Jon, that was the ultimate dishonor. He remembered his first contact with Dr. Miller, the phone call after the third feticide. And he remembered telling his nurse that he would not want to turn his back on such a man.

Donald Parker, obviously a talented director of the Clinic lab but an unhappy, gloomy, depressed individual. His comment about the Poet's intellect was actually a little scary, almost as though he somehow admired this monster. And was that a challenge when Mr. Parker said, "I don't think you'll catch him, Doctor?"

Intriguing, stimulating and a little mysterious—that was Jon's mental summary of the Special Procedures Clinic as he drove into the parking lot at St. Elizabeths Hospital.

CHAPTER IV

Early February, nearly a month since the last feticide. Despite the incessant rainfall, there were no reports of attacks on pregnant teenagers. Now the rain had stopped and the valley was experiencing the usual "false spring." The weather gods pulled this nearly every year. The sun came out, the temperature soared to fifty degrees during the day and little green tufts of the crocus and daffodil families peeked through the soil.

But long-term residents did not put their raincoats away just yet. And the Poet had been in the valley long enough to know the rains would return.

The typewriter was on the desk and it contained a foreboding message.

YOU'VE WAITED LONG FOR NUMBER FIVE
HERE HE IS AND NOT ALIVE
MOTHER AND SON WERE SURE TO BE
ANOTHER TAX SUPPORTED FAMILY
NOT NOW, FOR THE BABE LIES DEAD
NOTHING FURTHER NEED BE SAID

The calling card of "Number 5" was pulled from the typewriter and neatly folded into an envelope. But the Poet remained restless and rolled another sheet of paper into the old Royal. Thoughts and rhymes came easily and were quickly typed onto the page.

THIS IS THE SIXTH TO FEEL THE KNIFE
I FELT IT MY DUTY TO TAKE HIS LIFE
HIS MOTHER A TRAMP, HIS FATHER UNKNOWN
FOR THE WAYS OF THE DEVIL HE MUST ATONE
BEST HE DIE EARLY AND AVOID THE PAIN
OF YEARS WITHOUT HOPE AND LIFE'S JOURNEY IN VAIN.

This last effort seemed to end the flighty, jittery mood and bring a measure of contentment. An old photo album was pulled from the desk. It was small, thin; there had been very little money to waste on film in those days. Some of the pictures were of a small house, obviously in a rural setting and also obviously in need of repair. There was one picture of a family, two adults, one teenage girl and two smaller children perhaps eight or ten years of age. It was a somber picture, undoubtedly depicting the quality and substance of their lives.

No one smiled.

Still another picture showed the teenage girl holding twin babies. She looked worn and there was still no smile. The last picture in the album had obviously been taken from a boat. It was of the same home, but now it was entirely surrounded by water. The house was set at a weird angle. The porch was missing, the porch where the family had posed so stiffly and unsmiling for the camera. It was somewhere downstream, carried there by the surging flood waters that a month of heavy rain had created. Memories, almost all unpleasant. Time had only served to dull, not erase, them. Memories of the teenage girl in the picture—a sister—and of the twin babies, bastard babies born out of wedlock. There was shame and a sense of embarrassment in the family. There was also resentment toward an older sister who brought this shame and whose babies shared, indeed dominated, the very little attention and affection available from the parents. These babies, innocent little boys, became objects of hate. Almost daily their deaths were fantasized and always the world seemed better without them. Then came the torrential rains, washing away roads, crops and eventually their home. The two younger children in the non-gender overalls pictured in the photograph were separated and sent to different parts of the country. The twins and their mother remained with the parents in a sharecropper's house upriver and safe.

All this was years ago but the Poet, studying the pictures, could not forget. And there was the picture in the shoe box of James Leroy.

A week later the rains returned to the valley and the envelope with poem number five was dropped near the body of Janie's friend, Rachel Johnson. Rachel had turned, probably at the sound of a minor car wreck which occurred nearby, and the knife had struck in the front. Such was the force of this weapon that it passed entirely through the uterus and tore into her aorta. Mother and baby died almost instantly.

Reaction to the death of an unborn fetus was nothing when compared to the outcry of the public when they learned of Rachel's murder. Chief O'Neal announced by radio and television that he and other members of the police high command would hold a news conference at one o'clock the following day. Jon received a phone call late that night.

"Doctor Erickson, I'm Bill Arnold. Maybe you've seen some of my articles in the paper. My beat is the crime in this city. Ring a bell?"

"Yes, I've read some of your stuff."

"Good. You can help me. I want you to go with me to that news conference the Chief is holding tomorrow."

"Mr. Arnold—"

"Bill."

"Alright, Bill. News conferences aren't exactly my cup of tea, you know, and I don't have any business down at police headquarters tomorrow."

"Yes you do, Doctor. And I'll tell you three good reasons. One, you operated on two or three of the feticide victims. Two, you delivered Chief O'Neal's one and only grandson. Three, and most important, I understand you don't get along with Lieutenant Lenhart. I'm sort of making it my job to see if I can get him off these feticide cases.

"You're pretty well-informed."

"Spend some of my time at headquarters. Learn a lot there if you ask the right questions of the right people."

"Sounds like you know pretty much all you need to know now. You don't need me."

"Oh, yes I do. Believe me, I do. Meet me for lunch at the little café across the street from headquarters. I'll be there about twelve-fifteen. I'll even buy the meal."

"Tomorrow. Tomorrow's Saturday, isn't it?"

"Right. And you don't have any office hours."

"O.K., I'll be there. Think you can spring for a steak?"

"I'm a reporter, not some damn doctor. You'll get soup and a sandwich. See you tomorrow."

I just may like that son of a bitch, Jon thought as he hung up the phone.

The next day Jon drove down to police headquarters and parked near the café. It wasn't hard to find the reporter; a waitress pointed him out and Jon walked over and stuck out his hand. "I'm Jon Erickson," he said.

"And I'm Bill Arnold. Glad you could make it."

Jon did a quick appraisal of his luncheon benefactor. About forty-five years old, thin and with a somewhat sallow complexion. A press card was pinned to his jacket and a tin cup on the table already had two cigarette butts in it.

Before he sat down, Jon pointed to the ashtray, "Those damn things will kill you, you know."

"Gotta die some way. Sit down, and sign this." Bill pushed a piece of printed material across the table in front of Jon.

"Sign what? What the hell is it?"

"Makes you a temporary employee of the paper and entitled to a press card. I checked it out with my editor this morning. He thought it was a great idea to get a doctor to collaborate for no pay. Really appealed to his sense of humor. You ain't getting paid for this little venture, you know."

"I'll get paid."

"Bullshit. Not from my salary you won't, and no way you're going to get a nickel out of my editor."

"If Lenhart's at the news conference and you can nail his ass a couple of times, that'll be my pay. I don't know how you found out, but I really don't like that guy. I don't think he gives a damn if the Poet is caught today or a year from now."

"We'll see what we can do. I've met him and I think I can get to him. Here," he said, pulling a press card out of his pocket, "pin this to that tailored sport coat of yours. I suppose you drive a Mercedes like all the rest of the docs in this town?"

"Don't be so damned paranoid. No, I don't drive a Mercedes. If I didn't pay fifty thousand dollars a year for malpractice insurance maybe I could afford one."

"You're kidding. Fifty thou?"

"Fifty-one to be exact."

"That's quite a bundle but you'll make it back alright. Now, let's get on to Lenhart and see how we're going to mess up his day."

Thirty minutes later the newspaper's latest recipient of a press card along with his patron had finished their lunch and stood outside room 204 at City Hall. The reporter had succeeded in picking Jon's brain fairly clean of all relevant facts concerning the feticides and the role of Lt. Lenhart. "I think we're ready," he said. "Let's go in and find a seat."

It was a relatively small conference room, made even smaller by the presence of a long table at one end. Behind this oblong stretch of polished mahogany, seemingly protected by its very presence, sat the four major participants of the conference. Chief O'Neal, in full dress uniform, sat on the left. Next to him was Lt. Billy Ray Lenhart. The other two Jon did not recognize. Bill did. "The man sitting next to Lenhart is Doctor Clark, psychiatrist for the police department," he said. "and the man on the right is the police commissioner, Richard Braun. Do you know the doc?"

"No."

"Makes no difference. Let's see who all's here."

"Who all is here" basically comprised the *Who's Who* of local and state news media including various television and radio interests. There was also a scattering of out-of-state personnel attracted, no doubt, by the enormity of the crime and the national publicity it had received.

"Quite a group," Bill said as he gave a little half-salute greeting to a friend of his in the corner. Then he and Jon sat down in seats near the back row. "That's Don French. Hell of a guy from a newspaper in Seattle. And Jerry from United Press up there in the front row. Should be an interesting session."

The Chief stood up and the buzz of conversation slowly subsided. "I'm Chief Michael O'Neal," he said. "Most of you know me. And I have with me today Lieutenant Lenhart, Doctor Clark and Police Commissioner Richard Braun. The mayor has asked that I call this conference to answer any questions we can about this horror that has struck our city. Five babies and a young lady about to be a mother, murdered. Some of you may have heard the rumor that we had a suspect in custody late last night. I'll clear that up right now. Yes, a man was brought in and questioned. He was released without being charged.

"And one more thing before we take any questions. There has been an occasional newspaper article with implications that the police department is taking this so-called feticide thing rather lightly. Nothing could be further from the truth and I won't allow any questions that even suggest this. Every man in the department is involved in one way or another. Every man is determined to bring this depraved killer to justice. Now, who leads off?"

"Chief," it was the U.P. man, "I want to thank you and the others at the table on behalf of the news media for taking time out of your busy schedule to appear in person before us."

"The U.P. man is inclined to be a bullshitter," Bill whispered to Jon, "but his job is sort of political so I guess we can forgive him."

U.P. continued, "The problem is we really don't know where to start."

"Why don't we start with the man you had in last night, Chief?" Bill Arnold said. "Why was he brought in and why was he released?"

"Mr. Arnold, the police department will not be a party to starting a witch hunt concerning a man who is no longer considered a suspect, so I'd rather not try to answer your question. Maybe the best way to start this out is to have Lieutenant Lenhart brief you on the department's activities thus far, case by case. The Lieutenant has been in charge of the investigations from day one. Lieutenant."

Billy Ray slowly got to his feet. "Thank you, Chief," he said, "but before Ah get started, cain't help wondering why we have someone here who doesn't represent the press. Doctor Erickson, occurs to me you are out of your element."

Bill Arnold stood up immediately. "Lieutenant Lenhart," he said, "Doctor Erickson has signed on as a consultant to my newspaper. According to my editor, this entitles him to a press card. I have the legal document with me if you wish to see it."

The room was suddenly very quiet. It was unusual for hostility to develop early in a conference of this type. And it was quite obvious to all assembled that Lt. Lenhart and the doctor had established a distinctly adversarial relationship at some time in the past.

"Ah don't like it," Billy Ray said, "but the man said it's legal and that's what we go by around here."

With some reluctance then, the homicide detective turned his attention to the task assigned by his Chief. In just ten minutes he told of the intense police effort directed toward the Poet Killer. He reviewed every feticide, where and when it occurred, the comments of the various victims and the police activities relating to each case. Missing was any comment on motive. This omission brought a comment from Bart Connors of Channel 8.

"Any thoughts on what we're dealing with here. Why is the Poet attacking these girls? From the sounds of his poems he knows quite a bit about them."

"No, sir. We've drawn a blank on that."

"All the babies have been boys," Don French said. "Must be something you've come up with to help explain that. Can't be just coincidence."

Billy Ray shook his head. "We're workin' hard on that angle. Must be a connection. Just haven't found it yet. Maybe Doctor Clark can help answer that one."

"No, I wish I could," Dr. Clark said. "I agree the Poet certainly has some inside information, but just knowing that hasn't helped us catch him."

"I'm still a little curious about the man you had here last night," Bill Arnold said. "You turned him loose awfully soon. Was he just some wino you brought in to get the heat off the department for awhile?"

The Commissioner spoke up then, his voice grave and sonorous—very much like the politician that he was.

"As the Chief said, the police department is not going to be a party to the ruination of a man's life just to satisfy the curiosity of the press. Please, gentlemen and ladies, be more objective. Your profession has a history of not being too kind to the accused, be they guilty or innocent. Remember, our legal system presumes innocence until guilt is proven."

"We don't need a lecture on jurisprudence, Commissioner," someone from the audience said.

"Not a lecture. Just a reminder."

For the next twenty minutes there was an exchange between members of the press and the assembled police authorities which yielded no additional information. There was a sense of growing frustration among the reporters. Finally, it was Bill Arnold who summed up his peer group's dissatisfaction with the press conference, and most particularly with Billy Ray.

"A question for the Lieutenant," Bill Arnold said. "I'm trying to figure out just why we're here. So far, nobody from behind that table has said anything I haven't already written for my paper. Or if I haven't, somebody else has. You've gone out of your way to tell us of the police department commitment and dedication to solving these crimes, but I hear your personal attitude toward the victims is not all it should be. Makes me wonder if the city if getting its money's worth for your overtime."

Billy Ray had been seated during the previous question and answer period but now he quickly stood up. "And Ah have a pretty good idea where y'all got your information, too. As a law man, Ah cain't help but think your source mouthed off with somethin' mighty confidential. Confidential enough, maybe, to get hisself involved in a lawsuit."

The reporter remained in his chair. He had struck a sensitive area and he knew it. His instincts told him to keep pressing. "Lieutenant," he said, "I'm guessing you think Doctor Erickson was my informant and you are absolutely right. Maybe you'd like to sue him. Maybe you'd like to hear him testify in open court and hear him tell of the conversations you and he have had. I believe, if memory serves me right, there was something to the effect that all the mothers were on welfare and the babies were destined to be losers anyway. Sounds to me like the Doctor is the one most committed to finding the Poet. And incidentally, I will certainly tell judge and jury that he breached no confidences in his talks with me relative to the young ladies involved."

Billy Ray was mad. He had not anticipated this hostile critique of his efforts and before he could respond a large black man seated near the front stood up.

"Lieutenant," he said, "you don't know me. My name is Ed Sandstrom. This city is not my beat but the feticide story and the grisly poems left by the killer have attracted national interest. I'm here from Chicago. We've had some pretty wild crimes in our windy city but none to match this. The slaughter of innocent babies is bizarre enough, now I hear the homicide detective in charge of the case is dragging his feet because the victims were not, in his judgment, some of the city's best citizens. All I have to say is wait 'till the cops in Chicago get a line on this. The next time some con artist gets a shiv in his back our boys in blue will be able to relax and go have a beer. That is, of course, if they follow what appears to be your example."

Flushed and sweating, a cornered Lt. Lenhart did not wait for any additional comments. "Ah don't know what you expect from me," he said, half shouting. "Sounds like you want me out on the street bayin' and runnin' around like Loosiana hound dog. Ah resent you pushin' me around. Ah represent the law in your city. The way you treat me here today is one reason we have little chippies runnin' around pregnant and in the last case, gettin' herself killed. Respect. If everybody had showed more respect for the law—'specially y'all who write the news and influence the public—if y'all showed more respect we probably wouldn't need a conference like this 'cause they'd be less crime in your city.

"And you, Mr. Arnold, you think we got desperate enough to go out and corral the first drunk we come across. Well, let me tell you something, Mr. Crime Reporter. We got ourselves a suspect who runs away from his job when it rains, won't let nobody get into his car trunk and who know'd some of them girls."

"Woops," Jon whispered to Bill Arnold. "Look at the Chief. That is definitely not a look of approval. Something just slipped out of Billy Ray's mouth that was not in the script."

The Chief stood up and held out both hands in an obvious move to cut off any further conversation along those lines.

"I'll clarify the Lieutenant's remarks," he said, "then we'll have no further questions along those lines. We have a number of people who are under investigation. All of them, at one time or another, have been acquainted with the girls in that Special Procedures Clinic at the medical school. The connection in some cases has been pretty remote but they are being investigated none the less, one at a time. So far we have nothing specific to go on. And that's all I have to say on the subject."

"I'd like to have focused my television camera on the man's car trunk," Channel 8's man said. "You did open it up, didn't you, Chief?"

"We did," the Chief replied. "It contained a spare tire only."

"One final question, if I may, Chief. I think you know my friend here," and Bill pointed to Jon. "When he isn't wearing a press card he's a local obstetrician. Well, he tends to think in terms of the female gender and wonders if there were any women on your list of suspects."

"As I said, anybody who has known these girls will be questioned. Obviously there are many women in that category; we hope to check them all. This takes time; takes a lot of police hours. We understand your frustration. Try to understand ours. And that, ladies and gentlemen, concludes the conference."

Short and sweet," Jon said as he and Bill made their way down the stairs and out to the parking lot.

"Short, maybe, but not so sweet. Just about a total waste of time except we did manage to get to the Lieutenant. You're right, Jon. That guy is a real asshole."

"We didn't learn much, that's for sure. But strictly from my standpoint, it was very interesting—I mean the interplay between you reporters and the cops. Years ago I went to a police academy down south. So this little episode sort of took me back to my youth."

"The hell you did. What were you doing there?"

"Studying."

"To be a cop?"

"Sort of. My dad was a detective before he went into the service and it seemed like a pretty good life."

"How come you quit?"

"Oh, variety of reasons. But it was sort of exciting and I learned a lot about investigative police work. Enough to know it takes a lot of time and effort."

"Well, I wish their time and effort would pay off here in river city."

"So do I. I don't know how hard they were trying before, but I'll bet they try harder now. Nothing like a murder of a real live, walking, talking adult to stir them up. But Bill, call me any time. This was fun."

"I might just do that, but for now I'd better get back to the plant and try to write this up so it'll sell in tomorrow's paper. That's my stake in all this, aside from needling the Lieutenant. What's yours?"

"I think you pretty well summed it up when you nailed Billy Ray. I want the Poet out of commission. I don't want to see any more of his work."

"You've been involved with the bloody part of it, no question about that."

"Right. I'd better get going. I still have afternoon rounds to make at the hospital. And I have a karate lesson at four-thirty."

"A what?"

"Karate lesson. I try to get down to the 'Y' every week. Three professionals down there. Good teachers."

"Sounds like a waste of time to me."

"Oh, maybe. Good exercise, and who knows, I might get a chance to use it some day."

"You and Kung Fu. Well, don't get hurt. I'll see you around."

When Jon got home he sensed that something was different. He couldn't quite place it, but it just seemed as though there was a festive air about the place without any apparent reason. There was chicken for dinner with a brandy and cream sauce, and Kathy had opened a bottle of four-year-old Chardonnay. Kathy herself acted no differently than usual, chatting about her morning in the psych clinics and quizzing Jon about his visit to police headquarters. But Jon remained curious and when they had taken the last bit of wine and moved into the living room he broke the spell.

"What's up, Kate?"

"What do you mean?"

"I mean what do you have up your sleeve? Something different around here."

"I'll give you credit, Jon. You can be a very discerning individual. Here, discern this." And she brought out a glossy photograph-like image from her purse.

"No problem. It's an ultrasound picture of an eight- to ten-week fetus. So what's the big deal?"

Then it hit him. "That's yours," he said in a voice mixed with shock and accusation.

"And yours," Kathy said.

"I'll be damned. I thought your breasts were getting a little bigger. And those puffy nipples. I should have guessed a long time ago."

"Yes, you should have. But you do have a tendency to take your pleasures for granted. And if my enlarging breasts gave you more titillation—good word, don't you think?—I doubt if you'd stop to analyze why."

Jon's ego was not even slightly marred by the implication in Kathy's remarks. "Oh," he said, "I don't think I'm the only one who derives pleasure from our conjugal acts."

"I didn't say that. I am merely saying that for you, your gratification is of paramount importance. It just so happens that you're no slouch as a lover so I get a charge out of it myself. You may take that as a rather oblique compliment if you wish. But more to the point, what do you really think about my being pregnant?"

"Well, I don't know. It's going to sort of screw up your residency, isn't it?"

"My residency?" Kathy almost shouted. "Jon, I'm pregnant. We're going to have a baby. Don't be so damned—so damned—oh, I don't know what. Just try to show a little emotion. I know you see new mothers every day, but Jon, I'm your wife and I'm pregnant."

"Alright, Kate. Calm down. This just wasn't in my plans."

"Well, it was in mine. And we discussed the possibility last year. You didn't seem to have any objections then so I quit taking the pill four months ago."

"I must have been drunk."

"Damn you, Jon. There's something lovable about you but sometimes I can't figure out just what it is. You know, lately I've worried about that crazy Poet—not for me, but for you. After all, you deliver some unwed mothers and you've patched up a couple of his victims. I've wondered what I'd do if he stuck one of his knives in your belly. I think I'd cry but I'd sure hope your insurance was paid up."

"That's not very funny, Kate."

"It wasn't meant to be."

"And neither is your pregnancy. Bad timing, Kate. I can think of a dozen reasons not to have a baby this year. Why don't you have an abortion and try again in a couple of years?"

Kathy didn't reply for a minute. She picked up the ultrasound print, carefully put it back in its envelope and returned it to her purse. Then she turned to her husband and said very slowly: "Jon, that was cruel. You know very well I could never have an abortion unless the baby was abnormal. And for you to suggest it, and in such an offhand way. It's like you were talking to a total stranger, not your wife. I didn't know you could be so thoughtless, so selfish."

Jon had no ready answer for this accusation and watched silently as Kathy gathered up the few dishes and glasses in the living room and took them into the kitchen. He didn't see her tears.

The phone rang a short time later. Two of his patients were in labor and he was needed at the hospital. He did not kiss Kathy goodbye. Instead, anxious to be out of a very uncomfortable situation and avoiding the kitchen, he went out the front door to his car. All the way to the hospital he wondered why his wife, of all people, had to be so damned neurotic just because she was pregnant. It was going to be a very bad year.

And a dry one. It was the beginning of a drought destined to last into the summer carrying with it water rationing, dry lawns and dirty cars. People complained about the multiple inconveniences, but they were spared any evidence of the Poet. Rhyme number six remained in the tan coat pocket and was reviewed with every passing cloud. Rain would eventually come again but there was little contentment in this knowledge.

For Jon, a weed-free, carefully manicured lawn was almost a religion. He enjoyed backing out of the garage in the morning and pausing for a moment just to observe the fruits of his labor. Not this year—and brown grass was one irritant he appeared to take rather personally. Another was Kathy's pregnancy. He had not adjusted well to his wife's enlarging abdomen and associated physical limitations. The result was a continued tension between them which, given his attitude, could only increase. They argued more frequently and over matters that had never been of any importance before. And though Kathy rarely mentioned her work anymore, Jon knew the conflicts between her and Dr. Miller were continuing.

He wondered if the jealousy of the Clinic psychologist toward a female resident in psychiatry would actually develop into a pathological hatred. It worried Jon and though he would not show this concern to Kathy, he did to Bill Arnold. But even with a friend like Bill, he was careful not to show excessive anxiety though he did admit that the psychologist's belligerence toward Kathy could be dangerous. He also told Bill that when Kathy was four months pregnant she had undergone tests at the Special Procedures Clinic to rule out any abnormalities of the fetus. She was due to have a normal little boy sometime in September or October.

CHAPTER V

July arrived hot and still dry. Jon missed his partner, Ted Ashly. Ted was on vacation and the stress of covering the combined practices was beginning to show. Over the weekend he had delivered three babies via the normal vaginal route and two by cesarean section. It was five o'clock Sunday evening when he arrived home. Kathy had come in just a few minutes before. Some packages of frozen food lay on the counter when he walked in and without thinking Jon voiced his displeasure.

"What's with this crap?" he said. "I've been working all weekend and I hoped maybe we'd have a decent meal."

Kathy heard him and walked back in the kitchen. "I've been on the pysch wards all day, Jon," she said, "and under the circumstances, it's the best I could do."

"You're trying to serve two masters, Kate. Your pregnancy and your residency training. Can't be done. I told you before you should get an abortion but since you didn't, I think it's time you quit trying to take care of the crazy people in this town and confine yourself to the role you chose some months ago—being a mother—and maybe a little time being a wife."

"Being a wife?" Kathy said, "and serve only one master? Oh, no, Jon. I can take care of the first two very nicely, thank you." She picked up the packages then, replaced them in the freezer and without looking at Jon walked directly in front of him to reach her purse which was on the opposite counter. Now with a twenty dollar bill in her hand she turned to face her husband.

"I got paid Friday," she said, "and since I'm responsible for feeding you and since you can't stand the crap I planned to serve, take this twenty and go buy yourself a fucking steak. Just, please, get the hell out of here."

Jon ignored the proffered money but not the advice that went with it. Without a word he walked out of the kitchen, and back to his car. There was a restaurant a few blocks away but suddenly he realized his appetite was gone. The office paper work been neglected lately and it was to that haven he pointed the car.

By ten o'clock he had completed all his dictation and even browsed through a journal or two. The house was nearly dark when he got home. There was a small light on in the kitchen and another in the living room but the TV was dark and the stereo silent. The knot in his stomach was partially loosened by a large glass of milk—but only temporarily. It quickly tightened again when he went back to the bedroom. There was a note taped to the door.

Jon—if it wouldn't greatly inconvenience you I would prefer that you sleep in the guest room. Your phone is plugged in there.

K

"Temperamental God-damned pregnant women," Jon muttered as he went into the unfamiliar bedroom. The sight of his shaving kit plopped in the middle of the bed did little to relieve his depression.

The morning was no better. Kathy was gone to an early conference before Jon awakened. When he came home at or near his usual time of six-thirty the small table in the kitchen showed one place setting only.

Kathy was reading in the living room and looked up briefly to say, "There's a fruit salad in the refrigerator and a beef sandwich." Then her interest returned to the book in her lap.

"Did you eat, Kate?" Jon asked.

"Yes."

"Want a little wine?"

"No."

Jon suspected that Kathy really had not eaten, but it didn't seem an appropriate time to force the issue. He ate sparingly of the salad and only half the sandwich. Afterwards, fortified with a small glass of Chardonnay, he went into the living room. Kathy, pale and drawn from a sleepless night, looked up again from her book as Jon sat down in a chair and picked up the remote control to the television set.

"Don't turn that thing on for a minute, Jon. I want to talk to you."

"Okay."

"I'm leaving in the morning. I'm moving in with Sally Henning. She's another psych resident."

"Kate, for Christ's sake. A few little arguments and...."

"Jon," she broke in, her voice cold and bitter, "a few little arguments, you say. How can you be so blind? You'll never know how upset I've been over the past few months. You'll never know because you don't give a damn. Doctor Jon Spencer Erickson, you are without a doubt the most self-centered man I have ever known. If anything interferes with your little world, you act like a spoiled brat—petulant, sulky. I can't stand it anymore. I'm tired of saying I'm sorry. I'm tired of always being the one to start patching up after an argument."

"Kate—" Jon tried to interrupt.

"I'm not finished, Jon. All this was okay before I got pregnant. Sort of fun and games to cut you down to size every now and then. Not now. I have other things to think about. Me, for one. I need support. Not every day but when I need it I really do need it. But you are so blind to that, Jon. Or maybe you're not. Maybe you think you are so damned important that nobody else matters. Well, I matter and my pregnancy matters and I can't live with your conceit anymore. I'll be out of the house by tomorrow night. I'll need some furniture and I've contacted the moving people. They'll be here in the morning. Now, if you'll excuse me," and Kathy closed the book she had been reading and got up from her chair, "I'm going to my bedroom. I assume you'll stay in the guest room."

It was a statement, not a question and Jon did not reply. His mouth felt like it was full of cotton and the vise holding his guts had just screwed down two more turns.

There was a call to obstetrics at 4:00 a.m. so their paths did not cross in the morning. Just as well, Jon thought on his way to the hospital. Give her a few days, she'll change her mind. She'll get over this.

The maternity patient Jon had been called to see was slow to deliver and it was after nine o'clock by the time he was finished in the delivery room. He had made the rounds on his hospitalized patients while waiting for the delivery so he went directly to the office after a final check on the new mother and her baby.

Stephanie Van Osborn was his first patient and she expressed her displeasure at having waited twenty minutes for him to arrive. "I wish you'd be on time, Doctor. I don't like to sit out there with all those pregnant women. You don't seem to realize how much that hurts me. Here I am wanting desperately to have a baby in my own womb, to feel its little feet and hands. I almost cried sitting out there this morning."

Jon did not respond to her criticism and resisted the temptation to tell her to cut the dramatics. He was in no mood for any whines or complaints from Stephanie. Instead he picked up the chart and reviewed for her the lab work and ultrasound studies which had been done earlier. The family history was missing from her record. He noticed this now and asked, "I see we neglected to get your family history, Stephanie. Your father and mother alive and in good health? And how about brothers and sisters?"

"You didn't neglect to. I just told your nurse it wasn't important."

"It might be. You never know."

"I doubt it. My folks split when I was just a kid. I think my mother's alive. I haven't seen her in years. She may even be in jail for all I know. She was sort of headed that way the last time I heard from her. My father—I think he's in good health. Lives around here someplace. I don't like him."

"Brothers, sisters?"

"None. None to speak to. My father has a couple with his second marriage but I never see them. I'm sure I don't have any hereditary diseases in my background if that's what you want to know."

"I guess that'll have to do. Now, let's talk about your husband. Can we get him in for a checkup?"

"No. I told you he wouldn't come in. We live up close to the medical school. He even does some work for the clinics and I tried to get him to go in there to be examined. He says he's too busy. But I think it's a macho thing. Some macho. We made love twice last month."

"That could be a reason you don't get pregnant but let's x-ray those tubes of yours and have you keep a temperature chart to see if you ovulate. Check with my nurse. She'll give you the details. And I want to see you in about two months."

"I would like to get back to see you a little sooner if I can, Doctor."

"Make it six weeks, then, Stephanie, and be sure to keep an accurate temperature record."

"Oh, I will. And thank you, Doctor."

Nell came in shortly after. "Seductive bitch," the nurse said. "I wish she'd flaunt her bra-less body in somebody else's office. Causes quite a stir among the other patients out there."

"They'll get over it," Jon said. "Let's get on with the day."

He was upset after last night's scene at home and more concerned than he wanted to admit. He hurried through the remaining office appointments and left abruptly at eleven-thirty. Skipping lunch, he drove directly home and was three blocks away when he saw the moving van parked in front of the house.

"Son of a bitch. I can't believe that," he said. "What in the hell is she doing?"

He braked sharply and sat for a few minutes staring at the men loading items of their bedroom furniture into the large truck."

"Well, shit," and in sheer frustration he slammed the car into reverse, backed sharply and dangerously into a driveway then burned rubber for fifty yards down the street and out of sight of the ugly van. But mixed with his anger there now appeared an element of self doubt. It had never occurred to him his marriage might fail. Now his wife was gone. And the feticides. More frustration. Yes, he could repair the wounds in the uterus, but he could not bring back the life of the unborn fetus. And, the identity of the Poet remained a mystery.

His first patient for the afternoon was Sarah Tompkins. Her pregnancy had survived both the initial threat to miscarry and the medical school's Special Procedures Clinic. A full range of tests had been carried out at the Clinic, among which was the determination of fetal sex. Miss Tompkins was to be the mother of a baby girl and there were no obvious abnormalities. Her appointments in Jon's office were still a challenge. She was even more outspoken now, blunt at times, and her brilliant mind baited him constantly—usually with an element of vaguely masked hostility.

"What would you do if I had herpes, Doctor?" was her greeting today when Jon walked into the exam room.

"Well, first I'd prove that you really had it."

"How?"

"By taking a specimen from one of the sores and sending it to the lab."

"Then what?"

"Why all the questions? Do you think you have herpes?"

"No, but the fellow I'm living with right now thinks he might have had it last year. Maybe I should just kick his ass out but he's about the best stud I've come across. And he helped me get through that Special Procedures Clinic after you referred me. He works there. I guess I told you that before."

"Doing what?" Jon said, more to make conversation than seeking information.

"Oh, he's an orderly of some sort and works in the office. Frankly I don't give a damn what he does as long as he can perform at night."

"He's the father of the baby?"

"I don't think so. I think that honor belongs to one of your peers—an internist here in town. Met him in a bar one night. His wife had just left him and he needed some company. I'm pretty careful whom I screw, Doctor. This one was clean and carrying cash. I took him for five hundred and he got his money's worth."

"From the looks of things, so did you," Jon said as he checked the size of the developing uterus.

"We'll see. Oh, talking about money, I have good news for you. You're going to get paid for this delivery."

"That's always a happy thought. What happened? Did you run into the internist again?"

"No. I have a job."

"A job. Sarah, it isn't that I doubt your abilities, it just seems to me that your lifestyle is not one that lends itself to steady employment."

"There's a practical side to my lifestyle too, Doctor. I like expensive toys."

"Toys?"

"Stereo—computers—computers mostly, I love 'em. That's the world I fit in and that's my new job. I work for a company that does most of the computer programming for the medical school."

"What sort of an educational background do you need for that?"

"Doctor, you don't understand. I'm not interested in the front office of a computer company. I don't want to run the business side of it. And I really don't give a shit who invented the machines and who manufactures them. It's their job to make better hardware and faster machines for me to work on and I know just how to do that. I'm a natural. Don't ask me why—I just am."

"You must have had some classes, Sarah, or studied a lot about them."

"Oh sure, I've read all the stuff that's been written. And I lived with a guy in Berkeley who ran the University Computer Center. He was a smart bastard but, by Jesus, when I left him I knew as much as he did—probably more. He wanted me to stick around and get a degree. He also wanted more of my tail. But I don't give a rat's ass for a diploma. I just like to make those little microchips do my bidding."

"Sarah, I'll admit I don't know the first thing about computers. Do you actually learn anything while you're working or is it all mechanical?"

"Doctor, you can sit on your butt and program strictly by the book or you can use your brain and be innovative. My butt's big enough already so I use my brain. And I learn things. For example I've learned quite a bit about that Special Procedures Clinic that I didn't know before. A lot more than I learned when I was there as a patient. Just for instance, the software I work with tells me that Mrs. Jon Erickson had some tests done in the Clinic. Probably the same tests I had. Also tells me she has an M.D. and is training to be a resident shrink."

Jon was startled by this reply. Kathy was indeed a resident in psychiatry. That was no secret but though he could not say why, he felt vaguely uneasy. Here was a highly intelligent, basically amoral young woman with access to unlimited information about the medical school, some of which concerned his wife. He made a mental note to check further into Sarah's employment then changed the subject.

"Well, Sarah," he said, "I'm very pleased you've joined the work force—and not just because I'll collect my fee. Now let me check the fetal heart and you can be out of here. By the way, what happened to the young man in Berkeley?"

"I castrated the son of a bitch."

Jon dropped the instrument he was holding. "You what?"

"I cut off his balls. He beat me up one night and when he fell asleep I created a eunuch."

For the moment Jon was speechless and Sarah continued.

"You don't believe me, do you? Call the University Hospital in Berkeley and get the records on a Peter Sommer. It was about two years ago."

"Good God, Sarah. It's a wonder he didn't bleed to death—or did he?"

"No. I called the ambulance right away. I even went with him to the emergency room. Had the doctors fix my broken nose and take pictures of my black eyes and various bruises. For better or worse, Doctor, I've known too many men like Peter Sommer. I'd like to make geldings out of the lot of them."

"It occurs to me, Sarah, that you don't think much of your fellow human beings—male or female."

"Right. I think they're mostly ignorant slobs. But that's their problem. Now why don't you go ahead and check the heart tones on my little bastard here so I can get to work."

Jon did just that but he continued to feel some concern, some apprehension regarding Sarah and her activities.

The remaining patients that afternoon were not very exciting when compared to Sarah, and Jon managed to get through the office hours with his composure reasonably intact. Reluctant to go home, he stayed late at the office, reading, then made evening hospital rounds. It was after ten o'clock when he finally drove into the driveway and pushed the electronic garage door opener. Kathy's car was not there. Not that he really expected to see it but he was disappointed, nonetheless. The house was cold and dark and lonely. He had a quick bowl of cereal and went down the hall toward the guest room where he had slept the past two nights. Curious, he looked in the main bedroom—their bedroom. He barely controlled the lump in his throat as he took in the emptiness and quickly closed the door. It was the first time in their marriage that Kathy had not been in the house when he went to bed.

It was an unsettled night for others, as well. Poem number six weighed heavy in the pocket of its composer. It had rained briefly two nights ago but the intended victim had not followed her usual route home. Three precious hours had been wasted hidden in an alley, wet and angry. The anger was not new; it had smoldered for years. Now it seemed there was a chance to be free of all that resentment and an opportunity to repay society for the nightmare of an early life. And there were lessons to be taught. Immoral behavior must be punished by pain. The product of those immoral acts must be saved from anguish and heartbreak. The path of the steel knives was a proper one. God would approve; that was certain. The Poet occasionally considered how life might have been different if the twin boys had met a similar fate. And there was increased strain. The teenagers appeared to be more careful than before. They did not offer themselves as the exposed and defenseless targets the Poet was accustomed to. But number six must go—and soon. If it would only rain.

There was a strong element of pride in Jon's make-up which kept him from trying to contact Kathy during the next several days. He really expected her to call and at least give him her telephone number. She didn't. He knew her extension number in the psychiatry clinic and on several occasions he actually picked up the phone to call but never finished dialing. Judge Donovan called late one night. Said he hadn't heard from them lately and wondered if they would like to come down for dinner. Jon mumbled a feeble excuse for turning down the invitation and asked if he might call at some later date. The Judge had spent many years dealing with domestic problems. He remained astute enough in these matters to sense trouble.

"Jon," he said, "I'm available to you and Kathy any time. Please don't forget that."

Saturday morning, nearly two weeks after Kathy had moved out, Bill Arnold called. He told Jon that Chief O'Neal wanted to see them both down at his office that afternoon if they could make it. Jon said he had some things to do at home and at the hospital but could meet the reporter at four o'clock at the police headquarters.

Neither Bill or Jon had been to the Chief's fourth floor office before, but found it reflected his personality. Personal mementos and pictures dominated. On the wall immediately behind the Chief's desk was an enlarged picture of him as an infantry Captain receiving a medal from none other than General of the Armies, Douglas MacArthur. And, of course, there was the usual assortment of police department personnel, including the Chief, meeting with local and national dignitaries. His desk was large but uncluttered. A square, black onyx clock sat as the lone object on a small, handsome table just to the right of the desk. A replica of the Chief's gold badge was embedded in the base. It was an impressive looking timepiece and gave additional authority to the room in a very simple, and unpretentious way.

"Thank you both for coming," the Chief said, rising from the chair to greet his visitors. "Please sit down. The coffee will be here soon. My secretary said she was brewing a fresh pot."

"She told us you get the finest beans available, Chief," Bill Arnold said.

"She was exaggerating a little but I expect it is an improvement over that swill you have in the press room. And you, Doctor, I've had occasion to drink hospital coffee. I can do better than that."

"We'll look forward to it, Chief," Bill said, "but I don't think you invited us up here just for a tea party—or coffee. Right?"

"Absolutely. But before we get down to business, I'd like to show the Doctor a picture of that grandson he delivered for me. He's two years old now." Chief O'Neal handed Jon a photograph.

"That's a good-looking boy, Chief. Did I deliver a future member of the force?"

"Time will tell. It's not a bad life, except in times like these when you have a serial killer on your hands. It's tough right now." And the Chief was quiet for a minute. "Newspaper's been pretty hard on us lately, Mr. Arnold," he continued. "Can't really blame you, but it sure doesn't make our job any easier. And that's why I have you both here today. Frankly, I want you to ease off a bit on Lieutenant Lenhart. He really has conducted an intensive investigation into all phases of this crime. As you know, the Poet's been quiet lately. Now, some detectives would figure the guy has drifted off to some other city. Not Billy Ray. He's stayed right with it. But I notice he's been depressed lately. Even threatened to quit after that news conference we had a few months ago."

"I think you missed your chance, Chief. You should have paid him off and put his ass on the first plane back to Georgia."

"Now Mr. Arnold, you've got no idea what Billy Ray's gone through since that first baby was killed. Billy is a product of the South, as you know, and as such he shares that region's religious convictions and—"

"Wait a minute, Chief," Bill Arnold interrupted. "It's been a long time since I've been to Sunday school but I recall that you were supposed to show compassion and understanding to your fellow human beings. This attitude was sort of basic to the whole concept of religion. You know, 'meek shall inherit the earth,' 'do unto others'—all those nice little bones we throw to the 'have-nots' so they don't rise up and knock off the 'haves.' Well, your Lieutenant, fundamentalist though he may be, doesn't seem to subscribe to those principles."

One of the office personnel brought in a pot of coffee and Chief O'Neal took time out to pour a cup for his guests and himself.

"Billy Ray is having a tough time on this case," the Chief said after he tasted the brew and nodded his satisfaction. "I think anybody would. All I'm asking is that you don't go out of your way to bring him down."

"He's a tempting target, Chief," Jon said. "Especially the way he talks about the victims. Tough to overlook those comments."

"He was probably tired, off guard, and just came out with a gut reaction."

"Gut feelings are hard to hide, Chief. And remember, Billy Ray was born with his."

"I understand and I've talked to him about it. In my opinion it does not affect his determination to solve this case and at this point, I don't have any plans to assign a new man to head up that homicide team. And since you both seem to cross his path frequently, you'll just have to get along with him somehow. I think that sort of tells you that despite our sunny skies, I don't expect that rhyming son of a bitch to disappear in the near future. Doctor, I'm told that before you took to delivering babies you spent a couple of years studying law enforcement. Is that right?"

"Yes, sir. Two very interesting years. I think that's what makes me sort of schizophrenic when I deal with the Poet. One part of me is concerned about what kind of a professional job I do when I repair his victims. Then, there's that little part of me that's still a cop and I want to catch the bastard and rip one of those knives across his belly—maybe forget to sew it up."

"You're not alone in that feeling, Doctor. But you probably get to know those kids a little when you see them in the hospital. If they confide in you, something you can ethically tell us, my office is open. Please come down so we can talk."

"I'll do that, Chief."

"And Mr. Arnold, you've been reasonably fair with us in the past. If you'd rather talk to me than Billy Ray, please come on down. Some of what we talk about might be off the record but I'll give you first shot to write up anything that's important. And remember, both of you, it's my duty to give the information to Lieutenant Lenhart. I want you to understand that."

"Sounds like a good deal to me. Jon, what do you think?"

"I'm game. But, Chief, you really don't expect me to make a buddy out of Billy, do you? We've gone too far for that."

"No, I just want you to try to understand him a little better. This whole thing has upset him more than you know. He interviews those girls and he said they seem to delight in telling him of their weird sexual experiences. I guess in Georgia the girls of fifteen and sixteen just don't carry on that way."

"You know my profession, Chief, and I've either listened to or read about sexual deviation in nearly all its forms. So what do you mean by 'carry on that way'?"

"Drugs and sex, Doctor. The way it's told to Billy Ray it doesn't sound like there's one natural act of intercourse in the whole bunch when these kids get together and start shooting coke."

"Oh, I suppose they might get a kick out of exaggerating their sexual exploits a little. But I don't share your concern for Billy Ray's feelings," Jon said and paused for a moment to finish his coffee. "Cops are human and don't forget he represents an authority figure to them. Chief, you and I both know that authority means control. I'm not accusing him of taking advantage of his position as the interviewing police officer but the white man from the South has an ugly reputation when it comes to exercising his authority—sexual or otherwise—over the less fortunate members of society."

"Doctor, are you suggesting that Lieutenant Lenhart may have had other than a professional relationship with those young girls?"

"Some of those kids are kind of cute. Spend enough time around them and they get cuter and prettier every day."

"No. No, Billy's badge means too much to him. He'd never touch one of 'em."

"For your sake I hope you're right, Chief," Bill said, "but I've got to get back to the paper. How 'bout you, Jon?"

"I'll go along. I've enjoyed it, Chief," and Jon extended his hand.

"Thank you. I have, too. By the way, I just happened to think. Do you know a Lawrence Miller?"

"Yes, sir. He works as a counselor at the medical school. Also a state legislator."

"Same man. Well, he's been a great help to us. Organized interviews with the girls and seemed genuinely concerned with their welfare. If you happen to see him when you're at the medical school please tell him how much the police department appreciates all he's done for us."

"I will, Chief, and thanks again for your time."

"My pleasure. You boys have a good day, now. Oh, one more thing, Doctor. That daughter of mine is pregnant again. Be in to see you soon."

"I'll take good care of her, Chief."

On the street again Jon turned to the reporter. "Ever come in contact with this Lawrence Miller?" he asked.

"No, don't know him personally but I hear the political reporters talking about him. They don't like him. Has a reputation for being a real two-faced shit. I wonder how he snowed the Chief."

"Billy Ray did—and does."

"Good point. See you later."

Jon started to get into his car then, on an impulse, went across the street and back into the little restaurant. There was a phone booth in the corner. He dropped a quarter in and dialed Kathy's number at the outpatient department. There was no answer. He pulled out the phone book and looked up the number to Sally Henning, Kathy's friend, the one she said she was moving in with. He felt a little strange making the call. It was the first time he had tried to get in touch with Kathy at this number. Again, there was no answer and he let it ring at least five minutes. Depressed, and now a little angry, he called his partner's home number.

"Ted, this is Jon. Glad you're back. I need a favor. I haven't been drunk for a long time but I think this may be the night. How would you like to take calls for me until about eight o'clock tomorrow morning?"

"Sure. We don't have anything planned. You've been taking calls for about everybody in town lately, I guess you're due a night out. But I have a request."

"Name it."

"I don't know where you are right now but wherever it is, leave your car there and take a cab. I don't want to bail you out on a drunk driving charge tomorrow."

"Oh, I don't think it'll be that bad, but I'll take a cab just in case. Thanks. I'll call you tomorrow."

When Jon awoke the following morning, he was home. He established that by seeing a familiar picture on the wall. He was also aware of a terrible throbbing in his head. He started to get up, immediately thought better of the idea and settled back on the pillow. It had obviously been quite a night and as he lay there some of the more memorable events of the evening came flooding back into his conscious. If given a choice at that precise moment he would have certainly erased about six hours from his life.

It had all started quite pleasantly at an exclusive downtown restaurant. The bar was his first stop after taking a cab from the little café by police headquarters. He had knowingly chosen this particular eating establishment as it was famous for its food, its booze, and its attractive, unattached females. A small number of these young women would stroll unobtrusively throughout the lounge, subtly flaunting their sexuality. All were bra-less and their sheer clothing revealed nipples and flawlessly shaped breasts. They could, and did, bend over the tables to talk and it was a rare male who could maintain eye contact for any prolonged conversation.

Jon's entry into the bar had not gone unnoticed and after he had downed two martinis a slim blonde put her hands on his table, told him he looked a little out of sorts and asked if she might join him for a drink. It was the perfect approach. Not only did he feel "out of sorts," he also felt out of place and welcomed some company. In addition, as a natural egocentric, it came as no surprise to Jon that a beautiful young woman would desire his company. He quickly signaled the cocktail waitress and after a few more drinks they moved easily into the adjoining room for dinner.

The architect had designed the dining area to promote at least a semblance of privacy for each table. Visual isolation he had managed, but it was an economic impossibility to protect each dining couple or party from the conversation of any nearby group. Some of these conversations were to haunt Jon in the future.

His newfound feminine companion helped him select the wine—

a very fine ten-year-old Bordeaux—to go with the filets and the idle conversation expected under such circumstances. Jon was sober enough in the early part of the evening to realize he had never met this girl before, probably never would again, so there was little reason to be entirely truthful with her. In fact, there might be good cause to avoid the truth completely. She had introduced herself simply as Cynthia and he, in turn, said his name was Jack. He was, he said, a drug company executive in town for a few days and staying at the house of a friend, a doctor, who had gone to a medical convention. Cynthia did not establish any further identity other than to say she did some part-time acting for a small local film company. Jon—or Jack—casually discussed his role in the research division of a nameless pharmaceutical house. He was utterly shameless in his name-dropping of the various university centers he visited in the interest of the company. And he could do so with some authority and conviction as he had indeed visited most of these cities and schools during his years in pre-med and med school.

Somewhere between the last of the wine and after dinner brandy, Jon became vaguely aware of the diners—unseen—immediately behind him. There seemed to be a mixture of anger and despair in their voices. Such phrases as "I've got five, I need one more"—"you're crazy to keep this up"—"one more worthless whoring bitch"—"serious trouble"—all these and more seeped through the partition separating the tables and were heard above the din of other voices in the restaurant.

Jon's attention had never been seriously diverted from the face and body across the table from him so the departure of the unknown and unseen pair was merely welcomed as a timely riddance of an annoying distraction. Further brandy was ordered and when that was finished Jon suggested they go to his friend's house for a nightcap. Cynthia's smile signaled encouragement and a lavish tip to the waiter brought a driver to their table who led them out to the waiting cab.

It was nearly midnight when the taxi arrived at the Erickson home. Jon fumbled with his keys and continued the pretext of being a stranger in his own house. He "found" Jon's liquor cabinet and poured some ancient scotch for both "guests." Cynthia had kicked off her shoes and when she finished the drink announced she was going to take a shower and asked Jon to point the way. It was a heaven-sent opportunity. In Jon's mind there was nothing more erotic than a superbly fashioned female body, slathered and slippery with water and soap. He loved, almost more than life itself, the feel of firm breasts oily slick with a generous application of foamy suds. He showed Cynthia the way to the bedroom and bath, then returned to the kitchen to finish his own drink and put away the booze.

She was already in the shower when he came back to the bedroom. He quickly started to undress, but even in his haste, years of habit forced him to put his pants and coat on a hanger. Shirt, tie and socks were discarded on the floor of the closet and for once the ritual of placing shoetrees tightly within his heavy oxfords was forgotten. He had a moment of anxiety when he started to take off his shorts. He could hear the sound of water in the shower and could see the outline of Cynthia's nude body through the glass enclosure. Ordinarily, the anticipation of such a sensual delight would have stirred an obvious physical response. Under similar circumstances in the past he had even found it difficult to remove his shorts over the bulging erection. There was no such impediment tonight.

The sound of Cynthia moving around in the shower was too inviting for him to delay, and without his usual highly visible sign of sexual excitement Jon opened the shower door. The body that greeted him was a match for any *Playboy* centerfold. Her breasts were high and perfectly molded. The nipples, tight from the shower's stimulation, dug into Jon's chest as he embraced her. Then in a well-practiced move he turned her around allowing his hands to glide smoothly over her breasts and belly. Cynthia's response was to gently urge his hand to move lower and explore beyond the sculptured wedge of blonde hair. She gave a soft moan of pleasure as Jon's fingers expertly parted her inner lips, lingered briefly on the engorged clitoris, then probed deeply into the softness of her vagina. She brought his other hand into her crotch and came almost immediately as he started to rhythmically retract the foreskin of her swollen gland.

Breathing heavily, she turned to kiss him and with a soapy hand started to massage his unresponsive genital. Failing in this effort, she knelt down and put the soft organ in her mouth, but even this failed to produce any desired reaction. Hoping—almost praying—for some spark of manhood, Jon rinsed the soap off his body, helped Cynthia do the same and after quickly toweling they both got into bed. The positions were different, the results the same. During the next twenty minutes Cynthia had multiple orgasms, each brought about by the different and adept use of Jon's fingers. After her fifth or sixth climax, she suddenly got out of bed and went back into the shower, alone.

Finished with the shower, she came out of the bathroom and put on her clothes slowly, in full view of Jon. Her fire and passion were gone. She rather coldly asked for three hundred dollars and requested that he call a cab. He got up, put on his shorts and took all he had from his wallet—a hundred dollar bill plus a fifty. Silently he handed it over to Cynthia. She looked at the money for a minute, then took it and walked toward the door. She looked back just once. Jon was calling the taxi and she waited until he had finished. He would never forget her parting words. "You know, Jack," she said, "that's a real educated set of fingers you have there and if I ever want to get finger fucked again

I'll look you up. I really had expected a bit more from that thing between your legs."

And so had Jon.

Now, as he gradually came fully awake, he realized that, as painful as it might be, he simply had to get up. His bladder was full—that in itself was reason enough—but he also had to go back on call and make rounds. Slowly he eased out of bed and made his way to the bathroom. The towels were still on the floor and he chose not to stoop over and pick them up just yet. Maybe after coffee and aspirin, he thought.

As he started to void he stared down at the limp penis in his hand. "Well," he said aloud, addressing his remarks to the innocent organ, "you sure put on a hell of a performance last night. Not really up to the job, were you?"

Then despite the sober recollection of his humiliation he had to smile and make a little announcement to himself, to his penis and to no one else in particular:

"Some wiseass once said a stiff prick has no conscience. I'm not too sure just how to rephrase that to fit last night's endeavor, but," and again he spoke directly to the flaccid organ draining urine, "maybe you saved me from a peck of trouble. Sure can't get anybody pregnant with fingers."

A glass of juice, two cups of strong coffee with aspirin and a slice of toast enabled Jon to at least consider cleaning up the scene of debauchery. Cynthia's musty smell still permeated the sheets so he remade the bed from scratch. Next he went into the bathroom where he picked up the towels, tossed them into the laundry with the bedding and immediately started the washing machine. His conscience cleared somewhat with this effort, he shaved and took a long shower, emerging very clean, still a little shaky, but quite sober.

After he dressed it occurred to him that he had not brought in the paper nor had he checked with his answering service. He brewed another cup of coffee while he made calls to the answering service and to his partner. It was his good fortune to find no outstanding messages and no one in labor. According to Ted, it had been quiet; no emergencies and no deliveries. He did ask if the night off had been worthwhile. Jon evaded a direct answer by saying it had been interesting and expensive.

Ted chose not to continue that line of inquiry and asked instead, "Jon, do you need a ride downtown?"

"Oh, shit, I forgot all about that damn car. And how did you know I didn't drive it home?"

"Just guessing."

"Well, again, thanks for your concern, but no, I'll grab a cab. See you tomorrow and thanks for covering, though I'd probably feel better right now if you hadn't been able to."

"Okay, see you at the office."

Jon hung up the phone and decided to read the paper with his last cup of coffee. The Sunday edition was retrieved from the front steps and spread out on the kitchen table. He idly flipped through the pages seeing little of interest until his eyes caught a short item on page ten. It concerned the death of a teenager, apparently by suicide. The medical examiner reported that the girl was pregnant at the time of her death and that the baby was near term. There was a picture just below the article. It showed a body being carried out to the ambulance. The conspicuous bulge beneath the cover gave mute testimony of the double tragedy.

The story intrigued Jon, so much so that he put down the paper and called Bill Arnold. He caught the reporter at his desk.

"Bill, this is Jon. There's a little story in today's paper about a teenage suicide. Know anything about it?"

"Yeah. Quite a bit as a matter of fact."

"Can you talk about it?"

"What do you want to know?"

"Maybe I'm just seeing ghosts but I can't help wondering if that girl's death has any remote connection to the feticides. Does it?"

"You're sort of an intuitive bastard, aren't you? Well, I'll tell you what's going to be in tomorrow's paper. One of our best female reporters took that call last night—Joan Atkinson. The managing editor happened to be in and when he heard about the suicide, he sent Joan out. Thought she could handle the situation better than most of the boys. And she did."

"You haven't answered my question."

"Well, that was a funny kid. Did herself in with cyanide but actually took an enema before so she wouldn't crap all over the bed when the poison hit her. Her mother found a note and gave it to Joan, and because I do most of the feticide stuff for the paper, Joan left a copy of it on my desk. She figures the same as you do. There's got to be a connection here someplace. I'll read this to you. Won't make your day, I'll tell you that, and it won't exactly answer your question, but it'll make you wonder. Listen to this:

Dear Mom,

I just can't live in fear any longer. When this is found my baby and I won't have to worry about any threats. We'll be at peace. I'm sorry,

Mom, but I really don't think there is any other way.

You wondered what was wrong with me these past few months. All I can tell you is that I was scared. No, I wasn't scared of having the baby, I was scared of not having him. I'm too ashamed to tell you what all has happened to me. I got involved with some people that I thought I loved and thought they loved me. It wasn't the kind of love you'd understand, Mom, so I never talked to you about it. I wish I had now. It was weird and sort of wild at first. I was pregnant and guess I considered myself sort of an outcast. Someone offered to be my friend and I didn't ask any questions because I was lonely and needed a friend. Friends can hurt. Did you know that, Mom? This friend hurt other people, too—real bad.

For awhile it was kind of nice to have someone to talk to, someone who understood and who could protect me. But it didn't turn out right. I remember a poem or song or something that had a line like, "You stayed too long at the fair." And that's the way I feel and that's what happened. I just stayed too long and heard too much. Now my baby is in danger and I don't want to live without him. I know that sounds silly to you, Mom, 'cause I'm just a sixteen-year-old kid. But I love my baby and I'm going to die and take him with me so nobody can hurt him.

I love you, Mom.

And it was signed 'Mary Beth,'" the reporter said. "Not a very pretty story."

"What a waste," Jon said. "What a God-awful waste of young lives."

"I didn't tell you it would brighten your day."

"It sure as hell didn't. Sounds like there was somebody in that girl's life who needs a baseball bat between his eyes."

"Or a karate chop. How're you doing with that? Got your black belt yet?"

"No. Long ways from it. Maybe some day. Bill, I want to get together with you some of these days. I have some stuff I want to run by you."

"What kind of stuff?"

"I've been putting in some time on this feticide thing. Got a list of people. Nothing specific. Just want to get your opinion on what I've written down."

"Okay, Sherlock. Any time."

"It'll be awhile. I'm still adding to it."

"Well, everybody else has drawn a blank. Be glad to look it over with you."

"Thanks, Bill. See you later."

Jon put the phone down and taking his fourth or fifth cup of coffee, walked outside to sit on the patio. A bad night had not been improved by the phone call to the reporter. It was a beautiful morning, temperature about seventy-five degrees with hardly a cloud in the sky. The patio with its accompanying well-groomed backyard and floral beds was usually a place of quiet and rest, but not this morning. The neighbors, usually very restrained and private, were having a noisy argument. The voices were loud enough that Jon was able to hear parts of the quarrel as it ricocheted between husband and wife. And anger was evident when the woman told her husband he was crazy to continue his current activities. He told her, in an equally loud voice, that he had no choice, he must keep going for another five months, maybe six. He heatedly denounced a woman's organization which was standing in his way. "Damn them," he said. "And the chairman of that outfit, what a bitch." The wife warned her husband that he could be in serious trouble. Then a door slammed and Jon was left with his own thoughts. *Deja vu*, he had listened to a similar argument before. Where? He was painfully alert now, trying to remember and wondering why it seemed so important.

He was fairly certain it was recent and with that in mind he went over all of his week's activities starting with last Sunday. He reviewed every conference, every delivery and the multiple patient-doctor conversations in the office. Because of the booze and other distractions he was tempted to dismiss last night. But old habits die hard and the police academy had taught him to search all material carefully. He began with the bar and the drinks with Cynthia followed by dinner. Now, with intense effort, he discovered that the middle part of the evening, even with the wine and brandy, was not quite the blank he expected. He recalled a conversation in the next booth which had slightly distracted him from the barely covered breasts across the table and remembered the relief he had felt when the couple had gone.

Yes, it was a couple, male and female. He was sure of that and some of the words he heard last night were similar to what he had just heard from his neighbors. Something about the number five. His neighbor had said five months, maybe six. Five what? Someone said something about serious trouble and this was followed by a declaration concerning a bitch. His neighbor had used that term also.

The possibility was remote, almost outlandish, but it now occurred to Jon that he could have been dining next to the Poet. And as unbelievable as the prospect seemed, he knew he had to share his concern with Bill Arnold. And now. The cordless phone was on the table beside him and he touched the re-dial button to call the reporter.

"Bill, Jon. Sorry to bother you again but I want to run something by you and get your opinion."

As expected, the reporter exhibited some skepticism regarding Jon's theory, all the more so when told where the encounter took place and the amount of liquor involved. "Somehow, Jon, I don't think I'm going to stop the presses and declare an extra for this bit of news," he said. "But, I'm scheduled to see Chief O'Neal tomorrow morning and I'll tell him about it. I would think the first thing to do, and he'll probably order it done, is to check the credit cards in that restaurant and see who all was there last night, besides you."

"That should be easy for the police to do."

"Yeah, it's a start. And that's quite a restaurant, isn't it? Pretty obvious why it prospers. Only the rich and famous can afford those girls. I sure as hell can't."

"You have a point."

"None of my business, but you don't strike me as the type to establish a reputation as a cocksman just because you wife walked out."

"You don't know how right you are."

"Good. Unauthorized ass is getting pretty dangerous, anyway."

"Okay, Dad," and Jon couldn't suppress a chuckle. "I'll keep it in my pants. Now, will you talk to the Chief? Just tell him I really didn't dream all this up."

"First thing tomorrow morning. And Jon, I agree, little things like this occasionally break a case wide open. But the odds sure as hell don't favor it."

CHAPTER VI

It had been a month since Jon had heard from Kathy. She was getting close to term. He knew the picture as only an obstetrician would. He had tried to call, both before and after his unsuccessful foray into the world of expensive call girls. Sally answered the last time he had called the apartment and said Kathy was out but promised to have her call as soon as she came in. For the next week, each time the phone rang Jon picked it up expecting to hear his wife. Each time he was disappointed—and a little more resentful.

And he was tired. He usually shared night and weekend calls only with his partner. Recently other obstetricians had sensed his reluctance to spend much time at home and had prevailed upon him to cover their practice when they were out of town. Mondays were usually bad and today was no exception. Three nights with minimal sleep had put a considerable strain on a temperament which was already notoriously demanding. He even snapped at Nell during the morning office hours, a major breech of office etiquette, for which he somewhat begrudgingly apologized later. His spirits picked up a little that afternoon when Bill Arnold called.

"Jon, this is Bill. Check this morning's paper—page four. Then let's get together tonight, my office. If you can't make it just give me a call."

"Something to do with the feticides? Been a long time since we heard from the Poet."

"Just come on down to the paper this evening. Say about seven. I'll have a couple of sandwiches for us."

"Okay. You've piqued my interest. I'll be there unless I have a delivery. Should be clear. I had enough babies this weekend. Damn near filled the nursery."

"You sound a little weary. But you'll revive when you hear what I've got to say tonight. See you then."

Two appointment times remained unfilled as he had delivered these patients on Saturday. He noted this on the daily schedule then followed the advice of the reporter and picked up the morning paper from the waiting room. Page four contained mostly legal news and at first glance there appeared to be nothing of interest. Then, down in the left-hand corner he saw a small item, almost a filler. It mentioned the discovery of an unidentified female body in the basement garage of a large midtown apartment complex. The cause of death had not been determined and obviously the paper attached little or no importance to the passing of this middle-aged female. Just another statistic in this large city where drugs and alcohol made their daily contribution to the obituary page. She had been found by one of the apartment security personnel who promptly called the police. The body had been removed before the news people arrived, but a security man told one reporter that the woman looked about forty or forty-five. That was the only description of the victim at the death scene.

Page four had no other item of interest to the police—or to Jon. Five baby boys dead before they could take a breath outside the womb and now a forty-five year old female probable homicide victim—there appeared to be no correlating factors.

"Must be something the newspaper and I are missing," Jon muttered to himself as he went back to his office and started reviewing the afternoon charts. The list did not include any of his problem cases, but he did note that Sarah Tompkins had canceled her appointment. "What's with Sarah?" he asked his secretary. "I see she's crossed out on today's schedule."

"Something about being out of town," the secretary replied. "She's rescheduled for next Monday."

"Just as well. I'm not up to dealing with her today. She quit her new job?"

"No, I don't think so, Doctor. She just said it was some sort of an emergency. I didn't ask what. I don't like to get in a battle of wits with that one. She sort of gives me the creeps. I'm glad you don't have a practice full of 'Sarah Tompkins.'"

"One's enough," Jon agreed. "And by the way, don't let me get too far behind today. I'm supposed to meet Bill Arnold at seven o'clock and I have to make rounds first."

"We'll get you there, Doctor."

They did. Jon cleared the office by five-thirty and was through at the hospital an hour later. He had never been to the newspaper offices but knew the general direction and walked into Bill's office ten minutes early.

Status in this particular newsroom was measured by who did and who did not have a private office. Most of the reporters worked in cubicles in a large noisy common area. As Jon walked through this maze he was reminded of the scenes in *All The President's Men*. But he did walk all the way through as his man was the paper's top crime reporter and rated seclusion for his work. The door was open and with only a brief knock to announce his arrival, Jon entered Bill Arnold's inner sanctum.

Nobody had ever accused the reporter of being excessively neat—with good reason. He reported crime and his office walls were plastered with pictures of some of the scenes he had visited during his career.

Crime is rarely pretty and photographs of gunshot victims, hatchet murders, garroted young women, these and many more gave evidence that not everybody profits from crime. Jon looked for evidence of the reporter's family along with other personal memorabilia. These were missing. There were no pictures of children, no tennis trophies, baseball mitts or partially deflated footballs. Curiously, there was a small picture of a very pretty girl in a silver frame. She occupied the only uncluttered spot on Bill's desk.

"What's going on, Bill?"

"Jon, good to see you," the reporter greeted him then pointed to a chair close by his own. "Throw those magazines off and have a seat."

"You don't get any Pulitzer award for having the tidiest office in town," Jon said as he surveyed what to his orderly mind was complete disarray.

"I get paid for being meticulous in what I write, not where I write it. And did you read page four?"

"I did but I didn't gain anything from it. I presume that's why I'm here now."

"Right. You'll be interested to know the lady mentioned in that brief story died with a stainless steel knife in her heart. Stainless steel as in feticide. Same kind of a knife but no poem, no clue."

"I'll be damned. Copycat killer, maybe?"

"Could be. Doubtful. My sources tell me the knives that killed those babies and the lady in the apartment garage come off the same machinery."

"Was she pregnant?"

"Don't think so. Didn't look it, that's for sure. No, the cops tell me this lady was packing cocaine and had ten thousand in cold hard cash on her."

"And killed by the same weapon we find in the babies. What the hell's going on? Somebody get scared off during a robbery?"

"No, the police don't think it was a botched robbery. I've been sniffing around headquarters all afternoon and I'll tell you, that's a confused bunch down there right now. They have no idea on how to tie things together."

"Do you have any theories? You're not exactly a novice at this sort of thing, you know."

"Any coke in those kids who lost their babies? And how 'bout the teenager that was killed, any drugs in her?"

"There was a little in one of them, at least that's the report I heard. The rest were clean. Why?"

"Oh, just looking for angles. The drug world is full of weird people, but I'll be damned if I can get any sense out of this at all. The cops are sure of one thing, though, the Poet may not have left his calling card, but he was there."

Somebody brought some sandwiches and coffee in to Bill's office which prompted another remark from the reporter. "Now look here. I've prepared an elegant meal for you and I expect something in return. You're a doctor, you're a bright boy, pay for your keep. Give me a little help in writing this story."

Motive and connection, they were the problems and the next two hours were spent discussing them. Regarding the feticides, both agreed there was a real psycho at work here with a warped sense of social justice. But why the lady in the apartment garage? Jon voiced the possibility that the killer of the woman had been hired to do the job. He reasoned that the spring-fired knife need not be used exclusively on unsuspecting pregnant girls. Why not use the skill of this maniac to eliminate unwanted people? But unwanted by whom and why were they unwanted? Neither Bill nor Jon could answer this. There was a dead female on a slab in the police morgue identified only by a tag attached to the right great toe. There was a number on the tag plus the date and approximate time of death. All involved agreed that positive identification of the corpse might help prevent another feticide. It was not to be written off as just one more drug-related homicide.

"I'm sort of inclined to go along with you, Jon," Bill said. "I think there must be at least two people involved in this little caper. The Poet was there; everybody is pretty sure of that. But who sent him there? And I wonder if our lady corpse knew either of them. Certainly she had a brief acquaintance with the Poet but did she know him before they met in that basement? But why has he knocked off a non-pregnant adult female? Damn, can't figure this out," and Bill just sat in his chair shaking his head. "Sure doesn't look like he was after drugs or money. As you say, maybe someone paid him to do the job. Two people? Now we start thinking about that conversation you heard in the restaurant. Problem with that is you tell me the female voice was trying to talk him out of any more trouble. God, this gets more complicated every day. I think there's more than one person in this city who knows the Poet and knows all about him. Someone pretty close to him wanted to stiff the lady in the garage for some reason or other. Now, who? The lady who was with him in the restaurant? I don't think so. I don't think she wanted him to use his knives again. I think it was somebody else."

Jon didn't answer for a minute, then: "You sound like you believe my theory that I was practically eating dinner with the Poet."

"Not necessarily, but anything's possible."

"And that reminds me, what about Chief O'Neal? I never heard from you about that. Did you tell him about my little escapade and did he think it was worthwhile checking on?"

"At this point the Chief will check on anything and he did pretty much as I expected. He had his boys check on every credit card that went through the restaurant the night you were there. I hate to disappoint you, Jon, but he struck out. Lot of cash used that night, the head waiter said, so that didn't help and they were very busy so nobody stands out in his memory. He did think he remembered a couple who had an argument and two men who nearly got in a fight over one of the girls, but nothing the Chief felt was worthwhile."

"Well, shit."

"I told you not to get your hopes up."

"I know you did but sometimes I have a tendency to grasp at straws. I really want to see this guy on death row. Yeah, I'd like to be personally involved, maybe even physically involved in getting the bastard off the street. But at this point, I'll tell you something, Bill, I'd even shake the hand of Lenhart if he brought him in."

"That's going pretty far, Jon. And I'm sorry, I really am. This whole damn thing is frustrating a lot of people but I think you take it more personally. That worries me and I have a question for you. What are you going to do if this guy is never caught? That's not just an idle possibility, you know."

"I can't think that way, Bill. It would haunt me. I'd be looking for him every day for the rest of my life. That lousy son of a bitch, somebody will get him. You don't suppose he's quit picking on pregnant girls and is going to sell his marksmanship to the highest bidder?"

"I doubt it. If I were pregnant, especially if I happened to be full term with a male fetus and on welfare, I'd stick pretty close to home."

"I'm at that Special Procedures Clinic every week and I get the idea that most of those girls are doing just that. They've been scared but I'm afraid they're getting their nerve up again. Nobody from the Clinic has been hurt recently and I heard one of those rascals say she thought the siege was over. I don't know what they'll think when your paper tells the city just what killed the woman in the basement garage."

"Probably just give them all the more confidence. They'll think for sure that crazy had turned his attention to middle-aged women carrying coke."

"Did you happen to see Lenhart when you were at headquarters?"

"Briefly—that's about all I can stand of him. That smug son of a bitch seemed about half-pleased that somebody in the drug world got knocked off. And he told one of the sergeants they should look for a connection but doubted if they'd find one."

"Is that going to be the official police position?"

"I don't know. Right now they are concentrating on finding out who she is—or who she was. I think most of the cops hope the killer is the same old Poet and he just changed targets. They've taken a lot of flack from the news media, me included, about the unsolved feticides. We might be easier on them if they're a little slow in finding out who got the woman carrying coke and cash."

"Well, I hope you don't plan to ease up on Lenhart."

"I'm not going to let him off the hook, Jon. I plan to keep riding his ass until he gets something done—or he quits."

"I'll bet he gets canned if one more baby gets stuck with a knife."

"Let's just hope your theory isn't put to the test. And even if it is, don't bank on the Lieutenant leaving town."

Jon stood up and stretched then yawned. "Right now," he said, "the only thing I'm banking on is that I'll sleep through the night. My partner is taking calls and if we're about through here, I'm heading for bed."

"I think we've pretty well wrapped it up, at least for now. Not that we solved anything, but we had a good talk and I'll write it up best I can. Thanks for coming down, Jon. Why don't you join me Saturday? I have an appointment with Chief O'Neal. He won't object if you're there. His daughter being your patient doesn't hurt our cause. She must have some influence with the old boy."

"Let's hope so. I'll meet you down there. What time?"

"Two o'clock."

There was an air of frustration in the small, neat room that served as an office. Poem #6 remained in the raincoat pocket and the raincoat remained in the closet. Throughout the weeks—now months—of inactivity there had been no visible change in the behavior or work habits of the Poet. All duties were performed on schedule and without mishap or error. The inner turmoil was not apparent even to close friends. But the stress was there and was evident during those moments of isolation in the small office. The act of destroying a term fetus was a narcotic to this individual and a "fix" was needed. The weather report didn't help; sunshine was predicted for the next two weeks. But there was an item on page two of the entertainment section. This looked promising. It sounded exciting and held hope for conditions favorable to both hunter and hunted. There might be a problem with the raincoat while traveling on a warm, sunshiny day but somehow that could be solved.

Tuesday morning in the office Jon received a call from Judge Donovan. "Jon, I'm in town and hoped we might have lunch. Can you spare an hour from your busy practice?"

Jon knew he should not—indeed, could not—avoid this old friend any longer. "I didn't have any plans, Judge, but I do now. Where can I meet you?"

"There's a club next to the Federal Building on Fifth Street. I'll leave word at the desk I'm expecting you."

"I know the place. I'll be there shortly after noon."

There were no interruptions in the office routine and Jon arrived at the downtown club a few minutes before 12:00. A waiter directed him across the quiet dining area to the Judge's table.

"I've missed seeing you, Jon," Judge Donovan said as he rose from his chair and extended his hand.

"My fault, Judge. And a perceptive old devil like you probably knows why."

"Got a pretty good idea. Sit down. We'll order lunch and talk about it if you want."

It was time well-spent and as he drove back to the office Jon felt both relieved and a little wiser. Under the insightful questioning of the elderly jurist, Jon was forced to admit that he really was not anxious to take on the responsibilities of fatherhood. He was an only child of rather doting parents and had been allowed to adopt a very self-centered attitude. In his mind this was a reason, not an excuse, for being somewhat inconsiderate in his relationship to Kathy. Yes, he liked the free-wheeling life style a childless marriage afforded them and it would be very difficult to adjust. Difficult to accept a wife who now must share her affections with a demanding baby and difficult to accept the disruption in their lives that such an intruder would bring. He confessed to the Judge that he really didn't know if he could make this change. He didn't know if he could be such a hypocrite and pretend he enjoyed being a captive to a mother and her newborn. Now, as he backed into his parking stall at the office he remembered the Judge's final comment when they parted company on the sidewalk outside the club. Using all the wisdom of his seventy-plus years, Judge Donovan had told him:

"Jon, you are an intelligent young man. As such you are capable of modifying your behavior to bring Kathy back into your life. And to accept a child. Remember Jon, I'm not asking the impossible. I know you can't be a chameleon. You can't change completely every time your environment is altered. You're still going to be a little selfish. That's okay, that's Jon. But be a little considerate, too. It'll pay you large dividends. And that conforms to a rather narrow definition of being selfish—you get more out of life in the long run."

Sound advice and Jon would give it considerable thought over the next few weeks. He wondered if he was getting just a little tired of his reputation as an inconsiderate S.O.B.

The following Saturday Jon was the host when Bill joined him at the little diner next to police headquarters. Both settled for a chicken salad sandwich then went across the street and up to Chief O'Neal's office.

The Chief had experienced very few pleasant days since the Poet had dropped the first macabre little rhyme. Today was an exception; he was in a good mood and greeted his visitors accordingly.

"Welcome," he said. "Come in and have a seat. I have some news both of you will be interested in, especially you, Mr. Arnold."

"A little break in the feticide business, Chief?" Bill asked.

"Not exactly, but we do have an I.D. on the lady who was killed in the apartment garage. I don't know if it'll help us nail the Poet but by God we're working on it. Doctor, remember I asked you once if you knew a Lawrence Miller?"

"Yes."

"Well, our lady with the knife in her heart is his ex-wife."

"I'll be damned. He's not really one of my favorites in the Special Procedures Clinic, but I never tagged him as the violent type, either."

"No, no," the Chief said, "don't jump to any hasty conclusions. He's clear. We checked on that. He was married to the lady for only six months—many years ago. Divorced her, he said, when he found she had a drinking problem. Told us yesterday he hadn't heard from her in over twenty years."

"You believe him?"

"I think so, but cops are paid to have a suspicious mind so we'll follow up on it just to be sure."

"How'd you get her name?" the reporter asked.

"She didn't have a damn bit of identification on her when we brought her in. Drew a blank in the apartment house. Nobody knew her there, or if they did, they weren't admitting it. But she had some unusual dental repair work so we sent pictures, x-rays, and diagrams to every dentist in town and finally hit the jackpot."

"So you know her name. What else did you find out about her?"

"Not much. Found out where she lived but somebody had been there before us and cleaned out that apartment slicker'n a hound's tooth. No papers, no letters, nothing in the pockets of her clothing. No fingerprints, the place was wiped clean. Just like they wanted us to believe the whole thing was drug-related."

"Seems to me they'd use a gun, not that damned knife, if they wanted you to go chasing the drug angle. And besides the knife, can you dream up any connection between this killing and the Poet?"

"Nothing yet, Doctor. This can be painfully slow work but anything we learn eventually fits and helps. A little more time, somebody will get drunk and talk to the wrong person. We'll hear about it. Be a little break here or there and we'll find something more interesting about the former Mrs. Miller. The story, what there is of it, is yours, Mr. Arnold. And you, Doctor, I called you down here because you know this Miller fellow. At least you come in contact with him occasionally. I don't expect you to play detective but I would appreciate you keeping your ears open. Offhand remarks can be valuable. I wonder if he's telling the truth about not seeing his ex-wife for twenty years. When Mr. Arnold writes his article and this Miller's past shows up as front page news, he might just let something slip."

"As I said, he's not exactly one of my favorite people," Jon said, "but I'll hang around him occasionally and see if he has anything to say. You know Bill gave me a press card when I went to that news conference with him. Do I get a gold badge from you, Chief?"

"You get the pleasure of delivering my daughter again, Doctor, and maybe a sense of accomplishment if you help us out a bit. That enough?"

Jon smiled. "You bet it is, Chief. And I'll help any way you want me to. Thought I might make a contribution with that restaurant conversation but Bill said nothing came of it."

"Unfortunately, that's right. A few more credit cards and we might have had something there. As a matter of fact, I'm always a little suspicious of anybody who uses cash in an expensive eating establishment. I think he was there, Doctor, but we can't trace it."

There was a brisk knock on the door and one of the police sergeants came in without waiting to be asked. "Chief, I hate to interrupt you but we just got word there's been another attack on one of the pregnant girls. Ambulance is taking her in to University Hospital right now. The cop that called in said she really got stabbed. And Doctor, apparently the hospital knows you're down here. We got the word they'd like to have you come and help out."

"Damn," Chief O'Neal said. "I knew it was too good to last. My car in its usual spot, Sergeant?"

"Yes, sir."

"Take it and drive the Doctor up to the medical school. Flashers and siren."

"Yes, sir. Come along, Doctor."

Sergeant Morrow was a skillful and intuitive driver. He seemed to sense when the traffic would part allowing him to push the Chief's powerful Jaguar to its limits during the three mile drive to the hospital. And he was able to answer Jon's questions along the way.

"Why today, Sarge? Christ, it's clear as a bell. We haven't had a drop of rain for days. This is definitely not the Poet's kind of weather."

"It's where he struck—the location," Sergeant Morrow answered.

"They're making a movie up in the big park. Got permission from the city water department and turned the damned place into a regular rain forest. Helicopters and fire engines spraying water all over hell's half acre. Thousands of people up there today, some as extras but most just curious to see the movie stars. Noise, rain, lots of people—"

A semi-truck suddenly loomed in front, nearly blocking the narrow street. The Sergeant down-shifted the Jag, floored the gas pedal and slid toward the back of the trailer. The low-profile Pirelli tires screamed for mercy—but held. The Jag slipped around the end of the truck and accelerated. Sgt. Morrow glanced at Jon and winked. "Damn trucks," he said, "shouldn't allow them on the city streets. Now, where was I? What was I saying? Oh, yes—rain, noise and crowds. I suppose we should have been alert to a possible attack in a set-up like that but I guess the weather sort of lulled us to sleep. And it's been awhile since we've heard from that bastard."

"How do you work this radio, Sergeant? I'd better find out if she's still in the emergency room or up in surgery."

"Just lift it up and push the button. You'll get headquarters. They'll find out and call us back."

Jon followed the instructions and learned the patient had cleared the E.R. and was on her way to the operating room.

"Head for the main hospital building, Sarge. Let me out near the left wing. There's a staff elevator there. I can take it to the surgical floor. Incidentally," and Jon pointed to the Jaguar plaque set into the polished wood of the dash, "pretty fancy car. You drive it damned well but do all police chiefs rate this kind of luxury?"

"The boss married well, Doctor. Mrs. O'Neal gave him this little item last Christmas."

"Not bad. I sure as hell don't have to worry about that kind of luck."

Jon's arrival in surgery was only moments behind the patient's. He changed quickly, slipped on a cap and mask and went directly to the Supervisor's desk. Mrs. Connors was on duty and looked up when Jon walked in.

"They're prepping the patient in room eight, Doctor Erickson," she said. "You can scrub any time. Ben Sires, the Chief Resident is in there. I think he helped you before. Don Mason is a second-year man and he'll be assist also. Same type of case, though this one is a little different. I'm sure you'll see that as soon as you scrub. Incidentally, I am to tell you that Doctor Johnson asked that you be called. He's in a meeting."

"I don't mind. But what are you doing here on a Saturday, Mrs. Connors? I swear you must spend twenty-four hours a day in this place."

"Just charging you taxpayers double-time. Now get on in there."

The "little difference" was obvious when Jon finished scrubbing and went in to surgery. The patient was under anesthesia and except for a small blanket over her lower limbs was lying nude on the operating table. The usual "point of entry" of the weapon on the side of the near-term abdomen was absent. In its stead, the handle of the knife was visible in the midline just above the pubic bone. A thin, watery trail of blood continued to ooze from the wound over the freshly prepped lower abdomen and thighs.

"I didn't prep the knife handle, Doctor Erickson," the circulating nurse said, "just around the edges. I thought you could put a sterile plastic bag over it in case there were any fingerprints."

"Probably won't be," Jon said, "but damn sure wouldn't be if you painted the whole thing with betadine."

"What kind of an incision, Doctor?" the scrub nurse asked.

"I'd say our usual transverse, right above the knife. I'd like to get in there and see where the blade is before we pull it out."

"Through the bladder and into the skull, that'd be my guess," the Chief Resident said.

"Probably so. That blood looks a little thin. Probably a mixture of urine and amniotic fluid," Jon said as he slipped on his gloves. "Smells like it, too. I wonder what the hell happened. This isn't what we're used to seeing. Did you get some photographs, Ben?"

"Yes, sir. Several from all angles."

"Good. And you've checked thoroughly for any sign of fetal activity?"

"Not a sound in that belly."

"Okay. Everything under control up your way?" Jon asked the anesthesiologist.

"Vitals are good. She's lost some blood but not a huge amount. I remember one where the knife caught something and tumbled into the abdomen. Ripped the hell out of things. Now that girl really bled."

"You bet she did. Blood all over the place. Well, let's get going on this one."

Jon took the scalpel from the nurse and made a deep cut across the lower abdomen about an inch-and-a-half above the protruding weapon. The small bleeders in the skin and subcutaneous fat were quickly cauterized and the incision continued down through the fascia.

"Maybe we should cut those abdominal muscles and do a classic transverse incision," the Chief Resident suggested. "That way we wouldn't have to strip the fascia from around the weapon."

"Good idea." And using the cutting current of the cautery tip Jon incised the big strap-like rectus abdominous muscles on each side, exposing the peritoneum. This layer was slit transversely as well. With the uterus exposed, the path of the killing blade was confirmed to have first gone through the bladder, then through the thinned-out muscle of the lower part of the uterus to lodge in the upper cervical spine of the baby.

"Doctor Mason, do you know what the odontoid process is?" Jon asked the second-year resident.

"Yes, sir. I'm from a state where we still hang killers and horse thieves. So we know all about the anatomy of the neck."

Jon looked over at the scrub nurse. "Know what he's talking about, Miss Brown?"

"No, sir."

"Tell her, Don. Ben, you hold the retractor for him so he can show our scrub nurse."

The young resident, temporarily freed from retracting duties, took a thumb forceps from the Mayo stand and pointed to where the knife had entered the baby's spine. "Right there," he said, "is the second cervical vertebra. There is a little piece of bone on that called the odontoid process. A good hangman will place the knot of the rope right over that area so when the trap is sprung the knot will push that piece of bone forward. Theoretically, it severs the cord, and death is almost instantaneous. It's all a little neater than choking to death if the rope just cuts off your wind pipe."

"Very good, Don. Didn't you think so, Miss Brown?"

"A little gruesome but what's the point? I don't see any hangman's knot around this baby."

"I suspect when they do an autopsy on the baby they'll find the knife went right through the soft odontoid and cut the cord. Same type of death as hanging. Poor little devil didn't live long after that thing hit him."

When the baby had been removed and Jon's scalpel incision in the uterus repaired, the surgical team turned its attention to the damaged bladder. This was carefully closed and the suture lines checked by injecting a dye into the bladder. Satisfied that the closure was secure, Jon used copious amounts of a sterile fluid to rinse out the surgical area as well as the path of the offending knife. Drains were appropriately placed and the abdominal incision closed.

"Damnedest thing I've ever seen," Jon said just before the dressing was applied. "Look at that knife wound. I swear to God that son of a bitch hit her within a millimeter of midline. Hell, we don't do any better when we have them lying naked and asleep on the operating room table."

"Somehow I doubt if he was trying to impress us with his anatomically precise shooting," the circulating nurse said as she put the last strip of tape over the bandage. "She must have heard something and turned toward the killer. I wonder if she saw him."

"Probably have to wait for tomorrow to learn that," the anesthesiologist said, "but right now, let's get her off the table."

Jon stripped off his gown and gloves, tossed them expertly into the trash receptacle and walked out of the O.R. He checked with the supervisor and learned that Lt. Lenhart was not in the hospital.

"That's strange," he said to Mrs. Connors. "I thought sure he'd be here by now. Must be my lucky day. Probably hear from him later on, though. I'll dictate the surgery and he can have a copy tomorrow after I've checked it."

"I'll tell him you were looking for him," Mrs. Connors said. "Hopefully he's out trying to find the guy who sends us these patients."

"He'd better hurry. I heard the weather report on my way downtown at noon. We're due a little rain."

"Maybe the Poet doesn't listen to the weather man."

"Wrong. I think he studies the weather very carefully."

And Jon was right. Even though envelope number six had finally been dropped and the raincoat pocket emptied, the Poet was not completely satisfied. Number six had been difficult and that only increased the excitement. And there was satisfaction in predicting the behavior of the Clinic patients. Some, lacking entertainment elsewhere and feeling safe on a sunny day, had gone to the park to watch a movie being made. They, too, were watched and one nearly died.

But now the Poet saw dark clouds forming in the west; heavy rains were predicted. Time to think about another poem.

The fate of number seven was written out that night. The city would be shocked and puzzled when the rhyme was dropped. Shocked over the continuation of the crimes and puzzled that the Poet had selected a target, though pregnant, quite different from the previous victims. Something else was different, too, and unknown to the community. There was now a buyer for the knife, a vengeful, silent partner who had called one shot and would call yet another.

CHAPTER VII

Sunday morning when Jon arrived at University Hospital he called Ben Sires. The Chief Resident had delayed making rounds on yesterday's victim. Now he and Jon went in to her room together.

"Sherry," Ben said, "this is Doctor Erickson. You can blame him for that slash on your belly. Of course you can also thank him for saving your life. Doctor, meet yesterday's miracle child, Sherry Bourden."

Tiny and pale, intravenous lines still in both arms, a catheter in her bladder, her abdomen swollen with bandages where there should have been a pregnancy, Jon half expected tears and self-pity from such a picture. But that was not Sherry. Even the formless, dull hospital attire could not hide this girl's charm and wit.

"So you're the slasher who fixed me so I can't wear a string bikini anymore."

Jon smiled. "You're a mouthy little rascal, aren't you? Could have been killed yesterday, you know."

"Takes more than that nasty old Poet to kill me, Doctor."

"He tried."

"He? What makes you think the Poet is a man? My friends in the Clinic are betting on a female."

"That's interesting, Sherry. What makes them think so?"

"I don't know. Maybe it's because we have to deal with McGraw every time we go to Clinic. She's a bitch, you know."

"So I've heard, but I think it's just because she represents an authority figure. And make no mistake, Ms. McGraw is authority."

"She's a bitch," Sherry repeated. "But personally I don't think she's got the balls to shoot anybody. Besides, I agree with you. I think it's a man and I think I saw him yesterday."

"You saw him!" Jon and the resident said almost in unison.

"Do the cops know that?" Ben Sires asked.

"I don't think so and I'm not sure, anyway. But yesterday I was standing up there real close to the action, getting soaked to the skin but I wanted to see Tom Cooney. He's the star, you know. Boy, is he good-looking. I did get to see him but just for a few seconds. He's a real stud. I almost fainted when he stood there in his shorts with the rain coming down."

"Sherry," Ben said, "I don't think Doctor Erickson or I share your enthusiasm for seeing Mr. Cooney in his shorts, but we do want to hear about your encounter with the Poet."

"Well, I was standing by some of those fake buildings the movie people put up, you know. And there was sort of an alley or an opening between them. I guess it must have led back into the woods. Anyway, I was just moving over to get a better look—past this little alley—and I remember somebody said something like 'help me.' Said it a couple or three times and I turned to look between these fake houses and I saw someone kneeling down. Pretty sure he had on a rain coat and hat. That's about all I remember. It was awful noisy up there in that park. Helicopters and fire engines spraying water all over, so I'm not very sure of what I heard but I think it sounded like a man's voice. Then I felt something hit me in the stomach. Boy, it was a real wallop, too. Knocked me down and the next thing I know there's a lot of people around me and I get packed off into an ambulance. I don't remember much from then on in. A little bit last night maybe, when you guys got through with me. But I'm sort of okay this morning."

"And you don't remember telling any of this to the cops who rode with you in the ambulance?" Jon asked.

"I told you, I don't remember much at all about that ride but I don't think I talked to anybody."

"Ben, let's put a 'no visitors' sign on her door until this evening. There's a Lieutenant Lenhart who's going to want to question her and I'd just as soon she had a little more rest before he comes in."

"I'll see that it gets on the door."

"Let me sign the order. Lenhart will have a fit, but we'll let him in tonight or tomorrow morning if Sherry is up to it. Ben, why don't we write the order that one of us has to be in the room when Lenhart is with Sherry?"

"Okay with me if we can get away with it. I've only met him once. Can't say I was very impressed. Now, do you suppose we should take a look at last night's handiwork on Sherry's belly?"

"I don't want to see it," Sherry said.

"You don't have to, but we do. I'll have the nurse get us a dressing tray."

Late that evening Lt. Lenhart did arrive and after an attempt to bully Dr. Sires failed, he agreed to let the resident stay in the room during the time Sherry was questioned. The entire interview was transcribed, including the Lieutenant's objection to the presence of a third party. Ben described the scene to Jon the following morning and said he was surprised the Lieutenant did not spend more time quizzing Sherry about the voice and what she saw.

"He seemed reluctant to dig into it at all," Ben said. "Almost as though he didn't care."

"Well, Sherry admitted she couldn't see the figure in the alley very well," Jon said. "And she couldn't hear much either over all the other noise around there. I suspect the Lieutenant figured there was no way she could make an identification, so why spend any time on it."

"Maybe so. He did say she'd make a damn poor witness. Well, let's go see our little friend. Her chart looks good but I haven't seen her yet this morning."

"Suppose I should tell her about the attempted feticide last night? She might know the intended victim."

"I didn't hear about it. What happened?"

"Outside one of the downtown movies. Double feature, if you can believe it, an old Elvis Presley flick and another one starring the Beatles. Brought the teenagers out in droves and as the weather man predicted, it started to rain like hell while they were all lined up waiting to get in. A reporter friend of mine called me last night. He said the pregnant girl apparently bent down to tie her shoe at just the right second and the knife sailed into somebody else."

"Kill 'em?"

"No. Hit him in the back. I think he's okay. I'm surprised you didn't hear about it. Was on TV and the radio."

"Doctor Erickson, you've forgotten what it's like to be a resident physician in obstetrics and gynecology. It got pretty hairy around here last night. I haven't been near a TV set or a radio or a bed for the past twenty-four hours."

"Sorry, Ben. It's been a few years since I had that kind of a schedule. But you'll live through it. We all have. Now let's go see Sherry."

The recuperative powers of young people were always a pleasant surprise to Jon. Sherry was no exception. She was standing at the sink brushing her teeth when he and Ben came into the room.

"When are you going to take this hose out of my bladder so I can pee like everybody else does?" she asked as soon as she rinsed the toothpaste out of her mouth. "And how 'bout taking this dressing off so I can get in the shower?"

"I think we can take that hose, as you called it, out of your bladder in a day or two and you can probably take a shower tomorrow. And when you're all cleaned up I have a friend I want you to meet. He's a crime reporter for the paper and he wants to talk to you if you say it's okay."

"Will he put my name in the paper?"

"Sweetie, I hate to tell you," Jon said, "but you don't need any introduction to the people of this city. Your name was plastered all over the paper the morning after you came in here."

"Oh."

"May I bring him in?"

"Sure. But he'd better not be anything like that cop that was up here last night."

"Lieutenant Lenhart?"

"Yes. My belly was hurting when he was talking to me. He knew it, too. You'd think he'd at least say he was sorry I got hurt. Oh, no, not a word. I thought southerners were supposed to have good manners and be sexy. Not that guy. I almost asked him if his accent was fake but decided it wasn't a good idea."

"The Lieutenant is not known for his charm. If he comes back and tries to give you a bad time just get a hold of Doctor Sires. Now, let's take a look at that incision."

In the evening, Jon brought Bill Arnold up to Sherry's room. There was an instant chemistry between the two. The crusty, somewhat abrasive nature of the reporter was gone, replaced by a tenderness which Jon had not observed before. They stayed about half an hour and on the way out of the hospital Jon could not restrain his curiosity.

"That girl got to you, Bill. How come?"

"Oh, she's just a nice kid and she got hurt. I don't hand out shit to everybody I meet. I can be a decent sort every now and then."

"Yeah, I know she's a nice kid but you weren't just decent, Bill, you liked that girl. She remind you of somebody?"

"None of your damned business."

"I know that but why don't you tell me anyway?"

They were in the parking lot now and walking slowly toward Jon's car. The reporter did not respond to the question and neither spoke until they were in the car and moving out toward the street.

"Mind if I smoke?" Bill asked.

"No. Go ahead. You might crack the window a bit. Let the smoke out on your side. My lungs are still fairly pure."

Bill pressed a button to slide the window down then lit the cigarette with a small pocket lighter. He took a deep drag and exhaled slowly. The suction from the open window pulled the smoke out of the car.

"You sound like my daughter," he said. "She used to bitch when some of my smoke would intrude into her space."

Jon glanced over quickly at his companion. "Your daughter?" he asked. "Didn't know you had one. You've never mentioned her before. Didn't know you'd even been married."

"You speak in the proper tense. Had, is the word, past tense. She was killed in a car wreck four years ago."

"My God, Bill, I had no idea. That's her picture on your desk, isn't it?"

"High school senior."

"It still isn't any of my business, but how 'bout your wife?"

"You may not know it, Jon, but a lot of marriages go belly up after a child dies. We were no exception."

"Sounds like you've sort of had the shit kicked out of you a couple times. Sherry remind you a little bit of your daughter?"

"Oh, a little. Her mannerisms mostly. She's kind of flip, quick with her tongue, smart. I hope she learns something from all this. Be a shame to waste that brain."

Bill pulled deeply on the cigarette once more then flicked it out the window. "Jon, when we were on the phone the other day you said you wanted to get together. Had something to run by me, I believe you said. What was it?"

"Not quite ready yet," Jon said. "It's just a list of people that hang around that Special Procedures Clinic. I still have a little bit of cop in me left over from that police academy down south. When I flesh out the characters a bit we'll look it over. Okay?"

"Sure. And one more thing. Since you delved into my past history, I'll return the favor. What's with Mrs. Erickson? She back home?"

Jon shook his head. "Not good, Bill. I can't even get a hold of her. I've tried. Several times. I'm thinking about seeing a lawyer next week."

"She's pregnant, isn't she?"

"Yes."

"Forget the lawyer. Those sons of bitches won't help you. All they want is your money. Hang in there awhile. It might be worth it."

Like the words from the Judge, it was good advice. Jon knew it and he was reminded again when he drove home and entered the empty house. The weather was warm and there was still some daylight left so he took a Coke from the refrigerator and went outside and sat down on one of the patio chairs. He noticed a little rust forming on the wrought-iron table and thought to himself that he'd best get some paint pretty soon and fix it up. He couldn't help but remember how proud Kathy had been when the furniture store delivered the "rust-proof" assembly of chairs and table. She had bought it on sale, half price and it was their first outdoor furniture.

"Damn it, Kate," he said softly. "I wish you were home where you belong."

He read for awhile after finishing the Coke then went to bed early as he had a potentially difficult surgical case in the morning. Fortunately from the standpoint of his sleep—and his temper—he did not get called during the night and arrived in the operating room at 7:15 a.m. The anesthesiologist was able to get the case started ahead of time and by ten minutes until eight, Jon was standing, knife in hand, ready to start the operation.

It was an interesting case involving a huge ovarian tumor in a twenty-one-year-old woman. No malignancy was found and the surgery proceeded on schedule. As he was closing the long incision, Jon remarked: "Well, this turned out to be a fun case. I'll have time before office hours to go see that kid at University Hospital."

"Saturday's feticide?" the resident asked.

"That's the one."

"There was quite an article in the paper this morning. Told all about the one you operated on and also about the Poet hitting the wrong target in front of the theater."

"My daughter was at that movie," the scrub nurse said. "And you know, she may have seen the person who did the dirty work."

"She what?" Jon stopped sewing, the needle holder in his hand ready to place another suture through the fascia. "Say that again. Your daughter was in that mass of teenagers and thinks she saw the killer?"

"Well, she was pretty excited when she came home Saturday night. I haven't quizzed her much about it."

"I know someone who'd just about give his right arm to talk to her —Bill Arnold, crime reporter for the paper. And when he's through the cops would take over. Judy Ridgeway, if your daughter really got a good look at who's behind that spring-loaded knife she might be able to help catch him."

"Oh, she's just a kid. I doubt if she saw enough to be of any importance."

"Kids see things, too. And they have good memories."

"I don't know." The nurse seemed uncertain and fussed with the instruments on her Mayo stand. Finally she looked up at Jon and asked, "Will she be in any danger? She's all I have, Doctor. Her father was killed in a car wreck."

"I didn't know that, Judy. I'm sorry."

"I wasn't working then."

Jon was surprisingly gentle. "It's up to you, Judy," he said. "There's no way I can push her to see the reporter or the police. But I think she should."

"I'll think about it while we finish," she said. "You going to have a cup of coffee after you've written post-op orders?"

"Probably."

"I'll get in touch with you."

"Okay. Now let's get this belly back together again."

Judy called after Jon had dressed and was in the surgical lounge. "I can't do it, Doctor Erickson," she said. "It sounds like I could be putting her at risk and I just can't take the chance. It's only been a year since my husband was killed. You probably think I'm being over protective but I can't help it."

"I understand, Judy. If you change your mind, let me know."

"I will, Doctor, and thank you."

"Damn," was Jon's only response when he put down the phone.

"What's wrong?" one of the other doctors asked.

"Oh, nothing I can do anything about, at least for the time being. Anyway, I'd better head out of here and see that kid at the med school."

Sherry had just come from a shower when Jon arrived. With her curly red hair still damp, she looked like a freshly scrubbed little doll. "Look at me," she said. "I'm clean and no more tubes sticking out of me. I even got to pee in the pot this morning. That's a pretty big deal, let me tell you."

"You look great. You want to do me a favor?"

"Sure. Name it."

"I want to know about Frankie McGraw."

"Oh, shit. I was feeling pretty good 'till you brought up that bitch."

"You don't get along with her."

"I guess you could say that."

"Why?"

"I don't like to be bossed around. And she's mean."

"Is that all?"

"That's enough."

"Yes, she runs a tight ship. Anybody else on the Clinic staff give you trouble?"

"No. McGraw's the only one I couldn't get along with. I didn't hang around there much. Had other things to do. The Clinic was free and that's all I cared about."

"Well, let me put it this way. Were there any overt sexual advances from any of the male staff or medical students?"

"Overt? What's that mean?"

"Overt means something open, something obvious."

"Okay, sure. Mr. Good Guy—that's what we called him. Doctor Miller, he's one of our counselors, you know. Likes to get us in a one-on-one counseling session. Awful 'handsy.' Just can't keep 'em off you." The redhead gave a little shake.

"The students?"

"They're a horny bunch, those medical students. They think we'll be easy pickings since we've been had before. I went out with one once. Big shot, real smoothie, out to show the wayward little girl a good time."

"And did he?" Jon asked with a smile.

"Hah. Not with that attitude. He's the only one I got to know at all. They rotate through the Clinic, first one bunch then another. Attending doctors the same, come and go. The old standbys, the ones we see all the time are McGraw, Miller and Mr. Parker." She frowned a little. "Now Parker, there's a strange duck for you. Know him?"

"I've talked with him a little. What do you mean, strange duck?"

"I mean he rarely comes out of the lab. Never talks to us."

"The lab's his job, Sherry. He's not there to socialize with you kids."

"He doesn't have to. He's got a blonde chick who comes in after hours every now and then."

Jon's interest picked up. "Former Clinic patient?" he asked.

"Maybe. I don't think so. She doesn't act like she's ever been one of us. I don't like her."

"Sherry, how can you say that? I'll bet you've never met her."

"Doctor Erickson, you don't have to be formally introduced to some people. You just know you don't like 'em. I did sort of meet her once, though. It was about a month ago. I was in real late that night—had an extra ultrasound and a stress test. Must have been around six-thirty and they were just coming out of his lab when I walked by. I've had some ugly stares in my day—a pregnant teenager doesn't have much status you know—but boy, the evil eye I got from her. She didn't speak. Just looked at my big belly then at me. I can tell you she's not the class act she thinks she is."

"Well, she apparently doesn't bother anybody over there and Mr. Parker gets his job done so I guess what they do after hours is their business."

A nurse's aid brought Sherry's lunch in and Jon rose to go. "I'll see you tomorrow, Sherry."

"Whoa, wait a minute. Not so fast. When do I get out of here?"

"Wednesday or Thursday if all goes well."

"I farted this morning. The nurse said that was a good sign."

"And it is," Jon agreed. "We have some really special tubes for people who can't."

"I'll bet you do. No thanks. Bye, Doctor."

"Good-bye, Sherry."

"That little devil," Jon thought as he took the elevator down now. "I wonder what else she knows."

Afternoon office hours started out with a return visit by Stephanie VanOsborn. Preliminary evaluation of her infertility status had revealed that both fallopian tubes were blocked. At her initial office visit, Stephanie had denied the possibility of any sexually-transmitted disease but the damaged tubes were evidence to the contrary. Today she was scheduled to have a physical exam, then be hospitalized next week for a laparoscopy. The findings of this minor surgical procedure would probably confirm the presence of extensive pelvic organ adhesions. Even more important, by directly observing the damage through the scope, Jon could determine if major and prolonged surgery would improve Stephanie's chances for a pregnancy.

But on this office visit her attitude was different and she was not anxious to get pregnant. She seemed disinterested when Jon explained the various options to her. The pouty, spoiled appearance was even more conspicuous. She had changed her mind completely and if anything, expressed relief that she probably could not conceive. Certainly she did not want her husband to be the father of any child of hers. She had grown bored with him and openly admitted to Jon that she was seeking other sexual partners.

"I want to live a little," she said, "and I don't want to be tied down."

All this discussion was taking place in the exam room after Jon had concluded the physical. Stephanie had allowed the drape to fall to the floor and she sat on the table with two very shapely legs and hips completely bare. Her breasts were partially exposed with the gown hanging rather precariously on her nipples. Seductive patients were rare in Jon's practice but there were safeguards built into the physical structure of the office. Unobtrusively, he touched his knee to a small button located on the wall beside him. Seconds later, his nurse opened the door and told him there was an urgent phone call waiting.

"Thanks, Nell," Jon said when they were out in the hall. "Now what are we going to do with her?"

"Simple. I'll just tell her to get her clothes on and come out to the front desk so we can schedule her for surgery."

"No, she changed her mind. Doesn't want to have the laparoscopy."

"What does she want, then?"

"I think she wants to use that body."

"Not in this office. White trash—can't stand them."

Jon grinned at the nurse. "Don't be a bigot, Nell. Just tell her if she changes her mind to give the office a ring for another appointment."

"That one's trouble."

"Not as long as you're around to rescue me."

"I'll be here. Now you go to room three. Sarah Tompkins is there. You seem to enjoy jousting with her. I'll take care of Miss Stephanie and bring a new patient to your office when you get back there."

Sarah's greeting was characteristic. "Did you know this little fart kicks hard enough to wake me up at night?" she asked.

"You're not the first pregnant woman to have discovered that, you know, Sarah."

"Well, I wouldn't admit this to anyone but you, Doctor, but I sort of like it. Especially since I know it's a girl."

"You sound almost human today, Sarah. Can't tell, you might surprise yourself and do pretty well at this mothering business."

"Don't make book on that, Doctor. But I figure if I want to, I can sure as hell do a better job than my mother did."

"Let's hope you want to. Now let's check that little friend of yours."

Sarah's pregnancy, Jon found, continued to advance in an entirely normal fashion, but she had saved a little surprise for Jon. Just before he left the room she asked about Kathy.

"I saw your wife yesterday, Doctor. I think she's due about two weeks before I am. Or maybe you didn't know. I hear she has an apartment by herself. That right?"

Kathy's living arrangements as well as her pregnancy were none of Sarah's business but he resisted telling her so. He also curbed the desire to lie and say that Kathy had moved back home only yesterday. Instead, in a casual way, he asked if she was one of Kathy's patients at the Outpatient Clinic.

"No," Sarah said. "I don't go up to the medical school clinics as a patient anymore. I went up with a friend and your Doctor Kathleen Erickson was her shrink. But you didn't answer my question."

"Nor do I intend to. See you in two weeks, Sarah." And Jon walked out of the room.

Before entering his office, Jon picked up the file for the new patient. Her name was Opal Parker, age forty-five. Her occupation was listed as "housewife" on the office information sheet. The space for husband's name and occupation was not filled out. Jon briefly wondered if she could be any relation to Donald Parker, the Director of Laboratories, then looked up from reading the admission data when the nurse brought Mrs. Parker in. Hoping it wasn't too obvious, he hurriedly glanced back at the form to check the recorded age—yes, 45, but the lady who had followed the nurse looked at least ten to fifteen years older. Her hair was gray with no attempt at styling. She was also very thin and looked tired and listless. A mental patient was Jon's first impression of this drab-looking individual.

Mrs. Parker quickly dispelled this opinion when she introduced herself and sat down in the chair beside his desk. The voice matched the expression, flat without emotion, but she was surprisingly articulate and her grammar was flawless as she explained why she had requested an appointment today.

"I haven't been examined in years, Doctor," she began, "but I've developed a large swelling around my vaginal area. It's quite tender."

"How long has it been there?" Jon asked.

Opal Parker hesitated, nervously twisting her rings, then answered, "Just a day or two. It seems to be getting worse."

"Let me get some basic information for your chart," Jon said, "then we'll have you empty your bladder and the nurse will take you to an exam room."

"I'm having a little trouble voiding, Doctor. I think the swelling interferes."

There was something different in her voice, something that caught Jon's attention. "Do you want the nurse to catheterize you?" he asked.

"Yes. I'm afraid that will be necessary."

"You're pretty uncomfortable, aren't you, Mrs. Parker?"

She merely nodded.

"Okay. We can get the rest of the information anytime. Let's get you settled first."

Jon took the patient's arm and led her out into the hall. "I want you to cath Mrs. Parker before I examine her," he told Nell. "And be sure to measure the amount of urine."

Ten minutes later the nurse walked into his office. She shook her head slowly. "Something wrong there," she said. "I mean bad. I put a Foley in, got twelve hundred cc's. She's not going to be able to void for several days."

"What is it, a big abscess near the urethra?"

"Worse."

Puzzled, Jon said nothing more and went directly to the exam room. He was not quite prepared for what he found. Mrs. Parker had not been merely raped, she had been brutally torn and bruised. He rang for Nell and she came in with a box of tubes, syringes and glass slides. "Did you want these?" she asked.

Mrs. Parker sensed the meaning of the contemplated lab work. "Doctor," she said, "I appreciate your concern but you needn't bother with any rape tests. There'll be no charges filed."

Jon stripped off his rubber gloves and rose from the exam stool to walk around to the head of the table. "Mrs. Parker," he said and put a hand on her shoulder, "you have a very large hematoma— bruise—and several fairly deep tears."

"Will I need stitches?"

"I think they'll heal alright and I'd rather not suture them now. It's a little late. When did all this happen?"

She did not answer.

"Use some betadine and warm water," Jon instructed his nurse, "and wash the entire genital area. When you're through, help Mrs. Park-er get dressed and then I want her back in my office."

"I can dress myself," the patient said.

Jon's hand was still on her shoulder. He squeezed gently then said, "I know you can but the nurse will be here to help if you need it and to instruct you about the catheter. Then you and I will sit down in my office for awhile."

When Mrs. Parker returned to Jon's private office he advised her on how to care for the bruises and lacerations then suggested she begin talking. She was ready and it became obvious she had needed to talk for a long time.

First, in answer to a specific question by Jon, Mrs. Parker said she had called his office because she knew from the newspapers that he was a part-time, volunteer physician at the medical school. Unqualified doctors, she reasoned, would not be allowed an association with the University. She said there were personal reasons why she did not seek the care of a full-time professor at the school. Jon suggested that perhaps he should know these personal reasons and she replied simply that her husband was on the staff of the medical school and she did not think it was wise to take personal and physical problems of this nature to someone at the same facility. Jon did not press for any further information in this regard and Mrs. Parker continued her story.

Her problems, she thought, really started some twenty years ago when she delivered a little boy prematurely. His life was short—two days. She was surprised by her husband's emotional reaction. He was devastated and she remembered one evening when she was on her knees praying for the soul of her lost baby, he came in the room and interrupted her. "Your God is a fraud," she remembered him saying. "A just God would not have denied me again."

And in marked contrast to the man who was so loving and attentive before the death of his son, he suddenly turned off all signs of affection. Now, for nearly twenty years they had lived almost as brother and sister, and though they had continued to occupy the same bed, there had not been the slightest hint of a sexual advance by either. Her religious principles prevented a divorce, she said, and while her husband continued his studies, she devoted her energies to the care of their daughter who had been born before the boy, and to her church. At age twenty-five, she said, it had been very painful to be shut out emotionally from her husband. She had adjusted, but she admitted that the adjustment had taken its toll. She told Jon she presumed he was checking on her age when she first came into his office, then stated, quite bluntly, "The twenty years have not been easy, Doctor."

Continuing, she said she had recently noticed a change in her husband. Over the past few months he had occasionally put his hand on her in the middle of the night and even had drawn her close to him on one occasion. But she found it quite impossible to respond and had not encouraged him. Last night she admitted to actually rolling away from him after he had put his arms around her. Nothing was said by either at the time. Early this morning, she thought it was about four o'clock, she awoke with him on top of her tearing away her night clothes and physically attacking her. He had an erection, she said, but hurt her mostly with his fingers and fists. The assault was brief, perhaps three or four minutes, after which her husband got up and without a word to her put on his clothes and left the house. She had not seen him since.

She paused now and for the first time looked up at Jon. He nodded. "Please go on, Mrs. Parker," he said.

She reported feeling nauseated for awhile then got out of bed, removed the blood-stained sheets and took a warm bath to ease the pain. The bleeding had stopped rather promptly and it seemed to her that she could deal with the problem alone and without medical help. Later, she found she couldn't urinate at all and, unable to hide her shame any longer, called Jon's office.

Again she was silent and Jon asked, "Your husband is Donald Parker, Director of Laboratories at the Special Procedures Clinic?"

"Yes."

"I've met him. I'd planned to see him again tomorrow."

Opal Parker was clearly frightened. "Don't say anything to him, please."

"Mrs. Parker, you are a registered patient here and believe me, no information about your condition leaves this office without your permission. But it seems to me you have some decisions to make. Where are you going to stay, how are you going to live? How about your daughter? Can you go there for awhile?"

"Yes. I thought about that before I left home and have a small bag in my car. I called Christine, that's our daughter, and said I wanted to visit for a few days. I didn't tell her why, of course."

"Your husband and your daughter, do they get along very well?"

"No."

"That's a little unusual, you know. Fathers and daughters are very close as a general rule."

"No, I don't think my husband really liked Christine from the day she was born."

"Does she live near here?"

Mrs. Parker nodded.

"Do you want my nurse to drive you there?"

"No. Thank you, Doctor. I can get there. I got here," she said with a sad little smile.

"Alright, but I want to see you Monday."

"I'll make an appointment. You've been very kind, Doctor, and I appreciate it." She saw the gold band on Jon's left ring finger. "You're married, I see. What a lucky wife."

And with that final comment Donald Parker's wife got up from her chair and went out to the receptionist's desk. Jon buzzed and gave instructions for Mrs. Parker to have extra time on Monday, then hurried on to the next exam room.

When Jon arrived at the Clinic Friday afternoon he was surprised to find a note from Frances McGraw asking that he drop by her office when he was finished seeing patients.

"Boss want to see you?" the secretary asked.

"That's what it says," and Jon refolded the message and put it in his pocket. "Anything going on around here I should know about before I see her?" he asked the secretary.

"Not that I've heard about. But if there is, Ms. McGraw won't be the least bit reluctant to tell you."

"You know your boss, don't you," Jon said and went to check on his first patient. He was back at the secretary's desk in mid-afternoon checking on some charts when her intercom buzzed. It was McGraw. "Helen," she told the secretary, "don't forget to remind Doctor Erickson I want to see him."

"Yes, ma'am," was the response after which the intercom was promptly switched off by McGraw. "She's a woman of few words," the secretary said, "but you won't forget, will you?"

"Oh, no," Jon said and went back to see another patient. He was through by three o'clock and walked down the hall to the Clinic Director's office. The door was slightly ajar and he could see Frankie sitting at her desk. He knocked and walked in. She greeted him curtly and without getting up from her chair.

"Come in, Doctor," she said, "and have a seat if you wish. I thought you and I should have a little talk in private about how this Clinic runs. I meant to do it back in January."

The office furnishings, Jon noted, were Spartan. Few feminine touches had been added, though a large bouquet of mixed flowers did grace her desk. She was an attractive woman but appeared somewhat austere in a long, heavily starched white coat. And there were no smile lines around her eyes.

"I think that's a good idea, Ms. McGraw. I think we got off on the wrong foot my first day here."

"Oh, not necessarily. I put my foot forward and you put your foot on it. I'll remember that and you will please remember that I control the patients when they are in this Clinic."

"But you don't control me, Ms. McGraw, and you don't control the professional decisions I make regarding the care of these people."

"I'm aware of that but if I think your decisions are not in the best interest of the Clinic, I'll let you know."

"I'm sure you will. But don't ever forget, I have the final word on the obstetrical care of these young women."

"I know my place, Doctor. I'm hired to make this Clinic run like a jeweled watch. That's what I'm paid for. If that means pushing some of these kids around, then I'll do it. You, Doctor Erickson, are too easy on them. You're not as bad as their so-called counselor, that mealy-mouthed Lawrence Miller. He doesn't seem to believe in the value of discipline. I do."

"Proper discipline is one thing," Jon said, "being constantly disagreeable and inflicting physical pain, that's something else. And it's something I've been going to talk to you about for some time. I understand you're pretty rough when you examine these girls. In other words, you hurt them and they think it's done on purpose. If that's true, Director or no, it can't go on."

"Doctor, you haven't been around here as long as I have. These kids need to have their heads knocked around every now and then. I can do that. I've done it all my life. I'm the oldest of eight and I was sixteen when my mother died. My father was busy so I did most of the raising of seven brothers and sisters. They still don't thank me much but no one's on welfare and nobody's gone to jail. I was tough on them. I'm sure there were times when they thought I was too rough. And the girls in the Clinic—they think I'm a bitch. Doesn't bother me. But—" Frankie paused and looked at Jon, "I see it does bother you so I'll ease up a bit—but not much. They'll still do as they're told when they're around this place."

Jon rightfully sensed the meeting was about over and started to get up from his chair. "Well, Madame Clinic Director," he said, "you're right. It does bother me and I hope we don't have to talk about it anymore. You go ahead and run a strict Clinic but I don't want to hear another patient complain about any physical pain inflicted by you. Now," and Jon pushed his chair back to exactly where he had found it, "are there any other problems we can compromise on?"

Frances McGraw got up from her chair, too, and leaned over putting her hands flat on the desk. She looked straight at Jon again. "Oh, I don't know if I would call it compromise, Doctor," she said, "but if you can do anything about the Poet, it would make both our jobs easier."

"I'm trying, Ms. McGraw, believe me, I'm trying."

And with this both knew the conversation was ended. Jon said good-bye to Frances McGraw and walked down to meet with Donald Parker to discuss some of the laboratory findings on one of the patients.

This was Jon's first visit to the Laboratory Chief's personal office and he was not surprised to find the surroundings very similar to those he had just left. There was one major difference; where Ms. McGraw had a vase of cut flowers on her desk, Mr. Parker had a top-of-the-line electron microscope. The walls were bare, clear of any paintings or photographs. Other than the desk and two chairs, the only other furniture in the room was a free-standing closet which had been pushed against the wall.

Mr. Parker was studying a slide through the microscope when Jon appeared at the door. He gave a final quick look then rose to greet his guest.

"Come in, Doctor," he said. "You mentioned over the phone that you had some lab data you wanted to discuss."

"I have it with me," Jon said. "I saw the patient last Friday and I'm sure the blood was drawn that same day. Couple of things I don't understand."

Yes, Jon thought to himself, this is the same Donald Parker I met before—neat, efficient and inoffensive. It was difficult to see this man as the bully who had taken such violent advantage of his wife. But Jon was here to discuss laboratory findings, not family counseling.

"And I'm sorry I'm a little late," Jon said. "The Clinic Director wanted to see me after I finished seeing patients."

"Oh, Frankie? That's quite a woman. Beautiful, very bright, and an excellent Clinic head. But she's a bit of a bitch. In my spare time I study a little Shakespeare and Frankie reminds me a little of Macbeth's wife. Or maybe Bianca in *Taming of the Shrew*. She runs a tough Clinic."

"I know that. But here are the lab reports I'm a little confused about. I need your expertise to explain them to me."

The Laboratory Director looked over the forms and pointed out an error in the sheet of data. "This happens every now and then despite all our caution. But if you transpose these two figures, I think it will make sense."

Jon glanced at the corrections and nodded, "Yes it does," he said. "That takes care of my problems, thank you very much. And I'd better get going and let you get back to work."

"Do you have a few more minutes, Doctor? I have something I'd like to discuss with you."

"I'm in no hurry. What can I do for you?"

"It's personal. I'll get some coffee and we can talk."

"No, that's okay. Skip the coffee. What's on your mind?"

"I'd like to talk about my wife, Opal," Donald Parker said as soon as he had closed the door to his office.

"Mr. Parker, I can't do that. Your wife is a patient of mine."

"Yes, I know—privileged communication and all that. I think this will solve the problem." And he handed Jon a letter from his shirt pocket.

Jon quickly scanned the typewritten note:

> TO DR. ERICKSON:
> YOU HAVE MY PERMISSION TO DISCUSS ANY AND ALL ASPECTS OF MY CASE WITH DONALD PARKER.
> OPAL PARKER

The imprint and signature of a local notary public were on the bottom of the page.

"You are very thorough, Mr. Parker."

"It comes with the trade, Doctor. Most laboratory people are sticklers for details."

"I'm surprised at this," Jon said, looking at the note. "When I saw your wife it appeared to me she didn't want anything to do with you. She even asked me not to mention she'd been in my office. Granted she expressed that opinion when she was still hurting but she did appear rather adamant."

"And with good cause, no question about it. But I'm sure you've dealt with family problems before, Doctor. I hope you remember there are usually two sides to every story."

Mr. Parker went on then to tell of the problems in his marriage to Opal, problems, which, in his opinion, were undoubtedly present before he even met her. He said she was a victim of an incestuous relationship with her stepfather and two stepbrothers. Possibly because of this she had denied him any sexual advances during their courtship. This attitude did not change dramatically after marriage. "She became passive, submissive, and I used her," Donald admitted. "I was not allowed to touch her during either pregnancy and after the boy was born prematurely and died, she never turned my way in bed again."

"How old were you then?" Jon asked.

"Twenty-four."

"Most men can't turn off their hormones at that age."

"I didn't, not completely. An occasional laboratory technician, an occasional nurse, but no long-term relationships."

Lately, however, he admitted it had become more difficult to continue this semi-celibate lifestyle and had met another woman. She was much younger and also married. They shared what time they could together but she had only rarely allowed physical intimacy. Due to his frustration, Parker had recently made occasional subtle overtures toward Opal. She had been totally unresponsive. Matters reached their ugly conclusion when his newly-acquired companion suggested they keep seeing each other but not quite as frequently.

"She said it was too risky and there were things in her marriage that demanded attention. I think she is seeing somebody else," Mr. Parker said, "and just wanted me out of the way. At any rate, back to the other night. After she sort of gave me the brush off, she left me sitting at this out-of-the-way bar across the river. Frankly, I drank too much before I went home and Opal was still up when I staggered in. She gave me a disgusted look and went on into the bedroom. I watched TV for awhile then went to bed and tried to put my arm around her. She just grunted and rolled further away. I guess this must have been around one or two o'clock in the morning. I couldn't get to sleep after that and about four—I remember looking at the clock—I sort of went crazy. I think you know the rest."

"Not a pretty sight," was Jon's comment. "You're lucky she didn't call the police."

"Yes, I know and I regret it. I should have had the guts to walk out years ago but her religion wouldn't allow a divorce. I'm a religious man, too, Doctor, and I wonder if God has planned to send me to hell for what I've done to Opal. I've done some good things in my life so I don't think He'd keep me there very long, though."

"I'm not one to comment on religion," Jon said, "but you're right —you should have left long ago. Been easier for both of you."

"No doubt. But you know, human nature is weird. I spoke of using Opal when we were first married. Well, in a way, I continued to use her. Not sexually, of course, but I used her for meals, I used her for my laundry, I used her to take care of our house and daughter. And she was always there, complacent, compliant—and used. You might find this surprising, Doctor, but a man can adapt to that kind of a life."

"A man shouldn't, Mr. Parker, but I suppose it's like having a servant around the house twenty-four hours a day."

"Exactly."

"Most women, younger ones especially, won't take that kind of shit. Those kids you deal with in the Clinic, for example, they may not have much of a financial future but, by God, they know what an orgasm is and they won't miss out on many in their lifetime."

"I suppose. Can't say the results of their orgasmic pleasures contribute much to mankind. But," and Donald Parker just raised his hands in a hopeless gesture, "you've heard my soapbox story on that before so I won't bore you with a repeat."

"Oh, I think we both agree that their productivity doesn't help them or anybody else. But for now, we'll have to take care of them."

"Sort of a situation where you do your job and I'll do mine."

"Right. And I have some work to do over at St. Elizabeths so I'd better get going. Thanks again for giving me some needed education on all this lab work."

"My pleasure. Just give me a ring any time."

When Jon got to his car he just sat for a few minutes. It had been an interesting afternoon. He thought the time spent with Frankie McGraw, though brief, was well worthwhile. His initial impression of her was confirmed. They would not be friends but they could work together. The reports of her inflicting physical pain on the patients did worry him, though.

The apparent dual personality of Donald Parker was a little different. Possibly just a bad combination of booze and hormones but Opal Parker's genital injuries were a little scary. He had rarely seen evidence of sexual violence in his practice. It was never pretty and always upsetting. And once again, the Lab Chief had voiced his hostility toward the teenage pregnant patients. This reminded Jon of Mr. Parker's somewhat crude remark about the Poet when they were touring the lab.

A third member of the permanent staff at the Special Procedures Clinic had not gone unnoticed. How was it that Frankie had described Dr. Lawrence Miller? Mealy-mouthed, that was it. He was more than that. He was a sanctimonious fraud. Now as Jon backed out from the parking place he remembered Kathy complaining bitterly about her arguments with Dr. Miller. Worse still, as her husband, Jon knew he had done nothing to reassure or support her when the need was so obvious. Hopefully, there had been no further confrontations between the two. The obvious paranoia of Lawrence Miller and the inexperience of Kathleen Erickson could be a dangerous combination.

CHAPTER VIII

Mid-August and a recent rain shower did not bring out the Poet. Any respite, no matter how brief, from the horror of the continuing feticides did bring out the optimists in "Letters to the Editor." One wrote that he thought the Poet had died of natural causes and was listed among the countless obituaries routinely published in the paper every day. Another, a woman, thought the Poet was a female, now pregnant, and reluctant to take the life of an unborn as long as she herself had a growing fetus in her womb. It was positive thinking in the usual bright days of summer, even in the face of water rationing and brown lawns.

One who did not share in this optimism was Kathy's chief of the Psychiatry Service, Dr. Stenner. He had his theories, too, and frequently expressed them in the teaching seminars which he held daily with his resident staff. In this morning's meeting Dr. Stenner had invited the young physicians to express their own thoughts on the psychiatric implications of the fetal murders. There were many opinions but no one could put together a clear picture of the killer's personality. All agreed the killer must be psychotic and Dr. Stenner concurred. Schizophrenia, he thought, seemed appropriate as the individual involved was apparently able to function in some capacity other than a destroyer of babies. He went on to say that a history on the Poet would undoubtedly show severe emotional trauma in early childhood. And this trauma probably involved male infants, possibly a baby brother. There had to be rejection on the part of the parents as well. "If the police capture our rhyming killer alive," Dr. Stenner said, "I would give a year's salary to interrogate him."

"Him?" one of the women residents asked.

"If I were female," Dr. Stenner replied, "and spent my time upholding the right for women to be equal in all things good and evil, this is one time I might want to rethink my stand. Most of us just assume the Poet is a male. But you might be right. Women aren't necessarily kind to other women."

During the morning seminar the weather had changed and a summer storm was approaching. It was dark and raining when Dr. Stenner finished his lecture. The rain was unexpected and heavy. Anxiety would now return to the city.

Kathy's car had been serviced that morning and the driver for the repair department was not planning to bring it back until late in the afternoon. As a consequence, Kathy was riding with Jennifer Holford.

Jennifer was also a third-year resident in psychiatry; she and her husband were close friends of both Jon and Kathy.

"What's this I hear about you getting into another row today with that Miller guy from the Special Procedures Clinic," Jennifer asked as they drove up the winding, tree-lined back road.

"If he's around I'll get in trouble with him. He's been gone for awhile—some sort of sabbatical or something—so it's been pretty peaceful. But he got back last week and found out I had seen two girls from the Special Procedures Clinic. At least this time he had the decency to come into my office and yell at me instead of cornering me in the hallway. He's mad because he thinks I gave them bad advice."

"From what I hear about him, he doesn't know good advice from bad. But what can he do to you, Kathy? Does he have any authority over us? He's a Ph.D. on staff and we're only residents."

"No. It's all bluff. I checked with Doctor Stenner the last time Miller blew his cool. The Chief said just to ignore him. But that's not easy to do. I think the guy really hates me for some reason and I'm starting to be a little afraid of him. I hate to do it but I think I'll refuse to take any more patients from that Clinic. I hope Doctor Stenner will understand."

"He will. Incidentally, I hear your roommate is getting married—sort of sudden, wasn't it?"

"Very sudden. She wasn't even engaged when I moved in with her. Love can be like that, I guess."

"You guess? Don't you know?"

"If I did, I've forgotten. Its been too long since I've been in love."

"Kathy, that's bullshit. You know you're still in love with that arrogant obstetrician. Why don't you call him?"

"Are you kidding—call Gawd," and she stretched out the word. "No way."

"I think he misses you."

"I doubt it. I was never that important in his life."

"That baby's about due. Have you thought about moving back in with Jon before it's born?"

"I can't, Jenny. I just can't." And Kathy suddenly began to cry. She made no effort to stop the tears as they streamed down her face and dropped on her skirt. She simply sat with her hands folded in her lap sobbing.

"Kathy, why don't you stay with me tonight?"

Kathy just shook her head and after they had driven a few more blocks she turned to her friend and in almost a whisper asked, "Have you been to the house lately?"

"Yes. We were there a couple of weeks ago. Jon wanted to talk to Pete about something or other and invited us over for a beer."

"Is my portrait still there? It was above the fireplace. The one Mrs. Donovan painted of me? It was a wedding present."

"Yes, Kathy. It hasn't been moved."

She had stopped crying now and took a handkerchief from her purse and held it out the window. When it was moist from the rain she used it to carefully wipe her face and eyes.

"This is one advantage of driving in this lousy climate," she said. "You can always wash your face after you've been bawling."

"Lord, look at you," Jenny exclaimed. "If I cried like that my face would be a mess for hours. You—you look like you've just had a facial. My God, what a complexion."

"I'm Irish and Irish women cry a lot. We have to save face somehow. No pun intended."

"Well, here's your place," Jenny said as she drove in to the small complex of apartments. "You're sure you don't want to come home with me?"

"I'm sure. I'll be okay, and thanks. You going to be in Clinic tomorrow?"

"Yes."

"Good. I'll see you then."

Kathy waved good-bye to Jenny and glanced over to see that her car was sitting in its familiar spot. "I wish this place had a parking garage with locked doors," she said aloud, "and I wish they'd put more light out here. Can't see a damn thing, especially with this rain."

There was no light coming from her apartment window either. She thought she'd remembered to leave a lamp on in the small study but it could have slipped her mind or it could have burned out. She was not concerned when she unlocked the door and walked in.

The first light switch beyond the door illuminated the hall and living room. Kathy knew she had walked into chaos as soon as these lights came on. Evidence of unwanted, uninvited visitors was every place. The kitchen was an absolute disaster. Pots, pans, utensils, flower, sugar scattered all over the counters and floor. The living room had escaped the disarray but only because there were no bookshelves or drawers. Absolutely nothing was left untouched in the den. Books, papers, magazines—all on the floor. She went next to her bedroom and here it appeared the intruder had gone to extremes. Nearly everything Kathy treasured had been vandalized. Containers of perfume and powder were broken and their contents thrown about the room. Her clothes, many of them torn, had been taken from the closet and were lying on the floor.

There were tears in eyes again, but these were tears of anger and frustration. She moved to pick up the phone but it rang before she could reach it. For some reason she thought it was her friend who had just dropped her off from the seminar.

"Jenny?" she said.

"No, this is not Jenny." It was a male voice, muffled and not distinct.

"Who is this, please?" she asked.

"A friend. I've been calling. You finally got home."

"Your name, please," Kathy insisted.

"Doesn't matter."

She should have hung up right then. She knew that, but curiosity prompted one more question, a dangerous one and one which in retrospect she wished she had not asked.

"Why are you calling me?"

"I like women who live alone when they're pregnant. They are more—"

She slammed the phone down before he could finish. Now her anger was tempered with fright. A small glass-framed picture of Jon was the only item in the room which remained unbroken and it was to this she directed her outrage. First she swallowed her pride and called home, their home. No answer. Next his office number. The answering service said he was off call and could not be reached. She did not leave her name.

"Damn you, Jon Erickson," she said. "Damn you, damn you, damn you. You lead a charmed life. Even your picture—it's still on the wall and not a scratch on it."

The phone rang again just as she was going to pick it up to call the apartment manager and the police. It was the hospital reporting that one of her patients had become violent and the attending psychiatrist had requested she come in immediately.

"I'll be right there," she said, then phoned the manager and told him to come over and to please call the police. She would be back later on.

She quickly retraced her steps through the clutter and went out to her car. Kathy had called the shop foreman that morning and requested the driver lock the car when he returned. She could get in with her other keys and he was to leave the keys under the front seat. This had not been done. The door was unlocked and the key was still in the ignition. Annoyed, she looked even more carefully in the back seat. It was a safety measure Jon had taught her years ago. As expected, it was empty and Kathy slipped behind the wheel. She pointedly locked both the driver and passenger side doors and gave the standard twist to the key. There was no response, no sound from the high compression engine.

This was too much. The vandalism in her apartment, the strange call, the car not locked as expected and now it wouldn't start. Kathy felt herself at the very edge of panic. Sweat poured through her underarm deodorant as she tried the key again. Not a sound, not even a click. She flipped the light switch and the small enclosure was instantly illuminated. Next the horn. It was loud but not particularly reassuring.

"Okay," she said aloud, "my car is almost new, its just been serviced, the battery isn't dead—why the hell won't it start?"

For a moment she considered going back into the house and calling for help. She even pressed the button to electrically unlock both doors but found she literally could not make the first move to get out of the car. She quickly relocked the doors. There was a crashing sound in the driveway behind and her eyes shot to the rear view mirror. The light was dim but she was able to see that her neighbor had just slammed his trunk lid down. She was trembling now, every muscle tensed, but forced herself to concentrate again on starting the engine. Suddenly she noticed the automatic transmission lever. It pointed at 'D.'

"Oh my God. They left the damn thing in Drive."

Jamming the lever forward to Park, she turned the key for a third time. Instantly the throaty roar of twin exhausts greeted her. Weak with relief she held the throttle down listening to the powerful motor, then slowly eased up on the gas and backed out into the driveway.

Jon, contrary to Kathy's thoughts, was not exactly leading a charmed life on this night. He and Bill Arnold had driven over to Sherry Bourden's home at the request of her mother. Earlier that evening Mrs. Bourden had called Jon to tell him she had a hysterical daughter on her hands and didn't know why. She said Sherry had been up to the Special Procedures Clinic that afternoon to see a friend of hers and started to cry as soon as she got home. She hadn't stopped crying and just wasn't making any sense at all, Mrs. Bourden said. It didn't make sense to Jon, either, and he told the anxious mother he'd be over very soon and talk to Sherry. He also said he'd bring a friend of Sherry's over if that was okay. Mrs. Bourden had no objections and Jon immediately phoned Bill Arnold.

Mrs. Bourden had met Jon when Sherry was in the hospital three months ago. She was apologetic for having called but was obviously relieved to see him. She shook hands with Bill Arnold and welcomed them both into her apartment.

Sherry was in bed, her face to the wall and still crying. It was the reporter who knelt down on one knee beside the bed and put his hand on her shoulder.

"Sherry, it's Bill Arnold. Doctor Erickson and I are here and we want to talk to you. Do you suppose you could turn over so we could have a little chat? Doctor Erickson gets all upset when he hears young women cry. And so do I."

She didn't quite know if he was telling the truth but she did stop crying and turned toward Bill. Her eyes were red and tear-stained but a little of her mischief showed through.

"That's a b—bunch of bull, Mr. Arnold," she said.

"Well, you don't really know if it is or isn't. Now come on, it's too early for bed. Doctor Erickson and I are going to get you out of this bedroom and someone is going to make us some tea." He glanced back at Sherry's mother.

"I was just going to do that," Mrs. Bourden said and hurried out to the kitchen.

Both Jon and Bill helped Sherry to sit up, then each with an arm around her shoulders, escorted her into the living room. It was a small room, clean and sparsely furnished. A kitchen table, chrome and plastic, was in the dining area and Sherry's mother was busy setting out some cups and saucers. Two young boys stood awkwardly around their mother. They had been frightened by their sister's strange behavior and were now completely intimidated by the presence of a doctor and reporter in their home. Jon recognized their discomfort and moved over to stand beside them.

"Don't worry about your sister," he said. "Something scared her and we'll see if we can help. Now go give your mother a hand."

When the tea was poured Bill seated Sherry between himself and Jon. Her face remained puffy and red but she was quiet and sat drinking her tea. Suddenly she excused herself and went back to her room. She returned a few minutes later, her red hair neatly tied in a pony tail and wearing a new lavender bath robe. The transformation was completed by the liberal application of cold water and a little Murine to her eyes.

"Well," Jon said, "this looks more like the Sherry we all know. Welcome back."

And she was back, including her tongue. "Goodness, don't we have a lot of company here tonight? Including the Doctor. Mother, have you been ill?"

It was Bill who said, "Yes, you little devil, your mother's been ill. She's worried sick about you but it looks like you're pretty well back to normal so let's hear about today's adventure."

The boys, at their mother's insistence, had gone to bed. Now, with a fresh pot of tea, Sherry reviewed her trip to the Clinic. She said Virginia, one of her friends from school, was pregnant and wanted some company on her Clinic visit. It was her first trip back since being in the hospital, Sherry told them, and her status was almost that of a celebrity. Even Frankie McGraw stopped for a few minutes to ask how she was doing, and the medical students flocked around her like bees to the honey. Later in the afternoon, after her friend had completed all the tests required for that Clinic session, they met in a small lounge which had been set aside as a gathering place for Clinic patients. As soon as they were alone, Virginia partially unbuttoned her blouse and pulled a diamond ring from its hiding place between her swollen breasts. According to Sherry, she'd received it just four days ago and had been dying to share the secret with someone. She warned Sherry not to tell anybody at the Clinic because her boyfriend was an orderly there and she was afraid that McGraw would raise all sorts of hell if she found out about the ring.

"And let me tell you something," Sherry said. "That was no chip. That was a real rock. I wondered how an orderly could get his hands on something like that and figured he'd probably swiped it. I knew the guy. He'd made a pass at me when I first went up to the Clinic. I told him to get lost. Besides, somebody told me he was living with some broad who'd been a patient in the Clinic. She didn't stay very long, I guess, and I never knew her. Rumor was she got a job with a computer outfit downtown and now goes to a private doc."

Jon's eyebrows arched up sharply but he remained silent as Sherry continued her story.

The diamond, it seemed, had not been stolen. Sherry said Virginia bragged about her lover's connection with the drug world and the riches it brought. Virginia had told her of the high rise condominium along the river where she and her boyfriend spent their evenings. "I guess it was really something," Sherry said. And she described a living accommodation that was sumptuous by any standards and particularly impressive to a teenager who's only previous admission to a life of affluence had been through a nineteen-inch television screen. But the life of sex and drugs carried a risk. Her friend told of a night, recently, when her boyfriend had been in a nasty mood when he picked her up. One of his drug pushers had been killed. He was supposed to meet her in the basement garage of a local apartment complex but a homicide squad from the police department was already there when he arrived. The woman owed him fifty thousand dollars and he knew it was in her safety deposit box. But she had never shared a key with him and he didn't even know which bank the box was in. He was out fifty thousand and mad. "I guess he was mean to Virginia that night," Sherry said. "Hit her and threatened to hurt her real bad if she ever went to the police."

"Wait a minute, Sherry," Bill Arnold interrupted. "What about the safety deposit box? Do you know if Virginia's boyfriend ever found the key?"

"I don't think so. Virginia told me today that he's pretty worried about making up the money."

"Why is this important, Mr. Arnold?" Mrs. Bourden asked.

"The pusher that Sherry mentioned, the woman in the apartment garage, was killed with the same kind of weapon that hit Sherry. The police figure she might somehow figure in the feticide business. I'll bet with a little work the police can find that box. Might be important to find out if it has anything beside the fifty thousand in it. What else did your friend have to say, Sherry?"

"She didn't say anything more about the money. But I think she's my ex-friend now, Mr. Arnold. We got in a God-awful row when we were walking out to the bus. I sort of pissed her off when I said I wouldn't come up to this condo they hang out in. Coke, crack—just not my thing and that's about all they do up there. Well," and she looked at her mother, "I guess they screw around a little. But when I said I wasn't going to show up at the condo, she really scared me, I mean like panic time. She reached in her purse and brought out a switchblade, a mean looking mother. 'Sherry,' she said, 'my boyfriend put this thing against my boob that night. Then he closed it up and gave it to me. I sort of got the meaning. I want you to get the meaning too, Sherry. You're a pretty girl. Everybody always said you're the prettiest in the class. I think you want to stay that way, no ugly scars on that pretty face. But remember, I know how to use this thing. So does my boyfriend. You pop off to the wrong people and one of us will mark you.'

"Mr. Arnold, that's one mean cookie and she scared me. I don't need any more problems," and Sherry's eyes filled with tears. "I remember a kid I was sort of hot for in high school, we were sophomores—that's before I got pregnant—all he did was rat on some jerk who was selling pot in the school yard. Two days later he wound up with a broken leg."

"Did you say anything to Virginia?" Jon asked.

"I guess I sort of laughed it off. But I can tell you, it wasn't very funny. I like my face just the way it is. We took separate buses downtown, then when I got home and saw Mom I just lost it." Now Sherry began to really cry.

Mrs. Bourden reached over and took her daughter's hand. "Please don't start again, honey."

"I'll be okay, Mom." And in a minute or two she was. "Good thing I didn't put any eye makeup on," she said with a weak attempt at a smile. "Sure would've been a mess, wouldn't I?"

"Oh, I don't think so," Bill said. "Pretty hard to make a mess out of a face like yours. But Sherry, tough little nuts like you don't panic that easy."

"Oh, we try to act like bad ass kids most of the time but we can panic, too. Don't forget, where I go to school there aren't many Calvin Kleins in the lockers—just knives and drugs and maybe a pistol or two—so we sort of live on the edge half the time. We have to put on a show. Besides, it was the way she said it. She meant to scare the shit out of me—sorry, Mom."

"Sounds like you've had quite a day," Jon said, getting up from the table. "What do you say, Bill? Think we'd better get going?"

"Yeah, our friend looks a little tired. I'm going to get back to the office and make some notes on this. I plan to call Chief O'Neal in the morning and tell him about the safety deposit box. Don't worry, Sherry. Your name won't get mentioned. I'll just tell the Chief I have it from an unimpeachable source—that's you. Let him run with it and I'll bet he finds that box and has it open in less than a week."

Actually it was only four days later when Chief O'Neal called both Jon and Bill down to his office.

"Well, we have the safety deposit box," he said, very pleased. "And we have you two to thank for it. We'd never have known it was there. I guess there's somebody else we should thank, too, but Mr. Arnold is pretty closemouthed about his sources."

"As I told you, Chief, the source is someone who could get hurt if the name got around."

"And I respect that. Now let me tell you about the work we did in finding that box. And I'm damn proud of all the people involved. You might put that in your article, Mr. Arnold."

The woman in the story about the drug dealer had to be the first Mrs. Miller; all efforts of the police were based on that premise. Most criminals, the Chief said, use an alias at one time or another during their career. These aliases frequently bear a resemblance to the original name. Accordingly, all data previously obtained relating to the dead woman, including at least two known aliases, were fed into the big IBM computer at headquarters. Ten names came up on the screen as possible similarities. Armed with these, plus the reasonably life-like pictures taken of her before an autopsy was performed, a small army of detectives fanned out over the city to visit every bank, large or small. "We hit paydirt early this morning," the Chief said. "Damnedest thing you ever heard of. Here's this huge bank with thousands of safety deposit boxes—Ms. Miller, now Ms. Milton, thought she could keep a box here and nobody would ever know. But she hadn't counted on Edith Reeves."

Mrs. Reeves, the Chief told Bill and Jon, was in charge of the safety deposit box area and had been placed in that position because she had an uncanny ability to put names to faces. When the police arrived with their pictures and computer print-outs of a possible alias, Edith looked first at the photo then scanned the list of names. A few minutes later the detectives were taking fingerprints from the front of box number 1008. These were sent to headquarters and in thirty minutes a report came through that some of the prints were identical to those taken from the woman whose life had ended on the floor of the apartment garage. The legal hurdles were quickly cleared and bank officials removed the box. The Chief had made it a point to be there when it was opened.

"Your source had it right," he said to Bill. "There was fifty thousand in one hundred dollar bills in that box. But below the stash, tucked away in the corner, we came across letters and pictures. Here, look at this." And he handed Jon a black and white print.

"It's a little fuzzy," Jon said as he studied the picture, but it sure looks like a young Doctor Miller."

"Yes, I think you're right and of course we already knew she was married to him at least twenty years ago. But look at this one."

The second picture was recent and showed Lawrence Miller and his ex-wife on a bed in what was obviously a motel room. They were in position number 69 and appeared to be enjoying each other immensely.

Bill Arnold examined the picture along with Jon. "Chief," he said, "I thought Miller's story was he hadn't seen this woman since they were divorced."

"That's right," Chief O'Neal answered. "And here's another one."

This photograph was also relatively recent. It was taken in a motel again and this time Dr. Miller was with a much younger girl. They were standing near the bed, naked, and he was obviously entering her from the rear. One of his hands covered a breast, the other was cupped over her pubic area.

Jon held the picture under the light for a minute. "That's a teenager," he said. "She looks pregnant and I'd swear she's one of the feticide kids I operated on a few months ago."

"I'd be the last to doubt the eyes of an obstetrician in such matters and if it's important, we can prove it later. Here, these are the last three pictures in the box. They were in a separate envelope. All of them show a little girl. She looks about three or four. The dates have been cut off but our photography expert says the paper was popular eighteen to twenty years ago."

Jon took the pictures. "Cute little thing," he said. "Could be a daughter, I suppose." Jon held on to the pictures and looked at them closely for another few minutes. "You know," he said, "I'd swear I've seen that face before. Some people seem to keep an almost eerie resemblance to their baby pictures, even twenty and thirty years later. I've seen this one but I'll be damned if I know where or when."

"We've thought of the daughter angle. Already have a man assigned to study the state birth records around the time that little girl was probably delivered."

"Sure wish I could put a name to that face,"

"Take one of the pictures, Doctor," the Chief said. "Maybe it'll come to you if you look at it every now and then."

"Good idea. I'll do that," and Jon slipped the picture into his shirt pocket.

"Chief," Bill said, "you mentioned some letters that were in that box. Anything important?"

"Oh yes. A little blackmail going on. Listen to this." And the Chief read from the top letter in his hand:

Dear Larry,

I've had a few pictures taken recently by a friend of mine who specializes in getting the more difficult shots, if you know what I mean. I thought you'd especially enjoy that one of you and me. Brings back a few memories doesn't it? Old 69 was our favorite in those days and I was happy to see you'd kept up with the technique.

And I knew you'd want a memento of one of your protegées. She looks a little startled. Sure you got that thing stuck in the right place? I remember you were a little careless about that in the old days.

Now Larry, I just know you wouldn't want the negatives to fall into the wrong hands. Don't worry about the photographer. He does this sort of thing for a living and is very discreet. But he is quite expensive and is pressing me for payment. Apparently he is short of cash. I've run into a little bad luck myself, recently. I thought maybe a thousand a month would keep everybody happy for awhile. Let me know what you think. And I wouldn't waste much time if I were you. These things have a way of going public if they aren't taken care of right away.

Love,

Lillian

"Carbon copy, isn't it?" Bill said when he looked at the letter Chief O'Neal laid on the desk. "Neat handwriting, neat and to the point—one grand per month."

"And you notice there's no cutoff date. Miller picked up on that right away. Here's his return. It's a masterpiece. Typewritten, no signature and no fingerprints other than hers."

The Chief read aloud again:

Lillian,

Your recent communication is acknowledged. It was sweet of you to write and I did enjoy our little get-together last month. Your reference to the financial plight of cameramen and their friends was hilarious. You always did have a good sense of humor. The cameraman didn't seem to know just how long he would need help. I found that particularly funny.

I do look forward to seeing you again and I agree with your sense of urgency. But I would caution you, old and dear friend, a hasty decision or action could be so unfortunate, even disastrous.

I'll be in touch and arrange another time and place for us to meet.

"That's a very cautious man," Chief O'Neal said. "Didn't sign it. Didn't even type his name."

"So when do you bring him in?" Jon asked. "Isn't that the proper police parlance?"

"Take another look at those pictures, Doctor. Can you be absolutely sure the man is Lawrence Miller?"

"Well, not absolutely. But it sure as hell looks like him."

"And the letters. Does either one of them definitely identify Lawrence Miller as the object of blackmail?"

"No, but Jesus, Chief—"

"Don't misunderstand me. I think he's the one caught with his pants off alright, but proving it might be a little tricky. And here's something you didn't know. Lawrence Miller has a good alibi for the night this Lillian person was murdered. He was at a seminar all afternoon and far into the night. We can't account for every second but he was definitely seen there most of the time."

"That letter is a little threatening. Does that mean anything?"

"Those are subtle threats. Any lawyer would tell you that. And by whom? No, Doctor, we can't 'bring him in,' as you say, for the murder of his ex-wife. But, by God, he's implicated and that ties him in somehow with the feticides. We'll watch him. He'll have a hell of a time shaking the tail we put on him."

The Chief put the letters and pictures away and carefully locked the drawer. "And that, gentlemen," he said, "is all I have to offer today. I don't know what kind of a story you can make of this, Mr. Arnold, but I trust you to be careful."

"I think it'll be an article about money, Chief. Money and greed—all those good things. After all, we have a stiff with a knife in her heart and a safety deposit box with fifty grand. We have a hood who thinks that fifty thousand is his and we have letters indicating the woman might have been knocked off because of an attempt at blackmail. Sounds good to me, Chief. It'll be a hell of an article, that I'll promise you. Stories about dirty money always sell well. Don't know just how I'm going to write it to protect both Sherry and this Virginia person, but I'll think of a way."

Though it was not referred to in those terms, dirty money was the topic of discussion elsewhere in the city between the Poet and a guest. A future target for the Poet's knife had been selected some weeks before and final plans were being drawn today. Five thousand dollars occupied a prominent place on the Poet's kitchen table and there had been a promise of fifteen thousand more when all conditions had been met. It was strictly a business proposition between two people whose prior cooperation had resulted in the death of a woman in an apartment house garage. This time still another baby would be destroyed but that was not important. The motive for the attack was retaliation for previous slights and challenges, some imagined, some real. As Poet and guest shook hands to bind the arrangement, the Poet asked: "And you have other plans involving these people?"

The guest merely nodded and proceeded downstairs.

CHAPTER IX

```
NUMBER SEVEN, AN ANSWER TO A CALL
   POVERTY AND BASTARDY NOT AT ALL
HIS DEATH NOT MY CHOICE
   BUT ANOTHER'S VOICE
MY SKILL WAS SOUGHT
   INDEED IT WAS BOUGHT
KNIVES DON'T CARE
   WHOM THEY TEAR.
```

This message had been typed previously. The Poet reread it, was satisfied and satisfied also with thoughts of what the additional money could buy.

Now planning and stalking must begin. The intended victim would be followed on weekends and if an opportunity was presented, there would be fifteen thousand more in the secret bank account. It was doubtful that such a stroke of luck would occur soon as it was September and the Poet knew that was usually a dry month.

But this had not been a normal year and was to remain abnormal. September arrived on a Saturday with heavy rain.

Kathy and her friend Jennifer had planned to go shopping at a new outlet store and Jenny was due to pick her up at noon. Kathy had been attending a Saturday morning clinic which had run overtime and she had to hurry back to her apartment to change clothes before Jenny arrived. As was her custom when late, she drove with a conspicuous lack of caution.

Her hasty exit from the hospital parking lot did not go unobserved. A nondescript gray car followed her and parked down the street from her apartment. The driver of the car had correctly assumed that Kathy was dressed in hospital garb and was probably headed home. Hopefully she would change clothes and go out again soon. It might pay to wait and see. The rain was heavy now, splattering water on the windshield of the gray car, partially obscuring the sole occupant. Carefully folded and laying on the passenger seat was an ordinary raincoat. Barely visible, protruding from one of the sleeves was the point of a small, stainless steel knife.

Kathy dressed quickly and was waiting outside when her friend drove up. The gray car was a mere blur through the rain, unnoticed and unnoticed still when the driver engaged the clutch and slipped into the traffic behind Jenny's Volvo.

There was considerable congestion near the rural shopping center where the baby clothes outlet store was located and they were lucky to find a parking place only two blocks away. The Poet quickly drove into a nearby parking lot and handed the keys to an attendant. The offer to help with the raincoat was politely refused. It was light tan, similar to literally hundreds of London Fog raincoats sold in the city each year. It was quickly pulled over a brown cashmere sweater and the hunt was on.

"What all do you need, Kathy?" Jenny asked as she locked the car and the two women started for the store.

"Oh, I don't know. Just a few extra things for the baby. Somebody said there's a new baby store down here and I'm sure I can find something I think I need. Besides, the insurance check came through for that mess in my apartment so, right now, I have a little extra cash."

"Did the police ever come up with anything on that?"

"No, not even any fingerprints worthwhile. No doubt one of my crazy patients. Guess we'll never know for sure."

"Have they ever been back—the police?"

"No," and Kathy just shrugged her shoulders. "It's obvious a vandalized apartment doesn't rate very high with them."

"Does Jon know about it?"

"I doubt it. I don't know who would tell him."

"Okay, back to the baby. You're about ready to drop it, aren't you?"

"Any day now. That's why I want to look around and see if I'm missing anything I can't get along without. Baby clothes are no problem. Mom is going to send a whole box full later on. She wants to wait and see if it's a boy or a girl."

"I thought you already knew."

"Oh, I do. It's a boy. I had it checked at the Special Procedures Clinic. But I haven't told my folks. They're sort of old-fashioned. They think you should find out the sex when the doctor holds it up and you can see for yourself."

"Didn't you tell her you had all those tests earlier?"

"No way. Mom and Dad are very Catholic—I mean real Irish Catholic. Abortion just isn't a word in their vocabulary. No need for them to know I was planning to have the pregnancy aborted if the tests showed the baby was abnormal."

"Aren't you the same religion as your parents?"

"Sure, but I'm no right-to-lifer, and frankly I'm just a little leery of a God or a religion that would force you to go to term with an abnormal baby."

"No argument from me but it seems too bad your mother doesn't know. She'd have a great time going to sales and buying everything in blue."

"Jenny, believe me, it's better this way. My mother is a very nice lady and I love her dearly but when it comes to state-of-the-art obstetrical care she's about as enlightened as a witch doctor—maybe less. Her letters are full of warnings—'don't do this, you might die.' 'Don't do that, the baby will die.' Oh no, Mom is better off blissfully ignorant of what's going on out here three thousand miles away."

"Do you ever think about that, Kathy?"

"Think about what?"

"That some people have serious trouble during their pregnancy. That they die or their baby dies."

"Not for a second, and don't be so morbid. We're here to go shopping for this little fellow." And Kathy gave an affectionate pat to the bulge that seemed to precede her.

There were shops and merchandise of all sorts to be investigated. Perishables, for the most part, were displayed outside under awnings while the durable goods were in an adjacent building. This large barn-like structure was divided into cubicles and stalls for individual proprietors. The rain had slacked off, momentarily allowing the crowd to mill around the vegetable and fruit stands, but an ominous clap of thunder and gathering black clouds signaled another downpour. Kathy and Jennifer lingered awhile in front of an exhibit of roses. All types were displayed, hybrid teas, climbers, miniatures. And there was even an amateur horticulturist giving a lecture on the care of the various species. Kathy had recently acquired two miniatures, a Yellow Doll and a June Time. She hoped the man would mention them and possibly give some tips on promoting their health.

Despite the rain, now in a veritable torrent, a fair-sized crowd had gathered to hear the expert. And the crowd included the Poet, who, feigning interest in the lecture and seemingly straining to hear the pertinent points, moved to within a few feet of where Kathy and Jennifer stood. The right arm of the tan coat raised slowly as if to ward off the continuing downpour. Kathy chose that particular moment to move under the awning away from the rain. Jennifer quickly stepped up to join her. Unknowingly she had moved in a position to protect Kathy's pregnancy from an unseen danger. The right arm of the tan coat dropped down.

The lecture over, Kathy was tempted to buy another miniature but thought better of the idea and followed her friend into the shelter of the main building. Here it was dry but the storm had knocked out some of the electric power. There was enough to run the cash registers but not enough for adequate lighting. During the next hour Kathy and Jenny wandered from one concession to another, filling their shopping bags with various items which were on sale and getting closer to that area reserved for maternity and infant wear. Kathy found the outlet she was looking for, a store labeled simply "The Layette." It had just about everything for a baby plus a crowd of pregnant women milling around in the semi-darkness looking for bargains.

"The Layette" was located in unfinished quarters, actually an extension of the structure housing most of the shops. The roof was completed as well as the front and back but one side wall was merely canvas sheeting hung as a temporary shield against the wind and rain. Immediately behind this protection was a deserted softball diamond which fronted the river. The unfinished nature of the building was evident wherever one might look. There were dolls and toys hung from the ceiling as well as bassinets and scales, all destined to occupy shelf space when the side wall was completed. Kathy had lined up her purchases on the counter and was reaching for her credit card when the clerk shouted at her to watch out. Startled, she stepped back just as a heavy baby scale came crashing down at her feet.

In the confusion that followed no one noticed the anger and frustration evident on one face in the crowd. The right sleeve of the tan coat came down once more, this time with a small tear in the cuff where the missile had marked its path.

"Are you hurt, ma'am?" the clerk asked.

"No, I'm okay. It missed me," Kathy said. "But let's write up these items before something else attacks me."

"Certainly, Ma'am, right away. And I'm awfully sorry."

"It could have been a lot worse so don't worry about it. Better have someone check the rest of the nails and hangers up there, though. And get some more light. 'Bout half dark in here."

"Oh, I will, I'll call right away," the clerk said. He nervously finished writing up the sale and slid Kathy's visa card through the credit machine.

The transaction completed, Kathy turned and walked around to a nearby bookstore where she had left Jennifer.

"Got everything you wanted?" Jenny asked.

"Almost more than I bargained for," Kathy replied and told of the incident at "The Layette."

"Maybe your little passenger wanted to get weighed," and Jenny poked a finger into Kathy's swollen abdomen. "Hey, did you know you're missing a button on your coat?"

"No. Where?"

"Right there, where you stick out the most."

Kathy looked down to inspect the damage. "Well, damn," she said. "I'd swear I buttoned that before I left my apartment. And look at this, Jenny. Its been cut off. The threads aren't even torn or frayed. It's like a knife just sliced that button right off. I didn't feel it but I'll bet that scale had a sharp edge on it and just grazed me."

"If that's all the damage it did I guess you don't have to worry about it. We'd better get out of here. Company coming tonight and I don't have anything to eat yet."

"And I have a report to write. It'll take me the rest of the afternoon and evening to get it ready."

Late that night the owner of "The Layette" noticed a small hole in the canvas wall and promptly patched it with adhesive tape. It did not appear to be a matter of major interest, certainly not to the owner who had repaired holes before, and it did not even occur to him to inform the police. Three days later, an outfielder for the Portland Seals found a slightly rusty, dagger-like object in the softball diamond which adjoined the store. It didn't look like anything he needed or wanted so he tossed it into the nearest trash can.

A large sale along the waterfront park area, a summer storm which affected electrical power, these were not particularly newsworthy items and, accordingly, the newspaper concentrated on other matters. These matters did not include the Poet as his recent activity had gone undetected.

The Lieutenant remained in his role as Director of Homicide and Jon continued to study each case, as an amateur, he admitted, but he knew the time was not wasted. He was nearly ready now to have the meeting with Bill Arnold and discuss his findings and suspicions.

None of these had been shared with Lt. Lenhart. Their paths had not crossed since Sherry was in the hospital, but the antagonism and ill feelings persisted between the two. Down at the station, Billy Ray never missed an opportunity to ridicule Jon. He did recognize the bond of friendship between Chief O'Neal and the physician and withheld any criticism if the Chief was present. Jon rarely mentioned the Lieutenant's name except when he was in the company of the newspaper reporter whom he knew to be a kindred soul and who also kept him informed regarding the world of crime.

Bill and he were to meet for lunch today and Jon was hurrying through the office when he just happened to glance at Kathy's picture on his desk. Abruptly he sat down and dialed the psych department at the medical school. She had failed to return his previous calls and his ego had been bruised. But it would stand one more call.

"Hello," he said when the department secretary came on the line. "This is Doctor Erickson. Could I speak to Doctor Kathleen Erickson?"

"I'm sorry, Doctor. Doctor Kathleen checked out about an hour ago. Two of her patients canceled their appointments and she went downtown to do some shopping. She's due back around three. I'll tell her you called."

"In this rain? She went downtown in this rain?"

"Yes, sir. I told her it wasn't very smart but she said today was the only day she had time to get some things she needed."

"Thank you," Jon said and hung up the phone. She's probably lying, he thought; I'll bet Kathy's sitting right there beside her. But he felt ill at ease, strangely so, and found it difficult to concentrate on his patients.

Have you seen this Ridgeway nurse lately?" was Bill's opening question even before Jon had time to sit down for lunch. "You remember, she's the mother of that kid that was around the movie house where the last attack occurred. At least that's what you told me."

"Oh, I remember," Jon replied. "And no, she hasn't scrubbed with me since that case last month. Why?"

"I was just wondering. Nothing much happening lately and I need some new angles. Thought I might interview the girl if her mother would allow it."

"I don't even think it's worth a try, Bill. Mrs. Ridgeway is going to protect that daughter if she possibly can. Besides, she reads the papers. All's quiet and everybody thinks the Poet has written his last little rhyme."

"I've got ten bucks that says he hits again."

"I hope you're wrong. But I won't risk the ten spot. What else is on your mind?"

"The pictures the Chief gave you. You said the little girl looked like someone you knew. Come up with any bright ideas on that yet?"

"No, but I will."

"Any chance it could be one of the kids in the Clinic?"

"I doubt it. You figure the girl in the picture was about three years old and that must have been at least twenty years ago. No one in the Clinic over seventeen or eighteen. Probably a private patient of mine and I just can't put it together yet."

"Well, tell me what you know about this Miller character and his job at the Clinic."

"The last I heard was what the Chief told us. Remember, he said he'd put a tail on Miller that he couldn't shake. Have you talked to O'Neal since then?"

"No," Bill said, "I haven't seen him. So I guess there's nothing new on Doctor Miller."

The discussion continued through lunch and for awhile after. It was mostly a rehash of what was already known and they both left the restaurant about at about 1:15. Kathy was on Jon's mind again when he got to his car. Rather than head to his office he turned directly into the heart of the downtown shopping area. Maybe she really did have a couple of hours to spare and wanted to pick up something from the store. He drove slowly through the rain and traffic lights, his attention directed toward the shops. He barely missed a rear end collision when he thought he saw the familiar face he was searching for. She was gone when he looked again. The depression he felt was not overwhelming, but it was there, and he couldn't deny it as he drove back to the office.

The emergency room physician from St. Elizabeths called just as Jon was putting on a fresh white coat for the afternoon. "I just sewed up a young woman who says she's a patient of yours," the E.R. doctor said. "Name of Sarah Tompkins. Know her?"

"Sarah? Sure we know her. What happened? She in an accident?"

"Well, I guess you might say that. She had a knife slash across her belly."

"Knife slash. How the hell did she get that?"

"She wouldn't tell us."

"Why didn't you call me?" Jon asked. "I was wearing my pager."

"She asked us not to bother you. She thought we could sew it up and we did. Wasn't very deep, just through the skin and a little sub Q fat. Fetal heart was good. No sign of any trouble with the pregnancy. But she's quite a character, isn't she?"

"You don't know the half of it. She give you any trouble?"

"Oh, no. But she told us what suture to use and said it was a clean knife so not to bother with any antibiotics or tetanus shots. Didn't want any local anesthesia either and refused to take a prescription for pain meds to take at home. When we were through, she just jumped off the table as if nothing had happened, then asked to see our computer setup here in the E.R."

"I don't know as I'd let her."

"We didn't."

"Is she still there?"

"I think so. Probably somewhere out front filling out some insurance forms."

"Would you send her over to my office?"

"Sure and you can take a look at our handiwork. We flushed the wound with a gallon or so of rinse solution then closed it with a subcuticular stitch. She didn't want much of a scar and insisted we use 5-0 dexon. She'll probably sue us if it gets infected."

"I doubt it. She's got the morals of an alley cat but there's a smattering of responsibility lurking in that wild brain of hers."

"If she's still here we'll see she gets to your office. Let us know if there's any problem, Jon."

Sarah arrived thirty minutes later. She was a little embarrassed but covered it well with a mask of resentment at having to come to the office.

"Who the hell do you think you are?" she demanded of Jon. "I just got checked completely in the emergency room so what do you want me over here for? I have work to do, you know."

Jon let her rave on while he took her blood pressure then lifted up the dressing and examined the wound. She quieted momentarily while he checked the fetal heart with ultra sound. Both doctor and patient recognized a pattern free of any abnormality.

"Okay," Jon said before Sarah could restart the harangue. "Want to tell me about it?"

She did and it took a half-hour of office time. The knife had been wielded by her current live-in boyfriend whom Sarah had previously described to Jon as a fantastic lover. They were both home for lunch today and it was revealed that Sarah was not the only girl in town to admire this gentleman's sexual prowess. According to her, she and her friend were involved in a little before lunch screwing around and she felt a bump on his penis with her tongue. Gripping his erect organ firmly in her hand she led him over under a bright kitchen light. She was not inexperienced in the art of inspecting male genitalia and she knew a herpes lesion when she saw one. There was an instantaneous brawl involving two nude bodies. He was able to get his cherished member out of her grasp and knowing her temper and mindful of the fate of the Berkeley computer professor, he was the first to find a kitchen knife laying on the counter. The only weapon readily available to Sarah was a large fork which she had used to poke holes in the potatoes before putting them in the microwave oven. When she came at him with obvious intent to harm, he ducked and swung the knife across the most obvious target—her pregnant and protuberant belly. The effect was immediate. Sarah was drained of all fight when she saw an open and bloody wound across her pregnancy. The fork fell to the floor and in near hysteria she dialed 911 for an ambulance.

"I guess the emergency room Doc called you so you know the rest," she said when finished describing the scene in the kitchen. "Wish I'd known that knife had just cut through my fat. There's a butcher knife in one of the drawers. I'd of nailed that son of a bitch."

"You might have killed him, Sarah. Or he might have hurt you much worse. Better this way."

"Maybe. But he was fucking around with those chicks at that Special Procedures Clinic. He's an orderly at University Hospital—I told you that. Well, he got himself assigned to that Clinic so he could hustle some of the girls. I hope they all give him herpes or worse. Maybe it'll rot his damn dick off."

"That's not likely, Sarah. But at any rate, we'll keep a close watch on you to see if you've picked up the virus."

"And if I have?"

"Don't worry. It's easy to manage if we know about it."

"Okay. Well, I've got to get back to work. I'm an hour-and-a-half late now. How would you like to write a note so I can give it to the boss? Tell him I got hurt at home and had to come into your office."

"I can do that."

"Good. I don't want to lose that job. Love those computers."

"Sarah, what do you do with all the information you get from those things?"

"Doctor, I know that big main frame like nobody else. I can do anything I want with that information."

"Some of the stuff you have stored in there is from the Special Procedures Clinic, isn't it?"

"Sure."

"Be careful with it, Sarah. Some of the those statistics could be useful in the future. Don't foul up the work they've done."

Sarah gave her Doctor a disgusted look. "I don't plan to fuck up their research data," she said. "Now, are you through with me?"

"For today, yes, but I want you back in a few days. And if the skin around the wound gets red or hard, you call right away. And Sarah—"

"Yes."

"Try to be a little more choosy with your male companions."

"Doctor Erickson, I'm going to make like the Virgin Mary for the rest of my pregnancy. Doesn't hurt me to masturbate, does it?"

And without waiting for an answer she was out the door.

Jon wondered briefly if Sarah associated masturbation with Mary's presumed virginal status but he was already far behind in his appointment schedule so he dictated a very complete note for her chart and went to the next exam room. The patient there was one of the joys of practicing obstetrics. She was about eight weeks pregnant with her first baby, a baby that was wanted, a baby that would be loved. Her delight and excitement were contagious and Jon lingered a few extra minutes just to chat. This business could be fun.

There was a different atmosphere in the operating room at University Hospital. They were expecting another feticide victim. The report from the ambulance, radioed in, was terse:

> *We have a female, pregnant, with a projectile wound in her abdomen. She's a little shocky. Pulse 140, blood pressure 95 over 70, respirations 25. We have started an intravenous and will be at your emergency room in ten minutes.*

The emergency room attendants met the ambulance and moved the patient to a hospital stretcher. From there she went to the waiting elevator and up to the sixth floor operating room area.

"I thought all those feticide cases were teenagers," one of the orderlies said to the ambulance driver. "That one looked a little older."

"Yeah, I think she is. We didn't ask. Just clamped an oxygen mask on her and headed up here."

Ben Sires, chief resident in obstetrics, was the first to see the patient when she was wheeled off the elevator and into the operating room area. He thought she looked a little different than the usual feticide, too, and bent over to check her pulse and blood pressure. An anesthesiologist came by at that time and replaced the oxygen mask with one that better fit the patient's face. The mask was off for just a few seconds but Ben could clearly identify this latest victim of the Poet.

"My God," he said, "it's Kathleen Erickson. Get Doctor Johnson right away," he told a nurse, "and then radio page Doctor Erickson. Tell him there's an emergency over here in the operating room and we need him. For Christ's sake don't tell him it's his wife—he'd pile up for sure on his way across town."

Jon tried to beg off when the call came to his office from University Hospital. His office schedule was full and he hoped they could find somebody else to see the patient. But the caller was the operating room supervisor and she insisted. Reluctantly, Jon left the office and hurried down to his car.

The University's chief of obstetrics and gynecology met Jon in the hall outside the doctor's lounge. He was in a scrub suit and Jon was obviously surprised to see him. "Doctor Johnson," he said with a smile, "are you trying to horn in on my specialty? I thought you told me I was the expert in these cases. It is another feticide, isn't it?"

There was no returning smile on the Chief's face. "Yes it is. Let's get out of the hall, Jon. I want to talk to you."

Puzzled by the department chairman's presence as well as his attitude, Jon followed him into the staff dressing room.

"Doctor Sires had me called as soon as he saw the patient," Dr. Johnson said when the door was closed. "It's your wife, Jon. It's Kathy."

"Oh, Jesus." Jon slumped onto one of the nearby benches. "Is—is she alive?"

"Yes, I think she'll be all right. The baby is dead. I'm terribly sorry, Jon."

Jon continued to sit, his shoulders slumped and he seemed unable to speak.

"I've got to go in now, Jon. She's under spinal anesthesia—apparently just had lunch and the anesthesiologist didn't want to chance putting her to sleep. Do you want to change clothes and come on in?"

Jon took a deep breath and let it out slowly. His hands were shaking as he held tight to the sides of his head. "I doubt if she wants me there, Doctor Johnson."

"She asked for you, Jon."

"Damn," Jon said as he blinked back the tears. "She's something special, isn't she?"

Jon Erickson's professional abilities were held in high regard by the department chief but he knew the younger physician's frailties as well. This was evident when he handed him a scrub suit and said, "When this is all over, Jon, Kathy might like to hear those very words from you. See you inside. We're in room eight."

Methodically, almost by habit, Jon took off his clothes and put on the blue scrubs. After adjusting his cap and mask he left the dressing room and started down the hall toward #8. The O.R. supervisor looked up as he walked by. She had been the victim of some of his barbs and arrogance in the past, but her sympathy for him was evident today.

"Doctor Erickson," she said, "you forgot your shoe covers. I'll get some for you."

"No, Mrs. Connors," Jon said looking down at his bare shoes with some embarrassment. "Please don't bother. I'll get them."

He retreated to the dressing room to put on the covers and once more started down the hall. He didn't stop or look at Mrs. Connors, but in a gesture of friendship they both understood, he put his hand on her desk as he continued toward #8.

The operating room crew glanced up briefly from their work as he opened the door and walked quickly to the head of the surgical table, close to Kathy. The anesthesiologist, a friend of Jon's and very much aware of this couple's problems, unobtrusively reached under the drapes and released Kathy's left arm from the loose restraints which held it close to the table. She searched for Jon's hand, found it and gripped tightly. It was a scene few in the O.R. would ever forget.

The deadborn son of Kathy and Jon was delivered from the abdominal incision a few minutes after Jon came in. Dr. Johnson, holding the baby, looked over at Jon with just a slight shake of his head. Impulsively Jon released Kathy's hand and reached for his son. Without a second's hesitation, an understanding chief of obstetrics handed the baby over. Jon stood for a moment, openly sobbing, then brought the little boy to its mother. Kathy, her eyes flooded with tears, hugged the baby and put the pale little face to her lips.

"Kathy, I'm going to give you just a little pentothal now," the anesthesiologist said. "Won't be much but you'll be sort of drowsy until you get into the recovery room. Okay?"

Kathy nodded and after kissing the baby one more time let the nurse take it from her. Jon briefly held one of the tiny hands with both of his then kissed Kathy and walked out of the operating room.

"I don't ever want to see another day like this," was all Dr. Johnson could say as he continued the surgery in an otherwise silent operating room.

Jon was waiting when they brought Kathy into the recovery room. The pentothal had started to wear off and when she saw her husband she reached up and brought his head down on the pillow beside her. When she relaxed her hold on him, Jon kissed her again but still couldn't speak. It was Kathy who broke the silence that had existed between them for months.

"Jon," she said quietly, "I've never seen you cry before."

Jon didn't give any explanation. He just leaned over and said, "I love you, Kate," and holding her in his arms, put his head back down on the pillow.

The nurses in the recovery room came by frequently to check Kathy's intravenous fluids and vital signs, but interfered as little as possible for the two hours she was under their care. She slept soundly after being transferred to a private room but Jon stayed with her until after midnight. Reassured then by her even breathing and steady pulse, he took the advice of one of the nurses and left the floor.

There was a bar a few blocks from the hospital and as Jon drove by he was pretty sure he recognized one of the few cars in the parking lot. It was a Porsche 911 Targa and he had seen a similar car at police headquarters. He was too tired to give the matter much thought and continued on home.

The owner of the car was inside the bar and was very drunk. He had arrived early in the evening and tossed the keys at the bartender. "Here, y'all keep these for the night," he said. "The machine that goes with 'em is mah pride and joy. Saved about every dime Ah ever made to buy it. Ah plan to get plastered but no way I'm gonna plaster that car against some bridge railin' on mah way home."

"I don't suppose you want me to take it out for a little spin, so what am I going to do with the keys?" the bartender asked.

"Just put 'em where Ah cain't find 'em. And gimme a sandwich every now and then so's I don't fall off this damn stool."

And for the next several hours Lt. Lenhart proceeded to do just what he promised by drinking beer with bourbon chasers.

Early in the evening he acknowledged to those who would listen that he had just come from the hospital. He became the center of attention when he announced his name and said he was investigating a feticide which had occurred this afternoon. He was in his element. Most, if not all, of his fellow drinkers voiced their support of his feelings toward the teenage victims. All agreed the killer should be brought to justice but their red-necked qualities prevailed when, to a man, they hoped the Lieutenant wouldn't catch him until the "fear of God" was put into every little loose-living teenager on the street. One man, deep into at least his tenth beer of the night, did express a commonly held view of the group when he said, "Cute little shits, though. Wouldn't mind screwin' a couple of them myself 'cept the old lady would probably kill me."

"Yeah," someone chimed in, "and if your old lady didn't get you the Lieutenant here would put you in jail for pokin' your prick in underage ass."

Later, when the tavern was almost deserted, Billy Ray admitted that today's victim was not the usual case, not a teenager, but a doctor married to another physician who practiced in the city. It was suggested by one of the few who remained in the bar that the killer had probably mistaken her for one of the welfare kids. But the Lieutenant, now a little drunker than even he had planned, disagreed.

"No," he said thickly. "No way anybody gonna mistake that lady for a teenage brat. Too bad she's married to such a sum bitch. Saw him up there tonight. He din't see me. Damn near stepped on him in the hall. Wanted to tell the stuck up sum bitch he got what was comin' to him." Billy Ray drained his bourbon from the shot glass and with a vicious gesture ground out his cigarette on the bar. Then glaring into space with his puffy little red eyes, he added, "Shame that shiny lil 'ol knife had to go in her. Better off stickin' in his belly."

"What you got against the doc?" somebody asked.

"Smart ass, thinks he's a better cop than me."

"Wouldn't have to be very good," the bartender said.

"Watch your mouth," Billy Ray said, "you'll be wearin' the rest of this ham sandwich. Tastes like shit, anyway."

The bartender had obviously grown a little tired of the Lieutenant. "Take your complaints to the kitchen," he said. "And I'll apologize when I see you hauling the Poet off to jail."

"Barkeep, y'all cain't seem to understand that lots of folks think that Poet is solvin' some of our problems. Some of them same folks spendin' money right here in your bar. But whether he is or whether he ain't, the poleece force in this town doin' all they can to round up that boy."

"Maybe so, Lieutenant, but how long's he been at it now? Way over a year. Be fall pretty soon, with a lot of rain, and it'll be Christmas again before you know it. Maybe you cops can nab the son of a bitch and give us a little present—like peace of mind."

"He'll be past history by Christmas. Y'all can make book on it."

"Thanks for the tip, Lieutenant, but your track record so far isn't that good. Hope you're right, though."

CHAPTER X

Kathy's stay in the hospital was short, only two days, and Jon was with her most of that time. It was an opportunity for both to talk and the conversation was quiet and healing. There had been an irretrievable loss, that much was certain, but in the privacy of that room it was determined their bereavement would be for the death of a baby, not a marriage.

Roses greeted Kathy when she came home from the hospital. Jon had invited Judge Donovan to come by as he knew Kathy had missed him. The Judge accepted a key from Jon and had filled the house with his beloved flowers before the Ericksons arrived.

Kathy was delighted. He didn't stay long, just long enough to let both Jon and Kathy know that something good and decent had come from a tragedy—the Ericksons were home. Before he left he made a little toast:

"To Kathleen Erickson," he said, "you've made this house a home again. Now, please, let the strength—and obstinacy—that kept you two apart be used to keep you together."

Jon had made arrangements for a housekeeper to stay with Kathy during the day, and the following morning he went back to the office. He met briefly with his staff and thanked them for the flowers as well as their messages of sympathy for Kathy and himself. He asked them to cancel all appointments for the next afternoon as there would be a small, very private memorial service. "The Judge will be there," he said, "and a few very close friends. Kathy's mother was thinking about coming out but she changed her plans. I think Kathy will fly back there for a couple of weeks. So," and Jon's voice broke for just a second, "life goes on for most of us. Let's get with it and thanks again."

When he went back to his office to start making phone calls the receptionist looked at Nell. Both were blinking back tears.

"This may change him a bit," the receptionist said.

"A little, maybe," the nurse agreed. "Not too much, I hope. I sort of like him the way he is, but a dash of humility wouldn't hurt, I guess."

It took awhile to complete the calls which had piled up in his absence, but finally Jon turned to his crowded office schedule. **"Feticide Is Doctors' Son"** was the recent newspaper headline and every patient had read the story. All expressed their sorrow and some admitted fear and apprehension for their own safety. And they were beginning to doubt if the Poet would ever be caught. But it was Sarah Tompkins, his first patient in the afternoon, who, in her eloquent but purposely tactless manner, voiced what every one had been thinking.

"You sort of got the shitty end of the stick last week, didn't you, Doctor?"

"Sort of," Jon agreed.

"Poor little fucker. Never knew what hit him, did he?"

"Probably not."

"I'm telling you, Doctor, one of the good citizens out there has a thing about babies with a penis. Makes this little bitch in here pretty safe, doesn't it?" She stabbed a finger into her uterus. "I told you I didn't want a boy, didn't I?"

Jon gave a gentle slap to her exposed belly. "That you did, Sarah. And quite emphatically as I recall."

"Damn right. Boys are a pain in the ass. Piss all over the place with that little thing they're so proud of, then later on when they grow up most of them don't really know how to use it."

"Sarah, you do lighten my day a bit," Jon said as he reached over to pick up some instruments. "Now let's check those stitches and while we're at it, we'll check this little female fetus you seem to be so proud of. See if she's progressing satisfactorily."

"She is," Sarah said with conviction. "I know that. I have a scope at home and listen to her heart rate. And remember I had that ultrasound just the other day. She's due to poke her head one of these days."

Jon made some notes on the chart as Sarah pulled up her slacks and jumped down from the exam table. "Oh, by the way, Doctor," she said, "I understand your wife moved back in with you. Congratulations. See if you can take better care of her this time."

Jon turned quickly. "How the hell did you know that?" he asked, his tone of voice neither professional nor joking.

Sarah arched her eyebrows over unsmiling eyes as she replied, "Oh, some of us are just more aware than others. See you next week, Doctor, unless this little character wants to get out early." And she was gone.

"That is a she-devil if I ever saw one," was Jon's inaudible comment as he continued writing in her chart.

Opal Parker was in the next room. Jon examined her very carefully and found the savagery inflicted by her husband had resulted in little permanent damage. She told Jon that she had moved back home after Donald had rented an apartment downtown.

"I rarely see him," she said, "and really don't expect to ever live with him again."

Jon didn't say anything about his talk with the Laboratory Director but did tell Mrs. Parker that he thought she was healing very well and shouldn't have any complications. "And I want you back next week for a little more thorough exam including a regular physical. I'll bet you haven't even had a breast exam or a mammogram for years, have you?"

"No."

"We'll get that done next time you're in. Be sure to stop by the front desk and get an appointment."

"I will. And thank you, Doctor."

By five o'clock the last patient had been seen. Jon was exhausted from receiving and replying to repeated but sincere expressions of concern and sympathy. He sat down at his desk to complete three charts but his first thoughts were of Kathy and he immediately dialed home.

"Good to hear your voice when I call this number, Kate," he said when she answered.

"It's a nice number, Jon, and I'm glad to have it back, along with its co-owner."

"You're a good kid. How about dinner? Did the housekeeper fix it or do you want me to bring something home?"

"She has a pot roast going. Smells good. Will you be home right away?"

"I'm going to get hold of Ted to see if he'll take calls again tonight, then I have to see a couple of patients he delivered for me over the weekend. It won't be long."

"Jon."

"Yes, Kate."

"I know you like to talk to the resident staff and interns at St. Elizabeths, but would you try to avoid them tonight? I need you around as much as possible for awhile."

"Kate, I remember a scene not too long ago when I came up pretty short on the support side. That won't happen again."

"Thanks, Hon." There was a pause and then she asked, "Still take your martinis dry and with two olives?"

"Some things never change."

"I'll have it ready. See you soon."

Two weeks later Judy Ridgeway called Jon at the office. "Do you remember me, Doctor?" she asked. "I've scrubbed with you a couple of times and was there when you rolled out that big ovarian tumor."

"Yes, Judy, of course I remember you. We talked about your daughter during the surgery, as I recall."

"Yes, that's right. I got pretty upset that day. I was still a little shaky when I got off duty and went home. Debbie, that's my daughter, asked me what was wrong and I just told her I had a bad day in the operating room. I knew I was wrong when I said I wouldn't let anybody talk to Deb, but I was scared. Still am, scared for her, but my conscience has been hurting lately, especially after reading about your wife. I'm awfully sorry she was hurt, Doctor Erickson, and that you lost your baby. Maybe if Deb tells what she saw it'll help prevent another tragedy. That's a long shot, I know, but I think I'd feel better if we tried and I know Deb would."

"That's great, Judy. Let's start with this friend of mine. He's the number one crime reporter for the paper. You've probably read some of his stuff—Bill Arnold. Bill's very careful. He won't put her at any risk and probably can tell us if she really saw enough to go the police with."

"How do I get in touch with him?"

"Let me set it up, Judy. Are you working today?"

"No. It's my day off."

"I'll get ahold of him and then call you back with the time and place. Okay?"

"Sure."

Debbie had seen the Poet. Bill Arnold was sure of it after he heard her story. She told the reporter that she was standing fairly close to the person who got hit with the knife. And she remembered seeing the preg-nant girl stumbling over her shoe lace, then bending down to tie it just before the boy got hit with the knife. But when Bill pressed her, Debbie really couldn't be sure if the Poet was a man. "He was a grown-up, the only one in line for the movie and I know he didn't have a beard or a mustache," she said. "And I know if you showed me ten pictures I could pick out the Poet. I'll never forget that face. He, or maybe she, was sort of frowning. I guess because the knife missed the girl who was pregnant."

Bill took Judy and her daughter down to police headquarters the next day to be questioned by Lt. Lenhart and despite the Lieutenant's objection, he stayed with them during the inquiry. Judy Ridgeway was an attractive and personable young woman, qualities which did not go unnoticed by the reporter, who insisted on buying lunch after they left the police station. He also made it clear to mother and daughter there would be no mention of Debbie's name in any article he might write about the ongoing investigation of the feticides.

Bill made this commitment to Judy on a Wednesday. Thursday he called Jon. "I need a favor," he said. "I want you to call Judy Ridgeway—right away. Tell her some son of a bitch at police headquarters spilled his guts and Debbie's name will be in the paper tomorrow morning—front page. Identifies her as the girl who can describe the

Poet. It's not my story, Jon. I didn't write the damn thing but I couldn't get it pulled."

"Why don't you call her?"

"I'm afraid she won't believe me. She'll think I lied through my teeth just to get another headline. Now, God damn it, you know I wouldn't do that. I want you to tell her."

"I'll call her, Bill. I'll call her right now. You'd better give her a ring tomorrow."

"I will. Thanks, Jon."

Judy was angry and frightened for her daughter when Jon phoned, but at least she was forewarned about the morning paper.

The Poet was frightened also. Now, for the first time since the terror in the city began, someone had come forward with an accusing finger. Someone had actually seen the Poet in action. More had to be learned about this child and her habits before any plan for control could be devised. But the Poet sensed that time was running out and plans would have to be hurried.

The following week was a busy one for Jon, unusually so, but by Sunday night he was able to relax and enjoy his home and the company of his wife. She was scheduled to take off in the morning for a flight back to see her mother and father.

"Jon, do you want to do me a favor?" Kathy asked when they had finished dinner.

"Not fair, Kathleen Erickson. You know you could ask for the moon and I'd at least get you a chunk of cheese."

"Well, I may want some cheese. Some cheese and wine, maybe some fancy crab dish, over at the coast. I want to go to that big resort where we stayed two years ago. I want the same room, too."

"You want a lot."

"I can give a lot."

"You devil. You trying to seduce me?"

"No, not yet. But I'll bet I can when I get back in two weeks. Especially if we go to the coast. Why don't you meet me at the airport when I get back from Mom and Dad's and we can take off from there? Remember, there's a good place to eat about half way over. We both liked it."

"Hell of a good idea, Kate. I'll get that room you want if I have to pay double for somebody to move. Now, you can do me a favor. Give me your professional opinion on the Poet. And tell me if you think that young Debbie Ridgeway is in any danger."

Kathy's reply was to get up from her chair and come over to kiss Jon.

"What was that all about?" he said.

"Jon, you asked for my opinion, my professional opinion. I don't think you've ever done that before. Do you have any idea how good that makes me feel?"

"I think so, Kate. But I didn't do it just to make you feel good. I really want to know what you think." Then Jon smiled and added, "You can take it as a compliment if you wish."

"Oh, I do wish. Your compliments are sort of oblique but there are more of them lately and I love it."

"So I'm waiting for your discourse on the Poet. But Kate," and Jon was serious, "if you'd rather not talk about it I'll understand."

"No, I can talk about it. But about Deborah Ridgeway, yes, I think she is in danger. The paper made her name a household word. And it's a pretty safe bet the Poet reads the news. He either has to hide or he has to hide Deb. If I were her mother, I'd watch her like a hawk."

"Frankly, I think the police owe her some protection. The leak came from there, not Bill Arnold."

"Do you think they will?"

"Oh, they might assign a patrol car to run the neighborhood a bit more frequently but I guess they really can't be with her every minute."

"Well, somebody better warn that child to be very careful about where she goes and when she goes."

"I think Bill Arnold will do that. The devil may just have a dual purpose. He likes Deb alright, she's a sweet kid, but I think he's really attracted to her mother."

"Good for him. I met him, you know, when he came to the hospital to talk to me. Judy dropped by about the same time. I thought I saw a little chemistry there. But about the Poet. Jon, I just don't know. There are times I think it has to be a man. Then, something comes up and I think we have a psychotic female running loose. If you remember any of your elementary psychiatry you'll remember that psychiatrists are great for symbolism and the knife is a symbol for a penis. Thrusting, poking, jabbing, hurting, drawing blood—everything a penis is supposed to do. But again, symbolically, it's a little difficult to see the Poet's knife in this light. He doesn't hold it and do the damage, he throws it. And that throws the psychiatrist a real curve ball. Just doesn't fit. That's why I think it might be a woman, a woman with a deep-seated hatred of men. Probably one who's been sexually molested as a child. I do know she's crazy—or he's crazy. Either way, the Poet should be caught, have a quick trial and die."

"Kate, you just said the guy is crazy. You can't hang a murder one charge on a psychotic, a wacko."

"I would, Jon."

It was a beautiful September morning when Jon drove Kathy to the airport the next day. An occasional maple tree had a hint of color change and the temperature was a little cooler early in the day, warming up to a comfortable seventy-five to eighty by mid-afternoon. Kathy's plane for Boston was due to take off at nine o'clock and Jon planned to make rounds on his patients after she was gone. Morning office hours had been canceled, but he was expected in by early afternoon. It was Friday and not a good day to eliminate the office completely.

The Poet found it to be a pleasant day, as well. There were plans for Deborah Ridgeway today and these plans called for sunshine, not rain; bright, almost blinding sunshine was needed. The past few days had been spent studying Debbie's activities. She rode a bike to and from school every day when the weather permitted. The Poet had learned her habits by following her for several days, time enough to memorize almost every foot she traveled. Friday was selected as the day to execute the plan as it seemed young people were a little more careless on the last school day of the week. Her route home always took her across a viaduct that arched over a busy freeway. There was a spot on this crossing, where, with precise timing, she could be crushed against the concrete railing. It was ideal. Debbie rode this way heading west late in the afternoon. The Poet had noted that just as a driver topped the crest of the viaduct the sun was almost blinding. This would prevent the motorists behind from seeing the action very clearly, and hopefully they would be less apt to give chase. It might even look like an innocent accident.

This particular day had started like any other for Debbie: to school in the morning, gymnastic practice after classes, then back on the bicycle and home. The bicycle ride to and from school was the source of a major disagreement between her and her mother. She was a confident, careful bike rider and had no fear of the traffic. Traffic wasn't Judy's worry either—it was the Poet. She knew there was increased danger now that the newspaper had exposed her daughter's name to this maniac. Despite this, Debbie continued to ride her bike to school. And she was anxious to get home today. Her mother had said Mr. Arnold was coming over later on this evening and bringing another kid about Deb's age, someone he was sure both she and her mother would like. She thought of the reporter now as she pedaled home, frequently glancing back to check on the cars. It was sort of nice to have him around occasionally.

Early that afternoon the Poet stole a car from a remote area north of the city. It had not been moved for over a week. Presumably the owner was out of town and the car could be taken for a few hours without discovery. The Poet looked at the clock in the car; time for the girl to be heading home from school. The trail was picked up a few blocks from the viaduct. The procedure, carefully plotted and planned, was to draw abreast of the girl, then, with a savage pull on the steering wheel, slam into her from the side. There was a narrow walkway on the bridge, consequently she would be thrown directly into the railing, then back into the street. The Poet reasoned that if the impact with steel and concrete was not quite fatal, the cars immediately behind, unable to stop, would surely complete the job.

Just before the crest of the viaduct and with the sun positioned perfectly, the Poet pulled out to pass a small yellow station wagon which was directly behind Deborah. The driver of the station wagon, at least partially blinded by the sun, did not see the Poet in his rear view mirror and started a move to the inside lane. This forced the Poet to accelerate rapidly around the yellow car and then make the swing in toward Deb. The meticulous timing which was essential for the plan to work had been disrupted by the innocent move of the driver in the yellow car. The blazing western sun had befriended Deborah, not the Poet. The stolen car managed only a glancing blow, knocking the girl off the bike and into a post supporting a fence, a fence which prevented objects from falling or being thrown onto the highway below. She was hurt but she did not bounce back into the street and into the path of oncoming cars.

It was just before five o'clock and Jon was still in the office when his secretary buzzed him. "Mrs. Ridgeway is on line two," she said. "Sounds hysterical. You'd better talk to her."

Jon cut his secretary off and punched in the second line.

"Judy?"

"Doctor Erickson," the scrub nurse was crying so hard he could hardly understand her. "Debbie's been hit—on her bike. The car didn't stop—just hit her and kept going. My God, Doctor Erickson, she's hurt so bad. She's—"

"Judy," Jon shouted to gain her attention. "Where are you and where is Debbie?"

"At the hospital. She's in the operating room."

"St. Elizabeths?"

"Yes."

"I'll be right there."

Jon pushed the intercom button and told his secretary to cancel the last two appointments, he was going to the hospital. "Try to get in touch with Bill Arnold," he said. "Tell him Debbie Ridgeway has been hurt and is in the hospital—St. Elizabeths. Tell him I'll be with Judy. Just have him page me when he gets there."

He found Judy in the main waiting room of the hospital and took her to a more private area near the surgical suites. From here he phoned one of the surgical residents he knew and asked him to go by the operating room and find out all he could on Debbie's condition. "Her mother and I are in the small waiting room just off the doctors' lounge," he said. "We'd sure appreciate some information."

An experienced trauma team was attending Debbie and the resident had good news to report when he came out of the operating room. "She's going to be okay, Judy," he said. "Couple of broken ribs, one punctured the lung, but our chest surgeon is taking care of that. No rupture of the spleen or liver and that's real good. Right leg is fractured but it shouldn't be any problems for the orthopedist. Her face is bruised, but no facial bones are broken, no lacerations and her CAT scan is negative. She'll look like hell for awhile, you know that, Judy, but she'll be as pretty and healthy as ever when this is all over."

"Thank you, Hank," and Judy impulsively hugged the young doctor. "My God, I've been so worried. The police called and told me a car had swerved over and hit her. They said it was bad and that's all they'd tell me. But you think she'll be okay, Hank?"

"That's what they told me in the O.R., Judy. But I'll keep checking on her and let you know how things are going. Oh, I almost forgot. The girl at the reception desk downstairs knew I was going to check on your daughter and asked me to tell you a police lieutenant was in the lobby and wants to see you."

"Lenhart?" Jon asked.

"I don't know, Doctor Erickson. The receptionist just said he was a lieutenant from police headquarters."

"Okay. We'll call down there later."

Bill Arnold walked in just as the surgical resident left. "They told me I'd find you here," he said. "One of the candy stripers brought me up." He nodded quickly at Jon then moved to put an arm around Judy. "What's going on? How's Deb?"

Judy was close to tears so Jon told what he knew of the accident and of Debbie's condition.

"You say it was a hit-and-run, Jon?" Bill asked.

"That's what the police told Judy."

"Bet my last buck the Poet was behind that wheel. Police here?"

"There's a lieutenant downstairs. Probably Lenhart. Wants to see Judy."

In a search for news, all reporters spend their time in many places and Bill Arnold was no stranger to hospitals. And he was familiar with the routine and protocol. Assuming a professional manner he leaned over to pick up the phone and dialed the operator. "Let me speak to the reception desk," he said. And when he had been put through: "I think you have a Lieutenant Lenhart waiting down there. Tell him Mrs. Ridgeway will see him as soon as she receives definite word about her daughter." He hung up the phone and turned to Judy. "What'd you think? Did I sound like a doctor?"

"Oh, yes," Judy said with a faint smile—her first that afternoon. "Authoritative and just very slightly obnoxious."

"Well, that's a good start anyway. But maybe you'd just as soon see that cop now, Judy. From what you tell me, you're pretty sure about Deb."

"Might as well get it over with, I guess. Hank will let us know when she's out of the operating room."

All three went downstairs to meet with Lt. Lenhart. He inquired briefly about Deborah, then discussed the accident. It definitely had been a hit-and-run—apparently deliberate. Witnesses reported seeing the car turn sharply to strike the girl, then speed away. The make and type of the vehicle had been identified and the police found it abandoned on a side street only ten blocks from where Deb had been hit. Not much doubt it was stolen as the registered owner was out of town and a preliminary search revealed the car had been wiped of fingerprints.

Jon had been silent for quite some time, allowing the conversation to involve the Lieutenant, the mother and the reporter. It just wasn't like him to stay passive forever, especially when in the company of Lt. Lenhart.

"Just a thought, Lieutenant, here we are sitting around in the hospital discussing an accident that could have killed Deborah Ridgeway. I have to wonder if we'd have any occasion to be here at all if the police had kept her name out of the paper."

"Ah didn't write the article, Doctor."

"I know that, but you were the officer who questioned Deborah. Isn't it strange that her name shows up in the next day's newspaper?"

"Don't accuse me of mouthin' off to the press, boy."

"I'm not accusing you of anything, Lieutenant. But you were the only cop present when Deborah was questioned and the next day her name appears in print. You're an officer of the law. What's all that tell you?"

Lt. Lenhart noticed Bill had his pen out and was making notes on a small pad. "Y'all better be careful of what you write there, Mr. Arnold," he said. "Accuse me of bein' responsible for that little girl's accident and y'all gonna find you sef in a mighty big lawsuit."

"Lieutenant, I've been a reporter every bit as long as you've been a cop. I know what my paper can and can't be sued for. And it can't be sued for reporting a conversation—accurately."

"Well, go ahead and write anything you want. Ah have work to do. Cain't stand around here arguing with you two." The Lieutenant rose to leave, then remembering his southern manners, he turned to Judy. "Good day to you, Ma'am," he said and walked away.

"Wow," Judy said. "No love lost there, is there?"

"Not a bit," Bill replied. "And Jon, you'd be interested in this. One of the other reporters told me she saw Lenhart and your Doctor Miller at a Right-to-Life rally the other night. What do you think of that?"

"Doesn't surprise me in the least. Odd couple, though. They don't have a great deal in common."

"Who is Miller?" Judy asked. "He's not a doctor at St. Elizabeths, is he?"

"No. He has a Ph.D. from some rinky-dink divinity school in the midwest. He's really quite a character. Far right preacher—that's one side of him. I suspect that side of coining a little extra cash from the faith-ful. He's also a counselor at the Special Procedures Clinic up at the med school—that's his liberal side. I don't know. He impresses me as someone who'd drop his pants in the back of the church or after hours at the Clinic. And I'll bet if he got some cute little parishioner pregnant she'd be sent out of state for an abortion, with him quietly paying the bill."

"You don't have much good to say for your fellow man today, do you, Doctor?"

"Not those two, Judy. Lenhart and I got off on the wrong foot early in the feticide business. I just don't like his southern philosophy. But Miller, he's different. Maybe even a little dangerous. He's clashed with Kathy a few times. Doesn't sound rational to me."

"I don't know him," Bill said, " but after our little meeting with Chief O'Neal, I'm sort of inclined to agree with you. But when you mentioned the Clinic, I remembered I was going to bring Sherry Bourden over to the Ridgeways' today. It'll have to wait. She's quite a kid, Judy. About Deb's age. Got the drive and the smarts but she needs someone like you and Deb to give her a little class. Polish up some of the rough edges so she can go some place with her brain."

"You talked about her the other day, Bill, and I'm anxious to meet her. Maybe you could bring her up to the hospital. Debbie's going to need a lot of company for awhile."

"I'll do it. Maybe Sunday if Deb's okay. But right now, I think I'll call Chief O'Neal. I think your daughter needs some protection—police pro-tection. As soon as the Poet finds out she's still alive, he's going to have to think about finishing the job."

"Oh, my God, I hadn't even thought about that."

"You've had other things on your mind, Judy. I'll give the Chief a ring. I think he'll agree with me about some extra precautions. Now, if you people will excuse me, I'd better head for the plant and get some of this ready for the good folk to read in the morning."

"Thanks for being here, Bill," Judy said.

"Hell, Judy, I was just here for the story." But he winked and gave her hug on the way out.

"Bill," Jon said, "before you leave. You going to have any time this evening after you get this thing ready for the press?"

"Sure. Want to get together?"

"Yeah. I'm moving along with that project of mine and I'd like to talk to you about it. Why don't you come over to my place about eight o'clock. Might pour you a beer?"

"I'll be there. You going to stay with Judy for awhile?"

"Yes, at least until Deb comes out of anesthesia."

"Good. And Judy, I'll give you a ring late tonight or tomorrow."

"Tomorrow, Bill. I'll probably be with Deb all night."

"Okay. And I'll see you at eight, Jon."

Jon left the hospital as soon as Judy was allowed to be with her daughter. He had the beer on ice when Bill arrived.

"Now, just what the hell is this all about?" the reporter asked as soon as he got in the door.

"It's all here on the kitchen table," Jon said. "It's a list of suspects. I've been putting this together for quite awhile and I need your advice— your thoughts."

"Great. Pour my beer and start down the list. How big is it?"

"Six people."

"Not too bad. Know them all?"

"With a couple of exceptions which I'll explain as we go along."

"Okay, shoot."

"First is Lenhart."

"Oh, Jon. Come on. Just because you don't like that asshole is no reason to suspect him of clobbering those kids."

"Now listen to me. I know my prejudice shows every now and then but—"

"Every now and then? Jesus."

"Okay, you're right, I can't stand him, but Lenhart has some pretty strong feelings about these teenagers and their unwed pregnancies. And he's a right-to-lifer. Also, and I think this is important, you never see the Lieutenant in the hospital right after one of these kids comes in. There's always quite a delay before he shows up. Now where's he been? What's he been doing from the time the girl is hit until he comes in to question hospital personnel? And he must have been notified right away about Deb. Sure took him awhile to show up at the hospital.

Remember, he's in charge of all this and the cop on the beat is going to call him first."

"Okay, keep him on your list. But I think you're really out in left field. Who's the next one?"

"Miller."

"Well, I don't know him and you may be right. Sure sounds like he's tied in with the murder of his ex-wife. But your prejudice could be showing here too, Jon. Kathy has been verbally roughed up by this guy and that can color your thinking."

"Not just verbally roughed up, Bill. Kathy told me about her apartment being trashed. That could have been Miller. And he has access to all of the Clinic records, knows the girls, knows their habits, knows the sex of their fetus and when they're due."

"Oh, sure, Jon, for a suspect, I'd trade him any day for the Lieutenant. Next."

"Frances McGraw, the administrator of the Clinic."

"Yeah, you've told me about her before. She does sound like a mean witch. But you have to be more than just nasty to qualify as the Poet. She sure as hell knows everybody in that Clinic so that puts her right alongside of Miller. Might as well keep her on the list. Keep going."

"Donald Parker, head of the lab in the Special Procedures Clinic."

"You've never told me much about Mr. Parker. What do you have against him?"

"Bill, it isn't as though I have a vendetta against all of these people. True, I don't like Lenhart or Miller but I don't actually dislike McGraw—she runs a good clinic. And I respect Parker's abilities in the lab. I don't dis-like him, either, but he has a vicious streak in him and he made the damnedest comment about the Poet the other day."

"Stop," Bill held up his hand. "How do you know about his vicious streak and what did he say about the Poet?"

"Can't talk about him being vicious. Involves one of my patients. But he doesn't think too much of the unweds in the Clinic and when we were talking about them the other day he mentioned that he thought the Poet might be smarter than the rest of us."

"Oh, hell, Jon. Face facts. There are a lot of taxpayers in this city who think the Poet is doing them a favor. Lenhart is the most vocal one and I guess your lab director is another."

"Unfortunately, you're probably right. But Parker, along with Miller and McGraw, sees those charts every day."

"So do a bunch of doctors and medical students."

"I suppose, but I haven't had time to track down everybody who's been in that Clinic; interns, residents, staff physicians. I've just picked out, or maybe I should say picked on, the permanent staff; the people like Miller, McGraw and Parker who have been there since day one."

"That's four. You said you had six. The last two have any connection to the Clinic?"

"Remotely. One of them is a patient of mine, let's just call her Sarah. I mean that lady is hard as nails. Cut the balls off a guy in California and has what I'd consider a pathological hatred for little boys. She's pregnant and planned to get an abortion if she was packing a male fetus. She works for a computer outfit that does work for the Special Procedures Clinic, programs for them. Smart as hell. Has a boyfriend—or did have—that works as an orderly in the Clinic. Same guy, I think, that Sherry was talking about when you and I were over at her place. Mixed up in drugs, lots of money, probably was using Miller's ex-wife as a pusher. I can't imagine he'd have any reason to do away with male babies, but he could have supplied Sarah with information about the place."

"Pretty remote. But I'm a little confused. How can this Sarah person hate little boys and get screwed by big boys? I assume this pregnancy was not by divine intervention or artificial insemination."

"Neither. She just likes to screw."

"Okay, I'll give you that one just because she's weird and knows all about the Clinic. But she doesn't go to the top of my list."

"Well, neither will the last one. Another patient, Stephanie. Stephanie is a spoiled brat. My nurse can't stand her."

"Jon, I've met Nell. Met her when I came by your office one time. She's pretty savvy, but just because she doesn't like someone is a pretty farfetched reason to put that individual on your most-wanted list."

"I didn't say she was number one. She told me her husband owns a small metal shop up close to the medical school. Makes things for all the clinics, including Special Procedures. I've never met him, but if he gets into that Clinic with the gadgets he makes—out of stainless steel, I might add—you never know."

"Boy, you are reaching for anything. But now that you have this list—unlikely as some of the members might be—what can you do with it? Are you just sitting on it, thinking about it? All you docs are supposed to be such great thinkers, you know."

"Don't be insulting or you won't get another beer. And yes, I have thought about it and have actually done something with it."

"Such as."

"Stephanie is a long-time Portland resident. The rest of them come from all over the country. It cost a buck or two but I managed to find out something about them. There are people who do that sort of a thing for a living, you know."

"Oh, I know. Some of them are even sort of ethical. But expensive."

"Right. Sometimes they're worth it, too."

"Okay, what'd you find out?" Bill asked.

"The usual. Learned about their friends, their education, legal troubles, if any. Teachers, employers—anybody that'd know more about them than I do. Sent letters out to some of these people and already starting to get some information back. Maybe I'll be able to narrow this list down a bit."

"Jon, I know all about your two or three years of training to be a cop but let me ask you something. When you got through med school, were you a good doctor? Ready to do major surgery and all that sort of thing?"

"Of course not. You have to have more training and experience." Jon paused for a second and looked over at his friend. "I know," he said, "I'm out of my element. Two years at a police academy just doesn't do it. Isn't that what you're thinking?"

"Not exactly, but I guess that's part of it. I worry about you, Jon. You might be getting in a little too deep, here. Let's suppose for the moment that you're right. Somebody on that list is the Poet. Now, let's take it a little further. Let's assume that one of the recipients of your letter of inquiry is a friend of the Poet. A close friend from some years back. Obviously he doesn't know his friend is our famous Poet. He's sure to contact his old buddy. Then what? Jon, that rhyming S.O.B. will be laying for you. I read a novel recently. Weird. The hero, a police captain, was killed in the last chapter. I don't like endings like that and I don't want any of that truth-is-stranger-than-fiction bullshit under my by-line. So watch yourself." The reporter was serious. "One of those stainless steel stilettos wouldn't look too good in your backside. Now, get me another beer."

The Poet was having a beer that night, too; alone, angry and frustrated. Radio and television news had covered the car-bike accident in great detail. By now the whole city knew there had been an attempt on the life of Deborah Ridgeway. And thanks to the news media, they were also reasonably sure the Poet was the driver of the stolen car. Providence, it was said by a newscaster, had obviously intervened and the one person who could make a tentative identification of the knife-wielding killer was still alive. Depressed and still furious, the Poet snapped off the television set and opened another beer. Fear was an added emotional element present in the room tonight. A letter from an acquaintance in the midwest had arrived that day and it was read as an ominous sign of exposure. Perhaps a challenge to the mastermind of this danger would avert possible trouble. A challenge in rhyme. It was worth a try. And a better method must be found to eliminate the

Ridgeway girl. Many things to do, and there was a feeling that time was running out.

CHAPTER XI

"EMERGENCY VEHICLES ARE BEING DEPLOYED AT THIS TIME TO MEET THE TRANSCONTINENTAL JET"

Jon was on his way to the airport to pick up Kathleen and had been listening to a taped obstetrical lecture in his car. When the tape was finished he hit the eject button and got only the end of a news bulletin regarding a plane in trouble. Apprehensive, he touched the scan lever hoping to learn more from a different station. Hard rock, Western and occasional classical music was all. He flipped the switch between FM and AM and still no mention of a crippled jet. Back to FM and his usual station for road conditions. At the same time his foot pushed a little harder on the accelerator and the Legend Coupe picked up speed. He had just turned off the freeway onto the exit marked "International Airport" when the news center returned with the chilling report that Boston flight number 487 was in trouble and had been cleared for a straight-in emergency approach. The announcer said that two of the four engines were out and the crew reported additional problems with the landing gear.

Flight 487 was Kathy's flight, that much Jon knew as he swung down the short-term parking ramp and grabbed a ticket from the automatic gate entry. From his position on the ramp he noticed backup lights on a car two lanes over. He sped past an elderly man in an old Pontiac to arrive at the parking spot just as the departing car cleared the way.

There were sirens off toward the runways and Jon ran over the pedestrian bridge that led to the main terminal. Once inside he glanced at the monitor and saw that Concourse C, gate 59 was the flight's destination. The metal detector guarding the concourse slowed him only briefly and once past this obstacle he made it to the gate in record time. The waiting room of gate 59 looked out over a major portion of the airport runways and Jon found most of the occupants of that area staring anxiously out the windows waiting for the plane to come into view. A straight-in emergency approach meant that all other air traffic would be diverted.

Five minutes after Jon had found a place at the window the loud speaker blared a message that flight 487 was visible off to the right and would land in thirty seconds. The woman at the microphone added a measure of relief for the people waiting when she said, "Ladies and gentlemen, the captain of flight 487 has acknowledged the emergency vehicles but anticipates a smooth landing."

It was not just bravado from the cockpit. A few seconds later the big jet touched down without mishap, the fire engines streaming in its wake. The pilot, possibly still concerned about the landing gear, used up runway instead of relying on his brakes and eventually slowed to a stop and began the lumbering trip into gate 59.

There is always an air of excitement and anticipation when the loading bridge locks onto the fuselage of a passenger plane and the occupants come up the ramp to greet waiting friends and relatives. It was even more evident today. The shouts of recognition were louder, the hugs longer and the kisses more fervent. Kathy saw Jon the instant she came out of the passageway. They stood just looking at each other for a second, then Kathy dropped the small bag she was carrying and used both arms to let her husband know how glad she was to be safe, back home and with him.

"You scared the shit out of me," Jon whispered in her ear.

"Oh, God, Jon, all I could think of was that we'd never get to that hotel at the coast. I've really missed you."

"Well, Mrs. Erickson," Jon said as they walked toward the baggage claim area, "other than the little problem of two dead engines, how did you enjoy the trip?"

"Fair food, bad wine. But, I think I know a young gentleman who plans to indulge me with nothing but the finest. Don't you, Darling?"

"You'd better believe it. No holding back tonight."

Like a pair of teenagers they continued to chatter on until the carousel delivered Kathy's suitcase and they walked out to the car. Jon unlocked the trunk and put his wife's luggage in alongside the bag he had packed last night before going to the hospital.

"Home first?" he asked. "Or shall we just head out for the coast?"

"No reason to go home. I have everything I'll need right there. Let's get to the restaurant. I'm starved."

An hour later they pulled into the parking lot of a locally famous fish grotto. Both wanted the house specialty, a filet of chinook salmon. They gave their coats to an attendant and stood for a moment waiting for a table. Suddenly, Jon took Kathy's arm and turned back away from the dining area. "Let's go to the bar first," he said and guided her toward the lounge.

"We can get a drink with our dinner," Kathy protested.

"I know, but there's a man in there I really don't want to meet tonight."

"Who's that?"

"Donald Parker, director of the lab at the Special Procedures

Clinic. I'm sure you've met him. He's with some blonde. I think it's Stephanie Van Osborn. Odd couple, but it does fit with what I know about both of them."

"Stephanie? You've mentioned her once or twice before. Nell didn't like her."

"Right. And with good reason. But you know something, it just occurred to me. I think I have a picture of her when she was about three or four years old. Chief O'Neal gave it to me."

"You're not talking sense to me, Jon. This must have been something that happened during that little interlude in our lives when we weren't speaking. Sort of the dark ages of our marriage."

"We in the Renaissance now?"

"You bet. Now before you tell me about that picture, why don't you catch the waiter's eye? He'll find us a corner table in the bar where we can talk and I'll bet we can order dinner there, too."

Kathy was right. When they were seated and their orders taken, Jon told her of the safety deposit box which had belonged to the former Mrs. Miller. And he described the contents of the box, including the little girl's picture. "You know, Kate, when Chief O'Neal first handed me that picture I was sure I'd seen that same person—grown up. Didn't really ring a bell until I saw Stephanie in there just now. Must have been the way she was sitting. May just be coincidence, but it does look like her."

"So what's all this mean?"

"Damned if I know. May mean that Doctor Miller is her father and the dead woman was her mother. The letters found in that box sure point to a little blackmail going on. Odds are that Miller had his ex-wife killed to shut down her scheme and save him some money."

"You're saying that Miller is the Poet. I can't quite see that, Jon."

"No, not exactly. He had an excuse for that night, or as the police say, his whereabouts could be accounted for. In short, he was nowhere near that apartment house. But Chief O'Neal figures Miller paid the Poet to do the job."

"How 'bout Stephanie? Doesn't she ever talk about her parents?"

"Just told me she rarely sees her mother and chooses not to see her father."

"I don't blame her if Miller really is her father. I wonder if she knows that woman was her mother—the one that got killed in the apartment house basement?"

"She's got to be suspicious if she reads the paper at all. But she's never talked to me about it. Oh, incidentally, Kate," and Jon gripped Kathy's arm, "I haven't told you this before, but the police also figure somebody got paid extra for the knife that hit you."

"I know, Jon. Bill Arnold told me. He's a good friend. Even

showed me a copy of my poem—I guess you could call it mine." Kathy was quiet for a moment, her head down and slowly sipping at her wine. Then: "I just don't know, Jon. How can all this be happening? Is there ever going to be an end to it?"

"I hope so, Kate. I really have to hope so."

More wine was poured, then the waiter came with the salmon. They were not disappointed, it was even better than expected and this helped lift their spirits from the threatening gloom. When they returned to the car Kathy put her seat back and closed her eyes as Jon drove toward the coast.

A storm was heading in from the Pacific and the sounds of crashing surf greeted them when they went out on the small deck off their room. The hotel's powerful flood lights illuminated the waves pounding the rocks below.

"We picked a good weekend," Kathy said as she stood protected behind Jon with her arms around his waist. "I've never seen it this rough before."

"Definitely not a night to walk on the beach."

Kathy shivered and slipped her hand inside Jon's shirt, pulling him closer to her. "So who wants to walk on the beach?"

"Lord, your hand is cold. Take an hour to warm you up."

"Oh, I don't think so. Why don't you start a fire in the fireplace while I brush my teeth?"

The noise of the storm was only partially muffled when they went inside and closed the sliding glass door and drapes.

"Going to be a bitch of a night," Jon said as he arranged the presto logs and lit the firestarter. He stood watching the fire gain momentum then turned around when he heard Kathy come out of the bathroom. She had done a little more than just brush her teeth. Her dark hair was down to her shoulders and she was wearing a white negligee and dressing gown—erotic but not cheap.

"God, Kate, you're a pretty thing."

"Remember this outfit?" she asked.

"Do I! You wore that up in Maine on our honeymoon."

"I found it with my wedding things back home. Mom gave it to me before we got married. She knew different but thought I should at least try to look virginal on my wedding night."

"You know something, Kate, you still do."

"You're sweet." She gave him a quick kiss. "Now go brush your teeth. You still smell like salmon and gin."

"Sorry I don't have any fancy pajamas to parade around in."

"You didn't six-and-a-half years ago, either. I don't remember it bothering you much then."

The lights were off when Jon came out of the bathroom and Kathy was standing by the fire. She had turned back the sheets.

"You do know how to set the scene," he said as he took off her dressing gown and slipped the negligee down from her shoulders.

With a sensuous movement of her arms and hips she allowed the silky garment to glide off her body then slipped her hands down Jon's back. His shorts came off with difficulty and his memory of a past sexual debacle was erased.

Marriage had never cooled their passions. They accepted uninhibited sex and sexual satisfaction as a natural part of their lives. But Kathy sensed a difference tonight and later, with Jon asleep, she put on her gown and stood by the dying fire. She felt calm, at ease. Their sexual union tonight had been immensely satisfying to both, but it didn't seem to her as though it had been a purely physical act. There was more love involved, more sharing, more commitment. She sensed they had started life together again, and with an intense wish to be close to her husband she took off her gown and lay down beside him. Conscious of her desire and her actions, she pressed her breasts into his back and let a hand fall over his hip. Jon stirred, then awoke. Almost instinctively he brought his thighs together. Her gentle and provocative efforts to free the hand provided all the excitement he needed. Fully aroused, he rolled over and brought her on top of him. Neither required much additional stimulation to reach climax and afterwards, sprawled and relaxed by their efforts, they slept until late in the morning.

Kathy was the first to get up. Enjoying the somewhat horny freedom of wandering naked through the rooms of the suite, she arranged their clothing and toilet articles, then dialed room service for breakfast. She showered, then kissed Jon awake, turning quickly to avoid the hands which were reaching for her bare breasts. "Food is on the way. No time for play right now," she told him, then hastily put on a raincoat to answer the door and sign for breakfast. The storm was still with them. Wind and rain lashed the glass door and windows. A good day to stay inside. They managed to get dressed later and browse through the shops in the lobby, and still later had dinner in the elegant dining room of the resort complex.

The sun was out and bright when they awakened Sunday morning. The sea was still angry, but there was a clean and washed look throughout the grounds of the resort. After another late breakfast they packed and reluctantly turned the car toward home. Nature continued to be at her spectacular best. The storm had brought an early scattering of snow to the mountains and sunshine reflected off the white-tipped fir trees which lined the highway. Neither Jon nor Kathy spoke as they drove over the pass and looked out on the pristine beauty of a forest with new-fallen snow. Once down from the twisting mountain road and approaching the valley, Jon reached over and put his hand on Kathy's knee.

"Great weekend, Kate. Probably the best we've ever had."

Kathy, nearly asleep in the sheepskin seat covers of the coupe, nodded her assent. "Not 'probably,' Jon. It was the best."

Both went back to work the following day. Jon started his with an eight o'clock surgery; a hysterectomy on a forty-year-old former exotic dancer. She had a large poppy bloom tattooed around her belly button and Jon's transverse incision had cut across the stem of the flower which extended down to the pubic area.

When the surgery was nearly finished Jon had a call from the obstetrical floor. Sarah Tompkins was in labor and the nurse would like to have him check her as soon as possible. Leaving the resident to finish, Jon had a final word of advice. "This lady is rather proud of that poppy," he said. "I don't want to make rounds tomorrow and find the stem going off in two different directions. Think you can manage that?"

"No problem, Doctor Erickson," the resident assured him.

Jon was stopped by the obstetrical charge nurse before he checked on Sarah. "You've had some pips in here before, Doctor Erickson, but this one tops all. She'd make a mule skinner blush."

"Colorful, isn't she," Jon said. "Learn any new words?"

"No," the nurse said with an indifferent shrug. "Just some unusual ways to bring them into the conversation."

"How's she doing?"

"Surprisingly, very well. When I first saw her—and heard her—I thought she would top the bitch list. But she's doing okay. You should see the guy that brought her in. He's one mean-looking dude."

"Boyfriend?"

"She said he's her brother."

"Didn't know she had one, but Sarah's full of surprises. I'll go in and see her."

"Piece of cake, Doctor," was Sarah's greeting when Jon walked in the labor room. "Big deal, this is. Nurse said I was over half dilated. Hell, I could have told her that. No sweat so far."

"You wouldn't pull my leg, would you, Sarah?"

"You know me better than that. If this was as bad as I've heard it's supposed to be, you'd know about it."

"I'm sure I would. Well, let me see what's going on. Maybe the nurse is wrong. Maybe you're in false labor."

Sarah's narrow-set eyes fixed on Jon. "Don't shit me, Doctor," she said. "Remember, I'm the one that's knocked up. I know when I'm in labor and I figure to be out of this little birthing suite in another hour—maybe an hour-and-a-half if you sit on your ass and smoke a big, black cigar. That's what obstetricians used to do, isn't it?"

Jon didn't answer but put on a glove and checked the progress of her labor. "She's about complete," he told the nurse as he did the vaginal exam. "Got a rim left, vertex and swinging up to an anterior position."

He withdrew his fingers from Sarah's birth canal and took off the glove. "Looks like you're right, Sarah. Piece of cake. And I understand you have a brother in the waiting room. You never told me about him."

Jon's exam had stimulated a particularly strong contraction and Sarah remained quiet for the full sixty-second duration. "That was a good one," she said and used the sleeve of her gown to wipe a trace of perspiration from her forehead. "And yes, that is my brother out there. And no, I don't have to tell you every damn thing about my life. You know far more than anybody else as it is. You know how I screw and you know whom I screw. Isn't that good enough?"

Again Jon ignored the obvious baiting from his patient and made a slight adjustment to the machinery monitoring the baby's heart rate. It showed the rate had slowed during the contraction but picked back up to 120 beats per minute immediately after. "Okay, Sarah," he said. "I guess your relatives are your own business and my business is to see that you have a nice healthy baby. Looks like you're on your way to doing just that. I'm going upstairs. I'll be back when the nurse calls me."

It was impossible for Sarah Tompkins to acknowledge any weakness. She was hard and she was tough but right now she did not want her doctor to leave. "You want to know about my brother?" she said holding Jon's attention and his presence. "Alright, I'll tell you about him. Name is Matt."

Matthew Tompkins, according to Sarah, lived in California and had visited his sister regularly during the past two years. He had also served time in San Quentin for attempted murder. He was a big man, not especially bright, Sarah told Jon, but very protective of his only sister. At age eighteen, and a high school fullback, he fell in love with one of the rally girls and promptly got her pregnant. The girl, Holly, insisted on getting married but left him three months after the baby was born. The way Sarah told it, the fall from being a prom queen to being a wife and mother in a small drab apartment was too much. Holly left Matt and moved in with a former boyfriend whose finances and future were much brighter than Matt's. It was only a few months later, Sarah said, that she and her brother were having a few beers in a local tavern when the former rally girl and her friend came in. "They saw us right away," Sarah told Jon. "I thought they'd leave but I'll be damned if they didn't sit down at a table right across from us. The guy with her was sort of a slick-looking asshole—little mustache and all. Holly had a silk blouse on, no bra and her tits showed right through it. I sort of hoped my brother would toss his beer at her but he just sat there until they started to taunt him. Asked him if he was still blowing up footballs for a living and shit like that. The little snot really put his balls in a vice when she said she'd finally found someone who could give her a good screwing. That did it. Matt got up and walked over to their table. All he did was ask them to leave but the jerk with the mustache just sort of sneered and told him to go to hell. That's when Matt ripped the table off the floor and tipped their beer all over them. Turned out Holly's friend wasn't quite the pansy he looked. He picked up a chair and started to swing it at Matt."

Another hard contraction interrupted the story while Sarah concentrated on breathing and relaxing. She continued as soon as the pain diminished. "Well, let me tell you something, Doctor. That's a real shitty part of town and I never went there without a little extra protection—like a damn sharp switchblade. When I saw that chair coming in his direction I pulled that blade out of my purse and tossed it to Matt. He knew what to do with it. The chair caught him on the left shoulder but it was the last chair that son of a bitch clubbed anyone with for quite awhile. He really hollered when one swing of that knife nearly took his arm off. If Matt had quit then he probably wouldn't have gone to jail, but he went for the guy's chest next and they got him for attempted murder. Nailed him for a concealed weapon, too, the switchblade. He said it was his. All this was about two months after I cut the testicles off that sadistic bastard in Berkeley and Matt didn't want me to get in any more trouble."

Sarah was quiet for a moment, then added: "Matt always covered for me when we were kids. I guess I could do anything and he'd take the blame if I asked him to."

It was a statement of fact. Completely unemotional. There was no hint of appreciation or gratitude for the blind devotion of the elder sibling. It was an attitude of indifference that Jon found disturbing.

Sarah knew her body well. A very lively seven-pound baby girl was delivered forty-five minutes later. It was a pure, textbook, normal spontaneous delivery.

"What kind of a mother will that one make?" the head nurse asked Jon as he sat writing up the record.

"Hard to tell. Sarah will never be at ease with her fellow human beings—too much resentment, too much intolerance, but what a brain.

If that baby has half the intellect of her mother she'll manage pretty damn well."

"Does Miss Tompkins know who the father is?"

"Probably a local physician. Doctors can be a little careless at times."

One of the nurses put her pen down and looked over at Jon. "You have us interested, Doctor Erickson. Anybody we know?"

Jon smiled and shook his head. "Good try," he said, "but no way do you get any of Sarah's little secrets from me. Tell you one thing, though," Jon closed the chart and pushed it toward the nurse, "and I hate to disappoint you, but it's nobody on this staff."

Matt was still in the waiting room and Jon stopped to tell him he could go in and see his sister and little niece. Sarah's description of her brother was pretty accurate. He did not appear too smart, but was amiable and seemed eager to see the new mother and baby. After he had chatted with Matt for a few minutes, Jon went back to surgery and a relatively easy removal of a benign ovarian tumor. Judy Ridgeway was his scrub nurse and because the case was uncomplicated and fairly routine they were able to talk about her daughter as the operation progressed. Deb remained in the hospital, her mother said, but expected to be discharged in another day or two.

Judy also mentioned that Bill Arnold had brought Sherry Bourden over to the hospital on Saturday and again on Sunday. "She and Deb got along real well," Judy said. "They're both real smart, eager kids. Sort of fun to listen to them chatter back and forth. Sherry promised to take Deborah shopping as soon as she gets used to her crutches, but that takes a little doing, thanks to her broken ribs."

"Bill is a good judge of character," Jon said. "Probably also figures Sherry adds a measure of protection for Deb if they go someplace together."

"I hope so. I know she doesn't want me hovering over her twenty-four hours a day and I know the police can't follow her everywhere. You know, Doctor, Bill frightens me when he talks about the Poet. He doesn't think Deb is safe at all. She's the only one who's seen the Poet in action and thanks to that newspaper article, everybody thinks she can identify him—or her, Deb isn't sure, you know. Bill thinks the Poet is running scared these days, scared of being recognized and scared enough to do something desperate and that would involve Deb."

"Have you considered moving out of town for awhile, Judy?"

"We've talked about it, Deb and I. Neither of us like the idea. All her friends are here and so are mine. But we may have to if they don't catch that madman."

"Lot of people going to be scared out of town if something isn't done pretty soon. But Judy, let me know if either Kathy or I can do anything to help you out. You know, take Deb for a day or two when she gets out of the hospital. Something to give you both a little change of scenery."

"I will, Doctor, and thank you."

The surgery finished, Jon stopped by the hospital cafeteria for lunch and then reported to the office. His first call that afternoon was to Sarah's boss at the Computer Center. During her delivery, Sarah had mentioned her job status was a little shaky. Someone had planted a computer virus in the medical school computer and she was the number one suspect. But as she told Jon, "if I'd infected any of their damn disks they wouldn't have discovered it for years. And that's what I told those assholes." When Jon asked how the virus got there in the first place she replied, "The cheap bastards use bootleg software. Some of it's sure to be fucked up."

Jon had some misgivings regarding his role in salvaging Sarah's job but was able to convince the computer boss to retain her on the payroll. It wasn't easy. Sarah's genius at computer programming was not the question. It was her intellectual honesty. A wayward brain of that magnitude was capable of infinite mischief. But she had just delivered a baby and it was very hard to fire a new mother. Sarah gained a reprieve.

When Jon got home that evening he found Kathy tired but exhilarated by the patient contact which she had missed for the past few weeks. Everybody she saw in the outpatient department welcomed her back, including Lt. Lenhart. She happened to see him as he was walking toward the Special Procedures Clinic and he stopped to offer his sympathy. "And Jon," she said, "I even saw the lab chief, Mr. Parker. He was very kind also. It was just a great day until I ran into Doctor Miller."

Jon made them both a cup of tea and they sat down at the kitchen table. "Better tell me about that encounter, Kate."

This time he listened as his wife told about a teenager from the Special Procedures Clinic. The girl had put her baby up for adoption shortly after delivery and now the depression which had been evident to a certain extent before the baby was born, had become severe. She was brought to the psychiatric clinic by her mother and assigned to Kathy. Her appointment had been at 10.00 a.m. and word had leaked back to Dr. Miller by early afternoon. He was enraged by this slight to his pro-fessional qualifications and confronted Kathy in the hall outside her office.

"Jon," Kathy said, "that man is crazy. He was shouting and screaming at me right there in the clinic. It was a real bad scene—much worse than the other times when he's come over and yelled at me. Same old story, though. Accused me of stealing his patients again. Said he knew more about those kids than I would learn in a lifetime. Wanted to know what a neophyte shrink—that's what he called me, a neophyte shrink—was doing interfering with his treatment program. He demanded I send her back to him so he could straighten out any damage I might have done."

"So what did you tell him?"

"Well, I was a little shocked, frankly. I'll occasionally shout at a disturbed patient to get their attention but I'm not used to having another professional almost physically attack me in the hall."

"Kate, this guy is not terribly well-educated. He's not a real professional and he's paranoid as hell. He's in trouble, too. Remember, I told you he's a suspect in the death of his ex-wife."

"Oh, Lord. I forgot about that. I don't know, love," and Kathy shook her head, "this is getting pretty deep for a third-year resident in psychiatry. You told me that once before but you weren't very nice about it." Kathy put her hand over Jon's on the table. "Want to try again?"

"Always available to help pretty girls." Jon took his wife's hand. "And besides, I owe you this one. What'd you do after he got through ranting and raving?"

"While he was yelling and screaming I kept telling myself I really didn't have to take this crap. Almost told him to go to hell but it didn't seem like the safe thing to do at the time. I thought he might really go bonkers. I told him I would talk to my Chief of Service and see what could be arranged."

"And did you?"

"You bet. Just as soon as I could. The Chief said he'd handle it and assign the girl to another resident. I hate that, Jon," and Kathy set her cup down hard in the saucer. "She's a nice kid and I could have helped her."

"I know you could. You're probably the best one in that clinic to take care of her. Sometimes things just don't work out that way. But believe me, you've already followed any advice I could give you. And I'm glad your Chief is playing it safe."

"Who all knows about Doctor Miller's trouble with the police?"

"Damn few. Nobody up at the school as far as I know."

"Oh, great. Maybe I am better off on the sidelines for awhile."

"You bet you are. Stay clear of that son of a bitch. It's pretty obvious he doesn't like you."

"Bill Arnold said something like that, too, when I was in the hospital. We weren't necessarily talking about Miller. You know the way Bill talks. He said it just occurred to him that there must be one or two people in this fair city who weren't too fond of me. Doctor Miller is most certainly one of them but I can't see him as the Poet. And you told me he had a good alibi for the night his ex-wife was killed."

"Right, a very good one according to Chief O'Neal. But I think he's somehow connected to the Poet. May even be paying him to do his dirty work. I really don't think he handles that knife himself. Now," and Jon added some sugar to his tea, slowly mixing it in, "I've got something to tell you. Didn't want to worry you but I think you should know. Seems we both have an enemy or two in this city."

"Jon," and Kathy sat up straight in her chair, "what are you talking about? What's wrong? What kind of trouble are you in?"

"Here," and Jon handed her a piece of paper with a typewritten message on it. "Got it in today's mail at the office."

```
YOU'RE A DOCTOR NOT A COP
   KEEP PLAYING SHERLOCK AND
   YOUR LIFE WILL STOP
TO MY WARNING YOU PAY NO HEED
   A SHORTENED LIFE YOU WILL SURELY LEAD
WATCH YOUR BACK, WATCH YOUR FRONT
   I TELL YOU NOW I'M ON THE HUNT
WATCH ABOVE, WATCH BELOW
   WHERE I'LL BE YOU'LL NEVER KNOW.
```

Kathy read it, threw it on the floor and burst into tears. "Oh my God, Jon. What next? What do we do now?"

Jon got up from his chair and went over to put his arms around her. "I don't know, Kate," he said. "Several options, I guess. I've been thinking about them ever since I opened that letter. I obviously got somebody's attention."

"What do you mean by that?"

Now, for the first time, Kathy heard of the list of suspects that Jon had developed and the meeting with the reporter. "Bill warned me," he told Kathy, "said there could be some repercussions. As I recall he even said something about watching my back. But it was a little late then. I'd already sent out some of the letters."

The tears were dry now and Kathy was angry. "That damned police academy you went to," she said, "Just can't forget it, can you? And what are these so-called options you mentioned?"

"We could move."

"No."

"Get us both out of harms way for awhile."

"No, Jon. I'm not going to move. I'm scared but not scared enough to have our lives completely disrupted."

"You could have been killed, Kate. That's a hell of a lot more disruption than I ever want."

"And you're in danger, Jon. I remember telling you once if the Poet ever put a knife in you I'd cry but wonder if your insurance was paid up. Our marriage is different now, Jon. We're different and I'd just die if something happened to you."

"Kate, I really don't want to move either. That's just one option. Another is for both of us to stop any connection to the Special Procedures Clinic and anybody or anything the Poet has touched. That would even include Sherry Bourden and the Ridgeways."

"Bad. You've gone too far in this, Jon. Somehow you've really alarmed the Poet. He, or she, is starting to show a little panic. You can't stop now. But listen to me, Jon. I don't try to dictate things around here very often but if you're going to stay with this—and that's up to you—you have to see Chief O'Neal. If you don't, I will."

"Alright, Kate," Jon squeezed her hand, then released it and smiled. "You win. I'll call him tomorrow. And you know I didn't want to give up on this."

"Oh, I know, alright. I know you. You'd be impossible to live with if you had to give up sleuthing. Now, where was I before you scared the wits out of me? Oh yes, I was talking about Bill Arnold. Have you seen him lately or does he spend all his spare time with Judy Ridgeway?"

"Talked with Judy this morning. She scrubbed with me and said Bill brought Sherry over to the hospital to meet Deb this past weekend. I guess they got along pretty well. Apparently Sherry plans to be sort of a helper and protector for Deb when they go out."

"Good. That poor kid needs somebody her own age to be with her and from what you and Bill say, Sherry would be perfect. Should be a policeman not too far away, too."

And that was the scene three weeks later. Debbie had mastered her crutches and with her other wounds healing satisfactorily, she and her new friend were in the pre-Thanksgiving shopping crowd. Sherry, with an almost motherly concern, helped Deb off the bus in front of the city's newest shopping center. There was snow mixed with the rain which added to the festive air.

Bundled up in heavy coats, wool hats and scarves, the two girls were window shopping, for the most part, though each had one or two items they simply must find before returning home. Debbie had one additional objective; she wanted to select a small gift for her friend. It could not be too extravagant; she knew Sherry was quite sensitive when it came to their different place on the economic ladder. Debbie's father, long before his death, had listened to the pleadings of an overenthusiastic life insurance salesman. As a result, she and her mother were not exactly among the nation's poor and homeless. Sherry's father was an unknown factor. She hadn't seen him in years and any contribution he might have made to the family was not measured in dollars and cents. The issue of money between Sherry and the Ridgeways had surfaced only once. She had arrived at their home late one evening shortly after Debbie's release from the hospital. Judy, grateful for the girl's attention to her daughter and in an innocent gesture of friendship, offered to pay the bus fare. It was evident that Sherry's pride had been wounded when said she didn't need a handout, she could pay her own way to see her friends.

The subject of finances had not been brought up since, and now they were standing outside a computer sales store admiring the marvels of the computer and electronic age.

"Can you run a computer?" Deb asked.

"Oh, a little. We have some at school, but my thing is math. Don't ask me why. I just love it. I've already put a good pocket calculator on my Christmas list but I know I'll get clothes instead. Mom figures I need them more than a fancy adding machine. One of the kids in my class has one like that," and she pointed to a fairly standard model. "I think he probably stole it but, boy, can he zip through his math assignment."

They wandered down the street adding to their wish lists here and there until they saw a tiny restaurant, sort of tucked away between two giant department stores.

"Let's get a Coke," Deb suggested.

"And a hamburger," Sherry added. "I'm starved. Missed lunch today."

They ordered at the counter then headed for a nearby table. Before sitting down Debbie said she was going next door where she knew they had clean toilets.

"Want me to clear the way for you?" Sherry asked.

"No thanks. I can manage, but don't eat my hamburger if it comes before I get back."

She returned a few minutes later at about the same time the sandwiches arrived. They were small but well-prepared and it didn't take long for the girls to finish them. Just before they were to leave, each having paid her share of the check, Debbie looked at her friend and asked, "Want to do me a favor?"

"Name it and it's yours."

"I have something for you and I want you to take it just because I want to give it to you."

Sherry's face clouded for a moment, her usual smile gone. "Deb

Ridgeway," she said quite firmly, "if you bought me something, you take it back right now."

"No, I won't—ever. And you'd better take it, Sherry Bourden, or I'll be awful mad at you."

"Well, I don't want you to be mad at me so dig your hand out of that raincoat and let's see what you have."

It was a small calculator with far more features than they had seen in the display.

"Oh, my God," Sherry said when she opened the package. "Deborah, you really picked on my weak spot, didn't you?" And she actually started to cry.

"Think you can get an A in math with that?"

"An A plus," Sherry said, wiping the tears from her eyes. "And I'm going to keep it, too. You sort of got around me with this thing."

Both laughing, they started to get up from the table when there was a shout of recognition from a girl in the next booth.

"Hey, aren't you Sherry Bourden?"

Sherry turned and recognized two of her acquaintances from the Special Procedures Clinic. She had not known them too well, but the Clinic had a "clubby" atmosphere and there were no strangers there.

"Joan and Tammy," Sherry said.

"Right on," the taller of the two replied. "We thought you might remember us, seeing as how you were the smartest one of the bunch up there."

Sherry shook her head. "I don't know about that. I don't think any of us were terribly bright or we wouldn't have been there in the first place. But how are you anyway? You both look like you're about ready to pop."

"Any day now," Tammy said. "Can't be too soon for me."

Sherry introduced Deb and rather breezily explained away the crutches by saying her friend was a klutz and had fallen off her bike on the way from school. It didn't seem to be a matter of concern to either Joan or Tammy and at Deb's suggestion, they all joined forces and continued their "*tour des shoppes*."

Raincoats were not exactly unique wearing apparel in this city on a rainy, snowy afternoon. Accordingly, none of the four girls could be faulted for failing to observe one particular tan coat which appeared a size or two larger than the wearer needed. And as teenagers are prone to do, they were all talking at once while they moved slowly from store to store. A foursome when they left the restaurant, they were now, unknowingly, a group of five; the owner of the large tan coat lurked a discrete distance behind.

They soon found another fascinating window display, one which appealed to them and to countless other shoppers. At least a hundred people, some spilling out into the street, were watching the birth of a baby. A real live "physician" was in the act of delivering a "baby" from an extremely life-like mannequin. It was an exhibit—a performance—put on by a local birthing center depicting the safety of that particular organization in its care of the mother and infant. All the equipment of a modern delivery room was on display and the "homey" atmosphere of a non-hospital setting was emphasized. The "husband" was present as were the two other children, all comfortably arranged on furniture specifically designed and manufactured for the occasion. This birthing center wanted more business and no expense had been spared to entice the unwary woman into this rather faddish method of becoming a mother. Even a small—acceptable—trickle of "blood" was seen to ooze from the birth canal as the "baby" was delivered. It was at this point that Debbie turned her head away and through the rain and snow she saw the Poet. It was the face she had seen in front of the theater. She also saw the arm of the tan rain coat raised quickly to point directly at the silhouette of Tammy's distended belly. She screamed a warning and with all her strength brought one of the crutches up under the extended arm of the would-be killer.

No baby, real or plastic, has ever been born into such instant chaos. The stainless steel missile, redirected by the force of Debbie's crutch, struck and shattered the plate glass window in front of the maternity exhibition. Miraculously none of the live participants in the show were hurt. The knife fell harmlessly among the scattered shards of glass, but its full significance was instantly recognized.

Debbie, favoring her injured leg, fell to the sidewalk. In the few seconds before Sherry could rush to help, mass hysteria had broken out among the predominantly female onlookers.

It had been Patrolman Grant's assignment to "watch over" Deborah Ridgeway for an eight hour period of time. In plain clothes rather than in uniform, he was less than a hundred feet away when he heard the cries and the sounds of panic. He was assaulted by a sense of foreboding and guilt as he ran down the street and into the crowd. He saw the broken window, he saw the knife, and he saw Debbie still down on the sidewalk with Sherry kneeling beside her.

By training, he went first to the one who appeared to be injured. He showed his badge, then assisted Sherry in getting Deb to her feet with the crutches securely in place. "Are you hurt, Miss?" he asked.

"I don't think so," Debbie replied. "I think I'm okay, but did you get him?"

"Get who, Miss?" He didn't really need to ask. He knew the answer.

"He was going to kill my baby." It was Tammy. She had heard Debbie's shout of warning and glanced around just in time to see the tan-sleeved arm pointed directly at her, then forced upward by Debbie's crutch. Others, too, had heard the scream and turned to see a slightly built girl suddenly and violently use her crutch as a weapon against a man—yes, they thought it was a man—in a tan raincoat. Those who saw the action realized now what they had actually witnessed and clustered around, shouting questions at both Debbie and the policeman. Someone else hailed a passing patrol car and it seemed in only seconds the shrieks of multiple police sirens drowned out all other noises from the city.

By prearranged plan, the police quickly cordoned off a five-block area. Nearly every available cop in the city became involved in a frantic effort to encircle the area and corral the Poet. Traffic was stopped, cars and buildings searched. Anyone, male or female, wearing an oversized light raincoat became a suspect with the result that many an innocent citizen had a brief interruption in their civil rights that afternoon.

Bill Arnold was parked at a local drive-in calmly eating a sandwich when his police-band radio told of the Poet's latest public appearance. Fortunately he was near the action and drove as close as he could get to the crowd of people and the ever-growing number of police. Forcing his way through to the center he found Deborah and Sherry being questioned by a detective he knew.

"What in the hell are you two doing here?" he asked.

"I'm about finished with them for the time being, Bill," the detective said. "And since you seem to know each other why don't you take them home? You'll get quite a story on the way. We can always get more details down at headquarters if we need them."

"Good idea. Deb, can you make it though the crowd with those crutches?"

"Mr. Arnold," Sherry said, "my friend Deborah can do anything with those crutches."

Jon had been at home that afternoon leisurely watching football on television when the station suddenly interrupted the game and announced that their cameras were enroute to the downtown area to cover the near certain capture of the infamous Poet. A news broadcaster told of the episode in front of the window display and within minutes, the entire five-block area of the search was pictured from every angle. The television screen was ablaze with flashing red and blue lights and

Jon leaned forward in his chair, hoping to see the actual arrest. An hour went by, then another, and still no announcement or picture of the Poet in chains. The television reporter continued to make promising and hopeful comments but Jon did not share his enthusiasm. Totally discouraged now, he knew he was witnessing still another failure to silence the rhymer.

Bill phoned his story into the paper from the Ridgeway home. It would be page one with an appropriate headline. He took great care to credit the crippled teenager who had prevented another feticide. This time there was no attempt to shield Deborah Ridgeway. She was named and depicted as quite a young heroine, having previously survived an attempt on her own life by the Poet and now saving another. Bill was quite sure the Poet knew who deflected the knife and any attempt at a cover-up could only increase the agitation of this psychotic killer.

Two hours later Bill stood in Judy Ridgeway's kitchen with a beer in one hand and a spatula in the other. He was in charge of the hamburgers and Judy was fixing a salad. The girls were watching their afternoon's excitement being replayed over and over on the evening news.

Not all of the news was televised that night. Almost at the same moment that Bill was turning the hamburgers, Patrolman Grant was facing a very angry Chief O'Neal.

"An oversized, light raincoat. Jesus, man, how many times has such a description been drummed into you? Where in the hell were your eyes?"

"I'm sorry, sir. At least nobody was killed."

"Nobody was killed." The Chief was tired, his big shoulders slumped as he sat behind the desk. "Yes, nobody was killed—this time. But merciful God, man, we could have been through with this horrible business. We could have had that killer. You had a simple task to do—watch that girl. Watch her and all the people around her like your life depended on it. I don't know where your mind was, but one thing's damn sure—it was not on your job."

Without saying anything further the Chief turned his attention to the mounting paperwork on his desk. It was an effective dismissal. Patrolman Grant walked out of the office and quietly closed the door behind him. The Chief was right. He could have made the arrest of a lifetime but had chosen to spend a few minutes chatting with a friend.

That brief conversation, that momentary lapse of attention from his job, meant that his dream of sergeant stripes was now a nightmare.

Bad dreams were not the exclusive right of Patrolman Grant that night. The Poet's sleep was interrupted constantly by visions of the girl with the crutches. She was a reminder of a failure in the past and the cause of yesterday's debacle—the third knife to go astray. More care, more planning would be needed for #8. Somehow it must be sensational. Maybe a prediction, a forewarning would add to the drama. And today's mail had brought still another letter. A literature teacher from high school had written asking permission to forward information to a Dr. Jon Erickson. Only two letters so far and the Poet remained hopeful the warning poem would eliminate the need for more lethal measures to deal with the meddlesome physician.

CHAPTER XII

Jon hadn't purposely ignored Kathy's advice—her warning—that he take his poem, his list of suspects and all related matters down to Chief O'Neal; he just hadn't found a convenient time. Now, several weeks after showing Kathy the poem which threatened his life, Jon drove down to police headquarters.

The Chief didn't look up until he had read all of the material which Jon had placed on his desk. He was not smiling when he finished and told Jon, "Doctor, it's a wonder one of my boys hasn't found you in some alley with your throat slit from ear to ear."

"I know, Chief. I should have talked to you before I got so involved."

"Well, its done now. And we might be able to use some of this," and he passed his hand over the papers Jon had given him. "But there's no question in my mind that you're in some danger, Doctor, and the Poet's already given you the best advice possible, so watch every step you make. I'll assign a patrol car to cover your neighborhood more frequently than usual."

"Thanks, Chief. And if I get any return correspondence from any of those people I'll bring it down to you."

"Doctor," and the Chief's tone softened a little, "I know you want this bastard off the street. So do we."

They shook hands then and Jon left for the hospital, a little more concerned about his personal safety than when he had driven to police headquarters thirty minutes earlier.

Jon was not the only occupant of the city to now walk the streets with fear. Two hundred extra police had been hired but their visible presence served only to increase the apprehension among all the citizens. The additional blue uniforms circulating through the Christmas shoppers were mute testimony to the skulking danger which everyone knew was waiting to take another life. It was the day before Christmas and there had been no sign of the Poet since the aborted effort just before Thanksgiving. One enterprising reporter suggested placing a number on the front page of the daily newspaper. This numerical headline would denote the days since the last appearance of the killer. Older and wiser heads prevailed and this grisly reminder of the city's shame was never sent to press.

A pall hung over police headquarters. A week ago someone had brought in a small noble fir. Now, Christmas Eve day and the little tree remained bare of any ornaments; an exhibit of the general mood in the building. All were aware of the criticism pointed at them by various levels of society. The newspaper editorials had been particularly harsh, even to the point of a personal attack on Chief O'Neal. There were rumors of a lawsuit against the city and police by the parents of the boy who had been the accidental victim in front of the Elvis Presley movie. And within the past week the business community joined in the assault. Pre-Christmas sales were down 2.9 percent from last year and quite naturally the police were blamed.

Against this background of aggravations, a package arrived for Chief O'Neal. As a rule, any delivery, large or small, addressed to the Chief of Police was carefully inspected before it was delivered to his office. Somehow this parcel managed to avoid scrutiny by x-ray and other detection devices. Probably this was because of its innocent and attractive Christmas wrappings.

Chief O'Neal was alone when he started to take off the ribbons and bright paper. **Peace On Earth, Good Will Toward Men,** he remembered later, was emblazoned in blood-red print on the white ribbon.

The Chief was ordinarily a man who exercised sensible precautions, but today his guard was down and he started to open the box with all the enthusiasm of a small child on Christmas morning. Expectantly, he removed the tissue paper, then let out a bellow of rage which was heard two floors down: "Somebody get in here—now!"

They did. Sergeants, lieutenants, and secretaries all came rushing into his office.

"Look at this," he yelled. "That son of a bitch, I'll get him. I'll hang that bastard if it's the last thing I do."

Shaking and nearly apoplectic with rage, Chief O'Neal sat down and shoved the box over where the others could see.

Inside was a doll, a delicate little blonde-haired doll dressed in white. A small pillow had been appropriately placed to simulate a pregnancy. Stabbed through the pillow and into the body of the doll was a stainless steel knife. Red ink stained the dress around the edge of the blade.

One of the secretaries paled and sat down in a nearby chair. A tough old sergeant, hardened by years on the force, turned away swearing softly to himself.

The Chief, his composure only partially restored, stood up and barked out an order: "You," and he pointed to one of his lieutenants, "get the lab people up here to go over this thing with a fine tooth comb. I don't want it touched until they have checked and photographed every inch of it."

"There's a note in there, Chief," someone said. "You can dig it out without disturbing anything else. They can fingerprint it later."

Carefully, using a pair of tweezers from his desk drawer, Chief O'Neal extracted a piece of writing paper and laid it on his desk. "It's the Poet, alright," he said. "Listen to this:

MERRY CHRISTMAS, CHIEF

IT'S THE CHRISTMAS SEASON AND A CHILD
IS BORN
DEAD AND FORLORN
CHRISTMAS BRINGS NO JOY
IT'S ANOTHER BOY
NO VIRGIN BIRTH IS THIS
NOR DID THE ARROW MISS
PRETTY GIRLS WHO LIVE IN SIN
FIGHT A BATTLE THEY CANNOT WIN
LITTLE BOYS WITHOUT A FATHER
NO ONE WANTS TO BOTHER
I KNOW THEIR WAYS, I'LL TRACK THEM DOWN
ONE LESS BASTARD IN THIS TOWN
THE SKIES ARE GRAY, THE WEATHER COLD
PRECIPITATION HAS BEEN FORETOLD
BEFORE THIS YEAR DOES GO
LOOK FOR BLOOD UPON THE SNOW

The Chief looked up from the paper, his face set and grim. "All Christmas leaves are canceled," he said. "I want half the patrolmen in uniform and half in civvies. And I want this little message," he pointed to the poem, "to be seen by the experts who have seen the other little philosophical jewels that maniac has left."

By that afternoon most of the reports were in. As expected, there were no revelations. The outside wrappings of the package were smudged with prints of postal employees and members of the police force who had handled it. Inside was sterile. The doll was one of literally thousands on sale for Christmas. The print of the poem was by typewriter, probably an old portable, and the paper common.

These were not the only disappointments the Chief was to suffer this day. Months ago the police had established a register on certain individuals who might have ties to the Poet. Three from Jon's list of six were added to the file following his visit to headquarters. The other three were already on the police file of suspects. Over the past two months there had been a twenty-four-hour watch on some of these people, ordered by the Chief. Now, the day before Christmas, he personally interviewed every officer who had been involved in this assignment. Their daily reports dating back to before the pre-Thanksgiving episode had been carefully studied, but now, more desperate for positive findings, he decided to hear from them directly and question their activities on that particular Saturday. The discussions were not productive. A few of those on the list were proven clearly innocent, while for others doubts remained. But the surveillance was far from perfect. The team assigned to Dr. Miller, for example, had followed him to a Church meeting on Saturday morning then picked him up again when he and his family came home that evening. This left a gap of several hours during which time the aborted attack on Tammy had taken place.

"What church was it?" the Chief wanted to know.

"Pentecostal, out on Sunnyview near the park."

"I know where it is. What makes you think he stayed there all that time?"

"We didn't see him leave, sir. He's quite a religious man. We interviewed some of the parishioners and they all said some very nice things about him."

"And probably would lie for him. Do you think you can trust those people?"

"I think you can, sir. Particularly on something as important as this."

"You'd better hope so. But I don't like it. He was out of your sight for too damn long."

"Out of sight for too damn long" was the same conclusion the Chief gave to the team watching Donald Parker on that Saturday afternoon. They had seen him go into the Clinic building in the morning and come out late that night. "Could you actually see him in his office?" the Chief asked.

"No, sir. All he has is a little, bitty window in that office of his and there's something shoved up against that. But the lights were on until ten minutes after eight."

"But you couldn't actually see him in the office?"

"No, sir. We didn't honestly have him in view for several hours."

"That's too damned long."

The final group to report found the Chief in a sour and exasperated mood. But he couldn't fault this team for letting their quarry get out of sight. Their responsibility was a young man employed as an orderly at the Special Procedures Clinic. They had followed him day and night, the nights being more entertaining.

"We didn't lose him for one minute, Chief. Quite a cocksman. You know those special field glasses the department issued us? Well, this guy never pulls his window shades and hell, we could count the pimples on the ass of every broad he had in that apartment."

"I'm not interested in his sex life. Any of the other suspects come to his place?"

"No, sir."

"Did you have him under observation last Saturday?"

"Yes, sir. All day long. As I said, he doesn't cover his windows and we saw every move he made. He didn't go out until late in the evening and we were able to follow him then, too."

"Alright. This conversation has all been recorded, you know. So read it when my secretary has time to type it up. Oh, and one more thing. You didn't happen to see this guy buying a doll anytime in the past month, did you?"

"No, sir."

"Okay. Just grasping at straws. You might ask the other officers anyway. Never know what might turn up."

As he left the building late that night, Chief O'Neal simply waved to the desk sergeant. He knew she was on duty again tomorrow and would miss most of the Christmas holiday with her family. He didn't have the heart to wish her a Merry Christmas.

At the Ericksons' the next morning where there was no gloom or depression, it was a Merry Christmas. And it was a white Christmas. A light snow covered the lawn and trees. The Judge was coming for dinner later in the day and at Kathy's suggestion, Bill Arnold was invited with Judy and her daughter.

"I'm glad Debbie is coming," Kathy said. "She needs a little change in scenery from home and school, particularly with that policeman assigned to follow her around all the time. Does he go to school with her, Jon?"

"According to Bill, he does. Just sort of hangs around watching for anything or anybody out of the ordinary."

"Well, she's still a kid and they seem to get something extra out of Christmas. It makes it more fun for us, too."

"Oh, that reminds me," Jon said, "I forgot to give you this when we were exchanging gifts this morning." And he tossed a small package on the counter where Kathy was getting a pie ready for the oven.

"Jon, that's not fair. We agreed not to get anything extra this year."

"It's not much, Kate. Actually just a little symbolism."

"Symbolism?" Kathy frowned and looked at her husband. "Symbolism for what?"

"Open it up. You'll understand."

Actually more curious than pleased, Kathy cut loose the tape and tore off the paper. It was a dial pack for birth control pills—empty. She closed her eyes and shook back the tears. "Jon. Jon Erickson, you want a baby. You really do."

"But it'll have to wait 'till after dinner. We have company coming you know, Kate."

"You devil. I'm going to frame this and hang it in the bedroom just in case you change your mind."

"I won't. But seriously, Kate, I don't want any more poems dedicated to you."

"I know what you mean. Agreed. No little Ericksons until the Poet is caught."

It was a friendly and sociable group that gathered around the Erickson table that afternoon. The patriarch, of course, was Judge Donovan, Bill Arnold was the storyteller and Jon the near-perfect host. In the evening, with the company gone, the house quiet and the leftovers out of sight in the kitchen, Jon and Kathy sat in front of a roaring fire reliving a very good day.

"Nice to be with friends," Kathy said. "I felt sort of cut off from the troubles of the world today. It felt good, too."

"It did, didn't it? And did you notice, nobody even mentioned the Poet—not once."

"Nobody wanted to. Very pleasant to be rid of him for a day. Too bad he can't be erased that easily from real life."

But the Poet was real life. The Poet was also real death. And the day after Christmas, the day of major post-Christmas sales and large crowds, the spring-fired knife killed again.

Jon was off call, his office closed, and he and Kathy were having a mid-morning cup of coffee when Bill Arnold appeared at the front door. "I left my gloves over here last night," he said. "Knew you two were going to be home so I thought you might give me a little coffee and my gloves, but I don't have time now. Damn Poet got another one." Bill gave a vicious stabbing motion to his belly. "It's not too far from here. I'm going to cover it. Want to come along, Jon?"

Jon looked at his wife. She just nodded. He grabbed his coat, gave her a quick kiss and was gone. Kathy stood for a minute by the open door watching the car disappear down the street, the snow swirling in back. Then, almost by reflex she put her hands over her abdomen where the steel knife had killed her baby. She closed the door quietly and went back to the cup of coffee left on the kitchen table. She had managed to put all thoughts of that day aside, deep into her subconscious. But now they came rushing back, the pain, the loss. She had been the strength during those first few days following the death of their son as Jon struggled with his own emotions. She had even comforted her mother and father during the two weeks spent at home. No more. She was alone and she wept.

Bill put his "Press" sign against the windshield and double-parked not too far from the shopping complex where the Poet had struck; he and Jon walked quickly through the crowd that was, eerily, almost silent. An ambulance attendant recognized Jon and motioned him over to the all-too-familiar site of a pregnant teenager down on the sidewalk. But there were no cries of shock or pain. The girl lay motionless.

"'Fraid we can't use you, Doc," a paramedic said. "She took it in the front. Must have hit a hell of a big artery. She was dead when we got here."

"Son of a bitch," was all Jon could say and he knelt down and automatically checked the carotid pulse. There was no familiar thump beneath his fingers. He stood up and looked for his friend. "I want to leave pretty soon, Bill. I think I'd better get home and be with Kathy when this thing gets on radio and television."

"Okay. Just a few minutes."

They both watched as the emergency medical techs from the ambulance covered the girl's body with a blanket and tenderly lifted her over onto a stretcher. There was a small pool of blood underneath her and it was gradually seeping over to stain the white, fresh snow.

Kathy was slowly straightening up the kitchen when Jon came home. There were no tears, but he knew she'd been crying. Without a word he went over to where she was standing and put his arms around her.

"I heard all the news on the radio," she said quietly. "Did you know her, Jon? Had you seen her at the Clinic?"

Jon stared out the kitchen window for a minute. "Yup," he said, "cute little kid. I've seen her a couple of times."

Kathy leaned over the sink and bathed her face in cold water. When she had finished Jon handed her a towel. "How about another cup of coffee, Kate?" he said.

There is no attempt at subtlety when a newspaper covers the killing of a teenager and her unborn baby. A reporter somehow obtained a copy of the poem which Chief O'Neal had received and the following day the front page showed a colored photograph of the bloody snow beneath which, boldly printed, were the last two lines of that verse.

BEFORE THIS YEAR DOES GO
LOOK FOR BLOOD UPON THE SNOW.

Also on the front page was a picture of the victim taken from her high school annual, appearing typically pert and attractive. Surrounding this print of the smiling sophomore were multiple shots showing her as she lay sprawled and lifeless on the cold sidewalk. The Poet's calling card had been found and Bill Arnold included this under his byline:

THIS IS NUMBER EIGHT
A LITTLE LATE
MY PLANS AND ARROW WENT ASTRAY
I AIMED MORE CAREFULLY ON THIS DAY
CHIEF O'NEAL HAS MY POEM
WHICH FORETELLS THIS EVENT
IT MENTIONS THE TARGET
WAS NOT HEAVEN SENT

FOR THOSE LITTLE WHORES
WHO WOULD BEAR A SON
I AGAIN REMIND THEM
GOD'S WILL BE DONE.

Almost the entire first section of the paper was devoted in one way or another to this latest strike by the Poet. The editorial page continued its condemnation of the police force and indignantly demanded that the police commissioner fire Lt. Lenhart and consider asking Chief O'Neal to step down. Despite the harangue, there was no visible sign of change at headquarters. Commissioner Braun, showing considerably more fortitude than usual, ignored the paper's advice and stayed with Lt. Lenhart and the Chief.

In January, the Ericksons learned that Judge Donovan had suffered a heart attack. They both drove down to Salem that afternoon. They found their friend to be in good spirits, buoyed by the cardiologist's report of minimal heart muscle damage. And they were gratified to see how the elderly jurist maintained the dignity of the bench even as a patient in the stark, electronic surroundings of a coronary care unit. Of course the talk turned to the Poet as soon as the usual greetings were exchanged.

"You know, Jon," the Judge said, "I keep up with that God-forsaken feticide business and your name comes out in the papers occasionally. One time you were quoted as being a little critical of

Lieutenant Lenhart. Be careful of that man, Jon. Keep your skirts clean around him. Don't cross him, just do your job. It's okay to let your hair down with me and with Kathy and with that newspaper friend of yours —he seems pretty reliable. But leave the Lieutenant alone. Let him hang himself."

"I thought I might arrange the knot for him."

"No, leave him alone. You'll be in that city long after he's gone."

"I hope so. But you're right. And Kathy said about the same thing. It won't be easy but I'll watch my tongue when he's around."

The Judge's comments regarding Lieutenant Lenhart were on Jon's mind the next day as he drove to the hospital. The poem, too. And as much as he resented the necessity, he found himself checking his car more thoroughly before he got in and being very alert to the people around him. He was thinking of Kathy, too. They didn't talk about it much, but it was pretty obvious the Poet had been paid to put a knife in her. By whom? One of her patients? Doubtful, Jon thought. Dr. Miller? Possible. The violent death of his ex-wife placed the Clinic counselor in a possible alliance with the Poet. Such a union could have led to the death of Jon and Kathy's son. But how had Miller developed a relationship with the Poet? How had he met him—or her, as Kathy insisted? Too many questions and not enough answers.

One of the emergency room physicians was in the lounge when Jon walked in and poured himself a cup of coffee. "Hi, Jon," he said. "I admitted a patient of yours last night. She said she had been one of your infertility patients."

"Oh. I was out of town and didn't hear about it. Did you try to get ahold of me?"

"No, this wasn't quite down your alley. Name is Stephanie Van Osborn and she had the shit beat out of her."

"You're kidding. By whom?"

"Don't know, she wouldn't tell me. I turned her over to one of the trauma boys. I don't think anything was broken, just battered and bent. She'll be here a few days."

"I haven't seen her for quite awhile. Tubes were blocked from an old pelvic infection. But the last time I saw her she said she was leaving her husband and wasn't interested in any sort of a repair job. Good thing. I don't think it's possible to get those tubes working again—they're shot."

"Well, she was admitted to 6 North if you want to see her. I don't know what she looked like before, but she sure as hell didn't look very good last night."

Curiosity, plus at least a small degree of compassion, brought Jon to 6 North after making morning rounds on his surgical and obstetrical patients. He found Stephanie's name on the door and, exercising the inferred right of all physicians, walked in without knocking.

The emergency room physician had not exaggerated. It was actually difficult to recognize Stephanie, the spoiled, petulant beauty now an ugly mask of dark bruises. There was no mistaking her other visitor, however. Lt. Lenhart was seated on the edge of the bed. He dropped her hand which he had been holding and jumped to his feet. "Y'all forget how to rap on a door?" he asked.

Remembering his manners, and his recent resolve, Jon said, "Sorry. Just habit. I'll leave if you want."

Stephanie motioned him in. Her lips were swollen and cut and she spoke with difficulty. "No, don't go, Doctor," she said. "I'm glad to see you. I didn't think you'd come by."

"The E.R. doctor told me you were here. Sorry to see you got banged up." And still wearing a friendly smile, Jon addressed the detective: "This isn't the best of circumstances, Lieutenant, but better than the cause of most of our meetings."

Lt. Lenhart agreed. "That's true," he said. "Mah friend here didn't get killed. Sure got roughed up, though. Sure wish she'd tell me who did it. Ah'd get the son of a bitch jailed, that's for sure."

"You're right, Billy, I didn't get killed. I don't want the police involved and I don't want my friends involved and that includes you."

Jon felt himself to be the odd man out in this conversation and exited with as much grace as he could muster. "Let me know if I can help you, Stephanie," he said. "Nice to see you, Lieutenant."

Lt. Lenhart merely nodded in his direction but Stephanie asked him to be sure and return in a day or two. "I'll be more presentable then," she said.

Back in the hall, somewhat bewildered by what he had just seen, Jon took the elevator down and started for his office. In the car he was still muttering to himself. "I'll bet her husband did this. She leaves him and next I see her with Donald Parker and now Lenhart. Maybe Parker did it. That girl does get around, but somebody's going to kill her if she doesn't watch out."

It was Friday, which meant a full office in the morning and Special Procedures Clinic in the afternoon. Sarah Tompkins had an appointment for 11:00 and as usual his secretary had allowed extra time. She knew there was no way to get Sarah in and out in the space allotted for the average patient.

To all outward appearances motherhood had not changed Sarah

other than the physical fact of her carrying a baby girl. Healthy and alert, the infant was a miniature of her mother. Even at this age her narrow face held bright and inquisitive eyes. Mother and daughter arrived at 10:45 and at the first whimper the baby was promptly put to breast. Modesty was not one of Sarah's few virtues. She knew there were ways to suckle an infant with a certain amount of propriety and without appearing prudish. But Sarah chose her own method. Ignoring others in the crowded waiting room, including a few husbands, she unzipped her sweater to the navel and pulled it completely off one shoulder. Convenience dictated she not wear a bra and with the breast fully exposed the infant found the nipple with ease and began to noisily fill her stomach. A few stares of disgust and censure were snubbed and Sarah continued to nurse the baby when she was called in—before her appointment time—by a very alert office nurse who, with a smile, reported the scene to Jon.

"Why don't you just take the sweater off and let her have a go at both breasts?" Jon asked when he came in the exam room.

"It might be doubly offensive to some of the hoi polloi in your waiting room."

"Could be," Jon agreed with an indifferent shrug of his shoulders. "So what brings you in, Sarah? You pregnant again?"

"I thought you couldn't get pregnant when you're nursing."

"Less apt to, but it's always possible."

"If I remember right, Doctor, you also have to get screwed to get pregnant."

"Usually. There are other ways—rather mechanical and scientific—but it can be done."

"I prefer the old-fashioned way and I haven't been an old-fashioned girl since this thing came out." She gave her baby a friendly slap on its padded rear.

"You haven't answered my question. What brings you in?"

"I want my tubes tied."

"Let's see," and Jon looked at her chart which lay open on his desk. "You're twenty-five—twenty-six now, aren't you, Sarah?"

"What's that have to do with it?"

"I've known a lot of people your age who change their mind. Damned hard to get pregnant after your tubes are tied."

"They're my tubes. I can do what I want with them and I want them tied."

"And if I don't do it?"

"Somebody else will."

"I'll think about it, Sarah. I'd rather see you on pills. You probably won't ever change your mind, but at least the pills give you an option."

"And what do I do in the meantime? I want to nurse this little shit for awhile. Can't take the pills while you're nursing."

"Oh, you can, but it isn't a good idea. There are other methods, you know."

"Oh sure, rubbers," and she gave him a look of repulsion. "I like flesh touching flesh, Doctor. I don't want anybody wearing an inner-tube climbing on me. And don't give me your lecture on AIDS, either."

"I have a pretty good one."

"Save it. I don't do drugs. And anybody that gets in bed with me better not have any needle marks. Stupid habit."

"There are some bisexuals in this world. Did you forget that?"

"Remember, I have a few old-fashioned ways about me. Any hint the guy swings both ways and he's out. I think the penis belongs in a vagina not in somebody's asshole."

"So happens I share your opinion on that, but let's get back to the subject and the subject is pregnancy and how to avoid it. Just for laughs I could suggest abstinence."

"You're right. That's for laughs. Go on."

"Contraceptive creams and foams are fairly safe as long as you're nursing but whether you like it or not, condoms are the safest. And they usually protect you from all sorts of other things like venereal disease—including AIDS. You can get all those bugs from good old heterosexual intercourse, you know?"

"Okay, okay, you got your lecture in. So if I use all this advice and still get pregnant you going to hook up that vacuum and suck it out of there?"

"If that's what you want at the time, yes I will."

"I want that last statement on tape."

Jon was a little offended by her remark. "Come off it, Sarah," he said. "I've never lied to you."

"Not a good time to start, either." She was not joking.

Jon let this pass and changed the subject. "Did you ever give that kid a name? You hadn't by the time you left the hospital."

"Molly."

"Molly?" Jon asked, half frowning in surprise. "I can't believe that."

Sarah's defenses rose immediately. "What's wrong with that name?"

"Nothing, Sarah, nothing at all. I like it, but I think I expected something—something more exotic from the mind of Sarah Tompkins."

"She's the one who has to live with it. I considered Sabra or Scheherazade but didn't think it would fit. Her father's a redhead and I think she got his hair gene."

"Well, she's a good-looking little girl. Has her father seen her?"

"Only once. We had a little get-together in my apartment. His lawyer was there—my lawyer was there—and Molly was the guest of honor."

"None of my business, but sounds like your red-haired doctor friend is going to do some financing."

"Oh, yes," Sarah smiled. "For Molly and her mother, and for a long time."

"If I had any worries about your future, Sarah, I think you just dispelled them," and Jon folded the chart and started to walk out.

"Wait a minute. Don't run off. Didn't I see your picture in the paper the other day bent over that kid in the snow—the one that got wiped out?"

"Yes. That was sort of a bad day."

"For that kid, sure. But I don't know about the others. I think they're better off. They don't have a brat to pack around with them."

"How 'bout you, Sarah? Would you feel that way if Molly died tomorrow?"

"I'm not sixteen, Doctor. I take good care of what I produce."

"Not a very chivalrous attitude."

"Look at me. Do I look like the chivalrous type? If I had my way I'd abort every one of those little sex pots. Most of them are going to be shitty mothers and wind up on welfare taking my tax dollars."

"Sounds like you've been talking to the Poet recently, Sarah. That's his line you're spouting."

"I didn't say I'd spring a knife at them. I said I'd abort them."

"You might be stomping on somebody's constitutional rights, you know. Freedom of expression, freedom of choice, right to counsel, right to—"

"Okay, okay," Sarah interrupted. "If you won't let me do it my way, let the Poet handle it. Or if that doesn't suit your fancy, maybe a piece of barbed wire about half way up their vagina would help. You've heard the expression, 'tear off a piece of ass', Doctor?"

Jon acknowledged that he had.

"Well, I'd like to see something else get torn in the process."

Molly was asleep now; Sarah tucked her breast back into the sweater then reached for a Kleenex to wipe around the baby's mouth. Jon was surprised at how gentle Sarah was with her child. It was the first time he had seen any evidence of real love from this abrasive and frequently annoying woman.

"You like that kid, don't you, Sarah?"

Sarah, almost by instinct, hugged the baby close to her chest. "I love her, Doctor," she said, "and she needs me." Sarah looked over at Jon with just a hint of a smile. "Okay, so I'm not quite the hardass you thought. Now get your prescription pad out and write me some pills. I'll start them when I wean this little squirt."

In contrast to Sarah's varying moods, few of which were particularly cheerful, Jon found Frances McGraw to be almost effusive in her welcome when he arrived early for Clinic. She was in the staff lounge acting as hostess for Donald Parker's birthday party. Her usual severe hair style had been softened somewhat by the simple addition of a bright ribbon and even her voice had lost its commanding, authoritative tone. She was obviously enjoying her role. Donald had been coaxed away from his microscope and test tubes and was standing self-consciously over by a large plastic basin full of punch. There was a cake in the middle of the room with bright blue frosting which spelled out "**Happy Birthday Donald.**" With this as a tipoff as to the purpose of the party, Jon walked over to convey his best wishes to the guest of honor. Lawrence Miller was the last to join the festivities, but once there he moved quickly from group to group, chatting amiably with all who would listen. His smiles and overt display of good fellowship seemed a little forced and Jon wondered if it was all just an effort to cement his relationship with Clinic personnel. The most recent hallway scene with Kathy had not improved his position at the University and he apparently knew that he needed to regain favor and status.

The gathering for Donald lasted only about thirty minutes but it created a friendly and genial atmosphere throughout the Clinic that afternoon. It confused Jon. Three of his listed suspects for the role of the Poet were at that party and not one showed any hostility toward him. Frankie, he had never seen her more sociable and outgoing. Donald, the reluctant party recipient, had appeared embarrassed by all the attention and seemed to want to stay by Jon's side. Larry Miller gripped Jon's hand in greeting and acted like a long-lost friend. And again, the strange reluctance on the part of any one to talk about the feticides. Jon did notice how flustered the Clinic Director appeared when one of the medical students imprudently asked if a poem had been prepared for the occasion. Frankie muttered something about not doing poems and quickly changed the subject.

Jon was called to St. Elizabeths about midway through the Clinic and he delivered a healthy baby girl just before five o'clock. It was too late to go back to the University and after seeing his other patients he decided to drop by Stephanie's room. This time he knocked.

"Doctor Erickson, Stephanie. May I come in?"

"Just a minute, Doctor."

The door was slightly open and without real intention Jon noticed

Stephanie hurriedly replace her hospital gown and apply fresh lipstick before calling him again.

"You can come in now, Doctor."

She was alone and the new gown was quite chic and very low. Her face was recovering from the recent beating and the little pout was real, not just the swelling from someone's fist.

"I was afraid you'd forgotten me," she said.

"Oh, no, Stephanie. I knew there'd be lots of people to keep you company and you look much better. About ready to go home?"

"Tomorrow, if I can get somebody to take me. I don't want to ask Clark. I guess you know we've separated. I don't know what I ever saw in him anyway, Doctor. I like a good time. I like to go places. Not Clark. He's moody, doesn't want people around and spends all his time in that shop of his. At least I guess he does. I don't see him very often."

"Talk to social service. They'll find someone to give you a ride."

"No, I'll call Billy Ray. He's been real nice to me lately and I sort of like him, too. I guess you saw that the other day when you came in. I know he wants to arrest the guy who beat me up."

"How come you won't tell him who did it?"

"Personal. And I have some plans to even the score."

"That could be dangerous, Stephanie."

"A little, maybe, but believe me, somebody in this town is going to regret he ever laid a hand on me."

"Just be careful, Stephanie. You might wind up back in here a lot worse off than you were before."

"I don't think so, Doctor. I know just how to handle this one. But thanks."

"And I'd better be going. Have to check on that patient I just delivered."

As he got up to leave Jon noticed that the tiny straps of Stephanie's nightgown had fallen down on her arms. He resisted the temptation to give a parting and professional pat on her bare shoulder. "Take care," he said, "and good luck."

"Bye, Doctor. Thanks for dropping in."

Jon was out of a potentially compromising situation. He knew it and breathed a sigh of relief as he walked down the stairs to obstetrics before heading home. He hoped Kathy would already be there. It was always nice to see her car when he opened the garage door.

She was not only home, dinner was in the oven and she had ample time to sit with him over a glass of wine to discuss their activities of the day. Hers had been good. The psych department was testing a new drug for depression and the preliminary results were encouraging.

"I could have used some of that while you were gone, Kate," Jon said as he touched his glass to hers.

"Glad to hear you admit it, you rascal. Hate to think I was the only one going around in a perpetual gloom those two months."

"Oh, no. You had company. You just didn't know it. Now, you want some more wine or are we ready to eat?"

"I'm sure its ready. Come on, help me put it on the table."

During dinner Jon told of his visit to Stephanie's room and her not-too-subtle display of bare skin. "Damn it, Kate," he said, "I was afraid some nurse would come in and see that nightgown about to fall off and me eyeballing the whole scene. And that isn't the first time she's done it. Happened in the office and Nell rescued me then."

"Jon, that lady—and I use the term loosely—would screw you one day and sue you the next. She is definitely not your type."

"You're my type, Kate, and don't you forget it."

There was a call from obstetrics at 9:30. The intern reported that one of Jon's patient—a multip having her third baby—was in and already dilated to six centimeters. She was also bleeding far more than average.

"Think you'll be very long?" Kathy asked as Jon knotted his tie and reached for his jacket.

"Don't think so. Couple of hours, maybe. I'll call if it'll be any longer."

"It's windy out tonight, Jon. Maybe a few branches down, so don't try to break any speed records on your way to the hospital."

"Don't worry. I'll be careful. Which reminds me, you be careful too. The other night you forgot to set the security system alarm when I went to the hospital. I know we have that cop making frequent rounds in the neighborhood, thanks to Chief O'Neal, but I'd feel better if I knew that alarm was on."

"You sure its any good, Jon? We haven't tried it out, you know."

"That police sergeant told me it was the best in the business. Ties right into the police department and that can save time in an emergency."

"I think if I were a burglar sort of casing the area, so to speak, and saw that police cruiser making the rounds, I'd find another neighborhood."

"So would I, Kate, but let's face it, if all we had to worry about was the occasional stupid burglar I don't think the Chief would have that cruiser out here."

"I'll set it, Jon. Don't worry."

CHAPTER XIII

Cars were rarely parked along the street in this residential area. What few there were, Jon assumed belonged to neighbors or friends and never paid much attention to them as he drove by. Tonight was no exception; his mind was totally occupied with concern for the patient in labor who was bleeding. He hardly saw the older car which was parked about one hundred yards down the street from the Erickson home. As soon as Jon had passed, a man sat up in the parked car, a man wearing a Halloween mask. He took out a cellular phone from a small leather bag on the seat beside him, leaving a .38 caliber pistol and homemade knife in the satchel. A minute later Kathy answered the insistent ringing of her phone.

"This is Kathleen Erickson," she said.

"Is the doctor there?"

She thought the voice was vaguely familiar and without thinking she answered, "No, he's gone to the hospital. Who is this speaking, please?"

"I'm a friend of his. When do you expect him home?"

Kathy wondered if there was a deliberate effort on the part of the caller to disguise his voice. It seemed to come in short bursts and her answer to his question was purposely vague: "I don't know. He didn't say."

"Did he go to deliver a baby?"

Something wasn't just right about this call and Kathy felt a little uneasy. "I really have no idea," she said. "If you'll give me your name and number I'll have the doctor call when he gets home."

"Never mind," and the caller abruptly hung up.

"Probably a screwy husband of one of Jon's patients," Kathy said to herself as she replaced the phone. "Or could be one of my goof balls."

But memories came back—memories of a savagely ransacked apartment and of the knife that killed her baby. She checked the alarm system. It was armed but that did not completely stifle a growing feeling of anxiety. Exercise. She knew that most psychiatrists agree that if someone is worried or concerned they can usually get over it by intense concentration and effort on an unrelated matter. With this philosophy in mind, she changed into a sweat suit and climbed on her exercycle. "I'll run this damn thing 'till I drop," she said aloud. "Then I bet I can sleep and Jon won't catch me all in a stew sitting up waiting for him."

Ten minutes later, sweating profusely and her pulse rate over 150, she slid off the bike and turned on the shower. The intense exercise followed by literally gallons of hot water had the desired effect. She was relaxed and ready for bed.

She had just stepped out of the shower when the lights suddenly went off. Naked and wet, she groped for a towel and, thinking a fuse had blown, started for the living room. There was no light in the bedroom or hall. She remembered leaving the kitchen overhead on. It was dark there, too. She was frightened now and tightened the towel around her as she felt the way over to Jon's chair where there was a telephone. No light behind the buttons. And no dial tone. She was cold and shivering, the wet towel of little comfort. Then she remembered her panic when after seeing her apartment in ruins she couldn't start the car. And how foolish she must have looked while trying to start the motor with the automatic transmission in Drive. Just about as ridiculous as I look right now, she thought, standing nearly nude in the middle of a dark living room. There had been no cause for that previous fright and using this logic to calm her present fears she started in the direction of the kitchen to get some candles.

A noise from the bedroom alerted her. It was a scratching sound and was repeated when she listened more closely. It was windy outside, she had warned Jon about that; the noise must be a tree branch buffeted by the wind and scraping the window. In her familiar kitchen she quickly found the box of candles which were reserved for the dining room table. A minute later the warm glow of candlelight eased the darkness. Reassured, she decided against checking the fuse box, assuming the same wind which caused the noise in the bedroom had knocked out the power and telephone lines. Lights from the neighbor's house were burning brightly, but she failed to notice this and started back toward the bedroom. Sleep was out of the question now, but it might be possible go to the kitchen and read by candlelight until Jon got home. She was in the bathroom looking for her bathrobe when the imagined tree branch struck more forcibly at the bedroom window. Tucking the towel over her breasts she picked up her only light source and with reckless determination walked toward the presumed location of the annoyance.

The window crashed in just as she entered the bedroom. Shocked by the sound of splintering glass Kathy instinctively held the candle up higher to see what damage had been done. It was not a bright light which came from this dining room taper but it was enough, enough for her to see a knife slash through the bedroom drapes. She screamed and in a futile, impotent gesture hurled the candle at the hand which held the knife. When she ran down the hall she thought, or imagined, she saw still another figure at the front door. Trapped, afraid to go out the back, she crawled behind the large davenport in the living room and waited for the footsteps she knew would be coming down the hall.

Kathy had rarely thought of her own death. Even on the crippled jetliner coming in from Boston to meet Jon she knew a crash was possible but was fairly sure they would get down safely. And during the ambulance ride with the Poet's knife deep in her side her thoughts were of her baby. It didn't occur to her that she might die. But she was alone now and helpless. Calmly, peacefully, she began to whisper the almost forgotten words of her youth, "Hail Mary, full of grace, the Lord is with thee. Blessed art thou and the fruit of thy womb, Jesus." As she did so she also remembered that day in the operating room when she kissed her dead son.

Sergeant Cooney was following his Chief's orders and making frequent sweeps through the area in his patrol car when the police radio told him the alarm system had gone off and the telephone was dead at the Erickson home, 2250 Viewcrest. The Sergeant remembered the Ericksons. He had been there only a few days ago and at the doctor's insistence he had checked the entire alarm system, room to room, and made a detailed exploration of the exterior. He also remembered Mrs. Erickson; it was cold the day he'd been at the her home and she'd insisted he come in from the outside for a cup of tea.

"Send a backup to that address," he told the operator, "I'm close and going in right away."

He knew of a little-used roadway which went through the park. It was a short cut to Viewcrest and the Sergeant ran it at 60 miles an hour. He had a bad feeling about this call.

Shotguns were a part of every police car's arsenal. Sgt. Cooney had already unlocked the weapon and had it in his hand when he braked to a stop just short of 2250 Viewcrest, the only house that was dark. He was a big man, but surprisingly agile and quick. Thanks to his recent visit to the Ericksons he was familiar with the house and surroundings. He saw nothing suspicious in the front, so in a running leap he cleared a four-foot hedge and sprinted around the garage and into the back yard. There was just enough light for him to see the outline of a man starting to crawl through the bedroom window.

"Police," the Sergeant yelled. "Stand clear."

Slowly the figure backed away, first his chest, followed by his arms and head. He stood still for a second, then in a lightning quick move he pulled a pistol from his pocket and fired. He got off one round only. Sergeant Cooney brought the twelve-gauge to his shoulder, shot once, pumped and shot again. The man crumpled to the ground.

Jon arrived just twenty minutes later. He had finished his delivery but had somehow missed the police radio message to the hospital requesting him to come home immediately. Without this prior alert he was totally unprepared for the blinding display of police and ambulance lights which surrounded his house. He had one thought—Kathy.

A police car blocked the driveway so he ran the car up on the sidewalk and leaped out. People were everywhere—neighbors, strangers, cops, all with their faces eerily reflecting the multiple flashers. He was briefly detained by one of the policeman who asked him what his business was and why he thought he could park on the sidewalk.

"I'm Doctor Erickson," Jon said. "What the hell's going on? Where's my wife?"

"Sergeant, Sergeant Cooney," the policeman called out. "Doctor Erickson is here."

The Sergeant appeared at the open doorway, his big frame silhouetted by the battery-operated lights within the house. He beckoned to Jon and went down the steps to meet him. "Your wife is not hurt," he said. "Just scared out of her wits by someone who tried very hard to break in to your home. I have her in the living room where there's some light. Come on along. She's anxious to see you."

Two uniformed police were just coming from the bedroom, the bright beam of their flashlights preceding. Jon didn't even see them; he saw only Kathy lying on the davenport covered with blankets.

It was the second time she had seen him cry. This time she joined him.

Repair crews from the power and telephone companies were quick to answer the call. The lights came on a little after midnight. With electricity restored, the furnace started and Kathy began to peel off some of the many blankets the police had piled on her. "Jon, I'm not very well dressed," she said. "Would you get my robe for me? I think I can get up and make some coffee for everybody. At least I've quit shaking."

"You lie still, Kate. I'll get your robe and start the coffee."

"No, please, I want to do it and I want to make some tea for Sergeant Cooney. I remember he drank tea when he was here checking our alarm."

A short time later Kathy went to the kitchen. Once again she was in control of herself and her home. "I must look like hell," she said as she poured hot tea into three china cups. "Didn't even get a chance to comb my hair when I got out of the shower."

She turned to get some napkins and noticed a small hole in the Sergeant's jacket, a stain of fresh blood around it. "My God, Sergeant Cooney, you were hit. He could have killed you."

"Just a scratch. When some two-bit thief tries to draw on you, his first shot is usually wild."

"Not very damned wild," Jon said. "Too close, I'd say. Let me take a look at that."

"Nothing to bother about, Doctor. Just a nick, but I'll drop into the emergency room on my way back to the station. They can make it an official visit and that'll take care of some of the paper work. Frankly, I'm glad he shot first and nicked me. Makes it easier to explain why I killed him with two rounds out of that shotgun."

Other than the police, Jon was the only one allowed to see the result of Sgt. Cooney's act of self-defense. And he was the one who identified the body of Dr. Miller. "I don't understand all this, Sergeant," he said as he poured some coffee for one of the policemen who came into the kitchen. "I suppose this guy could be the Poet, but if he is and he wanted to kill Kathy, why didn't he finish the job when he destroyed our son? And why the mask?" Jon shook his head in disbelief. "We'll be grateful to you for the rest of our lives, but I don't think that body they just hauled away belongs to the Poet."

"More's the pity. I'm afraid you're right. The mask?" And he turned to Kathy. "He didn't want you to identify him. I think he just wanted to scare you within an inch of your life. And I think he very nearly succeeded. Now Ma'am, may I trouble you for a little more sugar for my tea?"

The morning paper echoed the question on the lips of every reader when the headlines blared:

IS IT OVER?

Most of the front page was devoted to the story. There was a full and graphic description of the shootout under Bill Arnold's byline. His sub headline read: Local Psychologist Shot Dead By Police and went on to read:

> Lawrence Miller, Ph.D., was shot and killed while breaking into the home of Jon and Kathleen Erickson at 2250 Viewcrest. Mrs. Erickson, a resident physician in psychiatry at the University Medical School, was alone at the time but was not injured. Her husband, an obstetrician and gynecologist of this city, told police and reporters of the frequent disagreements between his wife and Lawrence Miller regarding patient care. He said the psychologist had become somewhat irrational at times but no one had suspected him capable of violent behavior. One of Dr. Miller's associates, Avery Shaw, disagreed with this appraisal. When contacted following Dr. Miller's death, Mr. Shaw expressed his regret at the tragedy but did not appear surprised. "Larry didn't like that

> woman," Mr. Shaw said. "Felt inferior to her. Told me once he'd like to see her suffer."

Bill had interviewed Sgt. Cooney late that night also, and wrote of the Sergeant's confrontation with Lawrence Miller. In one paragraph readers were given a dramatic description of the gunfire in the backyard at 2250 Viewcrest.

> Sergeant Cooney responded to an alarm at the Erickson home and found a prowler climbing through a window in the rear of the house. He identified himself as the police and ordered the man to stand clear. Instead, according to the Sergeant, the intruder freed himself from the window and quickly fired one round from a pistol he had hidden in his coat. The bullet tore through the Sergeant's jacket, grazing his arm and he immediately returned fire with a twelve-gauge shotgun. Lawrence Miller died instantly with two rounds of double-ought buckshot through his chest.

Bill Arnold, savvy professional that he was, did not believe the long- sought Poet was dead. In his article he acknowledged that there were some similarities between Dr. Miller and the known facts about the serial killer of babies. As an example, he cited the knife found on Dr. Miller's body. But at least on preliminary exam the knife was not a close replica to the knives which had penetrated the wombs of previous victims. Kathleen Erickson had lost an unborn son to the Poet but Kathleen, in Bill's opinion as expressed in the write-up, was an aberration among the feticide targets. She was in her late twenties, married and not a welfare recipient. She had attended the Special Procedures Clinic early in her pregnancy but only to determine the status of her baby. And there was the poem left by her side after the attack which implied the Poet had been paid to perform this job. The final paragraph summarized his doubts:

> The police have not ruled out a personal vendetta against Dr. Kathleen Erickson. Lawrence Miller was known to be extremely insecure in his professional career, abnormally so according to Claudia Hillstrom, a spokesperson for the University Medical School. Ms. Hillstrom suggested that Dr. Miller envisioned Dr. Erickson as a threat to his position as counselor at the Special Procedures

> Clinic. A professor of psychiatry at the school, interviewed by phone at one o'clock this morning, described Dr. Miller's emotional status as 'fragile,' and that he could well have cracked under this imagined danger.
>
> Lawrence Miller, ill-trained Ph.D. and lay minister, may have plotted the death of an illusionary enemy but he does not seem a likely candidate for the role of the city's mass murderer. Chief Michael O'Neal was even more candid when he responded to this reporter's question early this morning. "No," he said, "Sergeant Cooney may have saved a very nice lady from serious harm when he shouldered that shotgun but did he kill the Poet? I don't think so. We don't have him yet. He's still out there."

It had been a restless night for Kathy and Jon and the morning paper was stale news to them. But they did read it and after breakfast both went their separate professional ways. In the psychiatry clinic at the Medical School Kathy was treated with something approaching reverence by her fellow residents and members of the teaching staff. But at the Special Procedures Clinic when Jon dropped by during his lunch hour, the atmosphere was more tense. Dr. Miller may not have been the favorite of many, but the violence of his death was shocking. Not all were exactly sad. One of the nurses caught Jon alone and said, "I'm glad your wife is okay, Doctor Erickson, and I suppose I shouldn't say it but I think it was a good thing that cop was a good shot."

"You think the feticides will stop now?"

"I don't know. I hope so."

"I hope so too," Jon said, "but I doubt it."

A few minutes later he saw Frankie McGraw in the hall. She agreed with Jon; Dr. Miller didn't fit her picture of the Poet. "I just don't think he could do any physical harm to these girls," she said. "He liked them, genuinely so. They couldn't hurt him and they listened to him. That helped his ego and his sense of self-worth. And you know, Doctor Erickson, his advice really wasn't all that bad, unless he was faced with a serious mental problem. Then he was over his head. I thought of him as rather ineffectual but gentle. And I can't imagine he wanted to hurt your wife."

"He did, Frankie. He really wanted to hurt her. Maybe not kill her, but hurt her emotionally and physically. No doubt about it."

"You might be right. But it's still a shock to some of us. Donald Parker and I were talking about him just before you came. We both think the Clinic will miss him. And that reminds me, Donald's going to be gone later this week and asked that you drop by the lab if you happen to come in before your regular time on Friday."

"Thanks. I'll go there now before my office hours start."

He found the lab director hard at work as usual, but worried about the publicity surrounding Dr. Miller's death. Among the many stories in the paper about the psychologist, one told of possible sexual liaisons between Miller and some of the teenage patients. Donald Parker considered this type of reporting irresponsible. He was most concerned that public opinion might bring pressure to close the Clinic. "This is innovative research," he said, "some of the best I've ever been associated with. Unfortunately there are a few crackpots in town that view us as just another abortion clinic."

"Abortion clinic," Jon said, surprised. "I didn't know we'd done any."

"Three, to be precise. Two for Down syndrome and the third for anencephaly. All were picked up on the lab tests we routinely run on the amniotic fluid. The patients requested termination of their pregnancy and the Clinic doctors obliged."

"Before my time here, I guess."

"Yes, I believe so."

"Doing an occasional abortion isn't going to lose your operating funds. And Miller's philandering makes for good newsprint."

"I suppose so." Donald rather absently twisted the adjustments on the microscope for a minute then asked, "Do you think the girls will be able to breathe a little easier now, Doctor?"

"I'd like to think so but I'm going to advise these kids to stick close to home for awhile."

"Yes, I would too. Especially if they're near term with a male baby."

They talked for a few more minutes about other Clinic functions, then Jon excused himself and drove to the office where he found Stephanie Van Osborn a surprising addition to the schedule. She had been released from the hospital in the morning and had called Jon's office saying she had to see him that same day.

"I don't need an exam, Doctor. I just want to talk to you for a few minutes," she said when Jon walked into the exam room.

"Sure, Stephanie. What can I do for you?"

"Well, first, I read the papers and I'm glad your wife wasn't hurt."

"Thank you."

"And I want to talk about my father."

"I don't know him."

"You did."

"I did?" Jon asked, puzzled.

"Yes, as a matter of fact, far better than I did. We rarely saw each other. Lawrence Miller."

Jon got up from his chair and faced a young woman who had just announced her father was the man who wanted to hurt, maybe kill, Kathy. This was not the same Stephanie Van Osborn he had seen in the hospital and in previous visits to the office. No petulance, no coy little flips of hair, no tears. She was harder, tougher.

"You're not kidding," he said.

"Of course not."

"And your mother was the lady found dead in the apartment garage."

"How'd you know that?"

"I know she was the ex-wife of Doctor Miller and I was pretty sure she had a daughter who would be about your age. The police found a baby picture of you in your mother's safety deposit box. At least it sure looks like you now that I know the connection. And whether you like it not, there is a family resemblance between you and your father."

"Yes, that was my mother. She wasn't exactly a lady, but that's no excuse for Lawrence Miller to kill her."

"That's a rather strong statement. I don't think the police are all that sure of who killed your mother."

"Did the police know she was blackmailing him?"

"Yes."

"I saw her not too long ago, I guess about a month before she died. She told me then that she'd seen my father and was going to squeeze some money out of him. At the time, it didn't occur to either one of us that it might be dangerous. Do you think he was the Poet, Doctor?

"No. I don't think so."

"Neither do I."

"You really didn't know him very well at all, did you?"

"No. Oh, we got together occasionally but I don't think he was ever very anxious to see me. I didn't exactly fit in with his new family. I'm Catholic you know. At least I'm supposed to be. Mother was. She was Italian—lived like one and I'm sure she died like one. I'll bet when that knife hit her in the chest her last conscious act was to look around for a priest."

"Are you very upset with his death, Stephanie?"

"Not really. But it's a little shocking, you know, to see your father's name splattered all over the front page of the paper."

"I can well imagine. No matter what you thought of him. Now, is there anything I can do for you?"

"I don't know. I guess I just needed to talk to somebody about it and you're pretty good at listening. And I wanted to ask you about birth control. Do you think I need it?"

"Your tubes look closed on the x-ray, Stephanie, but you can never tell. If it would really foul up your life to get pregnant, then you better use the pills."

"If you write me a prescription can I get it filled in Georgia?"

"Georgia?" Jon asked. "Why Georgia?"

"Billy Ray told me he may have a job lined up there. He doesn't like it here anymore. Wants to quit and go back where he came from. I think I'll go with him."

"I don't get along with Lieutenant Lenhart—you probably know that. But what's his hurry? Doesn't he want to finish up what he's started around here? The last I heard the Poet was still alive and well."

"Billy Ray doesn't think he is. He thinks my father was the Poet."

"He knows better than that. But did it occur to you, Stephanie, that people are going to wonder why the Chief Detective on the feticide case suddenly decides to call it quits and leave the state?"

"Oh, maybe. I'm not going to worry about it. But to be honest I'd rather believe my father did not kill those babies."

"You have a lot of company in that belief. Now, I'll write these out for you," and Jon reached for his prescription pad. "They may not fill them in Georgia so I'll give you enough samples to last three or four months."

"Thank you, Doctor," and she rose to leave.

"You're welcome, Stephanie," Jon extended his hand. "And good luck."

I don't like to see you behind closed doors with that woman," Nell said as soon as Stephanie had left the office.

"She's harmless, Nell. And she's in love with Billy Ray Lenhart."

"They deserve each other."

"She told me the Lieutenant may be leaving town."

"High time. We don't need his type. Hasn't been much good at catching the Poet, either."

"According to Stephanie, Billy Ray thinks the Poet is dead. Killed by that cop at my house last night."

"No way," Nell said. "No way that two-faced, no-good preacher shot those knives. We'll hear from the little rhymer again. I'd bet a month's salary on it."

Had anyone called her bet, there was evidence that afternoon that she would have had an extra month's salary to spend. For as the bet was being offered, Judy Ridgeway was getting off duty at the hospital and walking toward her car in the large parking garage provided by the hospital for employees. Good weather or bad she drove over to

Deborah's school at about this time. No more bike rides until all danger for her daughter had passed.

Today was like all other days since the attempt on Debbie's life except Judy's car was not in its usual parking stall. She checked the number on the pavement, yes, 132, and she was fairly sure she parked in this spot. But she had been called out in the middle of the night for emergency surgery and was sleepy when she came back on duty at seven o'clock this morning. There was always the possibility she could have parked one floor up or in the basement. She walked first to the next level up looking carefully along the way. Nothing. Next, down past her usual area into the basement and again no sign of the car. "Damn it," she said aloud, "that'll teach me to buy a sports car. Somebody must have stolen it. I'll notify security and I'd better find a phone and call Deb's school. They can keep her inside until I get a cab and come after her."

That "somebody" was the Poet and the large rain hat had been replaced by a wig, dark brown like Judy's hair. The car was proceeding cautiously and within the law toward a junior high building several miles away. From a vantage point two blocks past the school, the Poet had often observed the daily repetition of mother picking up daughter. It was worth a try. If she would get in the car the rest would be easy. The body and the car could be left on a side street before the police knew what was happening. Timing—so very important.

And timing favored the Poet. The school had not received the message from Judy and Deborah was among the crowd of children lining the sidewalk, talking to their friends and waiting for rides. The car lights were blinked, this was part of the routine previously noted, and a brief wave. Deborah waved in return and started out into the street toward the car. In a planned and cunning maneuver, the Poet turned to the left as if to see and avoid the other cars and of course to evade a face-to-face confrontation with the girl approaching the car.

Without warning, there was the shriek of a police siren from a car parked inconspicuously among the many others along the curb. The sudden blare, so close, literally froze the young people outside the school. Debbie stopped and turned toward the noise. The driver in Judy's car heard it too and knew the meaning. The engine was idling, ready to go as soon as Debbie entered. But now, without the quarry, the Poet floored the gas pedal. The car leaped forward, dangerously speeding through the children crossing the street in front. The source of the siren, an unmarked police car, was forced to proceed more cautiously out of concern for the students. As a result the Poet was quickly lost to pursuit. The driver of the police car alerted headquarters and returned to the school. His original mission was to pick up the plainclothes detective who watched over Deborah during school hours.

While parked waiting for his fellow officer, the policeman heard the radio alert regarding the theft of a car from a parking garage at St. Elizabeths Hospital. And suddenly it was there, right in front of him, not fifty feet away, same make and same license number. That was when he hit his siren, thinking he had an easy, routine arrest of an ordinary car thief.

Judy's car was found fifteen minutes later, abandoned. But if there was any doubt as to who stole the car and the motive of the theft it was dispelled by the poem which was found in the back seat, apparently left there when the driver hurriedly parked and ran.

THIS LITTLE GIRL SAYS SHE SAW ME
TOLD THE POLICE
LUCKY THE FIRST TIME
BROKE A LEG AND GOT A NEW LEASE
BUT THEN CAME THE INTERFERENCE
WHEN SHE DEFLECTED MY KNIFE
AND AS YOU CAN SEE
SHE PAID WITH HER LIFE

Bill Arnold cooked dinner that night for the Ridgeways. He had heard of the attempted kidnapping and was at the Ridgeway house when the police brought mother and daughter home from the school. Later he called Jon to get a sedative for Judy who was finding it very difficult to cope with this latest attempt on the life of her child. She was asleep by 9:30 and Bill drove over to see Jon. Kathy had taken one of Jon's sleeping pills, too, and was in bed by the time he got there.

"She might have slept without it," Jon said, referring to the tablet he had given Kathy, "but I didn't want to take any chances. I got a little rest last night, but I don't think she even dozed off for a second. She was still wired tonight."

"It's been quite some twenty-four-hours," Bill said. "And I still have to write up the Poet's latest caper. That little ode to Deb certainly puts to rest any thoughts about Miller being our feticide man."

"True, but I can't think of anybody I'd rather see with half his chest shot off."

"No argument and I could look favorably on the same fate for the Poet. I just hope the son of a bitch doesn't die in a car wreck. Incognito. I'd never get to write the story and we'd never be sure he was really gone."

"He doesn't deserve that kind of luck. Somebody will get him, Bill, and we'll know about it."

"I hope you're right. And that reminds me, how are you coming with your list? Any headway on reducing the number?"

"I'm sorry, Bill, I guess I forgot to give you a follow-up on those letters I sent out."

Jon reached into a desk drawer and pulled out the poem he had received and told Bill of Kathy's reaction when she had seen it.

"Jesus, I don't blame her. She's been through about enough. And did you take her advice? Did you go down and see Chief O'Neal?"

"I did, as a matter of fact."

"And what did he say? Did he give you the same recommendation you got in rhyme form, which was to be a doc and quit playing cop?"

"No, other than to be a lot more careful than usual. Did say he'd keep a patrol car out our way on a regular basis at night. I'm sure the Chief's idea of the car was to give me a little protection but it probably saved Kathy. Without Sergeant Cooney driving around close by, Miller would have had time to get in the house. Lord knows what would have happened then."

"Nothing good, that's for damn sure. How about your list of suspects? What did he think of that?"

"He kept it, if that means anything."

"Chief still think it's a male?"

"Wouldn't say."

"He's a sly old dog, but I think he agrees with me. I think we're getting closer to writing a finish on this story," and Bill started to get up from his chair. "And you know, Jon, I can sense a little added element of suspense here as the search narrows down. Can't help wondering what the Poet will do when somebody corners him."

CHAPTER XIV

It was a typical Willamette Valley February. There had been rain, lots of it, and now there was warm sunshine. Of course, everyone knew the wet weather would return for another three to four months, but the interlude of warm weather was having a favorable effect on the entire population.

Kathy and Jon had played golf on this particular Saturday morning and spent the afternoon working in the yard. Bill Arnold and Judy had been invited to dinner but, because Judy and her daughter had gone to San Francisco to be with Judy's parents for a few days, Bill came alone. Jon was off call and Kathy answered the phone when it rang just as dinner was finished. When the caller identified herself, Kathy muffled the handset and asked Jon if he wanted to take the call. "It's Opal Parker," she said.

"I'd better talk to her, Kate. I've told her she could call anytime."

A few minutes later Jon put down the phone and turned to their dinner guest. "I'll be damned," he said. "Opal just got a call from the hospital. Donald was brought in by ambulance with a knife in his back."

"Is he alive?" Bill asked.

"Oh yes. He's in the operating room now."

"What kind of a knife was it?"

"She didn't say. I doubt if she knows. Actually she was calling me to find out if I thought she should go in to see him when he recovers from anesthesia. The admission clerk in the emergency room called her. Apparently didn't know she and Donald have separated and without asking just called Opal and said her husband was on his way up to the operating room with a knife in his back."

"Well, I thought things had been too calm around the city. I think I'd better mosey on down to police headquarters and see what I can turn up. I wasn't listening to your conversation, Jon. What did you tell the lady?"

"I said it was up to her. I did say I would probably go see him in the morning. Told her we could meet, if she wanted, and go up to his room together."

"Do you know him pretty well, Jon?"

"Thought I did. Lately I'm not too sure. Lot of people around that Clinic I'm not too sure of any more. I see Donald every week when I go up there and he's been very helpful. Seemed a little down the last time I saw him, a little moody. But that was the day after Sergeant Cooney caught Kathy's friend trying to crawl through our bedroom window."

"Jon, that may be funny some day, but not yet."

"Sorry, Kate. But back to Donald Parker. He's on my list, as you know, and I'm fairly sure he's on Chief O'Neal's. The Chief didn't tell me who made the big three on his roster, but Donald and Frankie surely must be there. Miller was probably the third."

"So, the lab director and the Clinic Director. That's a pair to draw to. How 'bout those patients of yours? I think you had two of them on the list. They still there?" Bill asked.

"They haven't given me any reason to take them off. Frankly, I think both are capable of causing a lot of trouble, maybe already have. Sarah can be vicious. She's proven that."

"Do you remember, Jon, many months ago I told you and Judge Donovan not to rule out a female in the Poet's role. I still think that's possible, but from what you've told me about Stephanie and Sarah, I just don't think they fit. These are both young women, and yes, I've seen young women who would just as soon slit your throat as look at you. But to kill babies?" Kathy shook her head. "I don't think so."

"Frankie?" Bill asked.

"She's different. She's older, bigger, and according to Jon, she can be rather mean to the girls in the Clinic. At least that's what some of them say."

"Ever pick up anything from either one of them, Jon?" Bill asked. "Like a slip of some sort? Remember the press conference with Chief O'Neal? You were there when Lenhart got flustered and put his foot in his mouth. Something like that from Donald or Frankie?"

"Not Frankie. She's all Clinic. No chit chat, though she did talk a little about Miller the other day. Couldn't believe he intended to hurt you, Kathy."

"Hah, maybe she should go down to police headquarters and see that gun and knife."

"How 'bout the bruises you got on your knees when you were praying?"

"Jon!"

"You know, Jon," Bill said, "if the Poet doesn't get you some day, Kathy will. And I wouldn't blame her."

Jon just smiled. "Bill," he said, "I'm so glad to have that girl alive and well and home—if I didn't joke about it occasionally I think I'd just cry."

"And damned if I don't believe you. But speaking of the Poet, are you still being careful, watching who's around you?"

"Yeah, funny thing, though, I was talking to Donald Parker the other day—and I think he was saying something about Miller. But he looked right at me when he said some people can be dangerous when they feel threatened. Made me feel a little strange."

"Look, my friend, I've told you before, so has Kathy and O'Neal, you be careful. I'm as anxious as anybody to have the Poet put away. I have a story all ready to go—just fill in the details. And I've written about Kathy—twice. I don't want another Erickson's troubles to fill up my pages."

"I hear you. I'll be careful."

"But you're still going in to see Parker?"

"Bill, the guy had a shiv in his back. He doesn't sound very dangerous to me. Besides, he's a hell of good lab man. Works his tail off around that Clinic and I should go in and say hello."

"Okay. I'm off to headquarters. I'll let you know if I find out anything. And thanks for the dinner, Kathy. As usual it was delicious."

"You bachelors are all alike, Bill. Any food you don't have to fix yourself is always good. But thank you anyway and when Judy gets back we'll have both of you over. Does she ever go out for the evening and leave Debbie alone?"

"Never, but occasionally one of the cops will come in the house for awhile and we can get away. I don't blame her. I wouldn't let that kid out of my sight if she were mine."

"Going to be a lot of people with a little more freedom to wander around if this city ever gets rid of those poems."

"Don't worry, Kathy, they'll get him. But in the meantime, I think I'd better go on down to the police station to see if that was a stainless steel knife in the back of your lab man, Jon. See you later."

Sunday morning Jon got a call on his pager while he was waiting for Opal Parker in the lobby of University Hospital. His answering service reported that Opal had called and said she would not be joining him in a visit to her husband. Jon had checked when he first came in that morning and found that Donald had been moved out of intensive care and was in a private room on the sixth floor. Now with the message from Opal, he went on up to the surgical floor and found the lab director sitting up in bed eating an early lunch.

"Hello, Donald," Jon said. "You look pretty damned good for somebody who had surgery last night."

Donald Parker's greeting in return was somewhat subdued. The television was on and he did turn it down but not off. "I'm okay, Doctor," he said. "The knife didn't go into the lungs. Just bounced off my right shoulder blade. I'm going back to my apartment this afternoon."

"You're lucky."

"I suppose."

The conversation seemed forced and Jon was a little embarrassed. "Anything I can do for you?" he asked.

The lab director didn't answer for a minute. Then he flicked off the television and turned to face Jon. "Yes," he said, "as a matter of fact there is something you can do for me, Doctor. You can tell me what's going on in that mind of yours. You may not have noticed it, but I've been sort of disappointed in you lately, you and the cops. They were here earlier this morning. Wanted to know who put the knife in me. I don't know who the hell did it. My back was turned and it was dark. It was pretty obvious they didn't believe me. And I've been getting some pretty damned strange letters from people I knew many years ago. Apparently you've written to them. For some reason you're making inquiries about me. What the hell is this all about, Doctor?"

The verbal attack was startling, unexpected, but it was not Jon's nature to back away from confrontation. His reply was honest and direct. "Yes," he said, "I've written several letters. Some to your past employers, previous teachers, friends. But don't think I have singled you out, Donald. I'm checking on the past of a number of people who are involved in that Special Procedures Clinic."

"Well," and Donald Parker paused for a moment, "haven't learned much have you? Poet's still loose, isn't he? Sure didn't stop him from putting that stainless steel knife in my back, did you?"

"No, Donald, my letters haven't uncovered anything dramatic, yet."

"Probably never will. Seems to me you're sticking your nose in where you're apt to get it busted. If you say you sent out a lot of letters then you owe apologies to a lot of people. Me included."

"No, you're wrong. I don't owe anybody an apology. I'm involved in these murders. My baby died. That gives me a right—even an obligation— to do what I can to help the police. I'm sorry you're taking this so personally. You're on the permanent staff of the Special Procedures Clinic and whether you like it or not that lands you right in the middle of the suspects. You're smart enough to know that."

"Yes, I'm smart, smart enough to know that your meddlesome nature has put a number of innocent people through hell and we won't forget it. I don't think I would accept your apology even if it were offered." The lab director took a sip of his coffee then continued: "We can't help seeing each other in the Clinic from time to time, but just remember, Doctor, I won't be a friend."

"If that's your decision, so be it. But I came here as a friend and my offer of assistance still stands."

Donald picked up his fork and returned to his lunch. It appeared to be an abrupt finish to the conversation and Jon rose to leave. He was almost out the door when Donald Parker called to him. "Wait a minute," the lab man said. "I'll take that offer. I'll take it to mean you're sorry. You're sorry I got stabbed and sorry that I feel personally offended by your actions. But I think you owe me a favor."

"Donald, you don't seem to understand what I'm saying. I don't owe you anything but if you need something, I'll try to get it for you."

"I do need something and it won't put you out much to get it for me. I don't plan to come in to the Clinic tomorrow but I would like to finish up some paper work. Its in a big manila envelope sitting on top of my desk. Got a label on it, **"Cocaine And Pregnancy,"** you can't miss it. Frankie has a key to the office. I'd appreciate it if you'd bring that to my place tomorrow afternoon. Grandview Apartments—you know where they are?"

"Yes, not far from my office. I'll be there right after lunch."

Jon did leave then, not very certain of what he'd heard and not very certain of how he felt. But the next day, as promised, he did go to the Special Procedures Clinic and found the administrator in her office.

Frankie was surprised to see him. "Are you confused, Doctor?" she asked. "You belong here on Friday. This is Monday. Something special going on that I don't know about?"

"That'll never happen, Ms. McGraw. You keep pretty close tabs on things around here. But I'm supposed to pick up some material for Mr. Parker. He was in the hospital this weekend. Did you see him?"

"No, Donald and I had a falling out last week. I came back in about eight o'clock one evening and found him rummaging around in my office."

"I hope he had a good reason."

"Doctor, I can't think of any reason or excuse for someone to be in my office without my permission. That goes for you, that goes for Donald, that even goes for the Dean of the Medical School. This is mine; it's private, and nobody enters without being asked. I caught a junior medical student in here one night. Said he was working on a project. I don't know what the project was, don't really care, but I can tell you he's no longer working for a degree in medicine. I had him expelled the next day."

"Frankie, I didn't come to hear about your private property rights. I'd be the last to challenge you in that regard. But I told Donald I'd bring him the papers he wants and he said you have a key to his office."

"I do. I have a key to every office in this Clinic. That doesn't mean I go barging in any time I want something. I've never been in Donald's office except when he's there. I think he wishes he'd never been in mine."

"Maybe he was looking for something that would help him evaluate his lab work."

"No he wasn't, Doctor. I know what he was looking for. He wanted to see if I had any letters hidden away in here. Letters from teachers and friends in the mid-west when I lived back there. He talked to me just a few days ago and he was mad. Told me that he'd got some strange letters from people he knew before he moved here. Wanted to know if somebody was asking questions about me. I lied to him. Told him I didn't know what he was talking about. But I think you know what I'm talking about, don't you, Doctor?"

"Of course I do, Frankie. You wouldn't want me to leave you out, would you?" Jon allowed just a little smile to play at the corners of his mouth and Frankie saw it.

"I don't see any humor in this. I've told you about some of my past and that's all you need to know. Don't stick your nose into any other part of my personal life, past or present."

His smile disappeared and Jon said, "The only interest I have in your past is how it might relate to your present. And that's true for a number of other people who have been associated with this Clinic."

"I have a pretty good idea what you're looking for, Doctor. I don't think you'll find it." The Director looked at Jon for a second then reached into a drawer of her desk and pulled out a key with Parker's name on it. "Here," she said. "This is the key to Donald's office. When you get what you want just turn it in to the receptionist out there. I'll pick it up when I have time."

And once again a conversation with Frankie McGraw, B.S., R.N. was abruptly closed. Jon accepted the key and walked down to Donald Parker's office. A few minutes later he was back in his car heading toward the Grandview Apartments. On an impulse he picked up his cellular phone and called Bill Arnold. The reporter was in and answered immediately: "Bill Arnold," he said.

"Bill, this is Jon. Got a minute?"

"Sure."

"Just thought I'd check with you. I'm on my way over to see Donald Parker. Just got through talking to Frankie McGraw. She obviously knows I wrote some inquiry letters about her and is none too pleased."

"So? That's not very surprising. People don't like to be investigated for anything—robbery, rape, taxes, murder. Doesn't make any difference if they're innocent or guilty. Now, what's this about Parker? I thought he was still in the hospital."

"He was released yesterday. The wound in his back was not too deep. Didn't get into the lungs at all. What did you find out about the knife?"

"Classic stainless steel. Just like the ones we've seen before."

"Any prints on it?"

"No."

"I saw Donald yesterday and he told me it was one of the Poet's knives."

"How did he find out?" Bill asked. "I can tell you if somebody puts a blade in my back I'm not going to get a mirror and see what kind it is."

"He didn't say. He was in a bad mood. He's been getting some letters asking about those letters of inquiry I sent out and he's all pushed out of shape. They really touched a nerve, I guess. He wanted me to apologize for the hell I've put him through."

"Did you?"

"Of course not. I tried to explain to him that anybody closely associated with that Clinic would be high on the suspect list."

"Did he understand?"

"Hard to say. He did soften a bit and accept my offer to help him. That's what I'm doing now, I'm taking some papers down to his apartment."

"Jon, I'm not sure that's very smart. That guy could be dangerous."

"Dangerous? Not likely. He has a knife wound in the muscles of his back, you know. And by the way, the police didn't give you any hint about who put that knife there, did they?"

"No, and they don't believe Donald's story. He says he was attacked in the hallway of his apartment building and never saw his assailant. They think that's bunk but they can't prove it. You have any ideas?"

"Oh, I just wonder about Frankie. She was in a bad mood when I was in her office—and not just about those letters I'd written. She was pissed off at Parker. She'd caught him in her office and that's forbidden territory. I just wonder if she's mad enough to stab him. But on second thought, that's a big, strong woman. If she was going to use a knife on Donald she'd plunge it in to the hilt. She's not prone to halfway measures."

"Well, you're no help. I guess there's no story to write today, and it doesn't sound like you expect to produce any front page news when you visit Donald Parker's apartment. But Jon, you be careful and give me the name of that apartment complex. Call me back in a half an hour. If you don't, I'm calling O'Neal."

"Grandview Apartments. Thanks, Bill. I'll be in touch."

Jon found the laboratory chief to be in much better spirits than he was when seen in the hospital. He was relaxed, barefoot and lounging around in an old loose-fitting sweat suit. "My daughter was just here, Doctor," he said. "I'm sorry you missed her."

"I am too. I'd like to have met her."

"She's okay. Not easy to act as a go-between for two warring parents. But she does a good job and not too judgmental. She does get on my case for my country ways," and Donald waved a bare foot in the air. "But as I told her, I was born country and I'll stay country—bare feet and all." Donald noticed the large manila envelope in Jon's hand. "And I see you found my data on kids and cocaine," he said. "Thank you for bringing it down."

"No problem. As I told you, this place is right on the way to my office."

"Find anything else of interest in my office?"

Donald's voice had a different inflection and Jon immediately noticed the change. He frowned and looked closely at the lab man as he handed over the envelope. "No," he said, "I didn't look."

"Did you suspect you might find something if you looked around?"

Jon began to feel very uncomfortable. "What the hell are you talking about, Donald?"

"Here, I'll show you." And he thrust a piece of paper at Jon. "Take it. Read it." It was not a request, it was a command from the Poet. "This what you were looking for?" he asked.

```
THIS IS NUMBER NINE
    NO LONGER WILL SHE DINE
ON FUNDS FROM YOUR TAXES AND MINE
```

Jon saw the rhyme, knew for sure now whose home he was in and made a grab for the Poet's arm. But the move was a second too late. He felt his head jerked back and a knife at his throat.

"You went through my closet, didn't you? Told you to quit playing cop, but you want to be the hero, you want to catch the Poet. Dead heroes don't talk and we're going to make sure of that right now. Got this all planned out. Going to slit your throat over the bathtub. Easy to clean up the mess. Don't know what I'll do with you then. Dump you some place, I guess."

There was a high-pitched quality to the voice but Jon wasn't really listening. He did hear enough to know he had only seconds to live if the cold steel of that knife stayed in its present position.

In contrast to the Poet, the doctor was not a country boy—he always wore shoes. And the shoes he was wearing today were heavy brown oxfords with leather heels and steel clips. Many times in the past his friends had made fun of the authoritative, rather macho sound of his foot gear as he strode down the hospital corridors. Right now, right this very minute he thought about those shoes and he thought about his karate lessons. The proper use of both might give him a chance to live another day.

While Parker babbled on, Jon suddenly and forcefully pushed back toward his would-be murderer and planted a hard metal and leather heel on the top of Donald's bare foot. Over 180 pounds of pressure tore through the exposed skin and crushed the muscles and bones beneath. At the same time, with his right hand Jon seized the arm holding the knife and used his left to jam an elbow into Donald's groin. The lab director, in severe pain from his smashed foot and the blow to his testicles, dropped the knife and allowed Jon to spin free. Still gripping the arm which had held the knife and now facing his antagonist, Jon pulled him down by the hair and, using all of his power, brought a knee up into the side of Donald's head.

The Poet would live and he would later confess his crimes but it was Jon, pale and shaken, who was still standing when the police arrived in response to his 911 call. Bill Arnold walked in shortly after and saw Donald being carried out to a waiting ambulance. Bill looked at the semiconscious lab director, the knife on the floor and the thin line of blood on Jon's neck.

"Looks like you must have earned your black belt today," the reporter said to his friend. "And you sure look like you could use a drink."

There will be no number nine" was the opening sentence in Bill Arnold's lead article in Monday morning's paper. Then in classic newspaper fashion the reader was subjected to a review of the horror concerning eight feticides and two murdered teenagers. He wrote that it was a fitting climax to these many months of fear and revulsion when Dr. Jon Erickson phoned the police from Donald Parker's apartment and asked them to come by and take the Poet into custody. It was Dr. Erickson, the article went on to say, who had operated on many of the feticide victims and it was Dr. and Mrs. Erickson who had lost an unborn son to the killer.

Donald Parker's handwritten confession was another page one story. There was not one word of regret or apology. But there were signs, unmistakable, of a precariously unstable mind about to come apart. In his written statement, the former laboratory chief lashed out at the police, the Medical School, the Clinic and all its personnel. According to one authority, Donald Parker sounded like a trapped animal snarling and snapping at its captors. The confession left many questions unanswered, but there was hope of full disclosure when in a final, rambling sentence Donald demanded to appear before the news media prior to starting what he assumed would be a life sentence at the state prison. He also refused any legal assistance, saying he did not want to endure the farce of a trial.

That evening Deborah Ridgeway, unattended by the police, went to a movie with her friend, Sherry Bourden. Her mother and Bill Arnold were at the Ericksons'.

"Was it a little scary to let Deb out on her own tonight?" Kathy asked.

"Yes, I had a few qualms even with that monster in jail. I'm sure it'll take awhile before I can see her leave without some fear."

"How's Deb feel about it?" Jon said.

"She's like a little fawn turned loose in the woods. Can't quite get used to the freedom, but just dancing and jumping for joy."

"Do you suppose Donald Parker will say anything about Debbie when he talks to the press?"

"I hope he'll clear up a lot of things, Kate, including who paid him to target you."

"You're all assuming he'll get his chance to appear."

"Don't you think the judge will let him, Bill?"

"Oh, I suppose so. But it's going to be a damned circus. Television cameras, reporters from all over the country, but I guess one day of that's better than having some smartass defense lawyer trying to make a name for himself and posturing to a jury for a month."

"Did the judge say when he'll make a decision?"

"I was at the courthouse this afternoon and the word was he'll let us know next week."

"Next week? Why not tomorrow?"

"Legal precedent and all that crap, I imagine. Judges are lawyers at heart, you know. And lawyers live for the day they can complicate something simple."

A week later, Monday afternoon at three o'clock to be exact, word came from the state's third circuit court that Donald Parker had been properly arraigned on the charge of murder and further, that he had waived his rights to have legal representation as well as his rights to appear before a grand jury. The judge had pronounced a sentence of life in prison without chance of parole but had granted the prisoner's request to appear before the news media. The date of this news conference was set for a Saturday in late April at three o'clock p.m.

For Bill Arnold, the timing of both the announcement and Parker's appearance before the press was a flagrant and distasteful bid for publicity. "Good God," he told Jon by phone that night, "that judge must be planning to run for the Senate. Prime time television wins again. Three o'clock Pacific Standard Time. You know what time that is on the East Coast don't you? Six o'clock, when everybody is tuned into the news. And three o'clock Saturday afternoon—it might as well be a damned football game. I told you it'd be a circus. You still have that press card I gave you before the hearing at the police station?"

"Of course."

"Want to put it on and go with me when Donald Parker gets his chance to impress the news people?"

"Lord, yes. Wouldn't want to miss it."

"Good. Mark your calendar and I'll pick you up about one o'clock."

The former Laboratory Director confronted the reporters and television cameras within the paneled walls of the third circuit court, Judge Truman L. Harpole presiding. As Bill had predicted, a carnival atmosphere prevailed on the streets outside the courthouse. Even inside, there was a circus quality to the assembly. And the circus was like all others—it had a tiger, a captured tiger, a wild animal that everybody had come to see and hear.

No one was disappointed with the performance. Donald was led out in chains, flanked on each side by a heavily-armed officer of the law. And there were other police mixed in with the reporters, all with sidearms, all unsmiling and grim. A sergeant held up his arms for quiet and the show was on. The prisoner first read a prepared statement in which he detailed his education and research accomplishments—all without any visible emotion. His recent position as Laboratory Director, he said, allowed him access to the records of the patients in the Special Procedures Clinic. He knew each one of the girls, he knew their hereditary background, their faults, and he knew everything he needed to know about their pregnancy.

At this point he discarded the written comments and looked out at his audience. He actually seemed to make eye contact with every one present. He stood there for a full two minutes without making a sound or a gesture. Then he crashed his manacled wrists on the table and made a statement which would be carried by every radio station, every television station and every newspaper in the country:

"All of you, get the hell out of this room if you've come to hear me apologize. I am proud of what I did."

He paused again and it was obvious he was waiting for questions. A CBS television reporter was quick to accept the challenge. "I didn't come to hear an apology. I came to learn more about a man who killed two young women and eight babies. Where were you born?"

"Tennessee."

"I know you have a wife and daughter in this city. How about in Tennessee? Any family there?"

"Not that I know of."

"I'm sure God didn't just create you like he did Adam and Eve. So tell us, who all was in that family down south and what happened to them?"

"It's none of your damned business. But I suspect you and your network are anxious to lie about it, so I'll tell you how it really was in Tennessee when I was a kid. Probably make a better story than what you could dream up, anyway." Donald went on to tell of his early boyhood. It was not an easy time, no chance for childish games and play, his father and mother gloomy and depressed. "I had a brother and sister," he said. "We didn't have much fun together."

"Do you ever see either of them now?" someone from the front of the courtroom asked.

"I wouldn't walk across the street to see my sister. I don't know and don't care if she's alive. She was nothing but a whore."

"How 'bout your brother?"

"That big cop over there," and he pointed to Sergeant Cooney standing guard by an exit door, "he killed him. He's pretty good up close with a shotgun."

"Doctor Lawrence Miller?" Bill Arnold asked.

"Yes. He was my brother."

The reporter pressed him a little. "Different names—Parker, Miller," he said. "How come?"

Though frequently interrupted by questions, Donald told of the flood which had destroyed their home and of being separated from his brother when they were sent to live with different relatives. "I wound up with my mother's people and sort of got adopted. Larry went to one of our uncles and kept the family name. I never knew where he was, never saw him again until about four years ago. We met one day up at the medical school and got a little curious about our names and discovered we were brothers. We kept it sort of quiet. We lived different lives. Didn't really know each other. No sense trying to act like brothers after all those years."

This was the non-belligerent Donald talking. Easy, no shouting, no recriminations, just as though he was telling his family history to an interested group of friends, all in a matter-of-fact sort of way. Then the man from Public Broadcasting asked about the sister and there was an instantaneous change of attitude.

"Oh, you mean the whore," Donald said and he swung around to face his inquisitor.

"We're getting into something here," Bill whispered to Jon. "Look at the guy's face. He's angry. That sister is bad news."

"That was your description, not mine," the PBS man said.

"Well, she was. And her whoring around got her pregnant. She had twins—boys—right there in a bedroom on the farm. I remember hearing her scream when she was in labor and thinking it served her right for acting like a dog in heat. Never did know who the father was. Sure as hell none of the young studs around there came to the farm to claim responsibility for those brats and help pay for them."

"What happened to her?"

"Oh, she stayed with our parents. Right after the flood, Mother said my brother and I were old enough to be farmed out to some uncles and aunts but she couldn't bear to see the babies go. I remember her very words, 'Just ain't no way in the world I kin part with them little boys.' My father was a little more practical. He saw those little bastards for what they were really worth—an extra welfare check."

Jon penned a quick message to Bill:

> Ease up on him, Bill, he's apt to blow. Look at his hands, they're shaking like a leaf.

The reporter glanced at the note, nodded his agreement toward Jon, then turned back to the prisoner. "Mr. Parker," he said, "I read your confession but you left out a couple of things. Your calling card was found nearby when Doctor Erickson's wife was hit. She hardly fit the pattern of your usual victims and I think everybody would like to know why she was attacked. And there was the woman dealing drugs. Was that your knife?"

"There's a reason for everything. Didn't you read the poem I left by Mrs. Erickson?"

"Yes. It sounded like you got paid for it. Who paid you?"

"You can't hurt him now. He's dead. Larry Miller. My brother."

"Did he say why?"

"No. But I knew he was jealous of her. Hated her. Do anything he could to cause her trouble."

"And the woman in the apartment garage?"

"I told the police about all this. Must have left it out of the copy you read. Larry paid me for that one, too."

"Debbie Ridgeway. Does that name mean anything to you?" Bill asked.

"Sure. That's the kid who thought she could identify me. You have to understand I couldn't let her do that. I had too much to do. There was my work in the Clinic and of course I felt a real need to keep those little tramps from bringing more boys into the world."

What a sick bastard was Jon's penned comment.

"I've read your confession, too," the *Chicago Tribune*'s man said, "and I looked for some mention of the injuries which brought you into the hospital some weeks ago. Didn't see anything about it. You obviously turned your back on somebody who had access to your knives, maybe an accomplice or at least someone who knew of your double life and chose not to report you. Any comment?"

Donald opened his mouth as though he was about to speak. He stood there for a moment gazing out into the audience. At one point his eyes fixed in one area and it seemed he had found a particular friend. But then he looked back at the man from Chicago and just shook his head.

One of the NBC reporters was still curious about the relationship between Donald and his sister. "I wish you'd tell us more about your sister and your little nephews," she said. "You must have had some feeling for them."

"What's your name?" Donald asked the lady from NBC.

"Jasper, Barbara Jasper."

"Well, Ms. Jasper, you look like a young lady who has been surrounded by protection. I suspect your greatest problem in life is whether to order a twenty-dollar or a forty-dollar bottle of wine for dinner. I doubt if you've ever been in a home where moral decay has brought two extra lives into your own little world. Then have those two extra lives crowd you out of any love or attention from your mother. Yes, I had feelings for them. Damn right I did. I wanted to see the little bastards drown in that flood."

"Let me put this together," the *Tribune* man said. "According to your story, you have a moral degenerate for a sister—a welfare recipient—who is the mother of two little fatherless boys. These innocent little fellows, your nephews, through no fault of their own, manage to rob you of your mother's love—or so you say—and by their presence contrive to force you and your brother from your rightful home. You are asking us to accept this story and somehow relate it to your recent activities. Am I on the right track?"

Bill leaned over close to Jon. "Neat little one paragraph summary of the past forty-plus years," he said. "If Chicago is right, it's a pretty farfetched justification for the terror Donald Parker has caused."

"Psychotic people don't have to justify anything, Bill. They live in their own world. That's what you and *The Tribune*'s man are forgetting. But from the looks of Donald, we're going to hear more on the subject—and right now."

Jon was right. Donald stared at *The Tribune* man for a minute or two and once more brought the handcuffed arms down hard on the desk, startling all in the courtroom. "Well, aren't you a smartass," the city's infamous Poet said to the man from Chicago. "Think you have all the answers, do you? Well let me tell you something. You'd be a lot better off if there were more people like me in this country. Some of us see a bigger picture. It's clearer to us what's going wrong and we know how to fix it. There was no good in my sister. She brought unwanted life into this world by her evil and immoral ways. What chance did those little bastards have? None. Much better off dead, but there was no Donald Parker around to destroy them before they were born. But you can thank God there was a Donald Parker at the Special Procedures Clinic and he did you all a favor." And again he crashed the steel shackles on the desk. "There are seven less to receive a welfare check. Seven less to cause heartache and misery in their families, seven less to grow up and repeat the cycle, seven less to grow up in poverty and want. And despite what you think of me, I," Donald poked his finger into his chest, "I shall not want. The Lord is my shepherd and he leadeth me in the path of righteousness."

It was quiet in the courtroom now, almost as though the Poet's outburst had cast a spell. Then Bill Arnold broke the trance-like hush.

"Mr. Parker," he said almost with deference, "not only have I seen your confession, but the police allowed me to view the weapons which were found in your office. In the box with the knives there was an unusual picture. Would you care to comment on it?"

There was no fight, no defiance left in Donald Parker. He remained standing but appeared slumped and tired. "Yes," he said, "that's a picture of James Leroy."

"And?"

"I've been married twice, Mr. Arnold. I've never mentioned my first marriage to anyone in this city. Not even to my present wife and daughter. My first wife was a sweet little girl from South Carolina. I think she was sixteen and I was seventeen when we were married. James Leroy was born of that marriage and lived only two days. The hill people from around there used to take some strange medicines and I've often wondered if James Leroy's death might have been caused by a drug reaction. Maybe something his mother took when she was pregnant. At any rate, she committed suicide right after we buried our son."

With this revelation the news media appeared to have its fill and after a few more minutes of silence, Judge Harpole banged his gavel and Donald Parker was led away, head down and shuffling with the restriction of his leg irons.

"Get your questions all answered, Doc? Curiosity satisfied?" It was Lt. Lenhart. He was with a group of police officers slowly following the crowd out of the courtroom.

"Good afternoon, Lieutenant. Yes, I think I did, mostly. I would like to know who put the knife in Donald's back but it's pretty obvious he's not going to tell us."

"Oh, Ah have a pretty good idea. Cain't prove it. Don't know as how Ah would if Ah could." He made a move to rejoin the other detectives, then turned to give a little half-salute to Jon and Bill, "Y'all be good now," he said. "Won't be seein' you again. Headin' back to Georgia. Don't reckon Ah'll miss you much." He didn't wait for any comments from Jon or Bill.

Most of the press corps, Jon included, had been seated in the front of the courtroom. With his interest directed toward Donald Parker, Jon had not bothered to look around and see who else had come to see the show. He probably would have missed her anyway as Stephanie Van Osborn was seated near a rear door and left hurriedly, almost before the prisoner had finished speaking.

Once outside the courthouse Stephanie hailed a passing cab and directed the cabbie to a small Catholic church on the outskirts of the city. There was no conversation between driver and passenger on the long trip out to the Chapel of Immaculate Conception. Curious, the cabbie watched for a minute after accepting his fare and tip. The woman seemed to hesitate before entering the Church, then slowly ascended the stairs and opened the door. As he put the cab in gear and drove back toward the city, the cab driver still wondered why someone so young and smartly dressed would be going to Church at this hour of day—and not on a Sunday.

Had he been inside the Church the cabbie would have seen Stephanie hesitate again. She had neglected these surroundings for many years. It was only a brief moment of indecision; she walked quickly down the aisle and turned to go into the dimly lit confessional. Immediately she genuflected and her posture became that of the supplicant with her hands folded in prayer.

"Bless me Father, for I have sinned," she began when the small door slid open and the priest signaled his readiness to hear her. "It has been eight years since my last confession. Since then I have committed the sin of adultery many times. I have been unfaithful to my husband." For a brief second she paused as if uncertain whether to continue. Then slowly and painfully Stephanie told the priest why she was on her knees and in this confessional.

"Two months ago I stabbed a man. He didn't die but I confess to wanting to see him dead because he killed my mother and had beaten me many times. And I confess to having previously enjoyed the company of this man even though I knew he had taken the lives of innocent babies. I am sorry for these and all the sins of my past life."